C000135708

If Drowned

a story of lovers, mothers,
gods and monsters

If Drowned

or the Life and Adventures
of James Hawkins Seagrave
of Rawley Bay in the County of Yorkshire

An Autobiographical Fiction
Compiled from his Diaries,
Notes and Correspondence
by
Philip Harland

acknowledgments to Elaine Ianuzziello,
Dr Paul Calloway and Carol Thompson
for help in sourcing and editing the material

front cover *Hylas and the Nymphs* (detail)
John William Waterhouse
Mancheser Art Gallery

Wayfinder Press
London England

If Drowned
copyright © 2019 Philip Harland

ISBN 978-0-9561607-6-8

The right of Philip Harland to be identified as the author
of this work has been asserted in accordance with the
UK Copyright, Designs and Patents Act 1988

All rights reserved
Quotations for review and non-commercial purposes are permitted subject
to fair use and full citation otherwise no part of this publication may be
reproduced or transmitted in any form or by any means without the
permission in writing of the copyright holder and publisher

www.wayfinderpress.com
All enquiries to info@wayfinderpress.com

They vow to amend their lives, and yet they don't;
Because if drown'd, they can't – if spared, they won't.

Lord Byron, Don Juan

If Drowned

For Richard

Chapter 1

In Rawley Bay

I AM STANDING WIDE-EYED, CHEST-DEEP IN THE NORTH SEA staring at my mother, who is only feet away. The wind is whipping the waves into foam-crested harpies – those perfidious snatchers mariners call the Captain's Daughters. The salt sea stings, it fills my face, and suddenly – help! please help! – I am sinking. My feet feel nothing beneath them and all I can see is light and water swirling above me – unreachable, blue, green and grey swirls, eddies, whirls, churns, spiralling and seething. I am gasping for air, but swallowing water. The sea drags me down, my arms flail as I fall and all I can feel is a heavy, swirling, powerful force that is out of my control. There is pressure on my chest as if something, someone, is holding me down, but how can that be? I am helpless and drowning. I am four years old.

φ

Dear Julian,

YOU KNOW ME AS JAMES, sometimes as Jim, occasionally even as Father, but see me for a moment as young Amyas Leigh, lingering along the Bideford Quay listening for the cry of Westward Ho!; or Jim Hawkins, son of the keeper of the Benbow Inn, keen as a cutlass to join the crew of the Hispaniola; Horatio Hornblower, the seasick midshipman whose skill and daring has him promoted despite his poor beginnings and lack of influential friends to Admiral of the Fleet; lonely Rob Kreutznaer, known as Crusoe, making do and mending on the Island of Despair; Odysseus of Ithaca and the Island of the Winds; Jason commanding the Argo under the aegis of Athene. Like Odysseus I shall long for home, and like Jason I shall suffer the wrath of a vengeful woman.

"I looked with wonder," wrote Robinson Crusoe, "upon the sea that was so rough and terrible the day before, and could be so calm and so pleasant in so little a time after." This could be a parable of my time upon this earth. Crusoe was conceived in York of a sailor from Bremen. I was born in the York Infirmary of a seamstress and a merchant seaman. I can say with some certainty that George the Sixth hardly noticed. He had recently been crowned King and had a lot on his mind. German troops were occupying the Rhineland, Franco's troops were besieging Madrid and the Duke of Windsor was about to marry an American divorcée. I knew nothing of all this at the time, so I really can't be blamed. I was a boy growing up in remote little Rawley-by-the-Sea on the east coast of Yorkshire, adventurous and inventive as a boy with nothing to fear should be. It was from Rawley Bay that I left with Mr Oxenham to fight the Spanish Armada and as apprentice to Squire Trelawney set sail for Treasure Island.

> The Hispaniola rolled steadily, dipping her bowsprit now and then with a whiff of spray, while all was drawing alow and aloft.

A whiff of spray is the worst you would expect in the harbour before the heavy weather set in. Before my mother left – for good, as they say.

Rawley is a sprat-sized village with a dark harbour wall swept incessantly by the sea and set on the sides of a long, steep cleft that drops from the top of Crackwick Moor. In a hollow at the top lies High Liverside and from there runs the road to Nether Moor, where they say the body of a boy was found the day I was born. His arms were found in Downend Pond and his torso and legs in a bog on the moor. His severed head has never been seen. My friend Donald Nudds and I look for it when we are out playing in case we can claim a reward.

Nuddsy is an odd-looking boy whose mother puts a chip pan over his head once a month and snips any stray hair she can see. She says it's cheaper than sending him to the barber's in Thirby, when he comes home looking like a yard brush with no bristles. Nuddsy is daft and tough, and an excellent friend who will play anything I like. One of our games is to get lost on the moor. If you go up Long Lane past Ewbank Farm at the top end of Rawley all you will see are a few longwool sheep and a coarse carpet of heather and gorse that goes on forever. If you really are lost, of course, you can climb Black Rock at the top of the moor and look for the breakwater arms of the harbour and the grey wash of the North Sea beyond, then you will know your way home. Once on a clear day I swore I could see all the way over to Norway.

Rawley can be stormy, with waves of foam rolling in to the shore and nor-easterlies fierce enough to blow the sheets off the line. But it is a neighbourly place, and for Nuddsy and me it is a great place to play, with alleyways, cul-de-sacs, flights of steep steps, and snickets and ginnels so narrow you can run through touching the walls on both sides. In Rawley people will help you up if you fall and give you a glass of water if you are thirsty.

Four of the streets off the High Street up from the harbour are called First Street, Second Street and so on. They were named that way, says Great-grandma Barraclough, so that drunks like my father could find their way home from the Ship Inn at night. "All 'e 'ad to do was count from one to four," she says, "and some nights 'e couldn't even do that." She tells me about his eighteenth birthday, when he fell over in the pub and they asked him where he lived. "Four Seventh Street," he said, but they worked out he had to mean Seven Fourth Street as there is no Seventh Street, so they were able to get him home all right. Not long after he joined the Merchant Navy because it was rumoured they gave you a daily tot of rum as part of your wages, whereas that turned out to be the Royal Navy.

They had to carry him home, as no-one had a car. You hardly see a vehicle in the village unless it's the tractor that pulls the lifeboat, the doctor's Austin 10 or a hearse. I saw my first ambulance the day my mother came home with her leg in bandages. She was walking up Chapel Hill to the bus stop when she slipped on the ice and was hit by a car. Her bandages had to be changed when the wound opened up again. I had to avert my eyes. Blood was the first of my fears. It isn't the worst.

The houses in Rawley are built of stone from the Crackwick quarry, a gritty limestone, rough to the touch, blackened by exposure to air and the smoke of years of coal fires. On winter evenings the smoke lies low in the village, it smells strong and sharp, it thickens the air and tickles your nostrils, but when you smell the smoke you can picture the fires and know that people are home.

We live on Fourth Street, where the houses are built back-to-back with the houses on Third Street. They have front doors, but no back doors. Their WCs are little brick outhouses separated from the houses like orphans left out in the cold. Which is pretty much how my sister Jenny and I feel when our mother is away and our father is at sea, and we are sent down the street to live with Great-grandma Barraclough.

Who are these people? You might well ask. You met my mother once before your mother and I divorced. You never met my father. He remarried after his divorce to my mother and his new wife wanted nothing to do with us. Not sure if you ever met my sister, your aunt Jenny, who divorced, remarried and moved to Dundee. I hope that's enough divorces to be going on with.

I miss my mother – well, I miss the mother I see in the framed photograph on my great-grandmother's sideboard. The woman in the photograph is pretty, she is smiling, her hair is short and neat with small curls, brushed back from her forehead with a parting to one side. She looks present and ready to play, as though she were really there, when she rarely is. And when she is there she doesn't smile much.

Great-grandma Barraclough's house is like ours - one room and a pantry downstairs, two bedrooms too small to walk around the beds upstairs, an attic where my sister and I sleep, and a cellar with a ceiling so low that the grown-ups have to duck whenever they go down to bring up the coal. Great-grandma is as tough as a frozen haddock. Her grey hair is pulled back tight and held with a hairgrip. She has a lot of rules. We are forbidden to read comics, taste beer, put our feet to the fire in winter to warm them, go down to the dock at high tide, play on Second Street or visit Grandma Lily, her daughter, who lives in Thirby. "Why?" I ask about all these things. "Too many questions, lad," she says. "Tha'll understand when tha's older." "How old do I have to be to read comics?" I ask. "Too smart for 'is boots," she says to no-one in particular.

There is nothing worth bombing in Rawley, with the possible exception of the Methodist chapel, the Church of England primary school and the fish and chip shop. Even so we are issued with masks in cardboard boxes in case Hitler makes a gas attack. I put my mask on in bed to scare my sister, but it only makes her laugh. On the way to school Nuddsy and I pretend to be monsters who crawled out of the sea, but the masks are heavy, they smell of rubber and fit with a strap that traps your hair at the back, so we soon give up.

My sister laughs a lot. I have no idea why. One of the few times I hear her cry is when she drops a neighbour's baby on its head while she is playing with it and the baby's mother screams and swears at her. Great-grandma has to go round and apologize, which is something she is not very good at.

In one of Jenny's school reports, her teacher writes, "She makes frequent oral contributions, occasionally helpful." "That lass 'as the gift of the gab," says Great-grandma. When Jenny and her friend Rita Birtwhistle are chattering together they are like two endless streams tumbling over each other and never quite reaching the sea. All the women in Rawley do it. They can talk all day about practically nothing. The men are away fishing or in the merchant navy and when they are home there is not much for them to talk about except the weather and cricket.

One of my great-grandmother's sayings is, "I tek a man for what 'e is." I'm not sure what she means by this. She might be implying that other people – those who live on the wrong side of the Pennines in Lancashire, say – take a man for something else, perhaps for what he isn't, that is they are either stupid or hypocritical, whereas there is no question that Yorkshire folk are straightforward and sensible. I have not seen the evidence for any of these assertions.

"'Ear all, see all, say nowt," she says. "Eat all, drink all, pay nowt. And if wi' God's grace tha ivver does owt for nowt, allus do it for thissen." By slipping in the bit about God she makes it sound as though greed and self-interest are virtues to which we can all aspire. I think she must know what she is talking about, because she reads the Bible every day, kneels by her bed to pray at night and goes to chapel twice on Sundays, all signs of goodness and wisdom, I am led to understand, rather than ignorance and bloody-mindedness.

"Tha must NOT walk up Rawley Beck to school," she tells us. "Tha must go by the lane." She takes a grim delight in telling us of the time a two-year old infant was swept away when the beck burst its banks in a downpour. Most of the time it is a piddly little runnel, this stream, but it flows fast and it is impressed upon us that you can drown in the shallowest water. Having escaped the watery grave of the North Sea not so long ago I am not too bothered. Rawley Beck is a streamlet, a rill, it is nothing. If Jenny falls in I will rescue her and if I fall in I will get out again.

On the way to school one day after it has been raining I run to jump across the beck, slip on the grass and fall in. Jenny laughs like the Laughing Sailor in a penny arcade. I pull myself out and run home soaked and shivering and feeling sorry for myself. "What did ah tell thee, y'barmpot?" Great-grandma shouts, "y'could've drowned!" And then adds injury to insult by slapping me.

Mother is away for days, weeks, sometimes months, at a time. All Great-grandma will say is that she has gone to Leeds. Or sometimes Morecambe. It is wartime, so I think this might be code for parachuting behind enemy lines into France or patrolling the clifftops on the lookout for German spies. I am convinced that no-one will tell me more about where she is or what she is doing because it is a secret and traitors can be shot.

On the rare days when Mother is at home she sits at a sewing machine all day, unavailable to play, and when the item she is working on is finished she takes it to a woman called Agnes who runs a dressmaking business in Thirby. So we are told. Mother says that Agnes is more of a mother to her than an employer, having taken her on as a fourteen-year old when her real mother, Grandma Lily, was away. It is a plausible story, the sort a secret agent needs. I prefer to think that Agnes is the *nom de guerre* of a spymaster and that Mother is sewing her own parachutes.

Grandma Lily is a music hall artiste, so she is away a lot too. According to Great-grandma Barraclough, her daughter lives in Sin. "Where is that?" I ask. "All around us, young man," she says gloomily, smoothing the arm of her chair to comfort herself. She identifies the sins of Pride and Envy as committed by relatives on Second Street who are never to be visited; and Lust and Gluttony that can be laid at the door of her daughter, who is, she declares, next best thing to a tart. I take this to be a compliment, as I rather like tarts and cannot understand how being the next best thing to one would make her a sinner.

I have a note on blue paper that Grandma Lily sent to my mother, which my mother passed on to me before she left. It says

> Put this in Baby's hand for me, I wish it was a cheque I was writing instead.
> Lily.

The blue must be for a boy. It is an unusual idea to send a slip of paper in the post for a baby to grasp in lieu of a cheque, just as it would have been to send a cheque in lieu of a toy or a rattle, but it is explained to me on the premise that my grandmother is a bit 'funny-ossity' and we have to make allowances. I notice that she does not send her love to her daughter and that she calls herself not Mum or Mama, but Lily.

My mother purses her lips when she gives me this note, in the same way she purses them while reading the newspaper or answering the door. She has a frown line in her forehead as deep as the Rawley ravine. I think it comes from worrying about the war and what is happening in Leeds, or Morecambe, and from squinting at her sewing in the fading light.

She loses her temper easily. She can explode like the guns of a battleship and when she grumbles it is like the distant sound of bombs falling. Once I heard her say, "When I look at him, I see his father." She was not talking about my cousin Ivan or Nuddsy. She calls my sister a birdbrain and me incorrigible, which means, I discover, either 'incurably bad' or 'unlikely to change'. Well, which? I'm not sure about the second, but I resent the first. I am my mother's son, after all. And she is wrong to call Jenny a birdbrain. Jenny is really quite smart, although she hides it most of the time because she wants to be friends with everyone.

No-one in Rawley talks about feelings. I do not exaggerate when I say that I am not entirely sure what feelings are. If I were to ask Great-grandma Barraclough she would only say, "Don't be daft, lad." I know that I am confused by the situation, with my father away at sea more often than not (when will we see him again?), my mother at home one week and away the next (where is she?), my maternal grandmother *persona non grata* with her mother, my great-grandmother, (what went wrong there?), and some unidentified relatives who are out of bounds on Second Street (ditto). But is confusion a feeling? Can you differentiate it from shame or uncertainty, say? Why have Jenny and I been left with an old lady who makes us read the Bible every night and claims that comics are the work of the devil? Perhaps it is as well that no-one talks about feelings. There would be no answers for the questions they raise.

When Mother is away Jenny and I are instructed to write to her. I cannot write in joined-up writing yet and I have not yet been taught to use ink, so I draw capitals in pencil.

> DEAR MAMA
> I HAVE COME HOME FROM SCHOOL BECAUSE I DID NOT FEEL VERY WELL. YESTERDAY WE WENT TO GRIMLEY GLEN AND SAW THE CANAL. ON SATADAY WE WENT TO THE PICTURES AND SAW THE BEST HORSE IN ENGLAND IT WAS BLACK PRINCE OWNED BY MR JACK DOBSON WHICH WON FIRST PRIZE A SILVER CUP.
> LOVE FROM JAMES
> xxxxxxxxxxxxxxx
> xxxxxxxxxxxxxxx

Underneath I draw a picture of myself – sideways on, so that it will fit into the space at the bottom of the page. I look neat, with parted hair, a buttoned-up shirt, short trousers and ankle socks. I guess I want to remind my mother who I am and what I look like in case she forgets. The following week, still in pencil:

> DEAR MAMA
> HOW ARE YOU GETTING ON? ALL RIGHT? WE DO NOT GO TO WISBEY SCHOOL, WE GO TO WIGGLESWORTH SCHOOL.

Evidently she does not know we have changed schools.

> I GOT TEN OUT OF TEN IN TABLES AND NINE OUT OF TEN FOR SUMS AND 18 OUT OF 20 FOR SPELLINGS.
> LOVE FROM JAMES
> x x x x x x x x x x

Only one line of kisses now. I do not approve of her absence. She is like a ship sinking slowly from sight over the horizon, perhaps never to return.

By the time of the next letter I have learnt to use pen and ink, and I am experimenting with upper and lower-case, so there is something new to demonstrate.

Dear Mama

How are you getting on? We use ink at school now. yesterday all the other schools had holiday and we did not and that is not fair On sataday I am going to the Fair ~~wh~~ with Donald Nudds his dad and Jenny is it nice where you are? I am not useted to having only Flakes for breakfast. Do you have a nice big breakfast there? because we don't here we only have Flakes. We got a postcard of his ship from Dad.

Love from James

x x x x x x

Fewer kisses still. 'Do you have a nice big breakfast there?' – where? where? where is she? I know that Dad is away because of the war, though his ship docks in Grimsby and Liverpool and Hull and still we hardly see him. Great-grandma Barraclough says he is chasing skirts and exercising his elbow, so I assume he is keeping fit.

I see now how this might explain the Casanova letter – the one that leaves my mother feeling so bitter.

♀

Chapter 2

Sea Dogs and Libertine Adventurers

My FATHER HAS A FACE LIKE A PICKLED WALNUT and his ginger hair is combed back short and flat. He has a red nose, nicotine-stained fingers and a regular cough from never being without a Wild Woodbine, a Players Weight or a roll-your-own. I am impressed by his roll-your-own appliance. I watch as he takes the shreds of tobacco from a green and gold Virginia tin, spreads the tobacco evenly between the rollers, extracts a wafer of paper from a red Rizla packet, jiggles the paper in the rollers until it fits, then rolls the rollers with his thumbs, licks a line of glue on the edge of the paper, rolls a bit more, then flicks the bottom roller with his thumb and out it comes. When I succeed in rolling my first cigarette, it is the same feeling I had when I first tied my own shoelaces.

My father is like Jenny. He laughs a lot. He laughs when Mother is yelling that his brain is soft with salt water and rum. This upsets her even more. I have some of his charm, I think, though more of my mother's impatience and irritability. At least I can say after all the Latin and Greek and thinking a lot while cross-country running that my brain is my own, poor uncertain thing though it is.

I hear Great-grandma talking to her friend Mrs Kershaw about my father. "'E's a right wife in every port Don Juan," she says, pronouncing it 'Don Jewan'. "How many wives has he got?" I ask. They laugh. "And what is a Don Jewan? Is he Jewish?" "Nay, lad," says Great-grandma. "'E's Methodist, same as the rest of us, or 'e is when 'e's sober." "Why does he not come to see us more often?" I ask. She looks at me. I know what's coming: "Ee, lad. Too many questions."

I look up 'Don Jewan' in Pears' Cyclopaedia, War Economy Issue. And what I find between 'Donjon' ('the keep of a castle, a last refuge') and 'Doonga' ('a rough kind of East Indian canoe') is 'Don Juan, one of the libertine adventurers of literature'. That sounds more like it. I look up 'libertine' in the Modern Illustrated Home Dictionary, which defines it as 'a free-thinker who leads a licentious life'. I wonder if a free-thinker will be a good thing to be when I am older. 'Licentious', I find, means 'given to the indulgence of the animal passions', which I think has something to do with sex, so I expect to find out more in due course.

I mentioned the Casanova letter my father wrote. I find it in the fireplace.

Dear Mildred,

Do not know how to begin. You used the right word when you said Casanova. But I have never gone so far as to break any hearts, so do not start thinking I am a bad lot. It has only been a change from male company on board, although you can soon get a reputation of being a Casanova just by being able to get into conversation with the other sex. But let me leave my lurid past, we must think of

The rest is burnt. I look up Casanova, but can't find it. From the letter it seems to be about getting into conversation with the other sex, but I think there might be more to it than that. I notice that he does not write 'opposite', but 'other', sex. Does this show that he likes and respects women or not? And what does he mean by 'my lurid past'? 'Lurid' means 'shining with an unnatural red glow as of fire seen through smoke'. Is he referring to a burning ship he escaped? Why did Mother burn the letter? Why does he smoke and drink so much? What does Great-grandma Barraclough mean by "There's no smoke wi'out fire?" I know that fire at sea is a terrible hazard. Is he too cockeyed to care whether he burns to death or drowns?

One of his rare visits coincides with April Fools' Day. I want to make the day memorable, so I plan that he will find me slumped in a chair with a blood-soaked bandage around my head and that Jenny will say, "He hit his head on a spar when he was helping Mr Oldroyd launch his boat." There is a fundamental problem with this plan – a lack of blood for the bandage. I am loath to use my own blood, Jenny refuses to give me any of hers, not even a few drops, and there is no raw meat in the pantry, as we mainly eat tripe and sausages, and we are out of tomato ketchup, so I smear brown HP sauce on the bandage instead. When Dad comes to the door I slump in the chair and when he comes in, I moan. Jenny strokes my head and tells him I hit my head on the spar. "Good grief," he says, "we must take him to the Infirmary!" He comes close to inspect me, murmuring, "So Oldroyd has a sailboat, eh? I always thought it was a motorboat." "April Fool!" I cry and take off the bandage.

My father's breath wafts over me. He smells like a rum-soaked, chain-smoking, pickled-faced gnome, which is more or less what he is. "You are the April Fool, Jim lad," he says with unnecessary relish. "It is after twelve o'clock!" I have never heard of this preposterous twelve o'clock rule. You can never catch him out. He is as slippery as a fish.

To cheer me up he shows me a rude trick with a packet of Woodbines. "One hot day," he says, "a woman and her daughter are out walking in the woods ..." he points to the leafy-green part at the front of the packet "... when they come across a cool-looking pool." That is the bluey-green rectangle at the back of the packet. "They are very hot, but they do not have their swimming costumes, so they take off all their clothes and wade into the pool to bathe." I wonder to myself if they check first to see how deep it is or whether like Downend Pond the water is full of rusting bedsteads and bomb-damage bricks, but of course it does not matter. He continues: "Suddenly the daughter sees a stranger walking towards them and in a panic she says to her mother one of the words printed on the packet." I read and re-read every word on the packet, and finally have to give up. Dad points to the word 'diploma'. Apparently Woodbines have a diploma for something. I do not get the joke. "Dip-low-ma," he says, and laughs like a drain, as if getting one over on your young son is a great achievement.

When the time comes for him to leave, I ask him when he will be coming again. "We are an island nation, Jim lad," he says. "I have to go down to the sea and bring back sugar and spice and all things nice." "But when will you be coming again?" "Soon," he says. I persist. "When is soon?" I need a date to put in the diary I was given for Christmas. He will not say when. Slippery, as I say. As slippery as the seaweed on the rocks in the bay.

For a time I imagine that my father might be a pirate like Long John Silver, and that one day he will bring home gold plate and jewels and we will all be rich. Then I think he might be a nobleman held hostage like Don Guzman in Westward Ho! Or a prisoner-of-war, torpedoed and captured by the Germans and unable to escape. Any of these would be better than not knowing when I will see him again. Where is he? Who is he? Invariably I am drawn to Robert Louis Stevenson's brilliant picture of the Old Sea Dog:

> A tall strong heavy nut-brown man, his tarry pigtail falling over the shoulders of his soiled blue coat, his hands ragged and scarred, with black, broken nails.

This nut-brown man, not the libertine Don Juan, is the Dad of my dreams. I see him parrying the slash of a sabre with his cutlass while rescuing me and my sister from black-bearded ruffians intent on taking us into slavery on the Barbary coast. It seems to me that rescuing their children is one of the few things fathers are for. Yet here we are still, stuck with a praying, grey-haired old lady who won't let us read comics.

Do let me know if you ever want rescuing – from the influence of your mother, say. I'm serious. It may not be too late.

While waiting for my father to appear I collect cigarette cards of famous ships, planes and national flags, and read everything I can about the Call to Adventure. After Treasure Island I look in the library for more books on tropical islands. I am thrilled to find The Coral Island, A Tale of the Pacific Ocean, by R.M. Ballantyne. The story concerns a boy, Ralph Rover, who is marooned on a desert island and founds an entirely new state with two other boys. After a series of adventures they are rescued and return home wiser and more mature. I am disappointed by Coral Island. It is nothing like as blood-curdling as Treasure Island, which is surely one of the best books ever written, and I include the *Odyssey* and the *Iliad*, which are required reading at school, but which never thrill me, engage me or sadden and scare me as much as Stevenson's great tale of treasure and treachery.

If you have not yet read The Odyssey, by the way, you can take it from me that it is occasionally interesting but rather repetitive, like rowing a trireme across the Aegean in predictable weather. Westward Ho! and Treasure Island are far more compelling. Their stories soar and swoop like seabirds in a tropical storm, appealing and alarming in turn.

I read extracts from Treasure Island to Jenny at night by the light of a candle. She is terrified at the thought of the Seafaring Man with One Leg appearing, so I read that part over and over, particularly when the North wind is rattling the attic window and foam-topped waves are crashing outside in the bay.

> How that personage haunted my dreams, I need scarcely tell you. On stormy nights, when the wind shook the four corners of the house, and the surf roared along the cove and up the cliffs, I would see him in a thousand forms, and with a thousand diabolical expressions.

"Please do not read the bit about the leg!" she pleads, but I know she really wants to hear it.

> Now the leg would be cut off at the knee, now at the hip; now he was a monstrous creature who had never had but the one leg, and that in the middle of his body.

"Aha!" I cry in a fearful, piratical voice. "Aha!!"

I imagine my wounded father in a dozen such forms coming home from the sea. Even with the drunkenness, the typhoons and knife fights I believe that life as a Sea Dog would be so much better than life in a village on shore. It would, of course, be tough. And with the war getting nearer it might not last long enough.

φ

Chapter 3
Casualties of War

THE WAR AFFECTS ME about as much as it affects every other child who has no idea what is going on: very little at first and then in odd disjointed ways.

Mother takes us from Rawley Bay in Yorkshire to Scarmouth-on-Sea in Kent. At first I think it might be because my father's ship is due to dock in Scarmouth or Whitsea and we will get to see him before the pubs open. On a hill overlooking the harbour I find a tavern that reminds me of the Benbow Inn, so I go there whenever I can to keep an eye out for mariners with pigtails and parrots or eye-patches and missing limbs. My father might have been injured by exploding gunpowder, like Blind Pew, or had an arm shot off by a blunderbuss, like Black Dog. I am too young to go in the pub, so I fly my kite nearby on the cliff tops. I never see my father.

There is a war on and nothing is certain, but why are we here? We have been evacuated, I am told. Hitler wants to destroy all the factories and a bomb aimed at Thirby Mills might miss and drop on Rawley Bay. I do not follow the logic of this. If Scarmouth is as near to Germany as Rawley and Thirby, which anyone with an atlas can see that it is, how can it possibly be safer? A German pilot flying over Kent on his way to London might decide to drop his bombs on Scarmouth and go home early. And has anyone thought about the possibility of an enemy destroyer appearing in the harbour at Scarmouth with her guns ready loaded and blowing us all to bits? I certainly have. Perhaps we are here because Mother has some other purpose. Perhaps Scarmouth has something in common with Leeds.

I failed to learn to swim in Rawley Bay and I fail again in Scarmouth. "You are going to learn to swim," says Mother as she drags me to the beach. She will not accept that I am scared witless of the water. Am I the only one who pictures maritime monsters flapping their barnacled arms to create unstoppable undercurrents that will sweep me out to sea and into oblivion? If you have ever felt uncontrollable panic, even for a second, you will know what it is like to be suddenly out of your depth. My feet feel nothing beneath them. It is a premonition of death. The terror only subsides when my feet feel the sea floor again.

I refuse to go in over my waist. "That is not deep enough to swim," says Mother. "I do not care!" I cry. "Come out further towards me!" she calls. "No!" I cry.

"Come here!" she yells. She is standing in the sea staring at me. Suddenly a wave closes over my head and my mouth and nostrils fill with water. I retreat to the beach gasping with shock and revulsion, dragging my feet against the tide. My mother wades impatiently after me, cursing my unwillingness to subject myself to pointless torture.

I am relieved when we are banned from the beach because of mines in the sea. Is that mine floating only a few yards out British or German? It won't make much difference if someone sets it off. And by the way, I am thinking of writing to the Prime Minister to warn him that the single roll of barbed wire on the cliff top is nowhere near enough to repel a German invasion.

I see planes flying overhead and white lines of vapour criss-crossing high in the sky. Then G.I.s are walking around town. Jenny and I learn to call out, "Got any gum, chum?" I ask the teacher at school what G.I. stands for. She thinks it might be Government Issue or Galvanized Iron. I don't think she knows.

A G.I. calls at the flat where we are boiling winkles we have collected to eat with salt and a bent pin for tea. Mother is surprised, but she seems to know him. "This is Don, kids." "Hello, Mr Kidds," I say, having been taught to call men who aren't related to me 'Mister'. He laughs. "That is James," says Mother, "take no notice. And this is Jenny." "These are yours?" he asks Mother. "Well, they are today!" she says with a little laugh. "Would you like some winkles?" I'm glad to have a man to help me with the kite I made that I can't get to fly, even when the wind is blowing fiercely on the cliff tops. I tell him I want the kite to chase down seagulls, but it is really to give me an excuse to hang around the Benbow Inn. Unfortunately he seems to know very little about kites. He doesn't stay long. Either my mother hadn't told him she was married or he is a member of the U.S. Secret Service who came to pass over some codes and doesn't want to risk being identified.

The next time we are in town we see him walking on the other side of the street with some friends. Jenny and I call out, "Got any gum, chum?" but he doesn't respond. We never see him again and Mother never mentions him. He might have been killed in France or Germany. Everyone is coming and going – to the pub, to sea, to France, to Leeds or Morecambe - and there is no guarantee you will see them again.

Whenever we take a walk along the cliff tops near the Benbow Inn I look for my father. It seems to me that he should be doing my job of saving Mother from falling off the cliff. She makes me walk between her and the edge, presumably so that if the cliff ever collapses or there is a sudden gust of wind I will be the first to go. "It's what gentlemen do," she says when I question the practice. I wonder what it would be like for a gentleman to be smashed to pieces on the rocks and to land in a bloody pulp on the beach below. Would it be better or worse than drowning? Perhaps I would break my fall on a ledge half-way down and wait to be rescued while bleeding to death from a fractured skull. These are very high cliffs and I might never be found. Alternatively like Billy Bones I will be tracked to the Benbow Inn by my former shipmate, one-armed Black Dog, who will pass me the

Black Spot in the palm of his remaining hand. From that moment on my fate will be sealed.

In bed that night I down a bottle of rum in one go and read to Jenny in a pitiless voice.

> The mate was fixed by the bosun's pike
> The bosun brained with a marlinspike
> And cookey's throat was marked belike!

Then we say our prayers and open the Bible where we left it the previous night. We have reached the part of Genesis where a Great Flood prevails upon the earth.

> And every living substance was destroyed which was upon the face of the ground, both man, and cattle, and the creeping things.

It is wartime, so it is quite possible that every living thing will be destroyed with very little warning. At night I hear the V2 rockets flying overhead on their way to London. We are told you are safe as long as you can hear them, which is another way of saying you are in trouble if the sound stops. It means that a bomb is on its way down and if you are unable to get to a shelter or a cellar or under a table in time you could be blown to smithereens or buried alive. I wonder if being blown to smithereens would be better or worse than drowning while learning to swim or being smashed to a pulp after falling off a cliff. And would being buried alive be better or worse than any of these? What is the best way to escape from a burning ship? What would your last thoughts be as flames from burning oil race towards you on the surface of the water?

I lie awake listening for the sounds of bombs flying overhead until I think it might be better to listen for sudden silences. This is what reading about every living substance being destroyed does for you. I am forever expecting a sudden flood or for the roof to fall in, whereas what I ought to be worrying about is whether I will get a Meccano set or a cricket bat for my birthday and if there is enough treacle pudding for a second helping. I ought to have normal parents who are always there and behaving normally. Instead I have to be ready for anything, perpetually walking along the edge of a cliff while waiting for a sudden gust of wind.

After some months we return to Rawley without seeing my father. Mother goes away again. It is pointless asking where she has gone or why. Great-grandma will only accuse me of asking too many questions. She asks Jenny and me if we have been keeping up with the readings from the Bible. 'Too many questions', I almost say. "Oh yes," says Jenny, but the truth is hardly at all. We have reached page twelve of the Old Testament and there are eight hundred and seventy-eight more pages to go before the New Testament, which has two hundred and sixty-nine pages. I skip ahead to see what happens at the end of the Old Testament. Someone by the name of 'Malachi 4' is warning readers of

> the coming of the great and dreadful day of the LORD.

I guess this will happen sometime over the next two hundred and sixty-nine pages. The threat of a dreadful day is followed by

> And he shall turn the heart of the fathers to the children

which is a nice idea, though in our case unlikely. Something else is in prospect:

> Lest I come and smite the earth with a curse.

Isn't this meant to be the Good Book? There is far too much threatening, dreading, smiting and cursing. Jenny and I make a secret agreement: we will get to the end of Genesis and see how we feel.

Grandma Lily moves into a house around the corner in Third Street. Great-grandma, her mother, instructs us never to go there, so we go as often as possible. We call her Grandma Lily because her surname keeps changing. She was originally a Barraclough, then she was a Winterbottom, then a Peroni. Great-grandpa Barraclough was her father, who died in the front room a few days after his bed was brought down to be by the fire. Grandpa Winterbottom was her first husband, who was lost at sea. I wonder if any of the men lost at sea ever turn up and surprise everyone. And Mr Peroni – or, as Great-grandma liked to call him, Pepperoni – was a juggler Grandma Lily met when they were on the same bill at the Pontefract Hippodrome. I don't think they were married, but she called herself Mrs Peroni for a while. She also has a professional name. 'Lily Lemarr', it says in the programmes she shows me. 'Contralto, Comedienne, have a Laugh and a Singalong'.

Grandma Lily is as plump as a suet pudding and as jolly as a barful of sailors. She sings, she recites, she dances round the kitchen when the radio is on and rests her big bosoms on the table at mealtimes. Her favourite drink is Tia Maria. "If anyone asks you, James," she says when she gives me a sip, "this is *not* alcoholic." She holds parties where everyone has to do a turn and she is always top of the bill. Some of her songs and monologues are comical and some are sentimental. My favourite is Albert and the Lion, which is both cruel and sad. The little lad's fate, you will recall, is to be swallowed whole by a lion in Blackpool Zoo.

> Then Pa, who had seen the occurrence,
> And didn't know what to do next
> Said 'Mother! Yon lion's 'et Albert,'
> And Mother said 'Ee, I am vexed'.

I know very little about my male relatives.

Who are yours too, I'm afraid. Some were divorced, some disgraced, others died or disappeared. Here goes.

Uncle Arthur hasn't been seen since he went AWOL when his ship called at Halifax, Nova Scotia during the war. Uncle Jack Wibley served in the Middle East with the Royal Engineers and died of camel flu. Grandpa Winterbottom's trawler capsized in a storm in the North Sea when the skipper was driving too hard for home. There is a scandal of some sort attached to Grandpa Seagrave, who is never mentioned even though he lives two streets away. I hardly see my cousin Melvin because Great-grandma doesn't get on with his mother, Aunt Ada. Great-grandma also disapproves of my cousin Ivan's mother, Auntie Joan, who sympathized with the Russians during the war and named her son after Ivan the Terrible.

There. Best I can do, I'm afraid.

Auntie Joan, by the way, was originally a Barraclough, then she was Wilson, and when they divorced she married a Mr Wibley, and when he died she went back to calling herself Wilson. It was that or revert to Barraclough.

The war in Europe ends. Dad takes a shore job in Middlebridge docks, Mother comes back for a while from wherever she was, there is a street party and we all move into Seven Fourth Street together for several weeks. Dad is on the night shift, because of the money, he says, but I think it might be because of my mother. One morning he brings home a stray dog he found at the docks after a fire. Mother says he has to take it back immediately. Dad says he cannot take it back, because it has nowhere to go. Mother shouts at him, Dad strokes the dog so that it doesn't get upset, Jenny strokes the dog so that *she* doesn't, Mother stalks out of the room and slams the door behind her. She has no respect for doors. Dad goes after her, which leads to more eruptions and explosions and shouting and slamming. Jenny cries for the first time since dropping the neighbour's baby. Mother cries. The sea gulls cry. I take the dog outside for a run around the slag heaps. I vow that if I ever have a house of my own I will take off all the doors.

Jenny and I beg to be allowed to keep the dog and eventually Mother agrees to a trial period. We call him Ruff, because that is what he sounds like when he tries to bark. He can't bark, so he croaks. Ruff is another casualty of war. He is not a happy dog. I think if he could speak he would have something sad to say. Jenny and I take crusts of bread up to bed at night and when Dad comes home after the night shift he lets Ruff upstairs so that we can feed him. Unfortunately, when he goes downstairs again he is sick behind the sofa – Ruff, not Dad. Dad usually manages to throw up outside.

One day I come home from school to find that Ruff has disappeared. Mother says he must have run away to sea and changes the subject. It is another example of the fudging and dodging I have come to expect from every grown-up I know.

The war in the Far East ends. Dad leaves to seek work in the London Docks. Jenny and I move in with Great-grandma again and Mother goes away again. It might be to Leeds or Morecambe, but it could equally be John O'Groats or Mozambique, we have no idea. Grandma Lily moves to South Yorkshire to live with a miner called Bert. Auntie Joan and cousin Ivan emigrate to South Africa. Great-grandma has a vision of Jesus serving behind the counter at the Co-op and is taken to see someone. Mother comes home again for a short while, a man called Mr Sutcliffe comes to tea and Mother puts out her best china.

Zip-a-dee-doo-dah
Zip-a-dee-ay ...

After bearing involuntary witness to the madness around me, I am about to embark on an adventure of my own. I pass an examination called the eleven-plus and win a scholarship to the King's School, York.

Westward Ho! and Treasure Island are not required reading at King's, I discover. I am introduced instead to Virgil, Homer, La Rochefoucauld and Cicero. After the uncertainties of war, a fresh demanding breeze begins to blow.

φ

Chapter 4
Narcissus and Echo

A SALESMAN TAKES THE OXFORD COMPANION TO CLASSICAL LITERATURE and Harrap's Shorter French and English Dictionaries from his suitcase. "I can assure you, Madam," he says to my mother, "that no serious scholar should be without these." He is referring to me, I realize. I am the serious scholar. Great-grandma Barraclough tells my mother not to waste her money, but to give it to the church. "Jesus wants James to have a good education," says Mother.

The Oxford Companion is a treasure trove of information with incidents of murder, madness and drowning on every page, endlessly fascinating tales of gods, demi-gods, nymphs and monsters, superb drawings of Greek and Roman armour and fascinating maps of Asia Minor. I especially like the book's first entry, for 'Abdera'.

> A Greek city in Thrace, birthplace of the sage Protagoras and the philosopher Democritus, nevertheless proverbial for the stupidity of its inhabitants.

The sage Protagoras is quoted as saying that pleasure is the only true good; that good underlies all virtue; that all virtues reduce to one virtue; that the one worthwhile virtue is knowledge; and therefore virtue, like knowledge, can be taught. If this is the case I vow to pursue learning, which I believe will lead through virtue to the greater good, which I understand from Mr Dipshaw (Dippy), our Classics master at King's, to be pleasure. Dippy is at pains to point out that it does not follow from this that we should act selfishly. He seems rather to be saying that it is possible to pursue pleasure and get away with it. This is good news for me, if not for my pleasure-dreading, god-fearing guardian of a great-grandmother.

Dippy is a fan of Protagoras, who also says that things are only good or bad according to how you perceive them; that 'goodness' and 'badness' do not exist in themselves. Another surprise. I conclude that we should learn to distinguish good and desirable from bad and undesirable in our own natures, the better to know it in the world at large. It follows therefore, as Dippy says, that we should first pay close attention to ourselves.

He goes on: "A sea-nymph by the name of *Leiriope* takes her son *Narcissus* to a prophet and asks if he will die young. The prophet replies, 'Only if he does not know himself'. What does he mean by that?" The class offer various theories.

Dippy returns to Protagoras, who said that meaning does not exist independently; it is as subjective as 'truth', 'good' or 'bad'. To put it another way, meaning lies less in what you believe to be intended by the writer or speaker and more in what you understand as the reader or listener, which in turn means, at least to me, that we should first know ourselves before we know meaning; that whatever Protagoras and the prophet might have thought they meant it is their meaning to *you* that matters.

I apply this basic bit of linguistic philosophy to the French dictionaries my mother bought for me. These are heavy, handsome books with textured covers embossed in gold, but whenever I refer to them I wonder if I need to know quite so much about gerunds and derivatives, or to be offered quite so many alternative meanings for the simplest of words. You can go under in dictionaries like these. Take the first entry, for 'A'.

> A, a¹ [ei]. 1. (La lettre) A, a, M. It is spelt with two a's, cela s'écrit avec deux
> a, F. Not to know A from B, etre absolument nul. A1 [ei'wan], (i) …

It goes on like this for half a page. The entry for 'one' takes up two entire pages, whereas all I need to know for the moment is *'un'*. The dictionaries are called 'Shorter', but they are too long to be of much use to a young scholar, however serious he aspires to be.

They are not the biggest books I have ever seen. Bigger by far is the gilt-covered Daily Express Book of the Coronation of George the Sixth Crowned King of Great Britain, which Great-grandma keeps in a drawer wrapped in tissue paper. My sister and I are only allowed to turn its pages under strict supervision. One of the photographs is of the then Prince of Wales and Mrs Simpson passing the time agreeably by the sea on Capri or the Côte d'Azur. The Prince is floating in the water wearing extremely long shorts, while Mrs S. sits on a rock nearby in a swimsuit. The royal shorts are as long as the plus-fours he wears in other photographs. I am concerned that the sea might fill his shorts and drag him down.

"We see ourselves in all waters," says Dippy in reference to Narcissus. After my experience of rooting around in rock pools in Rawley Bay (not too scary at low tide), fishing for human heads in Downend Pond (scary but exciting and the prospect of assisting the police with their enquiries), and racing home-made boats in the beck (more fun if I concentrate on the boats rather more than the beck), not to mention walks by the River Yore and the Thirby to Middlebridge Canal (keeping well away from the edges), I find what Dippy says fascinating. "In warm baths, fountains, tears and oceans," he says. "Water can be supportive and cathartic, gentlemen. It can also be pitiless."

I have known for a while that after the incident in the North Sea, which is a mystery still, and falling into the beck, which was quite a shock, and being held under by a half-wit called Protheroe in the King's School baths, and all my life hearing talk of shipwrecks at Pendle Point and men from the village being lost at sea, I have a fear of the water. The Greeks called it *aquaphobia*, or more specifically, if they were talking about the sea, *thalassaphobia*. I am also not too keen on lakes (*limnophobia*), which are miniature seas, or on rivers and streams (*potamophobia*), without which lakes would not exist.

From the maps in my Oxford Companion I see that Greece is a nation of islands and that the Greeks, like the Brits, have a great deal of water to contend with. I am fine with water from the tap, by the way, which you might think just as well. Yet despite feeling anxious on or near bodies of water, I am also drawn to them. I fear and envy them. I am haunted and fascinated. I suppose the haunted part relates to my imminent sense of death in the North Sea and the King's School baths, and the fascinating part to the realization that I have to get over the haunted part. I have nightmares of drowning, but I also have intensely pleasurable dreams of swimming in a large outdoor pool, a dream so realistic that on waking I believe for a moment that I am at one with the water. The last thing I want to be is a marine biologist, but it is also something I would dearly love to be, if that makes sense.

Dippy is not like the other teachers, and not only because he believes that the meaning a teacher puts upon a thing is not the only meaning possible. The pens and pencils he wears in his breast pocket seem to be more for decorative than practical purposes. His face is full and his hair is carefully coiffed. "Narcissus is a beautiful youth, the son of a river god and a sea nymph," he tells us. "Everyone who sees him, youths or maidens, fall in love with him." I think Dippy thinks of himself as a bit of a Narcissus. He is not married, he tells us (Dippy, not Narcissus). He was asked once, but he turned the lady down. And when the nymph Echo falls in love with him (Narcissus, not Dippy), he treats her with some disdain. You might say he is a vain young man.

The prophet predicts that Narcissus will die young if he does not know himself, but the gods decide that self-love has its limits and he should be punished. They lure Narcissus to a pool and oblige him to fall in love with the reflection he sees there, which is, of course, himself. Love leads to fixation, fixation to a sort of insanity. "His fruitless attempts to possess this beautiful object lead to his death," says Dippy sadly. And he goes on to make an extraordinary claim, but it seems me that he is as much an authority on the subject as anyone can be. "Water," says Dippy, "is female. It may attract you, gentlemen, or anyway most of you, with the possible exception of Sheldon and Duxberry, but it is also unstable and dangerous." I am unable to suppress an image of my mother that comes to mind. Dippy continues, "When Narcissus breaks the surface of the pool the water-nymphs take their revenge." I am surprised and disappointed to learn that nymphs and gods have their less pleasant side, having believed that nymphs were all good-natured and accommodating, and gods high-minded and wise.

Dippy goes on about the lust for revenge of women who are unable to cope with their betrayal by men. "Betrayal," he points out, "is merely temporary disloyalty to a person, an idea or an ideal. We would be inhuman if we were wholly consistent. But if you were to suppose that men were not created by the gods to be loyal to a fault, gentlemen – and far be it for me to speculate, but it could conceivably be for reasons related to the perpetuation of the species – you might ask why should they be expected to go against their god-given nature?"

A word of warning. Some of this might have more meaning for you when I come to consider what happened between me and your mother.

"Sir, are there really nymphs, sir?" asks Brewster, who is a bit on the dim side. "What do you think, Brewster?" asks Dippy, and goes on without waiting for an answer: "Certainly there are nymphs." Brewster does not know quite how to take this. Dippy continues, "All of them female. In myth and epic poetry it is usually women who cause the trouble." That strikes me as unlikely, but I have a lot to learn. We discuss the case of *Medea*, the enchantress, who having been betrayed by her husband murders his mistress and as if that were not enough kills her own children too. She was the cause of a great deal of trouble, but was there some cause that caused hers?

I wonder about my mother's relationship with my father. Had she been tempted, if only momentarily, to hold my head under in order to wreak a bizarre kind of revenge on him? Does she look upon me as the personification of her punishment, her *Nemesis*? Surely taking revenge on your husband by attempting to drown his son would leave you with an empty kind of feeling, as well as frightful guilt.

Oh gosh, am I beginning to sound like a public schoolboy? No-one in Rawley would ever have said 'frightful'. In my defence, I hasten to add (actually, no-one in Rawley would ever say 'hasten' either, or come to that, 'gosh'), that I am the only one in my class at King's to vote Labour. I know this is so, because the result of the mock-election is Conservative 18, Labour 1. Before the ballot I ask Great-grandma Barraclough for a question to put to the Conservative candidate. "Ask 'im wheer t'money's comin' from," she says. "Money for what?" I ask. "For owt," she says. This strikes me as a really good question for a fearless scholarship boy to ask in a class of liberal-minded fee-paying boys, so I don't ask it.

On the way home I break the thin coating of ice on Downend Pond and look at myself in the water. And what I see there is a stripling looking winsome and pale. "Who are you?" I ask. "Are you, are you?" responds Echo, who unknown to me has been following me home. I look again and see my father grinning mindlessly back at me. I am *not* my father, I tell myself. His reflection dissolves into the pockmarked features of Long John Silver, which cheers me up somewhat, because that evening's homework is to write an essay in French on the subject of my favourite book.

It is time to put my new Harrap's dictionaries (Vol. I French-English, 688 pp; Vol. II English-French, 940 pp) to the test. 'Old Sea Dog' is not in the English-French edition, but sea-shore, sea-way and sea-faring are, and there are also several kinds of 'dog', such as fire-dog and dog-biscuit, so I put the words for old, sea and dog together to make *Vieux Chien de la Mer* and work them into my essay. The next day I find a red line through the phrase and a sarcastic comment from M'sieur: *'Do not reach beyond yourself, Seagrave'*. Beyond myself? That is not very helpful. Who am I? And how would either he or I know?

"In our overweening conceit all we see is a distorted reflection of ourselves," says Dippy, "and too often get it wrong." I take this to mean that we should not assume there is a single meaning to anything. What is important is the meaning we *make* of it – but more than that is the recognition that that is *all* it is – a reflection of ourselves. Have I got this right? I console myself with the thought that I will understand more when I am old enough to be a free-thinker, like Don Juan.

There is no-one at home who can help with these questions, no-one I know who knows the first thing about mythology, philosophy or French syntax. My friend Donald Nudds went to Secondary Modern school to study woodwork and nautical knots. He wants to be a boat builder. Great-grandma Barraclough is an expert on the Bible, the price of fish and the last hundred years of shipwrecks. I can appreciate there is as much meaning to be found in any of these matters as in anything else. My great-grandmother must think she is saying something self-evident when she says, "I tek a man for what 'e is," whereas in all likelihood her friends and neighbours have no idea what she means or another idea altogether.

Neither hunger nor the desire for sleep will tear Narcissus from his reflection. In despair he cries, "I see what I desire, but I cannot possess it! This face that looks back at me with love smiles when I smile and weeps when I weep. Why then must it always escape me?" In a final attempt to grasp his reflection, Narcissus falls into the pool and drowns. "He returns whence he came," declares Dippy. "We are made of water, gentlemen. If I were to grind your bones when you die, Seagrave, and dispose of your sinews, the rest of you would flow like a stream into the sea." We will be subsumed into the greater creation, he is saying, but meanwhile I have to accept that my life is at the whim of vindictive gods and capricious nymphs. I am powerless in the face of forces beyond my control.

It is a year or so later when I come across a boxful of papers that my mother left behind when she left – really left, as I shall explain. I am seeking information, any kind of information, about my life and clues to my fears. Among the postcards, school reports and photographs, I find a foolscap-size envelope containing a document with the title *Decree Nisi*. I look up *'Nisi'*. It is Latin for 'unless'. Unless what?

> This Humble Petition of Wilfred Seagrave showeth that your Petitioner lived and co-habited with the Respondent Mildred Seagrave *(what is the difference between living with someone and co-habiting with them?)* at divers *(various, not belonging to deep-sea divers)* places and there is issue to the marriage, two infants namely James Seagrave and Jennifer Seagrave, and that the said James Seagrave has been educated hitherto at Wigglesworth Council School Ramsbotham aforesaid and has recently begun attending the King's School, York.

It seems to be saying that at the time my father was almost, but not quite, divorced from my mother. *Nisi* must mean *unless* they decided *not* to, or *unless* the Court said they *should not*. There is a puzzle under 'Particulars'.

The Respondent who had on previous occasions asked your Petitioner to leave, informed him that she was going to live her own life and withdrew from co-habitation (*that word again*) with him notwithstanding attempts by your Petitioner to persuade the Respondent to resume co-habitation with him she has never done so (*finally I realize it has to mean sex*).

I realize this all relates to the differences and disappearances of Petitioner and Respondent, but offers no clue as to whether my father was a serial adulterer and chronic alcoholic, or whether my mother was irritable, impossible to live with and seeing someone in Leeds. Or all the above. Why did they get together in the first place? I try not to wonder if they passed their frailties and betrayals onto me.

An unequivocal *Decree Absolute* follows the *Nisi*. It is dated December of that year of the blizzards and snowdrifts so high that you could dig deeply into them and make a cave for yourself. When I read these papers I want to dig myself into a refuge and never emerge.

The Decree Unequivocal was issued by the High Court of Justice Probate, Divorce and Admiralty Division. How did the Admiralty get in on this, I wonder? Is it because my father served in the merchant navy? I wonder if that will affect my plan to join the crew of a freighter, sail to the Pacific, found an ideal state on a desert island and appoint myself sole ruler. Failing which I hope to get as far as Norway.

Neither Narcissus nor I can see the self that really is. We think ourselves virtuous, but as Protagoras says, virtue must be taught. Are the high-minded gods I used to see as models for humanity really such low-life hypocrites and egotists? I need to know whether the ideal me and the one I know can co-exist.

φ

Chapter 5

Duty and Liberty

AN ARTICLE IN THE DAILY HERALD says you can call yourself anything you like, so I try Dirk Kirkpatrick for a while, then Quentin X. Dirk is a Scottish explorer and Quentin a professional swordsman. But a wholesale change of name requires you to go to court, says the article, so I plan to slip in a middle initial instead. Everyone in my class has at least two initials, a few have three and one cousin of a viscount, if pushed, as he often is, confesses to four. I decide on aspirational Seagrave, J.H. rather than unexceptional Seagrave, J. The H will stand for Hawkins or Horatio, I have yet to decide.

James Horatio Seagrave, Lt RN, is a career officer in the Royal Navy, commissioned to serve King and Country with ambition and valour. Jim Hawkins Seagrave is a merchant adventurer, trading in spices and Spanish gold with a lucrative line in unusual fruit. I write my new name on the inside cover of my copies of Treasure Island and C.S. Forester's A Ship of the Line: '*This book belongs to James H. Seagrave*'. Now I must choose between joining the crew of the Hispaniola under Squire Trelawney or HMS Sutherland in the service of Captain Hornblower.

The Captain appeals to All Willing Hearts who Thirst for Glory.

> To all Young men of Spirit, Seamen, Landsmen & Boys, who wish to Strike a Blow for Freedom & to cause the Corsican Tyrant to wish that he had never dared the Wrath of these British Isles …

I see an azure blue sea, a high Peninsular sun and the seventy-four guns of a three-masted frigate standing in under easy sail for a rendezvous off Palamos Point. Ensign Seagrave keeps watch from the fo'c'sle with a nautical spyglass, sweeping the horizon for first glimpse of a Castilian sail.

Meanwhile eager ship's apprentice Jim Seagrave is beside himself with glee as he reads Squire Trelawney's letter to Dr Livesey on the eve of their departure from Bristol.

> The ship is bought and fitted. She lies at anchor, ready for sea. You never imagined a sweeter schooner – a child might sail her – two hundred tons; name Hispaniola.

I go down to the quayside for a long think and a whiff of the sea. There is a choice to be made: am I on the side of Duty and Glory or Liberty and Licence? What if I commit to one, but am later drawn to the other? There is a middle way, I find, which will give me access to both: ship's chaplain, with a cabin between the upper and lower decks, representing one side to the other, keeping the peace between quarrelsome shipmates, bringing warring families together, seeking a balance between the world as I would like it to be and the world as I find it.

In this pious new phase I suggest to Jenny that we take it in turns to read a chapter of the Bible out loud to each other every night. Great-grandma in her role as Defender of the Faith is encouraging. "If tha gets to the end of Deuteronomy," she says, "ah shall make thee some parkin." The prospect of her celebrated treacle-and-ginger cake, a dish normally baked only for Bonfire Night, is the deciding factor in getting us started. This promises to be not only a ground-breaking spiritual and cultural enterprise, but a culinary one too. Perhaps we can prevail upon her to make baked jam roll at a later stage of the journey, at the end of Joshua or Judges, say.

Our religious readings do not go as planned. Mother arrives on one of her visits and wants to hear us. We have reached the bit in Genesis where God is encouraging Abraham to make a burnt offering of his only son Isaac. I am appalled that a father could contemplate such a thing. "What sort of a Dad does that?" I ask my mother. "And what kind of horrible God orders a man to kill his own son?" Mother is dismayed and defensive. "God is NOT horrible and He has His reasons," she says. "He has given Abraham the chance to prove how much he loves Him." She means how much Abraham loves God, of course, not his own son.

Abraham cannot be allowed to get away with this filicidal crime, I decide. I can't be the only person to identify with the wretched son in the story. Genesis, whoever he or she is, only seems interested in the pathetic father. "Would you drown me or burn me to death if God told you to?" I ask my mother. "James!" she exclaims. "How can you say such a thing?" I notice that she does not say she would not, but I have to believe this is an oversight.

I venture another thought that I know will be far more distressing for her than the idea of sentencing a sick old man to community service for threatening to kill his own son. My readiness to express this is the equivalent of Jim Hawkins sailing into uncharted waters and stepping unarmed onto Skeleton Island. "Actually," I say, "I do not believe in God."

"James!" cries my mother. She is even more horrified than I thought she would be. "There are all kinds of gods, not just one," I say, with all the authority of a first-year student of the Classics. "There is only one God!" she exclaims. "Then why are there so many different good and bad things?" I ask, then answer my own question. "There have to be different good and bad gods to look after them all." My mother looks at me, mouth agape. "I do believe in Jesus," I say, in an attempt to mollify her, "though I am not too sure about the miracles." "You cannot have Jesus without God and the miracles!" she cries. "Of course you can," I say. "Jesus was only human." "Do not say that! He was the Son of God! And do not speak to me like that!" "Huh," I mutter. "I prefer Dandy and the Beano," I say, and push the Bible away. Unfortunately, it slides off the slippery eiderdown onto the floor, which was not my intention. My mother slaps me. It hurts, but I realize to my satisfaction that my denial of the Bible in favour of my favourite comics has upset her. She deserves to be upset. *I* am upset by her absence, her ignorance, her gratuitous violence, by the fact that I have to be billeted with a tyrant who was born hundreds of years ago, etc.

My mother slaps me rather more than my sister, because I am a boy and far more annoying. Her favourite place to hit me is the outside of the thigh, which hurts, but sometimes she hits me on the inside of the thigh, which both hurts and stings. If she cannot reach my leg she will aim for my head, although that often misses because I see it coming and duck. She learns to counter this tactic by hitting me from behind when I least expect it.

One day she is serving a special tea for Mr Sutcliffe, the man I mentioned earlier who is here on a visit from India to see his parents in Thirby. My sister and I are determined to entertain him, so I am chasing her round the table and we are laughing a lot. It is a very amusing game, as you can appreciate. Mother does not think so. "STOP THAT THIS MINUTE AND COME BACK TO THE TABLE!" she cries. Jenny sits, giggling, but I continue to run round the room, hee-hawing like a demented donkey. To her credit, Jenny finds this hilarious.

I am outraged when my mother grabs me, slaps me and tells me to go upstairs to my room. I go defiantly, slamming the stairs door behind me in the same way she used to slam the door – any door – when she was angry at Dad. In the attic I get out my navy frigate and pirate galleon and set up a battle at sea. Before long the pirates are winning. After a few minutes, Mother comes up to see me. "I am sorry," she says, "but you were naughty." "I was not," I say, "I was only playing." She comes to kiss me. I refuse to be kissed. "Oh James, you hurt me," she says and leaves. I continue playing. "You hut *me*," I say to the door. The captain of the galleon attacks the navy frigate and his pirates sever the limbs of a few able seamen with their bloody cutlasses – ha, not so able now – and sink their rotten ship.

Sometime later, my mother will say that none of this happened. Even though I still feel the slap. I now wonder if it might only be a representative memory, one that if not literally true is nonetheless entirely truthful. In any case how would I know the difference between something that actually happened and something I am certain happened? Just as I can picture Billy Bones looking nervously round the cove and whistling to himself as he awaits the arrival of the Messenger of Death; just as in my attic I see the torrential rain on the window and the puddles in the potholes on the unmade road below that I cannot see directly but know perfectly well are there, I know it happened.

It is at this moment, I think, that my mother's anger and frustration pass onto me. And the lesson is obvious: I should learn to have my own anger and frustration.

Now I know what my middle name will be. I no longer identify with Duty and Valour, which are so easily perverted into Treason and Treachery. Equally, I no longer see myself holding the middle ground. That would be to compromise myself, and myself is all I have. So I haul down the Red Duster and run up the Skull and Crossbones, and although I continue to say my prayers in case Isaac lives and Abraham recovers his sanity, I find myself saying them with mental reservations.

As for the great religious, cultural and culinary enterprise, Jenny and I give up after Genesis 43, 'And the famine was sore in the land'. It means there will be no Yorkshire parkin before Bonfire Night, but all that biblical incest, sodomy, iniquity, harlotry, flooding and famine are getting to us – even to Jenny, who usually laughs at anything she cannot understand.

There is something else in the air. Mother has bought a large metal trunk. And on the day it is delivered she presents us – bequeaths, it seems, given the unusual formality of the presentation – three of her most precious possessions: the Bible, which goes to Jenny, and Pears' Cyclopædia and the Illustrated Home Dictionary, which go to me. But why? And why now? I dare not ask.

I inscribe my books *James Hawkins Seagrave*. And then comes the day that changes everything, even more than I feared. My fate is in other hands, after all. The Black Spot appears.

φ

Chapter 6
A Walk in the Woods

I AM SCREAMING. Jenny has accidentally knocked over a kettle of boiling water that was standing on a grill thing on the fire and it spills over me. Mother rushes in, sees me and blames Dad, who has only just come into the house. She yells at him. He yells at her. It's not his fault. It is the first time I have heard him yell. I am still screaming. Great-grandma comes in from the toilet and yells at everyone.

A doctor arrives, puts something on me and gives me some tablets. I think he ought to give my mother some too, because I hear her yelling at Jenny, then hitting her, which I think isn't fair even though it was Jenny's fault. So now my sister is screaming too. Everyone is either screaming or yelling.

The day that changes everything comes soon after the business with the kettle, when I am almost better, which makes it worse. Mother takes me for one of her favourite walks by the Yore. It is not one of my favourite walks. I am expected to walk next to the river, just as I had to walk next to the edge of the clifftops in Scarmouth and on the outside of the pavement in Thirby. "It is what gentlemen do," says Mother. 'But I am not a gentleman', I want to say, 'I am only a boy', but all I say is, "Why do I have to walk next to the river?" I feel like Isaac being offered to God as a sacrifice. "Gentlemen walk on the outside to protect the lady," Mother replies. "Why?" I ask. "Because they are gentlemen" is all she can say. "But I am only …" I start to reply, but then give up. Rather than continue to argue the point I think it would be easier to drown.

A walk by the Yore into Birkenshaw Woods is meant to be a treat and we would usually bring home armsful of bluebells, but on this particular day we do not pick a single bluebell. Mother takes the opportunity to convey three unthinkable things in one heartrending sentence: "Your father and I are getting divorced," she says, "and I am going to marry Mr Sutcliffe and live in India." We are walking hand-in-hand at the time. I withdraw my hand in shock. She has transferred the Black Spot from the cold palm of her hand into mine. My fate is sealed.

It will be a year or two before I come across the court papers relating to this time; a year or two before I have to accept that marriage is not necessarily forever. But I am ten years old and my heart stops.

I do not understand why they have to get divorced. If they have a problem, why can't they argue about it or forget it, like Nuddsy and me? And why India? Even though she has been away before it was only for days or weeks at a time and then only to somewhere in England, or possibly France, and as far as I knew she was still married to Dad. I cannot understand why she is going to marry a man I met only once and hardly remember, and that she is going so far away it might as well be the moon.

The River Yore takes a great gulp and swallows me whole. I am sucked into a deep, dark vortex of dirty, dreadful, unspeakable feelings. This is a nightmare. I try to wake. My legs are shaking. I am very, very scared. "WHY?" I ask. She tries to explain that she and Dad do not get on. "*WHY* DO YOU NOT GET ON?" It is all I can think of, because my brain is melting. She cannot explain. "You will understand when you are older," she says. To hear these stupid, banal, demeaning, meaningless words again at this particular moment is infinitely worse than being fobbed off by Great-grandma Barraclough on the subject of Don Juan and whether my father is Jewish or Methodist. It is easily the worst thing anyone has ever said to me. "I WANT TO UNDERSTAND *NOW!*" I cry. "WHY CAN YOU NOT STAY TOGETHER? WHY CAN YOU NOT STAY *HERE*?" I am drowning in fear, fighting for air, desperately attempting to keep my head above water, reaching for the light before the darkness and dirt take over. I cannot breathe properly. I am coughing compulsively. I want to be sick, but nothing will come. A catastrophe is happening, a real one, not like those you read about in books

This will all sound self-pitying and bitter, I suppose. You might say I should put on record some of my mother's redeeming features. I'll try. Well, she worries a lot and makes a good suet pudding. Sorry, I'm not in the mood. This distant, irritable, unsuitable, unavailable woman is the only mother I have and I am about to lose her. If anyone tells me that what is happening is Fate or the Will of the Gods I will punch them on the nose or, better still, push them in the river and throw stones at them.

The next day I cannot speak and a few days later I am taken to hospital. When I wake, my throat is sore. They have taken out my tonsils, but it might as well have been my heart. I weep under the sheets where the nurses cannot see me. It is days before I can speak again and then there is nothing to say. I remember that old man on Third Street who to the despair of everyone who knew him stopped eating one day and went into hospital to die. I am no longer puzzled at why he did this.

How the information about the divorce affects Jenny I cannot be sure. She catches scarlet fever. I watch as the ambulance men carry her from the house wrapped in a blanket as red as her fever, as red as my throat after my heart was ripped out. I think things cannot get any worse, but they do. My books and toys have to be put in the oven to kill off any trace of scarlet fever and when they are retrieved they are all burnt.

After a couple of weeks when the unimaginable has shaded into the barely conceivable, Mother asks for my help with two large leather suitcases and the big metal trunk. "I want you to paint something on them for me," she says. "What do you want me to paint?" I ask, thinking if it were up to me I would paint a shipwreck or a drunken sailor. "I want you to paint 'Mrs H. Sutcliffe' on the suitcases and 'Not Wanted on Voyage' on the trunk." I am confused. "Who is Mrs H. Sutcliffe?" "That will be my name when I marry Mr Sutcliffe in Bombay," she explains. I am shocked. "What is the 'H' for?" I still don't get it. "Mr Sutcliffe's name is Harold," she says. I look at her in disbelief. "But your name is Mildred." "My official name will be Mrs Harold Sutcliffe." I look at her. I look at the trunk and the suitcases. She is giving up the last thing that might have identified her as my mother. Does she think that in some miraculous way this name-painting task will help me deal with her leaving? What it does is help me realize I am no longer part of a nightmare. You can wake from a nightmare and everything will be fine.

Mr Sutcliffe is the man who witnessed my mother's savagery that day he came to tea. How can he marry her after that? It can only be because he approves of domestic violence. And is it legal for her to call herself Mrs Sutcliffe before she is married? Of course she is entitled to call herself anything she likes, but is it decent?

When I come to paint 'Not Wanted on Voyage' I know exactly how the trunk feels. "Thank you, James," says Mother. "That is very neat."

Using the atlas in my Pears' Cyclopaedia of the World she shows me the route that her boat, the S.S. Cecilia, will take from Liverpool into the Irish Sea, south to the Bay of Biscay and the Atlantic Ocean, around Cape St Vincent to the Gulf of Cadiz and the Strait of Gibraltar, east through the Mediterranean, south through the Suez Canal and the Red Sea, and the final leg eastward across the Arabian Ocean to Bombay, where her fiancé Harold Sutcliffe will be waiting. She is excited. It must be exciting for both of them. It is not quite as exciting for Jenny and me.

My sister helps Mother pack. It is what girls do. They help, however they feel. I hide away on the Hispaniola moored off Skeleton Island and overhear the pirates plotting to kill me. Several days later, in a letter posted from Suez, my mother writes

> I was hurt when I came to kiss you goodbye and you carried on reading as though nothing had happened.

I do not know what to write back about how hurt she was.

In fact a great deal has happened. Hitler and Goering committed suicide. Mussolini was executed. A Chinese steamship blew up and sank after hitting a Japanese mine left over from the war and THREE THOUSAND PEOPLE DROWNED. The U.S. President dropped atomic bombs on Hiroshima and Nagasaki that killed and radiated millions of people. Gandhi was assassinated. Don Bradman retained the Ashes for Australia. *(Not sure if you follow cricket. Too complicated to explain here.)*

After the S.S. Cecilia has sailed I read about a boat called the Ramdas that capsized ten miles out of Bombay harbour, but the disaster only became known when the survivors swam ashore. The report made no mention of the non-survivors, presumably because they were not as interesting as the people who managed to swim ten miles to shore.

Then I learn that the S.S. Cecilia has been sunk by a German U-boat in the Red Sea and a Mr H. Sutcliffe has been found drowned in Bombay harbour after a mysterious accident for which no-one can be blamed. They say he is under suspicion of being a German spy. When I wake I realize that unfortunately none of this could have happened, as the war is over.

I think seriously about changing the H for Hawkins in my name to I for Isaac, the sacrificial son, but decide that although the future for J. Hawkins Seagrave might be lonely it will at least be adventurous – and possibly quite short, given Abraham's unforgivable dithering and the bloodthirstiness of God.

> Dear Mama
> How do you like it in India and what was it like on the ship – did you encounter any storms or did you get seasick? Thirby Town lost to Wigan Wanderers 3-1, but during the first half one of Wigan's team deliberately fouled Ward D.H. of Thirby who had to be carried off. I am writing this in bed. It is the old trouble with my headache and stomachache. I should be at school today playing cricket, but the doctor says I have to stay in bed all day. This morning I had a horrible pink tablet. Then at 10.15 I had five nasty white tablets and some medicine, then at 2.15 I have got to have five more white tablets. Then at 6.15 I have to have five more, and five more at 10.15, then I start having three. Phew! Do not forget to send some Indian stamps if you can afford them.

Our next-door neighbour hears Great-grandma Barraclough having another chat with Jesus and this time he is speaking directly to her from the radio. The neighbour calls the doctor, the old lady is taken away and we are sent inland to stay with Aunt Ada in Wyke.

> Everything went all right until this evening. I had a big swelling underneath my ear and Dr Sproat and Aunt Ada think I am down with the mumps. Anyway, Aunt Ada dabbed some black stuff on it, so it might be all right. She says I will live.

Aunt Ada likes telling people what to do. She doles out tablets for stomach aches and headaches, black stuff for mumps, butter for burns, steam for a cold, heat for a fever, cold keys down the back for a bleeding nose, Reckitt's Blue for bee stings and milk for growing bones. She collects kitchen scraps for her chickens and sends us out on the street to scrape up horse manure for her garden.

I do not feel like reading in bed at Aunt Ada's while I am ill, so I listen to my favourite radio programme, Much Binding in the Marsh, as I look out over Wyke

Moor. Every week the programme has a new song to go with the signature tune. I compose one myself for my next letter to India.

> At Much Binding on the Moor
> I'm lying in bed and rubbing my poor tummy
> At Much Binding on the Moor
> My Aunt thinks I've been a bit too chummy
> When Dr Sproat examines me he thinks I'm quite a freak
> And takes a look at my valves and pipes which are just beginning to leak
> While other people run away like frightened deer and say they'll come no more
> To Much-Binding on the Moor!

That is sad, I see now, though at the time I thought it was funny.

Are you following events so far? Let me summarize. My mother, your grandmother-to-be (as you haven't been born yet), has sailed to Bombay (Mumbai, I know) to marry Mr Sutcliffe, leaving me and my sister Jenny, your aunt-to-be, with your great-great-grandmother-to-be in Rawley until she falls ill and we are sent to your great-aunt-to-be Ada and great-uncle-to-be Ernie in Wyke while your grandfather-to-be, Wilfred, sorts things out for us to live with him and his new wife Edith, your no-relative-to-be-I-can-think-of. I hope that's clear.

Aunt Ada tells me a story about my mother and Harold, but before I pass it on you should know that Aunt Ada is my mother's sister-in-law and they do not like each other much. And Aunt Ada does not like my father, her husband Ernie's brother, either. Aunt Ada doesn't like many people. There is some history there related to what I am about to tell you about my mother and Harold. All four of them are involved: Dad and Mother, Ada and Ernie, or six if you include Harold and Auntie Joan. Although Aunt Ada is an envious woman, she does help my education about the world and the things people get up to.

Aunt Ada says that the reason my mother and her sister, Auntie Joan, do not get on is because Harold used to be Auntie Joan's boyfriend. When Harold went to India to work for the British Empire Corporation he assumed that Auntie Joan would pick up with him when he came home on leave, but the war started and he couldn't get home, so Auntie Joan began going out with Uncle Ernie instead. Then Uncle Ernie fell for Aunt Ada (do not ask me why), so Auntie Joan married a Mr Wilson and when Harold appeared again after the war Joan wasn't available, so he tried his luck with Ada, but she was engaged to Ernie, so he started seeing Joan's sister, my mother Mildred, instead, even though she was already married to my father Wilfred. Then Joan and Mr Wilson divorced, Mildred and Wilfred divorced, Ernie was unavailable, Ada was pregnant and Dad wasn't Joan's type, so Harold proposed to Mildred and she went off to join him in India, as you know, leaving Auntie Joan with my cousin Ivan, her son. Ivan is a twerp, so that was a poor bargain all round. Except, presumably, for Harold and Mildred. And Ernie and Ada.

"The upshot of this," says Aunt Ada, "is that in order to marry Harold your mother dumped you and your sister on your great-grandmother and then me." Aunt Ada is not one for niceties. According to her we were holding our mother back from improving her lot. I can understand that. Why would a man in Harold's position take on two kids who weren't his – a ten-year old who laughed at nothing and an eleven-year old who suspected him of being a German spy? It would certainly have affected his career prospects at the British Empire Corporation.

It is obvious that Aunt Ada resents having to look after Jenny and me and is envious of Mother for marrying Harold and sailing off, as she says, to a land of milk and honey. Aunt Ada wrings the necks of her chickens to show us how it is done, but I think it is more to warn us not to get on her wrong side. There is one good thing about Aunt Ada – she makes a good sour milk pudding, although the fact that the milk has to be sour says it all. Great-grandma used to say that Ada could make milk go off just by looking at it.

Aunt Ada tells me how my parents came to be married, and it relates to the reason I wasn't allowed to play on Second Street. Apparently Dad (long before he was, so I shall call him Wilfred) used to live on Second Street with his father and stepmother. Second Street is only two streets away from where my mother-to-be lived on Fourth Street, so little Wilfred and Mildred got to know each other while they were out playing, but their parents, the Seagraves of Second Street and the Barracloughs of Fourth Street, were in a feud over something or other and disapproved. Things did not improve when Wilfred and Mildred grew up and started going out. Then when Wilfred proposed and Mildred accepted, Wilfred's father and stepmother were not invited to the wedding and his stepmother let it be known that if they had been invited they would not have gone.

From what I learn from Dippy about the ancient Greeks, this is very much in the tradition of unscrupulous stepmothers urging their husbands to disown, or preferably kill, their sons by their former wives so that the stepmothers' own sons would inherit the lot and take over when the father died.

> For a stepmother comes as an enemy to the children
> of a former union and is no more gentle than a viper.

Euripides must have had a stepmother too, which would explain why he wrote tragedies. The disinheritance thing happened all the time in ancient Greece and more often than not involved poisoning and multiple murder, so you could argue that we have moved on a bit since, though not much. Today stepmothers use manipulation, humiliation and every other kind of abuse to poison the minds of feeble-minded fathers and alienate them from their unwanted children, as we shall see.

So when Wilfred walked out of the house one day with his wedding suit on a hanger over his shoulder, his stepmother said "Good riddance", his father said nothing and Wilfred never went back. It may have been this that drove him to drink and into the navy. Jenny and I had no idea we had a paternal grandfather living only two streets away. "People are odd," says Aunt Ada, and she should know.

There is something else I learnt from Ada – that she and my mother were in a race to see who would have a baby first. As luck would have it I was born a few weeks before my cousin Melvin. I think it is for this reason that Aunt Ada has it in for me and Melvin is so smug when he beats me at boxing, wrestling, French cricket and billiards.

> Dear Mama,
> How are you? I have a stomachache again. Aunt Ada says she is glad that you are not having as nice weather as us. For breakfast today we had flakes, and beans. Dinner was corned beef, peas, potatoes and peachers and custard.

A month or so later, I make a momentous decision.

> Dear Mother,
> I have decided to call you Mother. I think Mama was all right when I was younger, but not now I am eleven years old. By the way, the day after you went away I had a boil in my ear and my ear was full of blood. I hope you are having nice weather. Both my shoes need repairing. My Sunday shoes are wearing out at the toes and my other shoes the soles are wearing away. On Friday we had fish and chips and on Sunday ginger roley poley jam pudding and today we had sour milk pudding. Aunt Ada says Jenny and I have used all her writing paper so we have to buy more. So far we have saved 3/10d. Mrs Bernadelli the lady who lives next door gave us 3d each. So that is all for now.
> love James
> x x x x x
> P.S. What Jenny says about me in her letter is wrong.

I have to mention the colds that start around this time. Bear with me. They begin as itchy trickles that quickly turn into rivulets that overflow into unstoppable torrents, hot and cold cataracts of mucus that leave me with a red, raw nose, sore red eyes and sopping wet handkerchiefs. The days are unbearable, the nights merely painful. In the mornings I despair as the first wet trickle of the day descends. I understand that runny noses and sneezes are attempts by the body to rid itself of harmful toxins. My body has a lot to eliminate.

One of the dripping episodes falls on Melvin's eleventh birthday, when I am sent to bed in order not to infect the guests at his party. I can hear everyone shouting and laughing below. Jenny brings up Kim's Game for me to play, which is good of her. Twenty-one objects on a tray and two minutes in which to memorize as many of them as possible before the tray is taken away. Later Jenny has to tell me that someone downstairs – a hundred to one it is Melvin – has won. They might have given me a consolation prize, although there can be no consolation for being submerged in secretions and feeling like a drowning puppy who is surplus to requirements.

Shortly after the party there is another of those days that change everything. Dad's new wife Edith comes to meet us. Jenny and I know that we cannot call her mother. The Greeks had a word for the situation – *euphemismos*. Edith is a harmless word for an offensive idea, like calling a man-eating grizzly bear Teddy. This is what it says about euphemism in one of my books about the ancient Greeks.

> The goddesses of the Greek underworld who ascended to earth to pursue and punish the wicked were known as the *Erinyes* ('The Avengers'), but those who feared to speak their name directly would call them the *Eumenides* ('The Kind Ones') instead.

Rather than speak the 'stepmother' word directly, we seek to deflect the Avenger who has ascended from the underworld to punish us by treating her as one of the Kind Ones and calling her Edith.

A week before we meet, Aunt Ada sits Jenny and me down to write a letter of thanks to her. "For what?" I ask. "For marrying your father when your mother took off and coming all the way from London to look after you," says Ada. "Why should we thank her for that," I ask, "if she wanted to do it anyway?"

> Dear Edith
> We are writing this letter to say thank you for marrying Dad and coming to look after us. We are looking forward to meeting our step-brother Emil and playing with him.
> Love James and Jenny
> xxxxx

Not as many kisses as usual. We know you have to write 'Love' even if you are not related, even if you haven't met the person and were not invited to her wedding with your father. I suppose they did not want us complicating things. When we see the photographs, I notice that Edith's young son Emil is in almost all of them.

So Edith comes to Aunt Ada's in Wyke for an afternoon and Jenny and I behave as if we are at Sunday school. Predictably enough, I do not take to her. Her skin is pale, her face is thin and she has mouse-coloured hair. I surreptitiously check the palms of her hands for anything remotely resembling a black spot. Afterwards Jenny and I write to Mother and Harold in India.

> Dear Mother and Harold
> We hope you had a nice time at your wedding. Was it hot? Edith is very nice. We are looking forward to going to live with her and Dad and Emil in their new house in Thornton Moor.
> Love James and Jenny
> xxxx

Even fewer kisses. The letter is supervised by Aunt Ada.

> P.S. Aunt Ada has been very nice and is looking after us. Last week we had sour milk pudding again.

Later, I add a line.

> P.P.S. We watched her kill a chicken by wringing its neck and the chicken kept on running round the garden with no head until it died.

A month later, my sister and I move in with a woman we have met only once, a boy we have never met and a man who is almost a stranger. The Brothers Grimm would have made something nasty of this. Incredibly, we are looking forward to it. For a few days we even feel fortunate.

φ

Chapter 7

On Thornton Moor

DRIPS OF WATER FALL INTO THE BUCKET under my attic window. It is raining again. Did the Greeks make a deity of rain? I check. The *Hyades* (the 'Rainy Ones') were a sisterhood of celestial nymphs who wept with grief whenever they felt sad, which was frequently. Every day the rainy ladies weep for me in my attic, where I keep a diary on the inside page of which I have written: *'Nota bene*, diaries are meant to be secret and personal', in case anyone finds it hidden behind my Oxford Companion to Classical Literature and contemplates reading it without my permission, which I shall never give.

Thornton Moor is a desolate hamlet exposed every day to the teeth of the wind. My father has bought a house on a pre-war estate there for £900, a huge sum of money, it seems to me, for a place so lacking in warmth.

Edith has only been to Yorkshire once before. She does not like it. She does not believe that the neighbours are doing their best to be friendly when they say things like, "Wheer ther's muck ther's brass!" and "Well ah'll go to ahr 'ouse!" She entirely misses the point of their obscure attempts at humour.

How should I describe my stepmother without being unkind? It isn't easy. She is a hag, a hex, a harpy from Hades, a drab-haired mutant washed up from the slime-ridden depths of the Thames by impatient tides who could not wait to be rid of her. You might say I am prejudiced and I would not object. *'Facilis descensus Averno,"* I say with Virgil. Easy is the way to the underworld. I would ferry her over the Styx myself, pitch her into a pit full of vipers and paddle happily back through the shadows alone.

I know, I know. With my personal experience of exile and separation I ought to feel sorry for someone who has ended up so far from home. But I don't. I can't. My brain has not evolved enough for empathy.

There is not much I can say about Dad. He has been discharged from the merchant navy – with honour, he says, but I think it is with drunkenness – and now has a job as a machinist at E. Posselt & Sons, Middlebridge. Most of his spare time is spent in the Dreadnaught Inn and the Farmer's Arms. The only time I see him is first thing in the morning when I need a note for the P.E. teacher to get me off swimming, and I dictate most of those myself.

Sweets are still rationed. A dike burst on the Columbia River in America, drowning fifteen people and leaving tens of thousands homeless. Yorkshireman Len Hutton is England's leading batsman. Not so long ago he scored a remarkable 364 runs against Australia, which everyone says will be a record for ever, but according to the Daily Herald he struggles with fast bowling, the criticism is unsettling him and he is withdrawing into himself. I would say he wants to be back in Pudsey, where he was born. Personally I would give the ferryman everything I own, including my Everyman edition of Westward Ho! and my Cleartype copy of Treasure Island, to row me back to Rawley Bay. The Everyman editor has made me a promise and printed it on the inside cover:

> I will go with thee, and be thy guide
> In thy most need to go by thy side.

I want to be reassured, but mostly I feel bewildered. What does my father see in the She-Creature he married? Did they have sex when he was on shore leave in London and she became pregnant? He never has a bad word to say about her, but she has an inexhaustible supply about him. Mostly he takes her snipping and sniping quietly, absorbs it like a dishcloth, too soggy to defend himself or to have anything to say in response.

My father seems very fond of Edith's son Emil, who is three years younger than me, a gap wider than the mouth of the Yore. Among the papers Mother left behind is one of my father's letters to her in which he says

> Emil looks like he could be my own son – his hair is as ginger as mine was
> when I was young, he'll pass as my own.

I am offended. Emil does not look to me like he could be my father's son. Mind you, it is increasingly likely that I am not his son either. There is a distinct possibility that my real father is King George VI – if you study his profile on a penny or a half-crown you will see the resemblance. That would make me a royal bastard. Alternatively, I am a foundling and my parents are unknown. Anyway, who cares? If I run away to sea no-one but Jenny will miss me and she will soon get over it. So, yes, Emil could be his real son. They both have that smiling, dopey look, as empty as a promise. Dad's letter continues.

> Have no worries about my future happiness, I believe Edith will look after
> me, in fact I am sure. I do think she is wonderful for agreeing to marry me,
> when there's so many complications attached to it.

Jenny and I are the obvious complications, along with the dwindling stocks of rum at the Dreadnaught Inn. But is it not a wicked thing to say, that Emil could be his own son? Unless, of course, it is true.

What saves me from looking in the library for books on poisoning and arson is finding a substitute family on the streets. I am invited to join the Outlaws, a gang named after William's gang in the terrific books by Richmal Crompton. There are four of us: William, the leader (Tony Roper), who is a year older than me and meant to be reckless; his sidekick Henry (Kenneth Jupp), who has an air of wisdom about him, but is also a fighter; Douglas (Alec Jarvis), a bit of a misery but reputed to be good at spelling (actually he isn't – he spells knights as 'gnights' and knocks as 'gnocks'); and me.

"You can join the Outlaws," says William, "if you will be Ginger." My heart sinks. I want to be Henry, but Kenneth Jupp doesn't want to be Ginger and Alec Jarvis refuses to be Douglas, and although Ginger is supposed to have red hair and mine, I assure you, is not red but blonde – or possibly, in some lights, auburn – he is the Outlaws' second-in command and said to be as reckless as William. Yet as a newcomer I am honoured to be invited to join the gang and I would have taken any part available, other than the gang's arch-enemy Hubert Lane, of course, or sickly Violet Elizabeth Bott.

The Outlaws set fire to the moors with the flint sparks from a gas lighter, push fireworks through letterboxes, fight with flaming arrows against our rival gang, the Assassins, let down their bicycle tyres, tease the Co-op cat into upsetting the tins piled in the Co-op shop window, run around clattering on the garage roofs and smoke fag ends. With my experience of rolling your own, I take the lead in the smoking. I know that in the war they made ersatz coffee from roasted acorns, so I collect dock leaves and nettles from the common and dry them in the attic to make ersatz tobacco. It tastes terrible, so I collect the cigarette butts from my father's ashtrays and use half-smoked, spit-ridden shreds of genuine tobacco instead. We sit on the garage roofs smoking, hawking and coughing, and hatching plots against the Assassins.

The garages are not attached to the houses, which were built before people had cars, but grouped at the end of a dirt track on the edge of the common – ten or twelve thin sheds of corrugated iron, asbestos, tin and timber grouped so closely together that if you climb onto the roof of one you can get onto the roofs of the others by jumping the gaps between them.

Edith insists I take Emil with me when I go out to play, even though he is too young. My fellow Outlaws confer. "All right," announces William, "he can play with us if he will be Hubert Lane." Emil is pleased. He hasn't read the Just William books and has no idea that Hubert Lane is the Outlaws' sworn enemy. I do not tell him in case it gets me into trouble with his mother.

I help Emil climb onto the garages. William yells, "Ah no, it's Hubert Lane!" and runs off over the roofs clattering and laughing, followed by Henry and Douglas. I run after them and Emil runs after me. I stop to let him catch up, even though it means I will not be able to catch the others before they get to the end and jump off – and the whole point of the game is to get to the end and jump off in order to avoid capture. Emil tries to jump one of the gaps between the roofs, trips and hits his head on a raggy bit of corrugated iron. Blood pours from his head and sticks to his hair. I feel sick when I see it, but I take him to the pond to wash it off, which makes him muddy as well. He is crying a lot, so I take him home.

Edith goes loopy, as you can imagine. She accuses me of not looking after him. I am tempted to point out that I have been doing him a favour, but I tell her he simply tripped. She is seething and scathing.. When my father gets back from the pub she tells him to give me a good walloping. Perhaps the landlord refused to serve him after he had a tot too many that evening, but Dad is in a combative mood. He growls at her that it is against his principles to hit his children. It is the first time I have heard him talking back to her. So she comes up with a cruel and unusual punishment of her own. She sends me to Coventry. She does not utter a word to me for a week. It feels creepy, like living with a malevolent vampire who could turn on you, sink her teeth into you and suck you dry at any moment.

One day she is doing the washing in the cellar with Jenny and the door at the top of the cellar steps is open. "Your mother spoilt 'im," I overhear Edith say, managing to get at both me and my mother in the same breath. 'If only', I think. "Oh no," says Jenny, laughing. "I was the spoilt one!" She wasn't, neither of us were, and at first I feel sorry that she has had to lie in order to stay on good terms with her stepmother, but then I feel a kind of pride. If only my sister had been a boy, I think, she would have qualified to join the Outlaws. We could have absolutely depended on her in our bid to defeat the Assassins and dominate the estate.

I take some comfort in the thought that I do not have to conform to my stepmother's idea of how I should be. Mr Theobald, the Eng Lit master at King's (Baldy, of course, even though he isn't), has been discussing Polonius' line from Hamlet, 'This above all – to thine own self be true'. I would like my stepmother's acceptance in the absence of anything warmer, but not at the price of deferring to her cattiness and malice. And yet if *I* can be awkward, wayward and wilful, and still be true to myself, then anyone can. Edith can be true to herself and be as rancorous and poisonous as a coven of thirteen witches. 'O most Pernicious Woman!' says Hamlet in reference to his mother, but I'm sure he meant it to apply to stepmothers too.

Edith reserves her affection for her son. She talks to Emil, strokes his hair, shares little jokes with him and allows him to leave his greens. No-one else enjoys that kind of indulgence, including my father, who has taken to staying out later in the evenings. He has been banned from the Dreadnaught Inn, but is getting to know the regulars at the Farmers' Arms better than he does his own children. It isn't long before E. Posselt & Sons notice his trembling hands and transfer him from the machine shop to the warehouse.

A glossy little black and white photograph of a baby arrives in the post. Mother has written 'Rupert H. Sutcliffe aged 0' on the back. There is a note.

> Rupert was my choice, Herman (the H) was Harold's. Hope you approve!

Does she mean of the name or the baby? I want to reply, 'Neither, really'. It is like being given a shiny new knife with which to stab yourself in the leg. Somewhere a long way away where the blood runs thinly Jenny and I have a half-brother named after a cartoon bear in yellow checked-trousers and a Nazi war criminal addicted to drugs. Over the next months more photographs appear: baby Rupert laughing, baby Rupert crawling, baby Rupert being taught to swim in an outdoor pool. The sun is always shining in these scenes. In the background there are gardens and motor cars, grinning servants, tennis courts and a white-painted mansion with a wrap-around veranda.

When the Old Crone sees these photographs, she sniffs and mutters, "It's all right for some." She supervises our letters of thanks and manages to get in a hint of how pitiful things are for us in comparison.

> Dear Mother
> Thank you for the photograph of you with baby Rupert in the swimming pool. It looks lovely and warm there. You look like you are having fun. It has been quite cold here. I had another bad cold. Edith had to tear up an old sheet for me to use as handkerchiefs.
> Love and to Harold and to baby Rupert
> xxx

One kiss only for each of them. Edith looks over my shoulder. "You might as well send kisses for everyone else while you're at it." She means the servants and tradesmen who appear from time to time in Mother's photographs, identified variously as the *Bearer*, *Cook*, *Ayah*, *Driver*, *Sweeper*, *Chowkidar*, *Mali*, *Dhobi Wallah*, *Dherzi* and their assorted assistants and relatives. Edith is being sarcastic. I am sensitive to the envy that lies at the heart of her barbed remarks. That at least we can share.

There are three places I go to get away from my stepmother: Classics and Eng Lit classes with Dippy and Baldy, where I escape into other times and dimensions; the attic, where I write my daily diatribe against her and the world; and the streets and garage roofs with the Outlaws, where I am a more reckless version of myself.

The atmosphere in the gang is changing, however. Kenneth Jupp's bossy older sister Maureen has joined us and we can't work out how to get rid of her. She is followed by Mary Scully, Barbara Skidmore-Bews and my sister, none of whom has any interest in taking on the role of the Outlaws' lisping, snivelling *nemesis*, Violet Elizabeth Bott. But Maureen and Jenny make themselves useful by teaching us the lyrics of songs they have heard on the radio.

> If you roll a silver dollar down upon the ground
> It'll ro-o-oll because it's rou-ou-ound …

Maureen Jupp sits on a garage roof, her dress up to her thighs, flashing her knickers, singing this song as loudly and boldly as Grandma Lily used to belt out the Hallelujah Chorus in her kitchen on Third Street.

> A woman never knows what a good man she's got
> Until she turns him down-down-down!

It takes me a while to realize that Maureen Jupp is singing this song at me.

> A man without a woman is like a ship without a sail,
> Is like a boat without a rudder, a kite without a tail ...

Alas, it has me thinking of sons deprived of mothers rather than the star-crossed lovers Maureen has in mind.

> A man without a woman is like a wreck upon the sand
> There's only one thing worse in the universe
> And that's a woman without a man!

I like this twist to the lyric, although my mother already has a man and her universe is fine. And the Whore of Thornton Moor has a man too, of a kind – my father, whose continued lack of interest in what is going on at home encourages her to vilify or ignore me at will.

The other Outlaws want to get rid of the girls who have infiltrated the gang, but I am more equivocal. As Dippy once said about females in poetry and myth, they are not all to be feared, they can also be fascinating. Kenneth's sister Maureen, for example, has advanced ideas about sex. One day she organizes four of her girl friends to lie in a line in the grass on the common and persuades me – and I agree to this readily, I have to admit – to lie on top of each of them and kiss them in turn. The other Outlaws run off in disgust to throw stones in the pond.

The first two girls, Mary Scully and Hilda Brighouse, lie rigid with dread or excitement, I can't be sure which, while Maureen times the kisses using Barbara Skidmore-Bews' watch. I have no idea what I am doing, but Maureen seems to enjoy it and she isn't even in line. The next girl, Rosie Newton, giggles unstoppably, so that kiss doesn't last long. The winning kisser – she manages to hold her breath longer than the others – turns out to be Skidmore-Bews, a slender, athletic girl who ties her hair back with an elastic band and tucks her dress into her knickers to do cartwheels and handstands.

I like BSB, as we call her, because she is good at games, but she has been chalking 'BSB = SJ' on the garage walls and I am concerned. "Who is this 'SJ'?" I ask my sister. Jenny titters. She has been sworn to secrecy. I have never known this kind of suspense and confusion before. I have to acknowledge it as different in every way to excitement, fear, etc. Eventually Jenny takes pity and tells me that 'SJ' is actually 'JS' backwards. "But JS are my initials," I say. "So they are!" exclaims Jenny and runs away, still tittering.

Quid magnum facinus! What intrigue! as Dippy might have said. Nothing is for certain in this shifting world of sex games, secret graffiti, changing allegiances and popular songs. Every move made by an object of desire is subject to intense, sometimes savage, analysis.

One evening we are gathered outside the chip shop singing

> I wanna be loved by you!
> By you and nobody else but you!

while eating chips and batter bits, when Maureen starts arguing with Barbara. Mary Scully seems to know what it is all about. Referring to Maureen, she starts to sing

> She's wild again, beguiled again!

At which everyone joins in.

> A simpering, whimpering child again!
> Bewitched, bothered and bewildered!

Maureen goes off in a huff and sings to her reflection in the chip shop window.

> Do you smile to tempt a lover, Mona Lisa,
> Or is this your way to mend a broken heart?

Her attempt at an ambiguous smile implies it could be either.

> Are you warm, are you real, Mona Lisa,
> Or just a cold and lonely, lovely work of art?

Tony Roper suggests – unkindly, I think – that Maureen is more lonely than lovely. Things start to turn awkward, so I suggest a game of Teamball. My aim is to get Barbara Skidmore-Bews on my side and the means I contrive to achieve this are so blatant that I assume everyone will believe the result to be entirely coincidental. "Maureen Jupp and I will be captains," I announce. "My team will be all those whose surnames begin with S – Mary Scully, my sister, me of course, is there anyone else? Oh yes, Barbara. We shall be England. Maureen's team is the Rest of the World."

BSB and I excel at Teamball. We feint, dodge and pass with such accuracy and fluidity that before long we are not only outplaying the Rest of the World, but our own side, England, as well. We find ourselves passing and re-passing the ball to each other exclusively. It is an informal alliance as exciting as the time Alec Jarvis took three catches off my off-spin bowling at cricket. Actually it is better than that, because there is an element of fascination in my relationship with Skidmore-Bews that is wholly absent from my relationship with Alec Jarvis.

I watch Barbara as she runs like a gazelle to retrieve the ball … catches it, cups it, looks for me … I dodge into an unmarked space, she throws it … the ball rises and falls in an elegant arc into my willing hands … I toss it back … she catches it cleanly … and now we move further and further apart, challenging each other to maintain the connection until we can throw the ball no further without it bouncing, which is not in the rules. The others are not best pleased at this game within a game, although they recognize it for what it is – blatant flirting to arouse sexual interest, something they know well – and go off to play Sardines. Skidmore-Bews and I now work our way closer and closer, tossing the ball over a shorter and shorter distance until we are practically handing it to each other. And this is how someone from the posh end of the estate becomes my first official girlfriend.

Unhappily, Barbara doesn't only like skipping and ball games, she also likes swimming. The next day one of her friends invites me to join them on a trip to the beach at Sourness and I have to say I am otherwise engaged. As they troop off to the bus with their costumes and towels I feel useless, like Maureen Jupp's ship without a sail. The following week I am invited again and I have to concoct another excuse. I cannot tell them I have a morbid fear of drowning.

I attempt to write about my distress in an essay at school. The subject Baldy has given us is 'Alone'.

> Pirate Jim is fifty foot up on the yardarm hauling in the spinnaker.
> He pauses for a moment to welcome the dawn.

A spinnaker, as you may know, is a triangular headsail carried by a sailboat running fast before the wind. I realize that Jim would *not* be fifty foot up on a yardarm hauling in a spinnaker, so I cross out the line and start again.

> Pirate Jim stands firm in a force five gale.

Now what? There is no-one I can rely on in this gale – no shipmates, no friendly albatross. I am alone, as the title implies.

The special relationship between BSB and I comes to an end. Her skipping and ball skills, once so reassuringly normal and sporty, are no longer inviting enough, though Maureen Jupp's suggestive singing and simulated sex games are still too advanced for me.

Maureen's brother Kenneth, formerly my rival as second-in-command of the Outlaws, becomes my best friend. We make a wireless from a large cardboard box and sit inside it playing the gramophone, reading out announcements ("This is the News at Two. This afternoon it is raining") and telling jokes ("Have you heard the one about the empty lemonade bottle?" "No." "There's nothing in it.") for a captive audience – his mother and grandad. Then we write and produce a street newspaper using a John Bull printing outfit that Kenneth was given for Christmas, though setting the type is so laborious that we only manage one edition.

We organize a summer fête. To raise the money for this I retrieve a chipped plaster statuette of a boy on a dolphin that I won at a fairground and we tout it round the estate as first prize in a raffle. Tickets are threepence each. "Who gets all this money?" a man asks. "It's for local charities," we say, which is true enough. I have a stepmother and Kenneth's Dad died in the war. We feel over-qualified.

The fête's most profitable sideshow ('Sixpence for a Penny') involves a sixpenny piece placed in a bowlful of water. "If you can take the sixpence out of the bowl," we announce to prospective customers, "you can keep it." We make it clear that the wires from Kenneth's electric shock machine have been placed in the bowl, so that the effect when you touch the water is like being hit by a brick. It is a real shock. No-one manages to retrieve the sixpence, though the lure of winning so much for the outlay of so little (a penny a try, three tries for tuppence) proves so attractive that by the end of the day we have made seven shillings and sixpence from this sideshow alone.

Every such success pales in comparison to my failure to learn how to swim. Finding an excuse not to venture into the North Sea while playing with the gang on the sands is excruciating enough, but immersing myself at the shallow end of the King's School pool with the other non-swimmers every Wednesday morning is torture. Staying in the pool at the risk of asphyxiation is, I decide, insanity, so every other week I ask my father to write a note to the P.E. teacher excusing me. I dictate a form of wording that I know from experience works: 'Please excuse James from swimming today. He has a cold/cough/headache/verruca/chilblain /boil on his bottom'. The trick is to keep it simple and not to elaborate.

Those excused swimming who are not actually comatose are expected to go cross-country running, but even with a cold, a rash or suppurating sores on the soles of my feet I have no hesitation – the choice between running and swimming is like a choice between caning and hanging. One is clearly preferable to the other, yet neither is remotely desirable. There is no question, however, that my mental and physical health are better served by slogging away in the wind, rain and mud trying not to be last than cowering indoors in a pool reeking of chlorine while a troop of chimpanzees romp around me screaming, splashing and diving into the water without even thinking about hitting their heads on the bottom.

From my experience of the school pool I learn to hate confusion and cacophony, while cross-country running teaches me the virtues of persistence, silence and the consolations of loneliness.

One Tuesday night, knowing there is swimming the next morning and in danger of running out of imaginary ailments, I discover a way of giving myself a genuine cold. I pad around on the lino in the attic at bedtime, leave the skylight open, discard the eiderdown, shiver through the night and by the morning I am convincingly sniffle-nosed, red-eyed and knackered. It is not too hard to convince my father that I am in the throes of a medical emergency and might not survive unless I am excused swimming, but I cannot get away with this trick every week, so I have to alternate the colds with the bunions and boils. Dad obliges without question when I dictate these notes for him to sign. After shells and torpedoes exploding at sea and doors slamming at home I suppose he is ready for a quiet life.

He is not getting it with Edith. If Edith wants a quiet life she is going about it the wrong way entirely. I ought not to speak ill of my stepmother again, but before I do I should mention the one occasion on which she is almost kind to me.

I have taken off my bicycle's sit-up-and-beg handlebars and fitted them upside-down to look like racing handlebars, though after a while I realize they look more like sit-up-and-beg handlebars turned upside-down. The Outlaws are all speedway fans, so we make a dirt track around the pond and race round it, leaning over at the corners and throwing up as much dirt as possible. I come off on a corner at speed, scraping an arm and a leg on my way to sliding into the pond. It is not as bad as the Incident at Rawley Beck, because the water in the pond is still and shallow, but I know it is deep enough to drown in if I were knocked unconscious and no-one were there. The other Outlaws are on hand, but I am Ginger, reckless and fearless, so I rescue myself.

I am in pain. I can hear Dippy saying, 'You have been punished for your presumption, Seagrave'. All right, Dippy. 'You have broken the surface of the water without the invitation of the nymphs of the pond'. Oh shut up, Dippy. My leg hurts and my arm hurts. I limp home, bruised and bleeding.

Edith must feel a twinge of satisfaction at seeing me wince from the sting as she applies TCP, but her cleansing and bandaging have a soothing effect and I wonder if the warty Old Witch might not be so bad after all. It is a thought that lasts a good five minutes until her next scathing remark, which is on the lines of how selfish I am for not allowing Emil to ride my bike, even though it is too big for him and, as we know now, has next to no brakes. A scathing from Edith is far worse than scraping my skin on a dirt track. That wound will heal.

Her reign of terror continues. Mother and Harold bring infant Rupert to England on leave and call at the house to take Jenny and me out for the day. Harold parks at the front, knocks at the door and retreats to his car. "Don't you dare let 'em in!" shouts Edith from the kitchen as I run excitedly to the door. She comes into the front room and peers through the curtains. "'Oo the 'ell do they think they are?" I recognize a rhetorical question, one intended to produce an effect rather than elicit a response, but the atmosphere in the house is so thick with malice that rather than feeling happy with my analysis all I feel is ashamed.

The next weekend Mother and Harold come to take Jenny and me out again and this time Harold parks in the lane at the back. He doesn't get out. He sounds the horn. Edith is making dinner and sees the car through the kitchen window. She snarls at Dad. Unexpectedly he snarls back, so she throws a panful of gravy at him. It misses and hits the window, leaving the contents dribbling like diarrhoea down her new net curtains. Serves her right, I think. Then I wonder if Jenny and I might be next. If the Old Bag is prepared to throw the gravy at Dad, we might be in line for the meat and potatoes. Afterwards when we are well away from the house we can't stop laughing. We are hysterical.

I have told you almost nothing about Harold, or The Great Usurper, as I come to think of him. He is a heavy man with a discreet brush of a moustache on his upper lip, a gold tooth and a long fierce parting in his flat, black, combed-back hair. He has very little to say to Jenny and me other than 'How was school?' and 'Pick up your litter'.

On the day of the gravy he drives us all in his rented Vauxhall Velox down Coledale to the coast at Sourness. It is meant to be a day out for everyone, but I am worried in case Jenny and I are locked out of the house when we return. And there is a particularly unpleasant thing about Sourness-on-Sea: I am expected to go fishing for mackerel with Harold, who is attempting to establish some kind of second-hand relationship with me. I am resistant. In my book anyone prepared to call their son Herman is suspect. I do not wish to be difficult, but he has brought me on a killing spree and I find everything about it repellent.

I refuse to handle the worms and dead bits of things that the skipper of the boat keeps in a bucket for bait, so Harold hooks them on for me. And when I catch a mackerel – only too easy, as they are being hauled in all around me – I cannot bring myself to touch it, even to throw it back into the sea, so Harold himself yanks it off the hook and tosses it into the gunnels. The poor little slithery, silvery, shimmery-striped thing is fighting for its life, but it is an unequal battle.

Harold must think that his thirteen-year old stepson is a bit of a prat, and I care about that, but I am so haunted by the thoughtless slaughter going on all around me that at the same time I do not care. I am also concerned that our overloaded little bumboat will capsize and pitch us all into the sea. It seems to me that there are far too many overweight old men and obese adolescents on board. I check the whereabouts of the life jackets and ask myself who among us deserves to survive. Then I lapse into a sullen reverie, my rod draped unbaited over the side. I know now how Jim Hawkins felt when he was trapped on the Hispaniola with a gang of mentally unstable pirates and a fight broke out over a barrel of rum. In the blink of an eye the thieves and villains around me are slicing each other's throats and running each other through.

> The mate was fixed by the bosun's pike
> The bosun brained with a marlinspike!

I am elbowed in the face by the killer next to me as he hauls in yet another hapless mackerel. There are hundreds of his fellows – fish, not men, regrettably – dying on the deck. The romance of the sea has been greatly exaggerated. As we motor back to the harbour, Harold tells me a story about the fishermen of Sourness who do not learn to swim and sink rapidly in accidents at sea when their waders fill with water. It is a misjudged and completely superfluous attempt to amuse me.

On our next day out, we drive updale to visit the ruins of Beadle Abbey. There is no bridge over the river at Beadle. If you want to cross the river to take a walk in the woods you have no choice but to use the stepping stones, but on the day we are there the river is full and in places it slides rapidly over the tops of the stones. There are two ways to proceed: you can stop at each stone and think ahead to the next, as I do, or skip gaily from one to the other hardly thinking, like Jenny. Half-way across, I freeze. People are queuing up on the stones behind me, so I cannot go back. All I can do is take a step, stop, compute, take another step and try not to curse the nymphs of the river. Dippy would have sympathized. Mother waits impatiently at the other side. Harold is oblivious.

Then there is the Leap, a place higher up the dale where the rocky banks at each side of the rapids are so close that the gap between them looks almost jumpable. Harold tells us of drunken young men attempting the Leap and falling to their deaths in the torrent below. And there are tales of people jumping in deliberately. I stand at the edge and wonder what it would be like to fall in or be pushed. At best I would die and not have to return to Thornton Prison, and at worst I would survive, though that might be partly offset by being taken to hospital to recover rather than having to go back to jail.

Does Mother know that Jenny and I are unhappy? I look to her solicitors, Messrs Amble & Badcock, to take you through what happens next. Here is their account of the fight over custody between my mother and stepmother (my father playing only a nominal role, if any) as set out in an invoice I find in Mother's papers. She and Harold are in England on leave and they have rented a house near Grandma Lily's for Christmas. All I know about this at the time is the appalling thing that happens at the end of it all.

> To Mrs H. Sutcliffe, 12 Shuttleworth Lane, Beasley Bottom, Yorks.
>
> Item 1   Attending you relative to the refusal of the wife of your former husband Wilfred Seagrave to allow you access to your children and taking instructions to demand such access otherwise you would have no alternative but to apply to the Court   6s. 8d.
>
> Item 2   Writing to Mr Seagrave accordingly.   3s. 4d.

Edith is being uncooperative – more than that, obstructive. This could also be read as my stepmother wanting Jenny and me to herself, though that is laughably implausible, so what is she up to?

> Item 3   On receipt of letter from your former husband's solicitors Messrs Yalom & Co. asking what access you desired, writing to acknowledge and that I would enquire.   3s. 4d.
>
> Item 4   Attending you when you informed me you would like to have the children overnight each weekend and also half their holidays.   6s. 8d.

A modest enough request from Mother, though not much of a negotiating position, it seems to me.

> Item 5   Attending Messrs Yalom & Co. by telephone when they suggested it would disturb the children less if you would have them for the whole of the holidays and forgo any intermediate access.   3s. 4d.

Is Edith (for this is obviously her tactic, not my father's) thinking that this is a better way of getting rid of us for longer? Or is she continuing to be difficult for its own sake (not improbable)? Is it naïve or cynical of the Old Crow to suggest that we might be less disturbed if she has us for longer?

> Item 6   Attending you reporting that you did not like this idea and taking your instructions to enquire if you could have the permanent custody of the

children provided you thought when you had them for a weekend that they
would like to stay with your mother.   6s. 8d.

I begin to see the outline of a deep-laid plot. My mother is anticipating that if she
wins legal custody she will leave us in Beasley with Grandma Lily rather than take
us with her to India, but she is still not prepared to admit this to anyone, least of
all her own solicitors.

> Item 7   Later attending you by telephone when you instructed me to ask
> outright for custody.   3s. 4d.

Edith has refused to allow my mother and Harold even to see us, let alone take us
out for the day. But why? It could only be to save on gravy. And now she has the
opportunity to be rid of us permanently, will she finally concede? Or is there more
trouble to come?

> Item 8   Attending Messrs Yalom & Co. by telephone when they suggested
> on behalf of your former husband that you should have your son
> permanently and he should have your daughter but with no provision for
> occasional access of either.   3s. 4d.

What? God is insisting that Abraham offers a sacrifice. Edith is asking my father,
in effect, 'How much do you love me?' 'Enough to sacrifice my own son', is his
all-too-evident response. They are trading in children. The scheming stepmother
is plotting for the despised ex-wife to take the troublesome son in exchange for
the more amenable daughter. After all, my father has a ready-made replacement
for me in Emil. Note too that casual 'but with no provision for access of either',
meaning that my sister and I would be permanently separated.

> Item 9   Attending you on your calling when you refused this offer and
> intimated that unless you could have both children and your former husband
> contributed to their maintenance you would apply to the Court.
>   6s. 8d.

Righteous indignation. An ultimatum at last. And a powerful ploy. Going to Court
will increase the costs considerably and my father does not have Harold's
resources. In the other camp, meanwhile, the Shrew is playing a devious game. In
reality she is saying to my father, 'We have no choice but to let *both* of them go'.

And thus one drizzly winter evening with Christmas approaching, it comes to pass
that my father calls Jenny and me to him and with unusual clarity delivers a stark
choice: "You can stay with us here or go to live with your mother in India." I am
taken aback. It is put so bluntly and brutally. "We shall leave you to talk it over and
decide."

The irresponsibility of these supposed adults takes my near fourteen year-old
breath away. Edith puts on her coat. She is playing neutral observer in a situation
she has herself engineered. No cleansing of the wound now, no TCP. I expect
nothing more from the Daughter of Satan in relation to the choice that Jenny and

I have been invited to make, but it would have been nice if my thin-witted father had murmured, even under his breath, 'I want you to stay'.

It is raining outside. The Hyades are weeping again. Edith puts up her umbrella and leaves. My father hesitates at the door, looking contrite, then the Queen of the Shadows returns and ushers him into the night.

ϙ

Chapter 8
Scylla and Charybdis

A WARSHIP CALLED HMS DAUNTLESS collides with a Swedish tanker in the Thames and sinks. Sixty-four of the crew escape, only to die in the freezing cold. Not much of choice for the rest of the crew: drown or freeze.

On a class trip to see Hamlet Baldy asks us to consider Hamlet's choices: are they of his own making or is he at the mercy of darker forces? I am particularly struck when Hamlet's mother Gertrude describes what happens when her prospective daughter-in-law falls from a willow tree and drowns in the brook below. Shockingly, Gertrude makes no attempt to intervene. But why is Ophelia up a tree in the first place?

> There, on the pendant boughs her coronet weeds
> Clambered to hang, an envious sliver broke;
> When down her weedy trophies and herself
> Fell in the weeping brook.

Is this a melodramatic gesture on Ophelia's part? A cry for help? Or, like Narcissus, is she a bit of a drip who does nothing to save herself? Even a decision to do nothing is a choice. And yet I am moved. Even the brook weeps.

> Her clothes spread wide,
> Which time she chanted snatches of old tunes,
> As one incapable of her own distress.

Does 'incapable of her own distress' mean she is unable to do anything about her distress, like the fishermen of Sourness who do not learn to swim, or is she unable to do anything because she is too distressed? I can relate to either.

When Narcissus falls into the pool the gods intervene and transform him into the flower that bears his name. He will live on. No such luck for Ophelia.

> Her garments, heavy with their drink,
> Pull'd the poor wretch from her melodious lay
> To muddy death.

Metamorphosis for a vain youth who hardly deserves it, but no transformation, not even into a frog, for the fair Ophelia. Does she simply give in? Pull'd to a muddy death with no hint of resistance? I make a mental note not to wear a heavy dress when I go near the water. That would be a simple life-affirming choice. I could of course wear one if I did not wish to live or did not care.

I pray for intervention by the gods in the unthinkable decision that Jenny and I have to make. Will choosing one parent mean losing the other? If only the choice between an unwanted known and an unknowable unknown were taken away from us. Is a muddy death better or worse than a watery death? How would we know? Did Burgess and Maclean know what they were letting themselves in for when they opted for exile in the Soviet Union?

That night I dream of quicksands. To survive in a quicksand you must *not do nothing* or you will be sucked under and suffocate. And you must *not do too much* by struggling, or you will be dragged under just the same. What you must do, I understand, is to wiggle your legs slowly and gently until (hopefully) you rise to the surface, then wiggle them slowly and gently until (cross your fingers) they take you to safety. This makes exemplary metaphorical sense given the choice that Jenny and I have to make, though I hope never to have to test the wiggling thing out in reality.

The quicksands question is this: should we risk doing nothing – stay with Dad and Edith – or risk doing too much by disrupting our schooling, losing our friends and going with Mother? We have not stepped accidentally into this quagmire and nor are we there of our own volition. We have been pushed.

A mist of indecision descends upon us. Jenny looks to me to find a way through. If I make the wrong choice the day will only get darker. It would be easier if this were a Hobson's choice, that is no choice at all – you take the horse Hobson offers you or you have no horse. The easy way is to stay with what we know – familiar, disagreeable stepmother and emotionally unavailable father – while the more challenging alternative is to go over to the other side – indifferent stepfather and emotionally unreliable mother.

Earlier this term Dippy introduced our Classics class to the infamous myth of *Scylla* and *Charybdis*. Scylla is the daughter of the sea-god *Phorcys*, who also fathered the *Graiae*, who have one eye and one tooth between them, and the *Gorgons*, hideous creatures with spitting serpents for hair. "It is not a propitious start in life for young Scylla," says Dippy. "To make matters worse, her father Phorcys is away a lot. You sons of mariners will know how that feels." Thanks for reminding us, Dippy.

"When Scylla reaches marriageable age," he goes on, "she is seduced by *Poseidon*, a sex pest of a god – oh, shut up, Simpkins – who has the smack of the sea about him, charming and treacherous in turn. Poseidon's wife does not appreciate his seduction of Scylla, so in revenge she transforms the poor girl into a six-headed monster." We are directed to the passage in Homer that describes Scylla as having twelve flapping feet, and six necks enormously long, and at the end of each neck a horrible head with three rows of teeth set thick and close.

"Ashamed to be seen," Dippy says, "she hides among the rocks and emerges only to feed on whatever comes by – sharks, seals, dolphins, sailors. No passing ship is safe." Virgil imagines Scylla

harrying Odysseus' ships, and with her sea-dogs' fangs tearing at his trembling men! Ah, *timidos!*

In spite of the man-eating thing, I feel sorry for Scylla. But is it better for an unlucky mariner to be ripped to shreds or to die of drowning? I ask myself this because there is another side to the story. If you are a ship's captain in a hurry and do not wish to risk foundering on the rocks you might be tempted to tack to the other side of the Strait of Messina, but if so an equally undesirable fate awaits you in the shape of a whirlpool. Which is where the story gets bloodier still, because this whirlpool is no ordinary hazard to shipping. Its name is *Charybdis*. Dippy elaborates. "Charybdis is another lovely maiden – they do get into a lot of trouble in ancient Greece – who wishes to find favour with her father, Poseidon, the two-faced seducer who had his way – I've warned you, Simpkins – with Scylla. Charybdis offers to help her father fulfil his brother *Zeus's* master plan for the planet, which is for the sea to take over two-thirds of the land. But in her desire to impress her father she directs huge tsunamis and catastrophic waves to inundate whole islands and coasts. She shows no restraint."

It seems that it is not part of Zeus's plan for so much of the land to be taken over by the sea, so he punishes Charybdis by turning her into a monster and confining her to the same stretch of water as Scylla. "Charybdis is all mouth and bladder," says Dippy. "Three times a day she is condemned to swallow hundreds of gallons of water and spew them out again, creating conflicting currents that drag ships and their crews to a squally, watery death."

I feel even sorrier for Charybdis than I do for Scylla. At least Scylla has a choice of a kind. Instead of consuming the flesh (ah horror! ah *timidos!*) of shipwrecked sailors, she can wait for a shoal of red mullet to come along instead. Charybdis is deprived of all choice. Three times a day she must swallow, belch and swallow; gulp, regurgitate and repeat; condemned to do the same thing over and over without any hope of change. And that way, Dippy warns us, lies madness.

The sides of the Strait of Messina are said to be a mere arrow shot apart, so any ship that manages to evade ravenous Scylla cannot help but encounter voracious Charybdis, and *vice versa*. To be caught between the bloody jaws of the Sea-Hag and the coiling waves of the Whirlpool means choosing between being devoured or drowned.

I feel the tremendous burden of the choice that Jenny and I have to make: between a disloyal mother and an ineffectual father; between a stepfather we hardly know and a stepmother we know only too well. Contained in the universe of possible consequences to our decision are factors unknown and unknowable that will affect the rest of our lives. It is the kind of choice for which I imagine the word invidious was invented: unfair, offensive, intolerable and outrageous. Now I know how *Atlas* felt, condemned to carry the weight of the endless heavens on his shoulders in order to prevent them crashing to earth. I am almost fourteen years old and Jenny just thirteen. I am alarmed at the seriousness of our situation and ashamed – ashamed and embarrassed – to be a part of it. If we make the wrong decision the heavens will fall on our heads.

"If we go to live in India," I say to Jenny, "we will have to give up everything here." We are already familiar with the problems associated with moving. "If we stay with Dad in Thornton Moor," I say, "we will not have to change parents, friends, houses, schools, towns or countries." Settling for what we know will keep us on *terra firma*. The alternative is to take a leap into *terra incognita*. And leaps, as I know, can be suicidal. We need more wiggle room. By the time Dad and Edith return, we have found some. "We cannot decide," we say.

Messrs Amble & Badcock are getting restless. They report to Mother:

> Item 10   Attending Messrs Yalom & Co. by telephone to check on the position and they promised to take Mr Seagrave's further instructions.
>
>   3s. 4d.

> Item 11   Attending you reporting the position and arranging that you should call again later in the week by which time I hoped to have a reply.
>
>   3s. 4d.

Jenny and I are exercising the kind of control that neurotic indecision unwittingly creates.

> Item 12   On receipt of letter from Messrs Yalom & Co. attempting to contact you by telephone and leaving a message asking you to call.   3s. 4d.

Three shillings and fourpence for reading a letter and leaving a message? I would have done it for a lot less. Again Jenny asks me what I think. "Perhaps we could come back here if it does not work out there," I say. "But would they take us back?" she asks. It is a good question. "And meanwhile we would have no Dad." "We would have half a Dad, Harold," I say. There is a long hiatus. "You decide," says Jenny. It is all too much for her.

> Item 13   Attending you by telephone when you reported that your children are now prepared to go into your custody.   3s. 4d.

> Item 14   Attending you when you instructed me to accept your former husband's offer as conveyed by letter from Messrs Yalom & Co. for you to take custody of both children but to ask if you could have the children's beds and eiderdowns.   6s. 8d.

We have made a decision and yet feel powerless. The Evil Queen has won. Edith has managed to be rid of us. But why does Mother want the beds?

Item 15 Later attending Messrs Yalom & Co. by telephone to confirm the situation re legal custody but they promised to verify this and also to take their client's instruction with regard to the beds and eiderdowns. 3s. 4d.

Item 16 Attending Messrs Yalom & Co. by telephone when they informed me that an Order had been made giving you legal custody of the children and they agreed that the children should join you at your mother's in Beasley and start school there. 3s. 4d.

Hang on a minute – *start school in Beasley?? Is that why the beds?*

Item 17 Attending you reporting when you remarked that you would not get the benefit of the Family Allowance but you did not propose to let this interfere with the arrangements and I promised to communicate with you again when I heard from Messrs Yalom & Co. about the beds and eiderdowns. 6s. 8d.

Does this mean that we will be going to live with *Grandma Lily??*

Item 18 Writing Messrs Yalom & Co. to confirm arrangements for the beds and eiderdowns and also notifying them that your children would take their things to Beasley the following Saturday. 3s. 4d.

Beasley and the beds are surely intended as a temporary measure to fill the gap before leaving for India. Or are they?

Item 19 Postages and telephones. 10s. 6d
Item 20 Sundry payments. £1. 1s. 0d
Item 21 Sum total £5 10s. 6d

We have been sold for two pounds, fifteen shillings and threepence each, including postage and phone calls. A bargain. I reckon that Jenny might be worth a bit more than two pounds, fifteen shillings and threepence .

Why did my mother leave these papers – letters, invoices, decrees – behind when she left for India to marry Harold? Was it because she wanted to start a new life without the clutter of the past, or could it have been for our eventual education, for the genuine historical record? In which case, why not add a note of explanation or apology? Perhaps she believed that the documentary evidence was information enough, that it was up to Jenny and me to make our own meaning of it, as she had to. Or it could have been a simple cock-up – she intended to destroy the papers and in the hurry to leave she forgot.

Accompanying her solicitors' itemised account is a form from the Court House in Beasley confirming

that the legal custody of said infants be committed to the Complainant Mildred Sutcliffe and that the Defendant Wilfred Seagrave should henceforth pay to the Complainant the sum of NO pounds TEN shilling NO pence weekly for the maintenance of each infant whilst under the age of twenty-one years and that the Defendant shall have access to the said infants.

So Jenny and I pack our clothes and books and things and take the bus to Beasley Bottom. The beds go separately. Our father is in a hopeless dither, vacillating, I imagine, between guilt and relief: guilt that he is unable to maintain the already tenuous connection he has with his children and relief that he no longer has to. In a sense he has no more choice than we have. He will either be devoured by the Scylla-like monster he has married or be trapped forever in a Charybdian vortex of the law. For myself, I will soon discover that the whole legal process has been rotten to the core.

φ

Chapter 9
Mermaids' Tears

THE OCEANS ARE POLLUTED with tiny pellets of matter that do not degrade and form a deadly threat to life at sea. Mariners know them as mermaids' tears. Most reach the sea via contaminated waterways like the River Bease that flows through the wasteland at the bottom of Blackfoot Lane, Beasley. If you take the rotting footbridge over the river and make your way through the nettles and knotted briar you will come to the towering slag heaps of Beasley Main Colliery. We have moved to a coal town. On the day in December when Jenny and I arrive every chimney is smoking and all you can smell is coal smoke.

We are staying with Grandma Lily and her miner friend, Bert, who she moved in with a while ago. The front door of their terrace house opens directly to the street and the kitchen door to a steep back yard shared with three other houses. The place is as cramped as a rat trap in a coal seam, as small as Fourth Street in Rawley but without the sea view. On our arrival, Jenny and I have one consolation: the expectation that we will be leaving soon. We understand it to be a temporary stay while things are cleaned up and sorted out before leaving for India. But a pall of evasion hangs over Blackfoot Lane from the day we arrive.

On a frosty morning several days later, Mother takes us for a walk. I am already in a sour mood that day. The toilet we share with the house next door is halfway up the back yard and the next door neighbours make a point of running up and getting there first.

"It's nice here, isn't it?" says Mother, pointing to a tree or two as we walk by the scummy grey waters of the Bease. "Oh, yes," says Jenny, always ready to agree. For me it is another fateful walk along another grim river. It reminds me of the Yore. We pass a sewage outlet. There is a chill in the air. "It will be even nicer in the Spring," says Mother. "You mean in India?" ventures Jenny. Mother does not answer. Then: "Harold and I have had a difficult decision to make." She hesitates. "We think you will be better off here after all." "With you?" asks Jenny, puzzled, looking up at her, wondering if she has missed something. "With Grandma Lily," says Mother. "I have to go back to India to look after Rupert." "Oh," says Jenny. I am so accustomed to disinformation by now that the reality of the situation comes as no surprise. All the same, I am struck dumb. "Why can't you stay here?"

asks my sister, as near to tears as the day she was taken away with scarlet fever. I know what ought to come next – something on the lines of 'you'll understand in about twenty years' time when you are divorced and depressed, and in need of psychotherapy'. What Mother actually says, without a shred of evidence, is "You will like it here." She could equally have said, 'Sorry, Jenny, no, I am not taking you to the big house with a swimming pool and servants that you saw in the photographs. I am leaving you in a south Yorkshire slum with my ageing mother and her belligerent boyfriend'. "You will be going to nice new schools," says Mother. "Beasley Girls' High School for Jenny and Calverley Grammar for James. Thanks to Harold, it is all arranged." Mother wants to smile, but is finding it difficult.

Our stepfather does not want us. It is the only explanation for this twist to the plot that makes sense. With fewer teeth and scurvy he would have made a good Black Dog, as clearly he carries the mark that signals our fate in the palm of his hand.

I can only confide to my diary the bitter dark taste this information leaves in me. I have been handed a capsule of poison when the least I expected was a new suitcase. Not only have Jenny and I been deceived, but Amble & Badcock, Yalom & Co. and the Admiralty Division of the High Court have been led up the garden path too. Edith and my father must have connived in this lie in order to be rid of us. My sister and I are pawns, the least powerful pieces on the board, leftovers from the lives of others.

I guess that Mother is finding it difficult to acknowledge our vulnerability while being in such fear of her own. Moving to Beasley is not the choice Jenny and I made in Thornton Moor. After the long debate that went into making what we believed to be a grown-up choice, I see now that it was no choice at all, that only one option was available and it was not even on offer. No wonder I find spy films about double and triple bluffs and betrayal so compelling. I know how those loyal agents of the state feel when they discover they have been at the disposal all along of political forces beyond their control.

Mother writes to us from Port Said and Jenny and I write back. We are instructed by Grandma Lily to write separately and nicely to Harold. Here is what my thirteen-year old sister writes – either she is even smarter than I think or she has been taking dictation. Her letter does not contain a single crossing-out or misplaced comma.

> Dear Harold,
> How are you? We want to say how grateful we are to you for agreeing to look after us and being like a father to us, although you were no relation to us at all before you married Mother. I have only been to school for a week so far, but I think I will settle down alright, although I am not going to like the Latin, because the form are ahead of me in the work.
>   My art homework today is of a pobble (which is 'a thing you have never seen') and he is swimming the Atlantic Ocean behind a boat with his nose tied up in red flannel and a bell in his hand. He is yellow, with purple spots on and has black hair.

I think that is all for now. I shall have to stop, 'cos I have another letter to write to a friend and then my supper to have.
Love, Jenny
xxxxxxx

I guess that the letter she is planning to write is a real one, a heart-breaking note of farewell to Rita Birtwhistle, her best friend in Thornton Moor. On the same day I write

Dear Harold,
I am writing this letter to thank you very much for what you have made possible.

Blatant, blue-faced hypocrisy. Harold has denied us our right to a family life and to continuity in our education, but my complaint is so indirect that you might miss it altogether.

Calverley Grammar is quite a decent school, but in some respects rather sillier than King's. They have a custom here that when a master enters the room, the class must stand, which seems a bit unnecessary.

An equivalence for the unwanted authority Harold himself represents. Those 'quites', 'bits' and 'rathers' are my safe, sad way of duffing him up.

Well, it is getting on for supper-time, so I must sign off.
All the best, James

'All the best' is a handy alternative to 'Love' I have stumbled across and will increasingly fall back on. The Roman god of doorways, *Janus*, is the inspiration for my strategy of facing two ways at once. Like Len Hutton, who has averaged an astonishing ninety-seven runs on England's tour of the West Indies, I am building my attack on a sound defence.

P.S. I hope you are all minus illnesses etc. I only have a small cold at the moment.

Note that last little glance to leg (cricketing analogy, you might have to look it up). I am not yet ready to surrender my innings, but the weather is closing in and I will either have to retire hurt or bat on. What are my chances? I readily identify with the Greeks who knew the futility of outguessing the gods. "Are all events in our lives determined in advance?" Hadleigh-Dunne, a boy in my new class, asks Mr Underfield, the Classics master at Calverley. For some reason Undies looks directly at me. "What do you think, Seagrave?" I open my mouth, but nothing comes. "Personally," he says, "I believe that the future is determined by the present over which we exercise undoubted, if at times minimal, influence." Undies is not a fatalist like Dippy. The class discusses cause and effect. One boy, Trevellen, suggests that our brains are compelled to make connections between past and present events whether they are genuine connections or not. One thing puts us in mind of another and we come to believe they are necessarily related. Another boy,

Runciman, thinks that if a connection has been made it is perforce genuine, although it might not be significant or sensible. Undies puts it to us: can a solitary, so-called 'cause' ever be separated from the sum total of considerations and conditions combining at any given time to deliver an apparent 'effect'?

In other words, I should not be emotionally bound or unduly affected by what happens to me. My perception of a direct connection between events in my life and my unhappiness does not mean there is one. Yet my perception is the only reality I have to go on and, given that, I have no choice but to be unhappy.

If you're thinking of this as excessively self-pitying, Julian, you could be right, or you could be as hard-hearted as your mother. Sorry, I'm sure you're not. But have you ever considered how much responsibility your parents have for your present condition? Could a judge apportion it? Or do you see your life as the outcome of such a complex concatenation of events and decisions that no-one, least of all me or your ma, can be blamed?

Undies points out that the Greeks and Romans would only commit to a life-changing decision if the gods had advised them to do so via a dream or a soothsayer, which for me, as I guess for the Greeks and Romans, would pre-empt or at least heavily shade any idea of personal responsibility. But if my life is following a preordained path over which, contrary to what Undies suggests, I have little or no influence, does it matter a toss what I do or how I feel?

Yes it does, I decide. Jenny and I have to contend with real people who wield real power. That black-hearted pirate Harold Goldtooth and his thoughtless consort have torched our ship and left us for dead on a fever-wracked island in piranha-filled waters.

Grandma Lily has retired from the stage and is not as jolly and light on her feet as she used to be. She finds herself responsible for four motherless teenagers who aren't hers: perpetually smiling Jenny (laughing rather than crying), deeply neurotic me (occasionally manic, frequently depressed), and her widowed miner friend Bert's pale-faced, quiffy-haired, truculent twin sons, Roy and Ken (hostility and defiance personified). And yet Grandma Lily persists – she compliments us, scolds us, feeds us – as if we were her own.

Bert does not take well to having two teenage strangers foisted upon him and does his best to ignore us, but his combative sons are ready to engage at the least provocation. All I have to do is call them by their real names, Royston and Kenton. What happened to their mother, I wonder – the woman who must have chosen these aspirational names? She is never mentioned. You have to make up your own explanations in Beasley, just as you have in Greek mythology. I have two versions: in one she is murdered by Bert when he comes home early from the night shift and finds her in bed with a servant of *Bacchus* in the shape of the milkman; in the other she dies of a broken heart after Bert brings home the music hall star Lily Lemarr after a concert at the Miner's Institute, just as the Athenians brought back women from Sparta to be their mistresses.

Grandma Lily entertains us with songs and monologues in the evenings and as she goes about the household chores, but I notice there are fewer of the comical Albert and the Lion kind. More typical now is Seated One Day at the Organ, where she grieves the death of a loved one.

> But I struck one chord of music,
> Like the sound of a great Amen.

And her particular favourite, The Wreck of the Hesperus, in which she sings of a young girl's misplaced trust in her father, the vainglorious skipper of a schooner who takes his daughter to sea in atrocious weather despite having been warned of an impending hurricane.

> "O father! I hear the church-bells ring,
>   Oh say, what may it be?"
> "'Tis a fog-bell on a rock-bound coast!" –
>   And he steered for the open sea.

A decision that turns out to be a dreadful mistake.

> "O father! I hear the sound of guns,
>   Oh say, what may it be?"
> "Some ship in distress, that cannot live
>   In such an angry sea!"

He is speaking of his own ship! They are in terrible trouble.

> "O father! I see a gleaming light,
>   Oh say, what may it be?"
> But the father answered never a word,
>   A frozen corpse was he.

The girl has been lashed to a mast to save her, but the schooner sinks and the girl goes down with it. She cannot escape the ropes that bind her. At unbearably sad moments like this I feel that my grandmother and I share a desperate longing for something we have lost.

Every Friday Bert gives Lily his pay packet unopened. She checks the contents against his pay slip, counts out a few shillings for his beer and fags, and puts the rest in a purse in the sideboard drawer. Everyone knows where the purse is kept, but no-one dares touch it. Even Bert has to ask if he finds himself sixpence short for a pint or for his Capstan Full Strength.

Every Sunday morning Bert mixes the Yorkshire pudding before going off to the Grey Horse and at one o'clock my job is to run up to the pub and shout to the landlord from the off-licence bar, "Please will you tell Bert his dinner is ready!" After dinner he lights a thin roll-your-own and kips by the fire. The arm of the chair, the hearth rug and the eiderdown on his bed are full of charred holes from the burning fag-ends that fall from his fingers.

Whenever Bert has drunk a pint or two too many, say eight or nine in all, he becomes obstreperous, and as Grandma Lily is a stubborn woman they have endless, bellicose, over-my-dead-body debates. One evening the word 'plastic' comes up in the conversation while Grandma is talking to her friend, Mrs Duffield, about the ins and outs of Tupperware. Bert intervenes, something he would never have bothered to do if he had been sober. "The word's 'plahstic'," he declares. He pronounces the word with a long 'ah' as if he were a southerner. "Don't be daft, Bert, it's 'plastic'," says Grandma, using the no-nonsense, northern 'a'. "Ah said it's 'plahstick'!" says Bert. He is convinced that this is the only pronunciation possible.

"Plastic!"
"Plahstick!"
"Don't be daft!"
"Tha's the daft one! It's plahstic!"
"Plastic!"

They are playing out a version of their whole relationship. "Ah'll be off, then," says Mrs Duffield. Grandma accompanies her to the door while continuing to argue with Bert.

"Plastic, tha daft ha'porth!"
"Tha knows nowt, woman, it's plahstick!"

I am sitting by the fire doing my homework. I want to yell at them to shut the fuck up, but I look into the flames and imagine burning the house down. Now the twins start arguing and Grandma turns her attention to them. "Shurrup, the pair of you!" she yells. "You're as bad as two ferrets in a sack!" "Come 'ere, you two!" growls Bert and swipes them both round the head. Roy swipes his brother in turn "Oy!" shouts Grandma. "'E started it!" yells Roy. "Don't 'it yer brother!" yells Grandma. "That's yer dad's job!"

Whenever Roy goes out for the evening he polishes his shoes until the shine is as deep and enduring as the shine on Grandma's black-leaded range. The crease on his trousers is ironed-in with the steam from a wet teacloth until it is as sharp as a blade. And he shaves once a week until his cheeks glisten like apples. From the start you can see that Roy is out to impress girls and prospective employers.

In contrast Ken has more pustules than the rest of us combined and picks his nose more frequently than any nose-picker I know. He is younger than Roy by twenty minutes and skinnier and shorter. If you have ever seen the film Kes, he is Billy Casper, the boy who takes the brunt of everyone else's frustrations. His brother bullies him, his father wallops him and his nose drips like a tap with a worn washer.

Ken's morning job is to empty the chamber pots. Woe betide if he misses a morning and gets an earful from Grandma. His other job is to clean up anything that is spilt on the floor. My jobs are to sweep up the dead cockroaches every morning, operate the posser in the washtub on washing day and turn the rollers that squeeze the water from the sodden washing. My biceps are growing. I check them every week. When Roy farts at night and Ken lets one off in response, and they can't stop guffawing, I tell myself I might have to punch one of them any day soon. I mean, what is so hilarious about farting in bed?

Roy's job is to shovel Bert's ration of free coal from the colliery into the little brick outbuilding next to the toilet in the back yard. He also has to clean out the ash from the fire-grate in the morning, keep the coal-scuttle full and make sure the gas poker is connected to the gas tap and that there are matches within reach on the mantelpiece.

Jenny's job is peeling potatoes. We eat a lot of potatoes. She also has to whiten the edges of the front stoop and the windowsill at the weekend, and clean the front room window with newspaper and vinegar.

Everyone but Bert has to take a turn at washing-up and making sure there is enough newspaper in the outside toilet. We get through a lot of newspapers: the Daily Herald, the Beasley Chronicle, the News of the World and the Green 'Un. Real toilet paper is too expensive, though I know what it is like because we have it at school. It is very thin, shiny on one side, and every sheet printed with 'Beasley & District Education Committee' in case anyone is tempted to take a roll or two home.

The cockroaches come out at night from under the skirting. The way to deal with them is to put DDT around the skirting last thing at night, then first thing in the morning sweep up the dead bodies. If the fire is already lit I throw the cockroaches on and listen to them crackling. It is best not to come downstairs to the kitchen at night for a glass of water, because you can easily step on a scuttling cockroach that will make a crunching sound and leave a bitty brown mess on the lino. There are regular disputes with Ken around lines of demarcation here: does a squashed cockroach come under his area of responsibility or mine?

If you have to get up in the night and go downstairs, the best thing to do is ease your hand round the door to switch on the light before you take the bottom step into the kitchen. This gives the cockroaches time to scuttle back to the gaps in the skirting, scraping their thin little legs on the floor. They do not like the light. You have to be fairly desperate to go downstairs in the night.

At first I used to count the number of dead in the morning, but there were so many I gave up. I fear that if they can find no food in the kitchen they will start climbing the stairs and exploring the bedrooms, so now and again I leave a few crumbs out on the floor. I feed them, then kill them. I am facing both ways at once, like Janus, particularly when it comes to writing cheerful letters to my mother while in reality feeling resentful, and being polite to Bert and his truculent sons while actually hating them.

I ask myself if it would be better to die of drowning or from swallowing a live cockroach in my sleep. I choose choking on a cockroach while unconscious as the slightly less disagreeable alternative. Fortunately, there is little danger of drowning in Beasley after the health scare that closed the public baths. People were getting rashes and ringworm until the Chronicle ran a campaign and had the baths closed. Calverley Grammar has no pool of its own, so they lay on extra sports and cross-country running. I am instructed to run for the school, but there is no doubt in my mind that I am running for myself.

The loss of the pool is one of the few good things about Beasley. There are several not-so-good things for comparison. The mermaids can be forgiven their tears, as they foresaw what would happen.

φ

Chapter 10
Blood, Floods and Phobias

SUNDAY SCHOOL AT BLACKFOOT LANE Wesleyan Methodist Church is – how can I best describe it? – a hotbed of vice and intrigue. I first meet Janet Openshaw under a table when we are enacting something from the scriptures. We are hiding from Herod or sheltering from a plague of locusts, I forget, but we miss our cue to emerge and for several weeks afterwards we are the subject of wholly unnecessary innuendo from our fellow pupils.

On the following day I am on my way to school with my friends when I see Janet among a group coming from the opposite direction on their way to the Girls' High School. Our paths cross several times that week. On the following Sunday as we enter the schoolroom we exchange the single word "Hello" and the relationship is sealed. It is one of the better things about Beasley and has a slight but specific relationship to the sea, as I shall recount.

That evening I sit down to compose my first love letter. It expresses in the politest possible terms the fact that I have noticed Janet, wonder if she has noticed me, and raises the remote possibility that she might like to go out with me. To go out with someone is to have an exclusive but indefinable attachment. You can go out with someone without ever going anywhere. The important thing is that the exceptional nature of the attachment, however short-lived, should be acknowledged and honoured by your peers.

On Monday I give the letter to one of my friends to give to one of Janet's friends as the two groups pass. The next day Janet's friend gives my friend an envelope that reads *'Private: James H. Seagrave'* in small, neat handwriting. And here comes the really memorable and, to me, seaworthy part: the envelope has a drawing of a skull and crossbones and a treasure-chest in the sand with the word 'Secret' written on it. Janet Openshaw must have read Treasure Island! It is a special moment.

Inside the envelope is a piece of white notepaper, a piece of blue notepaper, a white card with the label 'Codebreaker' and a tightly folded piece of red notepaper sealed with the red sealing-wax used for parcels. The blue note has writing in some kind of code. The white note says:

> The answer to your letter is on the blue paper. It is in code. In the red note
> is the secret key for the code. Do not let anyone else see it. Turn the wheel
> on the Codebreaker until the arrow points to the code letter, then read the

answer letter in the little window. If you cannot work it out, write to me tomorrow – in code. Choose a key letter and write that at the top of your letter. Then write your letter using the code letters which appear in the little window on the Codebreaker. *Only write in code and do not let anyone else see the key.*

I am impressed. She must like me, I think. I work out the letter substitution methodology readily enough, but translation is a laborious task. 'Dear James', says the answer eventually, 'thank you for your letter. Yes, I have noticed you. I would like to go out with you if you would still like that. Yours sincerely, Janet Openshaw'. We go out for almost three weeks. It is an exciting but exhausting time, given the need to communicate everything in code.

Another good thing about Beasley is Grandma Lily's weekly wash. Every Wednesday the kitchen fills with steam and the scent of soap flakes as we take turns to work the copper, the posser, the paddler and the mangle in a sequence of simple, shared, satisfying chores. Drying day is Thursday, ironing Friday, so that by the end of the week everyone in the house – well, anyone with any sensitivity, that is, which excludes Roy and Ken – can enjoy the fragrance and freshness of clean, crisp, neatly pressed cotton. To me the work and the warmth involved are more than a distraction from loss, they offer the remission of sins. Trivial as it may seem, but holding a warm mug of cocoa or smelling the earth after rain help keep my deeper fears in check.

There are several less agreeable things about Beasley that serve to feed my fears: the outside toilet, bathnight, my nose bleeds, the blood of the butcher, the East coast floods and the terrifying nightmare of the flooding of the house. Before saying any more, I should mention Yorkshire fast bowler Freddie Trueman's debut for England, when he reduces India to no runs for four wickets in their first innings. I find huge solace in this unprecedented deed.

The outside toilet freezes in winter, much as it did in Rawley, but in Rawley there were only three or four of us using it and in Beasley there are twelve – six in our house and six next door. When the water pipes freeze and the toilet will not flush, waste and newspaper accumulate in the bowl and have to be sluiced down with a bucketful of water. The soggy solids that results often freeze too. You have to be alert and fit to take a trip to the toilet in winter. While you are pulling on a coat and filling a bucket with water ready to run out of the house the moment the toilet becomes free, it is not unusual to see one of the neighbours running out in a dressing gown or tracksuit and getting there first.

Friday night is bathnight. The water has to be heated in the copper. The zinc bath the size of a cattle trough has to be brought in from the back yard, where it hangs from a nail in the wall. The bath has to be filled from a tap at the bottom of the copper. There is a particular order for using the bath, based on the belief that girls are generally cleaner than boys: first Jenny, then Grandma Lily, invariably singing My Bonny Lies Over the Ocean or reciting Three Fishers Went Sailing …

For men must work and women must weep,
For there's little to earn, and many to keep

a line that seems to have a particular meaning for her, then Roy or me, whoever gets there first, and last of all Ken, who is usually defined as the dirtiest. Then Roy and I have to empty the bath into the drain outside, Ken has to clean it, and if any of us boys happen to have had a bath before Jenny or Grandma, more water has to be heated and the bath refilled prior to emptying and cleaning it again. Bert does not normally come into this arrangement. He has a pithead shower at the end of his shift and goes straight to the pub.

Bathnight is a trial, but my nose bleeds and colds are a real ordeal. I shall not go on about the colds again, except to say that a bath in Ken's bathwater would be infinitely preferable to a cold. The feeling of the first wet trickle of a bleeding nose is impossible to distinguish from the first wet trickle of a cold, but when it drips onto my shirt or the book I am reading in a sudden splash of shocking wet red it is inescapable. The trickle becomes a dribble, the dribble a stream. All I can do is mop up the flow with one rag or handkerchief after another until all the available rags and handkerchiefs are wet and red, then put my head back and swallow. Swallowing my own blood is a last resort. It feels perverse. I shall be punished for this, I think. For some reason the analogy of *Oedipus* marrying his own mother comes to mind. But I have no choice. A cold key down the back of my neck makes no noticeable difference. I suppose that a bleeding nose, like a streaming cold, is one of the ways I have learnt not to cry.

Mopping up the blood at the butcher's is another. I take a part-time job at the corner shop, never having given a thought to what goes on in the back room or the cellar. I find to my dismay that it involves a great deal of blood. There are spots and flecks and smears of the stuff that have to be cleaned from chopping blocks, counter tops, sinks and floors; blood that leaks and seeps from every joint, steak, chop and dollop of meat; buckets of blood for boiling with fat to make black pudding; and on one memorable occasion a droplet of blood from a nick in my finger, a modest enough cut that I think no more about it until a few days later when a red patch appears on my hand. "Streptococcal infection," says the doctor breezily. "Now what is our drug of choice?" He is being unnecessarily cheerful, I think. "You are lucky not to have necrotizing fasciitis!" he says and giggles as though this were the best joke of the day, which for someone with his sick sense of humour it probably is. "What is that?" I ask. "Flesh-eating disease!" he exclaims, accompanied by what I can only describe as a cackle. "Don't worry, you don't have it – yet!" Since that day I have always been grateful to doctors. This one taught me that my haemophobia was a rational fear.

The East Coast floods are a disaster, the biggest surge ever recorded in Britain since *Charybdis* reduced two-thirds of the world to sea. A huge area of low pressure over the North Sea sucks up a high Spring tide to form a wall of water twenty feet high that sweeps the coast from Tayside to Essex. Coastal defences are breached, low-lying areas inundated and thousands of homes destroyed. Three hundred and seven people are drowned, including a baby snatched from its mother's arms by a pitiless wave and swept out to sea. Everyone knows someone who was affected. I try not to hope that my stepmother went for a walk on the beach that day.

But the flooding of the house is the worst of all the bad things about Beasley. One night I have to go downstairs for a dry rag to stem a streaming cold. All the handkerchiefs I have taken to bed are saturated, and as you may know, though I hope not, there is nothing worse than having to mop a sore nose with a wet handkerchief. Sorry, I promised to say no more about colds.

That is a lesson I learnt as a child that you might take to heart too Julian: never depend on a promise.

During the night it rains heavily. I can hear it drumming on the roof and rapping at the windows. I switch on the light in the kitchen to give the cockroaches time to escape and see a puddle on the floor. A drip of water is coming from the ceiling. I run upstairs to wake Bert. The eiderdown is smouldering from one of his cigarette ends, so I grab the chamberpot from under the bed, fling the contents over the eiderdown and run to the room next door to wake Jenny, but she is doing her pigtails and tells me to leave her alone. I run downstairs. Water is all over the floor. It is streaming down the walls and rising through the floorboards. I go down to the cellar to see my mother standing chest-deep in the water beckoning me to join her. I run back upstairs and notice that the water dripping from the ceiling is red. It is blood! This is a recurring nightmare.

In the dream it is always raining and the house is always flooding. Water and blood are dripping from the ceiling and running down the walls. There is a variation in which water overflows from a stream in the basement and uproots the floorboards. All you can see through the hole in the floor is the flashing and frothing of the torrent below. The foundations of the house are being undermined, the cockroaches are swimming for their lives and the house is about to collapse. Are those foundations mine?

Yet I also dream of swimming effortlessly in a friendly open-air pool, a sensation so real that when I wake I am convinced I can swim. But where did I learn? Not in the North Sea, where I almost drowned; not in Scarmouth, where the beaches were mined; and not in the King's School pool, where I was held under by an ape called Protheroe who did it for a laugh and is top of my death list. I will give him a choice: assassination by drowning or by slow dehydration – an excess of water or a total lack of it.

I am unable to escape this tasteless, inodorous, insidious stuff that freezes and boils and surges and rages, that sustains life one moment and takes it the next. I have water on the brain. I take to staring at glasses of water at mealtimes. I calculate all the stages the water had to go through before it reaches the sea to be heated to rise and return as rain to be stored and piped to a tap in the kitchen ready for imbibing, bathing, boiling or steaming. I begin to seek reasons not to go to the toilet or to school in the rain. Then I am reluctant to go out to play with my friends or to church to sing in the choir, or to the Grey Horse on Sundays to tell Bert his dinner is ready. This is a new fear, half-brother to the others, but what is it? I refer myself to the Medical Section of my Pears' Cyclopaedia, the Introduction to which begins:

> First and foremost, let no one imagine that by referring to this book he [sic] will acquire information that would enable him [sic] to dispense with the services of the medical profession.

I check who has written this: 'A Prominent London Physician'.

> I have tried, on the contrary, to show that even the most commonplace and trivial-seeming symptoms may have grave underlying causes; that it is impossible – I wish to stress the word – absolutely *impossible* for an untrained person to assess the gravity of any illness.

Now I am *convinced* that I have no need of a London physician, prominent or otherwise, to assess the gravity of my condition. I can do it myself. I start to go through the medical conditions in alphabetical order, having no idea what I am looking for – abortion, abrasion, addiction, aerophagia – when I come upon *agoraphobia*, a morbid fear of the marketplace. That is it. My existing anxieties have been joined by a new one. I do not want to go out.

I know nothing of underlying causes, but I have found a way of living with my haemophobia by accepting that I can do nothing about it, and I resolve to do the same for my thalassaphobic response to the sea, although that is a big one and will have to wait a while. In the meantime the remedy for my problem with places of public assembly is obvious enough: I must match action to reason and get out more. It is my intuitive version of cognitive-behavioural therapy. I go on the Whitsuntide walk with the church, attend Beasley F.C. home games and join the Calverley school choir. These voluntary activities revive my internal debate about free will. Whether my sense of exercising freedom of choice is real or not hardly matters, I decide. Illusion and reality are two sides of the same coin. They exist independently but are inseparably attached, like Siamese twins who share the same brain. Whether the world I inhabit is real or not does not make the slightest difference to how I feel or behave in it.

This freedom to act on my feelings is not total, I know. It is more like wiggle room in quicksand – a restricted capacity to make limited choices. I am wandering around an open prison, aware that I can escape any time, but unable or unwilling – too agoraphobic, perhaps – to open the door. Free will or no free will, I cannot escape my own fears.

They appear again during rehearsals for a musical version of Coleridge's *Kubla Khan* as composed by Mr Fish (aka Stinky), the Calverley choirmaster.

> In Xanadu did Kubla Khan
> A mighty palace dome decree.

Stinky's atonal music waxes and wanes strangely.

> Where Alph, the sacred river, ran
> Through caverns measureless to man
> Down to a sunless sea.

This river runs deep and its sea is sunless. Coleridge read Robinson Crusoe when he was young and impressionable, as I did, and Crusoe first went to sea from the port of Hull, as I once thought to do. "Our ship had scarce left the Humber astern," wrote Daniel Defoe on behalf of Crusoe, "when there arose so violent a storm, that, being extremely sea-sick, I concluded the judgment of God deservedly followed me." Crusoe and Coleridge saw the North Sea as I do – perpetually leaden and sullen, then apt to rise without warning and drive poor mariners out of their minds. The protagonist of The Rime of the Ancient Mariner is clearly thalassaphobic. He shoots a friendly albatross that has led his ship out of dangerous waters, but only because his dread of the sea has unhinged him. When the ship runs out of drinking water, the crew blame the mariner – "water, water everywhere," they cry, "nor any drop to drink!" – and make him wear the dead albatross around his neck as a punishment. Am I condemned to carry forever the burden of my deepest fears?

My unhealthy obsession with the sea is for the time being in abeyance, however (I cannot see it from Beasley) and my incipient agoraphobia is under some kind of control (I go out only when I have to), but the relentless god *Phobos* persists in his attentions. He takes time off from the agenda he usually reserves for me – *aichmophobia* (needles), *acrophobia* (heights), *astraphobia* (thunder and lightning) – to introduce *claustrophobia*, unmarried sister to agoraphobia. I detest having to share the Blackfoot Lane attic with the sweaty, pissy, sneak-a-smoke-whenever-possible twins, who do not share my need for fresh air while I am doing my homework. And I feel trapped in the Calverley classrooms, with their chalky blackboards and stuffy central heating. I have difficulty breathing. The walls of the classroom are closing in on me. I visualize myself out on the playing fields with air and space. This brings some relief from the claustrophobia, but reminds me of the agoraphobia.

Calverley Grammar, nevertheless, is a school that tries, in spite of the school motto. At King's School, York, we were urged to *Nunc Agere*, 'act now', though no-one explained what we should do and why it had to be there and then. At Calverley we are required to *Fortiter Occupa Portam*, which translates in the daft little ditty that passes for the school song as 'hold the gate boldly'. Thus:

> *Fortiter Occupa Portam*
> Pray what is the meaning of that?
> Ever be bold the gate to hold
> There's the translation pat.

Pray what is the meaning of *that*? We are assailed by it daily at morning assembly and in a stultifying multi-verse version sung every year by the choir on Speech Day. The clumsy quatrain that makes up the first verse is a syllable short of a full helping, so the penultimate word of the fourth line has to be put on the rack and stretched

– trans-lay-ay-shun – in a bid to fit the dismal dirge that carries it. My life is in some disorder, but I ought to be able to expect the school song to scan or make sense or be cheerful or musical or motivate me to be a better person, and it does none of these things. I do well enough academically, because I am motivated to swot and swotting is something I can do on my own.

The Speech Day prizes in my final year are distributed by professor of poetry and celebrated crime writer C. Day-Lewis, who presents the Warner Memorial Prize for Classics to Seagrave, J.H., while Barnes, M.T., is awarded the Headmaster's Prize for Consistent Industry and Potts, J.D. Mrs Duckett's Prize for General Helpfulness. The address of welcome to the distinguished visitor is given, to the general bafflement, in Latin, though how Bamforth, G.M.T., who only came second in Latin, ever got chosen to speak it is beyond me.

> *Quoties patres nostros vidimus tuis libris toto animo deditos, et cenae et*
> *nicotianae et sui ipsorum omnino immemores …*
> How often have we seen our fathers, completely absorbed in your books,
> forgetting supper, tobacco, their very selves …

How often have I seen my father even partially absorbed in a book? Sex scandals and the soccer results were the only reading that engaged him. And he never forgot his tobacco. Yet it is entirely possible that his two children, who moved as much as ten miles away, somehow slipped his mind. He still has to visit us. I suppose that the demands of Dracula's Daughter and her bastard son, who could have passed as his own, you know, are taking up too much of his time.

My mid-teens have been spent in an open but inescapable prison. It is a time of freezing toilets, streaming colds, secret codes, floods, phobias, buckets of blood and unanswered questions. How many cockroaches do I have to kill before I can get away from here? What happens now that Britain has manufactured an atomic bomb? Where is Bert's missing wife and is there any connection to the body parts in the butcher's freezer? I pray that the next phase of my life will be freer and easier.

φ

Chapter 11
Restless Waves

MEN AND WOMEN ARE INCOMPATIBLE. I have come to this conclusion in the unlikely setting of Beasley F.C., the local football club known as the Blues – not because of the colour of their strip, which is red, but because they are a regular source of suffering to their ironically minded fans. The Blues usually end up in the bottom half of the Third Division, so there is always room behind the goal at the Brewery End for me to meet up with my soccer-mad friends. We are a witty, melodious lot, famed for our tribute to Harry Hough, the Beasley centre forward.

> 'Arry 'Uff, 'Arry 'Uff!
> We've 'ad enough, we've 'ad enough!
> Give us a goal or yer'll be on the dole!

On a pivotal day at the start of the new season, with the grass still green and hopes still high, I attempt to re-order the sexual politics of the Brewery End by bringing a girl along to the game. Elspeth Purcell is a thoughtful, beautiful sixteen-year old who is helping me get over my fear of going out and is, she assures me, quite interested in football. I believe she will be seen by my friends as rather special. Within seconds of our arrival at the back of the stand I realize I have committed an unforgivable gaffe. My friends make a point of ignoring us. I try edging closer to the group at an emotional moment in the game – a corner to the Blues at the Glossop Road End, a moment in which we would normally all share our anticipation, excitement and despair together – but my friends edge away and Elspeth and I are left standing apart.

Allegiances are changing. The focus of my interests is shifting from Homer and Horace to dancing, mixed doubles and kissing – the real thing, not Maureen Jupp's take-it-in-turns-to-be-timed competitive version. I learn to foxtrot. I practise my forehand against a gable-end wall. I discover an abiding interest in breasts. And I go to church with the grown-ups. Grandma Lily (contralto) prevails upon Jenny (soprano), me (tenor) and Roy (bass) to join her in the Blackfoot Lane Wesleyan Methodist choir. Ken (tone-deaf) is not invited.

I do not mind the sopranos, though they squawk a bit at times, and I have nothing against the contraltos, who generally don't make much of a fuss, but for some reason – and it is not, I assure you, because Roy is one of them – I develop an intense dislike of the basses. They have two volume settings: low-level grumbling and pile-drivingly loud. In comparison we tenors have colour and subtlety. We do *not*, as Roy is fond of quoting one of his colleagues, screech like the brakes of a freight train coming to an emergency stop at Beasley Bottom.

Joining the church choir means that Friday night choir practice has to be integrated into Friday night bathnight, a logistical nightmare, but there are compensations.

> Jesus, Saviour, pilot me
> Over Life's tempestuous sea!
> Unknown waves before me roll,
> Hiding rock and treacherous shoal!

Jesus helps me even out the emotional ups and downs of the week. He takes on the role of affectionate head of an exuberant family.

> As a father stills his child,
> Thou canst hush the ocean wild;
> Boisterous waves obey thy will,
> When thou sayest to them, 'Be still!'

For the first time in my life since leaving Rawley I feel contained but unconfined, like a willing young monkey in a well-run zoo. I also feel *good*, in a deserving and respectable rather than pious or zealous sense. For a while the notion of one steadfast, dependable God easily trumps my pantheon of wildly unreliable Greek deities as a metaphor for moral excellence, individual aspiration and community cohesion, and although Jesus seems to have his delusional side I am impressed by his ethics and feel sad when he dies.

A few things puzzle me about the hymns we sing. Who or what is the Holy Ghost? Is there such a thing as Eternal Pain? Why in all seriousness would we wish to extol the Stem of Jesse's Rod? My enjoyment of the experience of singing Songs of Praise (surely God has heard enough by now?) is greater if I concentrate on the harmonies rather more than the words, although there is one notable exception. I shiver when the basses get to the verse that goes

> Eternal Father, strong to save,
> Whose arm hath bound the restless wave,
> Who bidd'st the mighty ocean deep
> Its own appointed limits keep.

As far as I am concerned, eternal or temporal fathers and oceans deep or shallow can be trusted to keep to no limits whatsoever.

> O hear us when we cry to thee
> For those in peril on the sea!

Look what happens to the earth when *Zeus* leaves the aquaphiliac *Poseidon* to do his thing without supervision: violent storms, devastation and drowning.

Yet as Young Methodists we are rewarded when we turn up to the services on time, stay awake during the sermon and vow not to covet our neighbours' cattle – no problem there, as our neighbours are mostly miners and factory workers. Our reward is being given permission to meet in the crypt after Sunday evening service, when we play games that involve a great deal of kissing, hypnotising each other and acting out the dirty bits from Hank Janson novels. We also get to put on concerts, revues and plays.

I am currently working my way through Agatha Christie – five down, forty-five to go – so I set myself to write and direct a murder mystery for our next Youth Group show. This is the plot: Mrs Mortimer, a wicked woman with a terminal illness, invites all the people she hates and who hate her in turn – her faithful companion Miss Howard, her retired neighbour Dr Gough, her sensitive young stepson Rodney and his charming young wife Alison – down to her country house for the weekend. Each of her guests has a motive for murder. Her companion is exploited and badly abused, her stepson hates her for usurping his mother, her stepson's young wife feels disparaged and belittled by her, and her paranoid neighbour is out for revenge because she cheats him at cards. All this is established in Act One. In Act Two, the characters are gathering in the drawing room after dinner when a blood-curdling scream is heard. Mrs M has been found dead. No-one is grieving. Everyone is suspect. In Act Three, Inspector McCorquodale of New Scotland Yard (it takes me a long time to come up with the name for this character) arrives to investigate. McCorquodale, a shrewd man, is quickly on the case, eliminating the suspects one by one until in a final twist – gasp – we learn that Mrs Mortimer actually did it herself. Suicide by poisoning. The old bat knew she was dying, she wanted one of the people she hated to be hanged for her murder and it did not matter which. Fortunately, medical science and the forces of the law in the shape of Inspector McC combine to clear everyone and Mrs Mortimer is denied a church burial.

A dark plot for a sixteen-year old who is apparently sane and sociable. I don't have a title. My research leads me to believe that playwrights like to use well-known phrases for titles (And Then There Were None, See How They Run, etc.), so I try The More the Merrier and You Never Can Tell, but they sound like farces and my play is deadly serious, so I ask Grandma Lily if she knows of an old proverb I can use. After Many a Mickle Makes a Muckle (she may have made that up) and A Watched Pot Never Boils (meaning what?), she comes up with The Mill Will Not Grind with the Water that is Past. I ask her what that means. "Do not waste time wishing for what you no longer have, James," she says. That might be the story of her life, I think, or mine, or anyone's really, but it is too long for the play, so I abbreviate it to The Mill Will Not Grind ... I insist on the dots. No-one asks me why the title has to have three dots or even what the title has to do with the play. I have no idea myself until well into rehearsals, when it occurs to me that water is a metaphor for the torrent of fury that turns the mill of Mrs Mortimer's (and the author's) mind. And just as Jane Eyre is ostensibly about an orphan girl and her troubled master, but is actually about gender equality, my story of a batty old lady doing away with herself is saying that the world will not turn in your favour if you are stuck in the past. It is purely coincidental, what else, that the villain of my piece is a stepmother, and a pretty nasty one at that.

My mother's sister Auntie Joan is the next monster to put in an appearance, though she comes some way after my mother herself and the barely fictitious Mrs Mortimer – both monsters of my own creation, I should say – on my all-time list. When my mother moved to India she went up a couple of levels socially, but she kept the name Mildred. When her sister Joan emigrated to South Africa and made a pot of money in property she changed her name to Joanne. The news comes in a letter to Grandma Lily. "Joe-anne?" asks Bert in a tone of voice you could not mistake for simple curiosity. "'Oo the 'ell does she think she is?" If he had been an Agatha Christie character he would have been aghast.

Auntie Joan sails to Britain on a visit and comes to stay with us. She takes over Jenny's room, Jenny moves in with Grandma, Bert takes Ken's bed and Ken has to top and tail with Roy. Bert snores. Roy and Ken fart and guffaw. I console myself with thoughts of men and male children dead in their beds and a claw hammer found on the floor. Miss Christie would have approved.

One evening I find myself alone in the house with Auntie Joan. She is mixing herself a cocktail from a bottle of vodka she smuggled into the house and insists on concocting one for me. I do not like it. Do I have a girlfriend, she asks. No, I say, blushing (I am no longer seeing Elspeth Purcell after our humiliating date on the terraces). Auntie Joan tells me about her three ex-husbands in terms I would rather not hear and hints at an affair with Ernest Hemingway on the liner from Cape Town. Are these the kind of salacious games that the nymphs of *Nysa* played with young *Dionysus*? I am gratified that she assumes I know who Ernest Hemingway is, but I can't see such a sensitive writer sleeping more than once with a bossy woman like Auntie Joan. She would have told him off for smoking in bed or for not paying her enough attention and that would have been it. And having sex only once, I understand – though I need to do more research on the subject – hardly qualifies as an affair. I excuse myself, saying I have homework to do, and tip the rest of my Screwdriver down the kitchen sink.

She likes to make a point, does Auntie Joan. She refuses to change upstairs in the cold like everyone else and makes a point of stripping to her underwear by the fire downstairs. I find this gruesome. All that pink elastic. And she is old, at least thirty-five.

On the day my mother's sister leaves Beasley to return to her servants in Durban she leaves each of us young people a note marked 'Personal and Private'. I expect messages of encouragement and support at this tender and troubled time in our lives. Roy leaves his personal and private note out on the sideboard so that everyone can read what a level-headed, smartly turned out, good-looking young fellow she thinks he is. It goes without saying that she is wrong, but I guess it is good of her to flatter him in that way. Ken reads his note, shrugs, and goes off to kick a cat in the back yard. Jenny takes hers to her room and doesn't appear for a while. My note is a critical end-of-term report advising me, among other things, to get rid of the chip on my shoulder. Chip? *Moi?* This is not the encouragement I need. I need understanding and support. I need to be part of a family. Bert and his sons do not constitute a family. The church is no longer an adequate substitute for a family. My soccer-mad mates at the Brewery End never were.

I begin to spend more time on my own. I read a long book on the Peloponnesian Wars. I visit a military museum and take an unhealthy interest in battering rams and those heavy steel balls you swing round your head at the end of a chain. A clout from one of those would sort out Roy and Ken soon enough. And I take the bus to Sourness with a half-formed intention of enlisting in the merchant navy and attempting to reconcile my conflicting feelings about the sea. I linger along the quay with Amyas Leigh. I see Jim Hawkins hoisting sail on the Hispaniola and Robinson Kreuznaer hitching a lift to Kingston upon Hull.

It begins to rain. The romance of the sea would have been more apparent to the ancient Greeks, I reason, as more often than not the sun would be shining and their gods would be having sex and riding on dolphins.

I wonder what sex is really like. *Really* like. I need more information, more than my half-witted schoolfriends claim to have and more than the hints I have come across in stories by Somerset Maugham. It is hard to tell from those. There is a line from The Moon and Sixpence:

> As lovers, the difference between men and women is that women can love all day long, but men only at times.

How does that work? Will I ever find out?

Out of the blue I am approached by buxom, blonde Joyce Draper, who sings in the church choir (soprano) and excelled in the role of Alison in my play with the dots. She comes with an offer: would I be interested in auditioning for the Beasley Amateur Operatic Society with her and her friend, sultry, slim Celia Murgatroyd (contralto)? I imagine sex with Joyce and Celia – separately, my imagination does not extend to a threesome – and think it might be better with Celia. I know that my cricketing friend Mike Sykes (opening bat) fancies Joyce, so I invite him to accompany me to the auditions.

Mike lives in a semi-detached house with gardens front, side and back on the middle-class side of the common. His favourite oratorio, so he claims, is Bach's St Matthew's Passion, whereas those of us who live gardenless on the working-class side of the common think of Bach as beyond us and swear instead by Handel's Messiah. Given Mike's artistic preferences, I imagine that auditioning for musical comedy might not be high on his list of things to do this week, but Joyce Draper easily persuades him and Celia Murgatroyd reassures us that the Society is so desperate for men they will take anyone.

The audition consists of everyone sight-reading a number from the show while the musical director, Miss Iris Fisk, walks among us looking as though she is listening critically. No-one is rejected, however tone-deaf, underage or overweight. So at the age of seventeen Mike Sykes and I find ourselves dressing in tights and wigs and singing with the ladies and gentlemen of the chorus in the musical comedy romance, The Dubarry, a production sponsored by Beasley Beers, which as the programme points out may be obtained at the bar. The part of Madame Dubarry is taken by Miss Mona Little, a soprano from Sheffield with a mild speech defect; the role of René Leclerc, the penniless poet, goes to aspiring tenor Mr Clifton Pickles; and Louis XV is played by Mr Ivor Duffin, a diminutive baritone who has to be padded up for the part.

The show is not a runaway success. In terms of my pursuit of Celia Murgatroyd it has to be counted an outright failure. Her father picks her up after every rehearsal and is there or thereabouts after every performance. The nearest I get to carnal knowledge of Celia is catching a glimpse of her pantaloons as she changes into her crinoline in the wings. My friend Mike claims to have had sexual intercourse with Joyce during the last night party, but I know this to be an outright lie as no-one had sexual intercourse in the nineteen-fifties.

I move on. I audition for the school production of Pinero's Dandy Dick and am offered the part of turf-loving Sir Tristram Mardon, baronet. During the rehearsals I learn a great lesson. "We are not interested in YOU, Seagrave!" shouts drama director and Eng Lit teacher, Sugsie (Mr Sugden), from the back of the hall while I am struggling with my characterisation of an extrovert aristocrat, "only in the PART you are playing!" This wonderful note gives me permission to step outside myself, with all my agonies, allergies and chips on the shoulder, and be who I wish to be, in this case the kind and convivial, blue-blooded Sir Tristram.

How should I translate this learning into my life? It helps to be told by Sugsie, a kind and forthright teacher, that "unfortunately no-one out there in the audience and, indeed, beyond, is the least bit interested in who you really are, Seagrave, only in what they imagine or wish you to be." It is an assertion I will come to see, sadly, as true.

'Dandy Dick producer Edwin Sugden', trumpets the Beasley Chronicle, 'scored a remarkable triumph over stage and lighting deficiencies. James Seagrave's racy baronet was a gem of confidence, ease and polish. Stephen Pooley's Major Tarver provided a ludicrous mélange of foppishness, dyspepsia and musical pretension. The refreshments were superb'.

Sir Tristram's supposed confidence, ease and polish help him off-stage. I am promoted to prefect. I am given a badge to pin to the lapel of my blazer and a cherry-red tassel to attach to my cap. On the way home that day I am set upon by Roy and his cronies, who grab my newly tasselled cap and toss it about between them until it falls to the ground and I can retrieve it. I am angry and speechless. I punch Roy. He punches me back. His cronies join in. In the ensuing mêlée I mistakenly punch his twin brother, Ken, who up until then had not been involved.

The episode is brief, but has a long-lasting effect. Roy and I do not exchange a word for a year, even though we eat at the same table, sleep in the same attic and piss in the same pot. Our rivalry over the affections of one Sylvia Newbold, a well-built girl who plans to join the police force, hardly helps. I convince myself she is more attracted to me than to Roy, even when the evidence indicates otherwise. It is inconceivable that she would prefer his muscly, carefully Brylcreemed, slicked-back looks to my slender, tousled-haired, more informal appearance.

It has to be Roy who on more than one occasion secretly takes the dead cockroaches I have collected for the fire and scatters them back on the floor. All I can think of in response is to leave the lid off his dark tan shoe polish and hope that it dries out before it gets to his shoes. Self-respect is at stake here. Our sense of ourselves. Who are we? Two motherless youths wanting to make something of our lives. Roy knows exactly what he is going to be. He leaves school at seventeen to train as a builder. I stay on in the sixth form hoping that something will come up without me having to think too much about it.

My new best friend is Stephen Pooley, fellow Classics and Eng Lit scholar, who had such a triumph as Major Tarver in Dandy Dick. Our joint ambition is to finish The Times crossword before morning milk break, a task we achieve once with seconds to spare. Encouraged by this, we decide to write a sketch for the next Youth Group revue with the aim of educating our audience about some of lesser known aspects of Greek mythology. We call it Sex Slaves of Ancient Greece and it begins with a verse to the tune of The British Grenadiers.

> Some talk of *Alexander* and some of *Hercules* …

I want to replace the Roman 'Hercules' with the Greek original 'Heracles', but Pooley convinces me this would be too pedantic. The fact that Alexander was an historical character and Hercules is mythical also bothers me a bit, but Pooley argues that no-one will notice or care.

> Of *Hector* and *Lysander* and such great names as these …

A mythical Trojan with an actual Spartan. Same argument. Doesn't matter.

> But of all the world's great heroes, there's none so fair and brave
> As *Dionysus* and *Odysseus*, two Ancient Greek sex slaves!

I take the part of Dionysus (mythical) and Pooley Odysseus (probably mythical, possibly historical, certainly legendary; Pooley doesn't mind). We begin by comparing notes about how little the general public knows about the reality of our private lives. Although it is well documented that Dionysus was reared by the rain-nymphs of Nysa, it is not so apparent that they taught him the ways of *Eros* some time before he was ready to learn. In truth it was an early example of sexual abuse

– somehow less shocking when an under-age youth and a bevy of rampant nymphs are involved. We make light of this in a way one might not get away with today.

> Of Dionysus and Odysseus, the two, O
> Who is the more ill-used of this dubious duo?

Odysseus's travels and travails after the battle of Troy are common currency, we allow, and it is generally accepted that when his ship founders off the Isle of Ogygia he spends seven years on the island at the behest of the goddess *Calypso*. According to my expurgated edition of Homer she 'receives him kindly'. Odysseus tells everyone that he struggled for years to return to his wife, but who believes a word of it? Here is a man who feigned an episode of madness in order to avoid joining the expedition to Troy – he ploughed a beach of sand and sowed it with salt. Does he have an ounce of credibility left?

After spending a further two verses competing over who is the more enslaved and exploited, we own up to the audience to being the unscrupulous and heartless liars that are – sad and lonely old men.

> I, Dionysus, do declare
> That of all the self-servers I compare,
> I am the worst.
> > Nay, quoth I, Odysseus, if I may dare,
> To confess my distress, 'tis I who doth deserve
> The opprobrium of this gentle jury. Come, unnerve
> Me now and sentence me to the poetical end which in life
> I did forfend.
> > It shall be my fate too. You are bound
> To sentence us both – no fear, no favour – to be drown'd.
> But me first.
> > Oh no! I must suffer more!
> > > Then I go first!
> Let us go together.
> > To the pub.
> > > Or we shall die of thirst.

And we leave the stage as the curtain closes. I had wanted to work in a serious point about drowning as the commonest cause of death in ancient Greece, but Pooley persuaded me that death by drowning did not sound quite the right note for a comedy sketch about sex. I could put a note in the programme if I insisted or, better still, save it for my diary.

We turn our attention next to sending selective verses from the poems we come across in our Eng Lit studies to girls in the sixth form at the High School. One of these:

> Look, Delia, how we esteem the half-blown rose
> The image of thy blush, and summer's honour

contains a simile we analyse at length in class with Sugsie. "What do you think 'half-blown' means in this context, Seagrave?" Sugsie asks. "Was the rose picked on a windy day, sir?" I answer in all innocence.

But our favourite verse, inevitably, is Marvell's

> Then worms shall try
> That long-preserved virginity,
> And your quaint honour turn to dust,
> And into ashes all my lust.

The girls at the High School affect to be offended by this kind of thing and return the favour with witty literary extracts to show what crap men are.

> Sigh no more, ladies, sigh no more,
> Men were deceivers ever, –
> One foot in sea and one in shore,
> To one thing constant never.

The source of these ripostes, I discover, is more often than not Polly Unmore, Eng Lit scholar, Head Girl and High School tennis champ.

> Much ado about nothing

is my predictable rejoinder to her quotation from the play. She responds with lines from a sonnet.

> If my slight Muse do please these curious days,
> The pain be mine, but thine shall be the praise.

I come face to face with Polly Unmore at the joint organizing committee for the annual High School and Grammar School Ball. I am impressed that she has her own study with a two-bar electric fire and that she has arranged for a pot of tea and three kinds of biscuit. She chairs our meeting with patience and grace, sitting neatly in her grey uniform edged with gold, knees together, sensible hair, crisp and pretty, as sweet and appealing as butterscotch. She suggests we run a tennis tournament on the day before the dance and looks to me for a response. Does she know I have been practising my forehand? I hesitate. Someone suggests that she and I form a sub-committee to organize the tournament. I try not to catch the eyes of my colleagues, who are doing their best not to smirk, and agree.

On my way home I reflect on the exchange and on the crispness and prettiness of Polly Unmore. I look forward to the tournament and the ball. Some men and women, I think, might not be incompatible after all.

φ

Chapter 12
Eros and Psyche

THE TENNIS TOURNAMENT GOES PREDICTABLY: the boys fool about and the girls win easily. The dance on the following evening is not so predictable. Polly Unmore arrives in a deep aquamarine dress with a striking white sea-shell design. Her hair is cut in a fringe, her arms are bare, she is slender and elegant. The effect is spoilt only slightly by the matching sea-shell ear-rings, but I can see that thought had gone into the ensemble. She is making a statement: I am a tasteful, desirable eighteen year-old and I do not have a boyfriend. I remind myself that she is still Head Girl and not to be trifled with, even though I have no idea how to trifle.

One of my jobs as MC is to be first on the floor to get everyone dancing and for that I have a prearranged starting partner: polite, petite, light-on-her-feet Mary Entwistle. I am hoping that no-one else asks Polly to dance before enough couples are on their feet and Mary and I can decently excuse ourselves. One or two boys are brave enough to approach the Head Girl, but she is able to say "No thank you" firmly and sound as though she means it. After a while I think that she might be waiting for me. We dance together several times. I bring her a glass of orange squash at the interval and take no chances when it comes to the last waltz. I bypass Mary Entwistle and get to Polly first.

It is Paula Teresa Unmore who introduces me to George Gordon Noel, sixth Baron Byron, on our weekend walks. My reading of Don Juan challenges the received wisdom favoured by Sugsie and Great-grandma Barraclough and gives me a new perspective on my father. "This wayward adventurer is no womanizer," I aver, "but a weak, amenable man easily seduced by persistent women." Polly resists my interpretation and holds to the traditional line. "I want a hero!" she declaims. "One without shame!" She quotes from Don Juan's encounter with one of his many lovers.

> A little still she strove and much repented,
> And whispering 'I will ne'er consent' – consented.

I am surprised, almost shocked, but manage not to show it. Is this an invitation to intimacy? On our next walk along the banks of the Bease – I make a conscious effort to position myself between my girlfriend and the river as I understand a gentleman should – she comes up with a line from Byron's assault upon the Hellespont.

> Once more upon the waters! Yet once more!
> And the waves bound beneath me as a steed
> That knows his rider.

She looks at me. Is that an innocent glance or an enticing smile? We are in what Dippy would have called ambiguous waters.

The following Sunday we meet and walk along the Bease by the hawthorn trees and into the ancient glades of Wormley Woods, where we kiss and embrace, and sit on my new gabardine raincoat, the one I keep only for Sundays. We kiss again, lie down and hold each other so close that I dare not move or do anything more. In any case I really do not know what more to do. After half an hour of kissing, embracing, stopping and starting we fall silent and gaze at the tops of the trees. What on earth is this painful feeling? I guess it must be sexual frustration. Is Polly expecting something more after all that valiant poetry? We are steeds that know neither ourselves nor our riders. The prospect of loosening the reins is unimaginable. I recall that Winston Smith and Julia didn't have this problem when they escaped into the woods, made love and fell asleep. Since reading 1984 I believe that falling asleep afterwards must be an indicator of good sex, but Polly and I are still awake and I am baffled and embarrassed. I feel like a pantomime horse with its trousers down, except that mine are still up and this is not at all funny.

When it is time to go home I take up my raincoat, shake it out carefully and fold it over my arm in the way that one does, then we walk in silence back to the bus station holding hands. I am as much at sea as a Greek trireme that has lost its oars in a sudden squall. All I know is that Barbara Skidmore-Bews, Janet Openshaw and Celia Murgatroyd no longer count. I am in love for the first time.

My mother is in Beasley preparing to take Rupert out of prep school in the foothills of the Himalayas and leave him in the care of an order of monks in the North Riding of Yorkshire. I am accompanying her on a bus past the High School on our way to do some research at the Beasley library when Polly gets on. What a happy coincidence, I think as I introduce them. It saves me taking my new girlfriend back to Blackfoot Lane, where she would have to be nice to surly Bert and the terrible twins and listen to Grandma Lily reciting The Lady of Shalott or the Wreck of the Hesperus. It will also save her – *quel horreur!* – having to run up the back yard to beat the neighbours to the toilet.

I know that my mother will be thrilled to meet the first real love of my life. I wonder if it might even help Polly and I unstick the habit of stuckness we have got into on our Sunday walks in Wormley Woods. We get on perfectly well when we are walking, talking and sharing poetry, but the moment we stop and kiss something else happens. We hold each other tight, clamped together like a spam sandwich, feel frustrated, give up and go home. Could it be anything to do with that nightmarish walk in the woods with my mother?

This chance encounter on the bus feels like a defining moment. Polly is polite and behaves impeccably. Mother is distant and frosty. I want her to embrace my sweetheart, to wreathe her in smiles and ply her with questions such as 'How did you and James meet?' 'What are you studying?' 'How many children do you plan to have?' The least she could do is invite Polly to join us for a cream tea in town. Is she not impressed with my sweet, smart girlfriend in her grey and gold blazer and gold-trimmed grey felt hat? Something else is going on. It will take the next venture between our two schools to give me a clue.

When the Joint Sixth Form Committee next meet in Polly's study, I view the Head Girl, her teapot and biscuits in a new, more proprietorial, light. The Committee is planning a competitive debate in which a pair of celebrities find themselves in a hot air balloon that is plunging to the sea and must be emptied of ballast in order to rise to safety again. The sandbags have all been emptied, but the balloon is still falling and there are hungry sharks circling in the freezing Antarctic below. We do not question the logic of sharks in the Antarctic or the fact that there is time for a debate in the middle of an obvious emergency. One of the celebrities has to be sacrificed in order for the other to be saved, and each has to come up with an argument in favour of remaining in the balloon. The survivor will be decided on a public vote.

The girls elect Polly as their representative and the boys put up me to oppose her. Members of my committee who know of our romantic involvement do their best to hide their silly grins.

There are suggestions for the characters in the balloon: Napoleon and Josephine; The Emperor Haile Selassie and his fourteenth wife; Queen Elizabeth and Jomo Kenyatta; Christ and his mother Mary; Francoise Sagan and Charlie Chaplin. Someone proposes *Orpheus* and *Eurydice*. I suggest *Eros* and *Psyche*. I have a sense from Undies, my Classics teacher, that Eros, despite his reputation, is an interesting fellow, and I am curious to discover what Polly might make of the wayward Psyche, his lover. The committee agree to my suggestion. The debate will be held at the boys' school. Polly knows very little about the myth, but she is as confident in her powers of research and persuasion as the talented professor of Eng Lit she is surely destined to become.

Ten minutes before the start someone discovers that Calverley Boys have no toilets for girls. There is momentary panic. Next to the classroom where the debate is to be held are two staff toilets, which we hastily arrange to be labelled 'Ladies' and 'Gentlemen'. Committee member Hugh Newby, whose subject is Art History, is despatched to produce the labels as a matter of urgency. Five minutes later, I find myself suffering from a nervous need to comb my hair, so I slip into the toilet we have designated for Gentlemen. After a few seconds I hear a group of girls about to enter. Mortified, I nip into one of the booths. Either I have chosen the wrong toilet or the fool Newby has messed up the labelling. I try to lock the door of the booth, but it is broken, so I kneel and pretend to be fixing the lock. I am trapped.

If I leave now the girls will be outraged and my reputation will never recover. If I stay where I am, at keyhole level, forcibly holding an unlockable door against the possibility of someone – not just anyone, a girl! – attempting to enter, I shall be discovered and traduced. I face humiliation even worse than the episode under the table with Janet Openshaw. I can hear Scylla sharpening her teeth and Charybdis sucking in the sea. They demand a sacrifice. I must either bring my principled silence with Roy to an end or offer to take over Ken's chamberpot duties. After an agonizing interval trying to choose between two equally inconceivable alternatives the girls leave and before anyone else can enter I bound out of the booth and into the corridor like a March Hare. A girl is approaching. I recover my poise. With an insouciance derived from my acclaimed performance as Sir Tristram Mardon, baronet, I mention in passing that there is a small problem with the locks, but the flush is working and the towels are … and walk into the room where the debate is about to start, nervous and perspiring, completely unprepared for this key status and relationship defining – as I see it – debate. And I have not even combed my hair.

"Eros," I say, "must be saved." The pithy opening line I planned a week ago seems asinine now. He should save himself by not getting into silly situations. "I represent sexual desire," I say. "Where would we all be without it?" There are giggles from the audience, but I cannot tell if they are thinking me as outrageous (good) or foolish (bad). "I arrive on a plunging dolphin from the depths of the ocean," I declare, "range over the earth like a bee with golden wings and with my arrows bring true love." What am I saying – bees, arrows, plunging dolphins? Sugsie would be appalled at my reckless use of mixed metaphors.

I point out to my audience that as the son of *Aphrodite*, goddess of pleasure and procreation, I have a certain responsibility. I am obliged to avenge the injury done to my mother. "Once the world looked at her with wonder and prayed to her," I say, "offered her sacrifice and so on, until …" and I pause "… the usurper *Psyche* appears, claiming to be the new Aphrodite." "Quite right too!" interjects my supposed friend Pooley, who is showing off. "Granted," I allow, "that Psyche isn't bad looking and that she feigns a gracious disposition, but my mother is the true and only Aphrodite and she has been wronged!" I mentally compare Aphrodite to my actual mother and wonder what they could possibly have in common. Perhaps an envy of younger, prettier women.

It is Polly's turn. "Save me. I am Psyche, personification of the soul and guardian of reason. What would we be if it were not for our innermost intelligence?" She draws the audience's attention to what she calls the undercurrent of chauvinism, even misogyny, in my opening remarks. "Is Eros so naïve as to suppose that the normal process of a young woman finding favour with a young man over the young man's mother is mortally injurious to the older woman? How on Mount Olympus can he be a responsible god, lover, husband and father if he cannot think and act honourably?" There is applause from the girls and from some of the boys.

I affect hurt and surprise. "My mother," I say, "is not jealous." But she is, I tell myself, and she has no right to be. It is the only explanation for her frostiness on the bus. "She genuinely believes that the nymph Psyche is not a suitable match for her diligent, tireless, susceptible son – who is," I remind the audience, "a god with a god's work to do." I am trying to put the difference in Eros and Psyche's social status diplomatically and almost certainly failing. Then without thinking I come out with "Psyche is too beautiful to have need of a soul." I regret this immediately. "What I mean is that she belongs to us all!" I cry. I try to skip round the sink-hole that has appeared by checking my notes for something I can use to regain the initiative. "All my mother is asking me to do," I say, "is take up with someone who will gladly support the struggle for love and trust that is the ultimate reward for youthful years spent in erotic desire." I am not at all sure of the relevance of this, as I lifted it verbatim from my Oxford Companion only that morning, but I think it might give Psyche something to think about. She might suppose I have said something profound.

Polly ignores it. She picks up on my earlier solecism and snorts. "Beautiful women have no souls? What Eros's mother actually wants is for Psyche to fall in love with some other young twerp. I am to be punished for usurping her!" And she asks, "Is it my fault I am not ugly or worthless? There is good reason Eros is winged, it is because he is flighty!" There is laughter and applause, mostly, I believe, from girls who have been jilted recently. "And the reason he looses off arrows at people is not to capture their hearts," Polly cries, "but because they wound and inflame!" She turns to me. "Because of the jealous spell your mother has placed on me, all the eligible men are avoiding me." "No, no!" calls my former friend Pooley. Polly turns her attention back to the audience: "Sisters and brothers, I must be saved and the reason is clear – the need to further female emancipation in this chauvinist world with its obsolete belief in the myth of the dutiful wife!"

Huge applause. Nice try, I think, but the boys will be unconvinced and the girls will not be distracted for long. "Psyche is confusing male protection with domination," I declare. "Keep me in the balloon. I am a hard-working god. I respect *Zeus*, bring love to mankind and honour my mother. If the gods cause Psyche to be cast overboard because she is a nymph rather than a goddess I shall swoop down and save her!" I hope that the jury will see this pathetic promise as a generous offer, or at the least an ingenious twist.

Polly raises an eyebrow. "Here is a man who cannot stand up to his envious mother, makes me miserable with his obsolete notions of worth and needs some old has-been in heaven to tell him to be himself! Can I trust him? Can I cocoa! Save *me*! Sacrifice *him*! I may fancy him, but I do not need him!" More applause. The vote swings in her favour.

My girlfriend and I continue our weekend walks while I struggle in oceanic depths of complexity that I cannot begin to fathom. It is ironic that Polly's argument in the debate centred on the triumph of reason over feeling, because in Wormley

Woods it is the other way round. The more passionate we become, the less sensitive, and the greater the gap in empathy and understanding between us. I try to separate my romantic fantasy of love from the reality of lying with Polly in the woods, a love that is more about discomfort, frustration, the unknown and unknowable, and unfortunately leaves grass stains on my raincoat.

Polly is offered a place to read English at Oxford and I am accepted for Classical Studies at Upham. When we meet for the last time I am extraordinarily sad. The situation has faint echoes of my mother leaving for India and it leads me to make a reckless suggestion: "Let us get engaged," I say. Polly looks at me kindly. "Don't be silly, James," she says. It is her sensible side. I imagine she is planning to sleep with the first half-decent man she meets at Oxford and the idea of being engaged to a mildly entertaining nerd who can quote romantic poetry but knows nothing about physical love does not fit her picture of the foreseeable future. "We are too young, James," she says. She means me. I am too young. I am ten years old, the age at which my mother took me for a walk in the woods.

I have a sudden insight into how the unconscious exclusion of unacceptably negative thoughts about my mother has placed such a heavy constraint on my ability to act and think freely with Polly. Too late. My soon-to-be-former girlfriend and I say farewell in Beasley bus station, a fitting place for such a depressing event. "This is like Trevor Howard and Celia Johnson in Brief Encounter," I say, "but with buses." Polly smiles and makes to go, then turns and says quietly, "James, this is not *au revoir*, you know, it's goodbye." "No, no," I say, "I'll write witty letters, you'll send me postcards of dreaming spires, we can meet at half-term." She says nothing. I add, "We can get back together when we know more about ourselves and – what's that other thing we're supposed to know more about, oh yes – life." She looks at me, not with the amused interest she had shown over tea in her study that day, not with the erotic ambiguity she brought to quoting Byron on our walks by the river, but coolly and kindly – rather like, I imagine, for how would I know, a cool and kind mother.

She gets on the bus. I am unable to see her for the reflections in the window, but I wave as her bus rumbles off into the night. I feel betrayed – not by Polly, not by my mother. I hold back a tear. I may know next to nothing, but I know my betrayer.

φ

Chapter 13

In Upham

"'W HY DO YOU WANT TO READ CLASSICS AT UPHAM?' is the question you are bound to be asked," says Undies. He goes on. "And here is what you say: 'I am fascinated/enthralled/intrigued/compelled' – take your pick – 'by the relevance of the ancient world to the present day, particularly in terms of its politics/culture/sculpture/philosophy/philology' – any two of these will do – 'and excited at the idea of studying in such historic surroundings with such world-renowned teachers and researchers'. And if you mention philology make sure you know what it means." I look blank. "Stamp collecting, sir?" He sighs, "Why do I bother?" I pretend to look serious. "I think it's the study of language and literature, sir," I say. "Yes, sir, it definitely is," says he. At the interview I trot out some variation on what Undies has proposed and am offered a place.

All the digs on or near the campus are taken, so I am farmed out to a B & B at Spurnham-by-Sea, 1s 6d for a day return to Upham, or £2 7s 9d for a monthly pass. On my first night at Mrs Kolynos's I take a walk along the sea front as a storm approaches. Grey clouds scud across the darkening sky, surf rolls up the cove and stops at the cliffs. The next night is the final phase of the full moon and the wind whips in over the water. I have left Beasley behind and Mrs K has an indoor toilet, but I have no feeling of freedom. I write to Mother in India.

> Lovely weather here, especially when the icy wind blows in from the
> N-North Sea. Invigorating and exhilarating it ain't. I have not yet managed
> to take an early morning dip.

My first term sees the worst post-war maritime disaster in the British Isles when the M.V. Princess Victoria sinks between Scotland and Ireland in a storm. 133 lives are lost, though this is nothing compared to flood-rains in Iran that claim 10,000 deaths. TEN THOUSAND. Then Egypt's Colonel Nasser nationalizes the Suez Canal, which gives Mother a reason for staying put as she is unable to sail and reluctant to fly. I write.

> My apologies (again) for not writing. You say you are glad to learn from the
> tone of my letters how much happier I am. Wrong end of the stick, dear,
> though I intend to stop smoking, drinking, churchgoing, and all the other

vices, including attending the opera, which I never did anyway, and I am sure my mood will improve.

After only a few days in Spurnham-by-Sea, I contract a cold. Mrs Kolynos brings me hot milk and brandy, but the infection takes its joyless course. On the following Sunday I attend evening service at a local church, where I learn for sure what until now I have only supposed, that I am not a believer. I have curiosity, depression and no faith. Not even the smallest residue of belief in the existence of some kind of Enormous Entity. This will be the last time I set foot in an English church other than to admire the stonework and identify it as Saxon, Norman, Early English, Tudor or Gothic Revival. I do, however, retain a certain regard for the Greek concept of *gods* as a convenient metaphor for the breadth and complexity of our perceptions and values, and all things good and bad in the world.

You will not be surprised to learn that I resolve early on that my dissertation at Upham will be on the high incidence of drownings in ancient and mythological Greece, and on the benign and malign influence of the gods in these sad and dramatic events. I am advised to keep my options open, but I will not be swayed. For the sake of comparison I do some research into the incidence of drowning in modern-day Greece. That is surprisingly high too, as much as double the world average. Why would that be?

Icarus is one of the first drownees I am drawn to, largely because of his relationship with his father, *Dædalus*, a master sculptor and inventor whose statues are said to be so lifelike they can move of their own accord. I believe without question that given a trick of the light or a momentary shift in perception a certain kind of father with an inflated sense of his own worth might persuade his susceptible son that his magic was real.

Dædalus takes on a talented apprentice, *Talus*, who devises a revolutionary stone saw superior to anything his master has invented. In his envy and rage at Talus's achievement, Dædalus throws him off the Acropolis. What is he thinking of? Couldn't he have found a less public place?

Rather than stay and face trial in Athens, Dædalus takes his son Icarus and flees to Crete, where *King Minos* grants him asylum on condition that he design an elaborate labyrinth to contain a savage bull-like creature known as the *Minotaur*. The design works perfectly and Dædalus prepares to move on, but the King is unwilling to lose him and confines him to the very labyrinth he has created. Not the brightest idea of the year, but – and this is so bizarre it has to be true – Dædalus *cannot find his way out.*

Consider your own cleverness, the gods seem to be saying, lest it does you more harm than good. Trapped in a maze of his own making, Dædalus decides to build wings for himself and his son to enable them to escape – an absurd idea, you might think, but he executes it brilliantly and soars off in the general direction of Sicily without checking to see if his son is following. Icarus has difficulty making his wings work. I prefer this explanation to the theory of over-ambition, as it fits my firm belief that his father is at fault. Icarus flies too high. You know the rest. The wax binding the feathers melts, the wings disintegrate and Icarus plunges to the sea where he drowns. Meanwhile his father flies on to the Strait of Messina, where he avoids the jaws of *Scylla* and the maelstrom of *Charybdis* by the simple expedient of flying over them. Dædalus does well for himself in Sicily. I can find no mention in Ovid, Apollodorus or my Oxford Companion of the father grieving for the son or even pausing for a moment to wonder what happened to him.

Make what you will of this story, but I find it depressingly relevant to my own. My father took off without me, left me to set my own course and made no attempt to see how I was getting on. You can call that love of a kind – at least I learnt to look after myself, if not very well – or you could call it wilful neglect.

You may know that the Old Testament has a reference to the sins of the father being visited on the children to the third and fourth generation, so with any luck this particular pattern of culpable negligence will have worked its way through the Seagraves by the time it reaches your children, if you ever have any, leaving them plenty of other patterns (anxiety, thalassaphobia, fear of flying and so on), to fall back on.

I make notes on the other Greek drownees I come across – *Vritomatis*, *Sharon*, *Taras*, *Arion* and the rest. And a tally of shipwrecks and ill-fated voyages, including *Jason's* crackpot quest in the *Argo* in search of an unlikely sheep's fleece. This research comes in handy when I am elected co-ordinator of the Classics Department float for Rag Week. I suggest Jason as our theme. No-one in the department has the slightest interest in debating the matter, as they are too busy writing essays, getting drunk and having sex, sometimes, I suspect, at the same time.

The theme for this year's parade is 'Ists & Ites', by which the organizers intend to mean sadists, masochists, sybarites and the like rather than sophists and socialites. The title I propose for our departmental float is *Jason and the Argonites* (nauts, nights …), in which Jason having been shipwrecked on a remote Aegean island entertains a succession of scantily clad, sexually predatory sea-nymphs. My premise depends on persuading three women in Year One to dress in diaphanous tunics of muslin and seaweed and to cavort around a sated Jason (me) while consuming sacred lotus and dancing to the music of the spheres. A woman in Year Three complains that this is a blatantly sexist scenario that does nothing to advance the cause of gender equality, but as sexism and gender equality haven't been invented yet, to our shame, no-one takes any notice.

I arrange for a crew from the Department of Engineering to construct the float, but the beer I agree to supply them induces the kind of dreamy forgetfulness you would expect of lotus eaters rather than serious engineers. I appeal to their better feelings. They assure me they have none. I am offended by their casual profanity ("Fuck me!" "No thanks!" and so on), having been taught by Sugsie at Calverley that a poverty of language invariably masks a paucity of thought. I ask the worst offender, Gareth, to clean up his act or leave. Gareth accuses me of being "a pious, sanctimonious, self-righteous Pecksniffian who couldn't organize a box of chocolates." I suspect he might be right, but my snippy response is to point out that Pecksniffian, being an 'ian', is at odds with the theme of the week, which is 'ists' and 'ites'. This is more provocative than I intended. "Pardon me, Jim," says Gareth, "I should have said you're a piss artist and a shite." I suppose I deserve this. I am still a virgin, and shockable, and when it comes to calumny and blasphemy ("Christ all-fuckin'-mighty, Jim, Jesus fuckin' wept," etc.), a prude. Despite my conversion to godlessness the picture of a pious old lady kneeling by her bed to pray every night still speaks to me.

The float situation deteriorates further. My Year One nymphs take exception to the quality of the muslin and the smell of the seaweed (gathered from rock pools at low tide in Spurnham-by-Sea and kept overnight in Mrs Kolynos's fridge), and refuse to cavort, not even for charity, so I recruit two less finicky Art students instead. They have one condition, that I buy a ticket for the Arts Ball. I agree.

How was I to know that this innocuous arrangement would change my life forever, and not for the better?

Our float raises £3 15s 0d for the Royal National Lifeboat Institution, by the way, a sum I believe to be reasonable given the inclement weather.

The theme of the Arts Ball is Black and White. Undergraduates dress as night and day, silent film actors, piano keyboards and so on. I fashion myself a toga from a bedsheet, stick a split-nib pen behind my ear and go as a Didactic poet of the Hellenistic Age. An earnest-looking girl in a long black gown and grey bonnet asks me to explain my choice. "It is about the certainty of moral instruction expressed in verse," I reply – "black or white, only one way to be or to behave, you know?" I am being cryptic and didactic, but after the unbidden farce around the float I want to show my serious side. "What are you?" I ask. She turns her back to show me a label on which she has typed 'Arrangement in Grey and Black, Number #1'. It takes me a while, but I work out that she has come as Whistler's Mother. This impresses her, although she has supplied a number of clues – untying her bonnet, sitting in profile, staring vacantly into space. Her name is Lydia.

This is, of course, or will be, if not for a while yet, your mother. Should I be circumspect about what else I say about her? I think not. You have a right to my biased, highly selective, self-referential, emotionally charged account of the relationship. To be fair, you should compare it to her account, though knowing her propensity for buttoning-up tight when it comes to personal matters you may not get it.

We talk. We dance. I buy her a beer. She buys me one. We dance some more. And so begins a relationship we will both come to regret – not your fault, son, entirely ours, I really wish things had been different – for the rest of our lives.

My first term at Upham sees me co-founding the Cabaret Club and joining Dram Soc, Film Soc and a Classical Studies group called the *Convivium*, which mainly studies wine. I attend lectures on the culture and architecture of Athens and Rome. I parse *Virgil* and *Homer*. I skim through *Cicero's* Orations and Rawlinson's translation of *Herodotus*. And I hold hands with Whistler's Mother. We look at prints of paintings by *Masaccio* and *Piero della Francesca* and watch foreign films like *Fanfan la Tulipe, The Seventh Seal* and *Pather Panchali*. I wear a college scarf and a duffel coat with wooden toggles. I smoke a pipe instead of eating breakfast. Not a good idea. And never having tasted anything alcoholic other than Grandma Lily's Tia Maria and Auntie Joan's Screwdriver, I find I can get nicely relaxed for the evening on a single Scotch and a pint of Upham Ale. This leaves me with a hangover the next morning, but by the evening I have recovered and can start relaxing again.

Lydia Ripley's wiry dark hair is pinned close to her head to keep it in check. She has a reluctant smile. Her mouth curls up at the corners and little dimples appear, but they do not last long. She is a serious artist, a painter of abstract arrangements in grey, brown and black. She plans her work carefully and takes a long time deciding on the titles. A typical title would be 'Arrangement in Grey, Brown and Black, Number #3'. After we have been seeing each other for several weeks I am granted the privilege of previewing a painting she is working on. I make to comment, but she stops me. She is highly resistant to influence.

Lydia lives with her widowed mother in a bungalow with a bay window, leaded lights and white-painted gable-end barge boards. High-voltage lines cross nearby. I might have taken this as an omen, but for the second time in my life I am in love. It has taken me unawares, though it is a completely foreseeable response to my need to fill the Polly-sized hole in my motherless life. For all my studies of the architecture of Athens and Rome, I have no sense of perspective.

There is a twitch in the lace curtains of the front room as I arrive to meet her mother. It is the start of a test that other boyfriends have, I think, failed. Mrs Ripley stares at me. She is wearing a powder-blue twin set and pearls, coral-pink slippers and spectacles with oversized tortoiseshell frames. On the mantelpiece are a number of pill containers and above these a framed reproduction of brightly coloured mountains in Switzerland with what appears to be a genuine stream tumbling from them. On the wall opposite is a reproduction of a cobalt blue-faced girl with blood-red lips by an artist called Vladimir something. I can see what might have led Lydia to paint small abstracts with a restricted palette.

"Would he like tea or coffee?" Mrs Ripley asks her daughter. For a moment I wonder if she is talking about her husband, Mr Ripley, until I remember he is dead. "He does not drink tea or coffee," replies Lydia. Another warning sign I fail to notice. I might as well not be there. Mrs Ripley's eyes narrow. "I have never heard of anyone not drinking tea or coffee," she says. In fact I don't mind tea and coffee, but I am going through an experimental phase in which I am attempting to find out what I like. A key aspect of this experiment means taking nothing for granted.

"Could I have a glass of milk?" I ask. Mrs Ripley mutters something to someone who isn't there and shuffles off into the kitchen.

Lydia sits in an armchair by the fire. I sit on the arm of her chair. After a long, silent moment in which I think of everything and nothing, she turns her face up to mine and we kiss. It is one of those moments one remembers forever, but which in this case I would really prefer to forget. The sea threatens to close over us. The rest we shall live to regret.

φ

Chapter 14

Riders to the Sea

LYDIA DOES NOT WANT ANY HINT OF COMMITMENT between us. It is all I want. I want security, certainty, stability – even, though I'm not so sure about this – what it is, how it works – fidelity. She wants an undemanding boyfriend who will be available on demand. Two conflicting forces are at work here: an inexorable move towards intimacy and an immovable resistance to it. "We are not a couple, James," she says. "You must trust that things will find their own level." That is exactly what I cannot trust. It might not be the level I want. But I try to back off. I read my Virgil.

Ducite ab urbe domum, mea carmina, ducite Daphnim!
Bring Daphne from the town, my spells, bring Daphne home!

The impotent cry of an impatient heart. If this is the domain of courtly love with its chivalric values of patience, courtesy and poetry, I am in the wrong domain.

My frustration spills over into political activism. The country has divided into those who support military intervention to take back control of the Suez Canal and those who are resolutely against it. A group of us from the Cabaret Club perform a satirical sketch about Anthony Eden and Colonel Nasser at the Rugby Club dance and are booed, which we take as a compliment, though it could be because we are not very good. Lydia does not approve of the actions of the British government, but will not accompany me to meetings and demonstrations.

All the same, I want to impress her. I play Gorodoulin in Ostrovsky's Diary of a Scoundrel, a satire, and Luka in Chekhov's The Bear, a farce. Lydia comes to see the plays, but is noncommittal. Either she is not impressed or she is and wishes not to show it, in which case she succeeds. She reminds me of the young Famine's on-off behaviour towards Felix, her would-be lover, in *Les Misérables*. "There is a manner of avoiding which resembles seeking," as the author puts it. Perhaps Lydia simply intends to arouse and maintain my interest. It is the best I can hope for. At least I can get us tipsy easily and cheaply, enough for her to be playful for a while and for me to suggest going further, at which point she sobers up and so do I.

I trust you will be more fascinated than discomfited by my writing about your mother and father-to-be like this. If not, my apologies, but I need to express it anyway. You can blame generations of equivocators and evaders before me who failed in their responsibilities to the truth – or rather to truthfulness, to the intention to be truthful, cf my earlier caveat. The hedgers and fudgers, well-meaning or not, spawned a generation with a desire to be less disingenuous. We don't always succeed, of course. Sometimes we make a mess of it, as you will see.

"Before the voyager may enter the *Euxine* from the Sea of Marmara," I announce to Lydia during one of our flirtatious evenings in the Students' Union – I have downed my tot of Scotch and am half-way through my Upham Ale – "he must first pass between two part-submerged adamantine rocks called the *Symplegades,* which guard the narrow strait of the Bosphorus and are impervious to persuasion. At one moment they will open up and move apart voluntarily, at the next they will close together with such force that anything caught between them – a bird, a ship, the hand of an anxious lover – will be crushed."

Lydia's cheeks flush. "James, are you talking about sex?" I want to say 'Yes, yes!' but don't. "I am the wary explorer," I say, "keen to enter the *Euxine*, but having no knowledge of the tides and the winds." I change tack. "Your moods are these rocks. One ardent, if wary, the other resistant and pitiless." Lydia raises an eyebrow. "Upon reaching the Symplegades," I say, "the voyager is advised to take a dove and set it free. If the dove succeeds in flying unscathed through the rocks, the gods will look considerately on the traveller's passage through to warmer waters." I flutter my handkerchief. Lydia purses her lips – reminding me, for a moment, of my mother. I toss my handkerchief into the air and it falls to the floor. "Your dove cannot fly," she sighs. "You have to release it at just the right moment." "When is that?" I ask, encouraged by the least hint of interest. "At the moment when the rocks are ready to move apart," she says. "How will I know that?" I ask. She sighs again. "If you really loved me, James, you would know."

If I really loved her. How would I know if I *really* loved her, or, indeed, really *loved* her? I have difficulty knowing the difference between love and obsession. Perhaps she has to see that I have other choices and she might lose me if I take them. I consider the other women I know. Fiona, one of the actresses in Dram Soc, seems to like me, but Fiona likes everyone. She is as loose as the literal translation of a classic text. Leanna and Diana, my nymphs in the Art Department, have boyfriends already and are almost certainly sleeping with them. Bernice in Year One of Classical Studies is a gorgon with an ice-cold gaze that could turn one to stone. Lydia, in comparison, is comely, complex and self-possessed, the perfect object of my neurotic desire.

One morning I wake with the thought that in order to sleep together we might have to be married. It is all too common in the fifties – you will have read about this and it really is true – for couples to marry in order to sleep together. Some of them are otherwise intelligent people.

The next time Lydia and I are in the Union bar I raise in a cheery, roundabout way the *notion* of marriage at some unspecified time in the future, supposing that the merest hint of it might be enough to intrigue her. She does not dismiss it outright, on the grounds that practically anything, however improbable, is thinkable, but dismisses out of hand any hint of the notion of getting engaged. "Don't be silly, James," she says. It is the same thing Polly had said. "It would put me under an obligation," she says. Well, yes. That is my intention. I do not say this. I suggest that we do not have to be engaged in order to spend the odd night together. "What are young people for," I ask, "except to sleep around and be silly while working out who they are and what they want in life?" "The difference between us, James" she says, "is that I know what I want."

Is this love, I ask myself, or a fixation born of frustration? I can no longer tell the difference. It might only be my need to be acknowledged, to be admired and desired, but is that so bad? I remember the interest that accrued to me when I was performing and directing my awful play with the three dots. I suggest to the Dram Soc Committee that we enter a production in a national competition for one-act plays and that I will direct it. .

I skim forty or fifty plays, and in the end the one that looks me in the eye, that demands an explanation of my intentions and will not be ignored – predictably, I see now, but could not so at the time – is J.M. Synge's Riders to the Sea. There is a fearful inevitability to this story of the struggle of men and women on the Isles of Aran against the relentless cruelty of the Atlantic Ocean.

> Cathleen Is the sea bad by the white rocks, Nora?
> Nora Middling bad, God help us. There's a great wind roaring
> in the west, and it's worse it'll be getting when the tide's
> turned to the wind.

The cruel sea has already taken Maurya's husband, her husband's father and four of her sons. Now the fifth son is missing. Maurya entreats the sixth, the youngest and most jealously cherished, not to ride his horses down to the sea to sail them to the Connemara Fair.

> Maurya What is the price of a thousand horses against a son?

But her son does not heed her and the acquisitive sea takes him too. Maurya gives in.

> There isn't anything more the sea can do to me, I won't care
> what way the sea is when the other women are keening.

The audience gives us four curtain calls. Actually it is an apron stage, but the actors milk the applause. The adjudicator awards the production an 'A', but her consideration is relatively lukewarm. 'The Irish brogue, on the whole, was surprisingly good', she writes. 'The production was a well-tasked attempt, but missed some of the gentle comedy of the play'. Well, for sure we missed some of the gentle comedy, going all out as we did for the awful perfection of the tragedy. 'A good opening was attained. Production 29/35. Endeavour 5/5, Attainment 4/5'. Not bad, you might say, though not brilliant.

Lydia's equivocal response to my moderate success might be a factor in the bout of influenza I suffer soon after the last night. I guess my immune system has been compromised by the tensions and frustrations of the year. A virus that originated in China arrives by way of Singapore and by the time it reaches my defences it is part of a full-blown pandemic that goes on to kill hundreds of people. I feel as near to physical death as I ever did in the North Sea, Scarmouth or the King's School pool. I flounder in the anguished secretions of my swollen mucous membranes. My head is hammered by a thousand callous blows. I know what Marcus Aurelius meant when he said that time is a violent torrent and every instant of time but a pinprick of eternity. The illness feels never-ending. I instruct Lydia not to visit me for fear of infection and she obliges without question. She is not one of nature's nurses.

In my fever I feel the powerlessness Maurya felt in the face of the demands of the Atlantic Ocean; the helplessness Ophelia felt when she fell from the willow tree, her saturated gown holding her under and down as an excess of self-pity holds me. I hear my anguished voice in the bluebell woods. WHY CAN YOU NOT STAY TOGETHER? WHY CAN YOU NOT STAY HERE? Through tears of pain and frustration I tell myself that I must not, will not, go through anything like that with Lydia.

Dimly I perceive I have a choice: to give in to the deadly virus of desire, be overwhelmed and die sexually deprived, or to stay afloat in a lukewarm pool of compromise that will at least keep me alive.

φ

Chapter 15

Hero and Leander

IT HAS BEEN SAID THAT HUMAN BEINGS FIRST LEARNT TO SWIM as a means of escaping their foes. A relief in the palace at Nineveh shows soldiers struggling to cross a river in an effort to distance themselves from enemy archers.

Hostile forces pursue me to the water's edge. I flail through the waves towards a distant shore that I cannot be certain is there. I am Leander in the storm-tossed Hellespont, glimpsing a light that will guide me to land where my lover awaits. But the waves and the winds, and finally even my will, are against me.

I perceive the ability to swim not as a source of fitness or pleasure, but as a primary means of escaping drowning. Presumably there is a corollary here: that in order to drown it is an advantage being unable to swim. This bleak thought occurs to me while I am desperately ill with influenza and contemplating death. I am in a coma, unable to make my own end-of-life decisions. I am nineteen years old. Who am I? What do I want? If I were to indicate to you as my parent or carer or partner that I wished to die and you were in no doubt that you had interpreted me correctly – though it is more than likely you had not – then you might arrange for me to be screened psychologically to ensure I was not depressed or suffering from some cognitive deficit that made it impossible for me to act in my own best interests. If I were diagnosed as too depressed or mentally deficient to know my own best interests, would I then have your permission to die? Who are you – not you, son, I hold to a fantasy that you would have a better idea of my interests than some others – but *you*, my doctor, counsellor, lawyer, lover, paramedic, passer-by. How do you perceive my best interests other than through a clouded window of your own? What if it is the flu and depression and nothing else that defines me, and I wish to kill myself because I am ill and depressed? For what other reason would I wish to kill myself?

The flu subsides and I return to my studies. Lydia remains pleasant but distant. She is working on her portfolio, painting in the usual muted colours, though now with an occasional splash of purple or burgundy. I suggest this might be a sign of sexual deprivation, but she will have none of it.

My academic researches are coming up with a variety of violent ends. Are the poisonings, hangings, drownings and stabbings of the Greeks and Romans affecting my state of mind or is it my state of mind that draws me to them? I am uncertain how to continue. My tutor is pressing me to make a decision on my final year specialization – will it be literary, archaeological or philosophical? I have shelved the limited idea of a dissertation on the incidence of drowning in ancient and mythological Greece and am contemplating something more elusive. I have given it the working title of The Modern Tragedy of Hero and Leander. Was Leander's death accidental, was Hero's death self-induced and did either have elements of both? If the story were a metaphor for today, how might I re-interpret it? I plan a structure where the probabilities of each step depend on the outcome of a number of earlier, not-so-apparent, but ultimately correlated, steps. Could the tragedy have been foretold and are there lessons to be drawn for a general pathology of attraction and rejection? Whatever conclusion I come to, my analysis continues to be fed by feelings of isolation and a morbid interest in death by water.

Leander is a beautiful youth who lives in Abydos on the Asiatic side of the Hellespont, the Strait that links the Aegean to the Sea of Marmara. He is in love with *Hero*, a beautiful priestess of *Aphrodite* who lives at Sestos on the European shore. You might have to make some allowances here. The protagonists in these stories are always beautiful and the reason is simple: it is because you and I, even at our most tiresome and troublesome, are beautiful too.

Every night Leander swims the mile or so of the strait that separates him from Hero. To guide him Hero places a lamp in a window of the tower in which she dwells. Marlowe describes Leander entreating Hero with sighs and tears to be allowed to make love to her.

> And yet at every word she turned aside,
> And always cut him off as he replied.

Such frustration as I know almost daily with Lydia. Virginity is an affliction of the time, the default state of the naïve, the fearful and the emotionally repressed, and I count myself in each of these categories. It is not quite the same for Lydia. Whenever I bring up the subject she says she has to save her creative energy for her work. She equates sexual arousal with intellectual turmoil, and is convinced that an intimate relationship with its inevitable upheavals will divert her from her degree. I attempt to persuade her that her responsibility as an artist is to express the fullness of her humanity, just as Leander assures Hero that the goddess of love, Aphrodite, will be less than impressed if her devoted follower continues in her chaste state much longer.

> Abandon fruitless cold virginity,
> The gentle queen of love's sole enemy.

Every night Leander swims the mile of the Hellespont that divides him from Hero. He wishes above all else to make love to this lovely woman. Is he one of those men who thinks he can convince a woman to submit by protesting his love long enough? Or does he wish to convince himself that his love really is lasting and somehow more elevated and sublime than simple desire? Sadly, he seems to have no-one around him – no father, I suspect – to reassure him that given the scarcity of eligible young women in Abydos his attraction to this young woman in Sestos is almost inevitable, that his impulses are natural, that the strait between them being both a metaphor for difficulty and an actual barrier has an attraction in itself for a determined young man, and that when all is said and done Hero is not a goddess but a complex human being with her own fears, frustrations and desires. And finally, to point out that if Leander's fascination has turned into overwhelming obsession the time may have come to call it quits.

Every night I am rebuffed. Night after night I give up and swim the long mile home. I am surprised I have the strength. My health must be affected. Hero's too. I would say we are in no fit state to continue this way.

"We should be hot or cold!" I say to Lydia. I know how St. John the so-called Divine felt in his gloomy cave on Patmos, railing against the spiritual deficiencies of the lukewarm Laodiceans. "We are in a state of spiritual failure to be neither!" I declare. "We have a duty to express our passion or life becomes tepid and featureless. Here are our choices," I say, on one unhappy evening in the Union bar, reducing them to one silly binary choice: "Sleep together or split." Lydia is bemused. She is Whistler's Mother again – rendered in shades of grey with a splash of muted colour here and there, then finished and framed. In the right mood Lydia can be sensual, even emotional, until some internal official appears and tells her to stop her nonsense and act rationally or there will be unwelcome repercussions.

Leander's habit of swimming the Hellespont every night in anticipation of making love to Hero continues through the seasons. It is the only way he can hope to bridge the emptiness, the chasm of longing, within himself.

It is the Easter break and Lydia has arranged to travel to Paris with a girl friend to visit the Louvre. She suggests we talk further when she returns. Of course that is reasonable. Of course it is not. She sends me a postcard from Paris with a drawing of a baguette and a croissant and the words

There must be more than *'oui'* or *'non'*.

What does she mean, 'more'? What could be more than yes or no – *peut-être?* That is not more, it is paralyzingly less. I am Leander making my way back to where I began, with only sighs and gasps and tears to express the depth of my frustration. For me there *is* nothing more than yes or no.

I phone Mrs Ripley to ask for the address of Lydia's hotel in Paris. She affects forgetfulness: "I had it, now where is it, I thought I had it, oh dear, I do not know where it is, I do not think she gave it to me." I press her: "You must have it, Mrs Ripley." Her manner changes. "Well, James, if I had I might have been told not give it to you." "Oh," I say, "I am so sorry to have troubled you" and ring off. Trying to be nice to Mrs Ripley is like stirring cocoa powder into cold milk – dry bits of goodwill float to the surface and never quite blend. I tell myself this is not how it is meant to be between a young man and his girlfriend's mother.

I go to the Fine Art Department and embarrass myself by asking Lydia's friends if they have her address. One of them takes pity on me and gives me the name of the hotel. I phone, book a room, leave a message and raid my grant to pay for the trip. My grant cannot afford it, but I do not care.

It is hard to tell if Lydia is pleased or not when I appear. "Are you happy to see me?" I ask. "I'm surprised," she says. "Is that more *'oui'* than *'non'*?" I ask. She smiles. Her friend Harriet appears. Harriet is not my friend, but she knows she has to play nonchalant student and to be cool about the situation. After a day or two she leaves to travel elsewhere. I suggest to Lydia that I move into the room they were sharing. "It will save us both money," I say. She does not accuse me directly of being silly, as she did a few weeks ago, but snorts in a 'Don't be silly, James' kind of way. At best I am romantic, I think; perhaps *un peu* idealistic; at worst, I suppose, pathetic.

I find a cheap hotel twenty minutes' walk away and move into a fifth-floor room with no window. The toilet is in a cupboard on the landing. I do not plan to stay there long.

Lydia and I spend the days together. I am charming and amusing. We visit the Louvre, buy cheese and wine, discuss Impressionism and Expressionism, view the statue of *Aphrodite* in the Department of Greek, Etruscan and Roman Antiquities, go to see Renoir's *Boudu Sauvé des Eaux* at the cinema and admire Baron Haussmann's boulevards. I learn the word for corkscrew: *tire-bouchon*. And every night after drinking cheap red wine in Lydia's room we kiss.

One hot summer night Hero's resistance melts and she succumbs to Leander's pleas. It is at this point that any parallel the story might have had with that of Lydia and James breaks down. Lydia will not – and I am coming to believe that in some ways she cannot – succumb. She is determined not to engage any further than she already has. Her dedication is to her art, as she puts it, or to the need to abide by some outdated ideal of self-denial, as I imagine she means.

One tempestuous night the wind in the Hellespont changes. I am in Lydia's room and we are kissing goodnight – a kiss that, as ever, holds the possibility of going further – when she stops responding. Not reluctantly or gradually, as is her habit, but abruptly. She stops. I move to maintain contact, but she flinches and moves away.

> And yet at every word she turned aside,
> And always cut him off.

The wind puts out Hero's lantern. Leander continues to swim in her direction, but he can no longer see the light on the shore he had been aiming for. There is no moonlight. He loses his way.

"What is wrong?" I ask. Usually Lydia says something offhand or perfunctory in response to such a question, but tonight she is silent. I persist. Again I ask, "What is wrong?" Suddenly she yells, "Leave me alone! It's over! Go away!" I am stunned. This is coming from a far, dark, uncharted place. There has been some kind of chemical reaction, and the kiss – or the wine – or something that sparked in her mind, or her body, or both – but what? – was the catalyst. I see my mother turning away to embark on the S.S. Cecilia, but all I hear is Lydia saying, "It's over! Go away!" I am confused. I walk away. So it is over. It really is over

Outside, it is raining. I take a wrong turning. I cannot find the bloody hotel. It had been there, a couple of streets from the river. I am alone in a strange – unfriendly – hostile – city. What the hell am I doing here? The delicate structure I had built to support my fantasy that things between us were tricky but okay, that she was awkward but okay, that I was mentally disturbed but okay, has suddenly collapsed, its foundations swept away, and the whole construct – every brick, every stair, every doorway – no longer there. The hopelessness, the pointlessness of my life is suddenly laid bare.

I stumble down the wet steps that lead to the river. The cobbles on the quayside glisten. A couple are kissing under a bridge. I look at the black waters of the Seine and all I can see is my own despair. I have a choice: I can give myself up to the river or return to my windowless room and take the bottleful of aspirin I keep for my headaches. I sit on the steps in the rain. If I go the way of the river there is a risk of surviving. I might be rescued by one of the lovers who come down to the quayside to kiss. There would be some irony in that. Or like Renoir's tramp *Boudu* I might be *sauvé des eaux* by a passing Parisian bookseller, adopted by his family, cleaned up and married to the housemaid. Drunk, I steal a rowing boat and float oarless downriver, a fool and a free man again. I might live, I might drown. If I survive it will only be to be alone. The river does not care either way. But ending it here will cause more trouble than if I return to the hotel. I would be the careless agent of chaos no better than Boudu. The right thing to do is take the aspirin. I shall write to Lydia and my mother, apologizing and explaining that it is not their fault, it is wholly my own. My spirit has gone. My mother should cherish her remaining children, they will need her care. Lydia should work at her painting, never mind the grade of the degree, she should cherish her art. My father will have to arrange for the body and my books and the diaries. What will he make of the diaries? I don't care. He will make of them what he will. Jenny will be sad, because we haven't been close since she went to Exeter to study family therapy. My stepmother and stepfather will feel a prickle of guilt, but they will get over it quickly. Grandma Lily will feel I have let her down after all she has done for me. She might be angry for a while. What a waste of potential, she will think. He couldn't sing, but he could recite The Wreck of the Hesperus. Aunt Ada, Auntie Joan and Bert will experience a moment of surprise and curiosity, nothing more. Royston and Kenton will hardly notice. Rupert will be fed half-baked scraps of information when he is old enough to wonder what he missed in not having known his mentally ill older brother. Mother will have to forego the funeral unless she forces herself to fly, which she probably won't. A pity. It might have brought her and my father together for an hour or two to consider their legacy. Would my death have some value if there were a learning for them in that? No, no – claptrap, bombast, to think I might have mattered. Taking the aspirin will be tidier altogether than drowning. I will be found dead in bed in the morning. The cleaner will call the concierge, the concierge the manager, the manager the police. They have seen it all in these hotels. They have my passport. *Les flics* will take care of everything.

It starts to rain again. I get up from the steps to seek out the hotel. I have to write to Lydia and Mother. For a time I am lost. I wander the streets until the dimly lit entrance to the hotel appears out of the gloom. I have come from the dank shadows of the *Quai des Brumes* and arrived at the door of the *Hotel du Nord*. Why am I seeing everything in terms of black and white films of the thirties? I identify with their characters – doomed lovers and drifters who lived on the margins of society, victims of violence and irrational passions, whose stories all ended in disappointment or death.

> Dearest Mother,
> This is the hardest letter I have ever had to write. I think it will hurt you very much. I can no longer accept what I find around me.

I think that blaming society in general might bring some small consolation to the one or two people who might be badly affected by what I am about to do. At the same time I owe it to myself to make an attempt at the truth. What was the catalyst that accelerated the reaction that led to this critical change?

> I have an intense internal physical pain. I had hoped that Lydia and I would be able to seek something more authentic together. Now she has decided that she does not want me. I loved her and I am ready to die, because only death can relieve the pain of more loss. This is not solely about Lydia, it is about my life. I realize this will hurt you, really hurt you. Please find some way to accept and forgive me. I am blinded by self-interest. How could it be otherwise? And I cannot see anything to live for. My existence has been short and pointless, one random event among countless others, so what does it matter? I shall be dead before you get this letter. You might be dead before it arrives. Life is short and vile. There must be something better. How do you measure pain? If you were to ask me 'How much does it hurt?' I could only say, 'As much as I feel it', because my pain is my own and you cannot share it. And I cannot help it if my distress distresses you, because your distress is the result of events in your life and mind over which I have no control and of which I am only one indeterminate and for sure peripheral part.
> I have re-read this and I know what I mean, but you may not. I am sorry if that is so. If you cannot understand, please just accept it. If you cannot accept it, that is your problem, I'm afraid, and I cannot solve it for you. How shall I

end this? There is no good way. All I ever wanted was to feel loved, or at least wanted, or at the very least accepted. If only I could have felt accepted.
Love, James

In the tales of the ancient world, the lot of infants who were put out on the hillside and left to die but survived was to suffer the kind of pain that could only be assuaged many years later by the victim taking revenge on the perpetrator. Can such revenge ever by righteous? It might arise from an outraged sense of injustice, but is it ever justifiable? My letter could be taken as my revenge on my mother, but that would only be an unintended effect of my attempt at the truth. I am attempting as best I can in my anguish to offer real information. It is the most and least I can do. I cannot be held responsible for any hurt or pain or shame or shock that others might experience as a result, because I have not lived their lives.

In my guilt at wanting to hurt Lydia, I leave something gentler, a pastoral poem from Virgil.

> *Incipe Maenalus mecum, mea tibia, versus ...*
> Reed-pipe of Maenalus, support me in my song.
> Let the relentless sea overwhelm the world.
> Woodlands, good-bye to you;
> I will go up to the windy lookout on the mountain-top
> and plunge down headlong to the waves.
> Let Nysa take this last gift from a dying man.
> *Desine Maenalus, iam desine, tibia, versus ...*
> Reed-pipe of Maenalus, be still: my song is done.

I place both notes on the bedside table. I am shivering. The idea of going out again and jumping into the river would only be to exchange bathos for melodrama, so I take every tablet of aspirin in the bottle, and there are a lot, lie down on the bed as I am, thinking that at least no-one will have to dress me before they take away the body, and let my thoughts wander, having accepted with certainty that I will not wake again. Great-grandma Barraclough would have wanted me to say the Lord's Prayer, but I cannot bring myself to do that. The most I can do is repeat one of the psalms to myself, the one that goes something like:

> Lord God my life draweth nigh unto the grave ... thou has layest me in the lowest pit, in darkness, in the deeps ... Lover and friend hast thou put far from me, now darkness is my closest friend.

I believe that what I am doing might even be seen as an altruistic act of self-sacrifice. The emotional resources of those nearest to me have run out – long ago, in some cases – and my absence will save them further hurt. The gods will be appeased. I accept that suicide is a serious existential problem, but if I can no longer justify my existence it should no longer be a problem. No longer *my* problem. My death is a logical consequence of the loss of the will to live and I cannot help that. This is no 'easy' way out. There is no other way. A liberation from desire and loss, but nothing special. I am not important, although I wonder – beyond hope, beyond reason – whether my life might have some meaning after death. But to whom? Not to me, for sure. And its meaning, if any, to others is beyond me. Sleep cannot come soon enough.

There was a High Court case in which the mother of a ten year-old boy with a tumour of the brain refuses to give her consent to a life-saving operation for the child. She is divorced from the boy's father. Is this her revenge on her former husband for not living up to her dreams? Is her outrage at the failure of her marriage leading her to visit mortal harm on her son? Every time she looks at him she sees his father. "I need more time to decide," the mother of the ten-year old tells the judge. "Your son has no time," the judge responds. "He is likely to die in a matter of days." The judge orders the surgery. The boy survives but is disabled and dies a few months later of an accident on the motorway. His mother was driving.

Hero in her despair sees the lifeless body of Leander in the broken waters of the strait and throws herself from her tower to be with him. I cannot see Lydia doing anything like that for me. She will have to live with her guilt.

> Whose was the scream that I heard
> In the midst of the hurrying air?
> Was it thine, lost bird,
> Or the voice of an old despair?

Am I dead? No, awake. I look at my watch. It is morning. I feel unbearably disappointed. I have failed. My cries were no more than those of an old despair. Is it always to be *neither* 'oui' *nor* 'non' then? Were the Laodiceans right, that there is neither good nor evil? Is it better to be in a state of half-hearted indifference at best; a vague, grumbling, tummy-rumbling discontent at worst?

> So then because thou art lukewarm, and neither cold nor not, I will spue thee out of my mouth.

He is unforgiving, this raving saint who has spent too long in a cave on an indifferent island, but there is extremism for you: where there is no suffering, bring some about. The Buddha said something about the cause of suffering is having preferences. I lie awake and sadly alive. The cause of my suffering is having parents. For a bitter moment I wish they had never lived, and theirs before them.

Lydia and I fly back together. She has recovered from her panic attack, as we are calling what happened that night, and we do not discuss it further. I say nothing about what happened to me. The notes I wrote I keep to myself. I have an ache in the gut that matches the one in my heart. It brings little in the way of sympathy from Lydia, who puts my symptoms down to cheap wine and cheese. One thing I know: my commitment to the relationship is over. I cannot conceive of a future with someone for whom I tried to kill myself and failed.

Soon after our return I go to see Olivier's film of Richard III and afterwards write to my mother describing the terrifying death scene on Bosworth Field. If she cannot mourn the death of the Prince, I reason, she can share that of the King.

> Richard is alone in a hollow shouting "A horse, a horse!" only to find himself surrounded by his enemies and his own men. His men have stopped fighting and have come to kill him. Lord Stanley clanks over, sword drawn, then everyone else rushes in. I see him lying there – someone slits his throat, his armour is torn off and scores of swords and knives are plunged into his body. Everyone steps back and the camera moves up and watches from above as he writhes in the last throes. The writhing stops and slowly he raises himself on one elbow, holding his sword in his withered left hand which has only two fingers ... the sword falls to the ground and he collapses, dead.

Not quite the modest, achingly poignant death I envisaged for myself, but I do not say that. I confide events on the Left Bank to my diary, but it is not enough, so I decide to write a play to exorcise the experience. This will not be a whodunit like my play with the dots, because nobody did it. The action is not set by the sea or the Seine, but in a bedsit in Upham. I call the characters John and Lorna in a half-hearted attempt to distinguish them from James and Lydia.

> Dim lighting. John lets himself in. He is 19 years old, slim and clean-shaven, dressed in a sports jacket, tapered trousers and black polo-neck sweater. He moves around the room sobbing quietly, moaning and hitting things. A woman's voice is heard faintly.
>
> LORNA'S VOICE
>
> Go away, I don't want to see you any more, go away, go away, I want you to go away, I don't want to see you any more ...
>
> JOHN
>
> No no no no no ...
>
> LORNA'S VOICE
>
> Go away, go away, go away!

That is as far as I get. Just as well, eh? Perhaps I could make Lorna Mrs Mortimer, have John call in Inspector McCorquodale and make the whole thing a farce.

> Please understand, Mother, please understand, Harold, I am giving up Classical Studies for the time being. It is too inward-looking. All I am learning is that we are constantly reinventing the past and I do not wish to do that. I might be confused, but I have to escape before I am completely stifled. I need to find something less predictable, a life that holds more opportunity for fulfilment and happiness. They say that the man with the fewest needs is the happiest. I do not believe there is any plan for this world or for me in it. I have to have the courage to trust my own sense of what is right.
>
> You will be thinking I have failed you. I know you had hopes, you wanted to see me doing well in a respectable profession, and until now my sense of duty to you both outweighed any thoughts I had of a different kind of

fulfilment, but lately I have seen that *because* I have this overwhelming sense of duty I must be rid of it! As Henry Miller said, *'Je m'enfou de votre civilization.'* You see my education has not been entirely wasted.

Please be at your most sympathetic and understanding – and if you do not fully understand all I say you will realize this is no phase I am going through, it is a fair account of the conclusions I have come to as a direct consequence of my life so far. May I say right now that I intend to pay back the money Harold invested in my education, for which I shall always be grateful. I must repay it to satisfy my sense of duty – there I go again – and to prove, as I must, for you will not take it for granted, my gratitude. And Mother – please, if you love and believe in me you must desire my happiness and fulfilment more than any expectation of conventional success.

They gave me an education rather than acceptance and in my unhappiness at my lack of acceptance I am rejecting their education.

Right now I need sympathy, lots of it. I am seriously contemplating the idea of doing nothing much – travelling, living off the land. Lydia has decided that she does not want to join me.

No wonder. I am about to embark on a quest as ambitious, speculative and poorly planned as that of *Jason* and the *Argo*.

I loved her too much. I believe I shall get over it. I was so much in love that I hate myself for saying that.

I guess I am severely depressed. Too depressed to see beyond my immediate past to what determined it. And now my quest is not for knowledge or a degree, or an intimate relationship, it is for the sun reflected on water and for the earth – or perhaps sand, a remote beach – beneath my feet. It is for something as ephemeral as a fragrance on the breeze. A return to simplicity will help me learn from my suffering, I imagine. One self-help book I read said that those who are depressed do not necessarily think of themselves as depressed, rather that they feel worthless, emotionally starved or hugely confused. To *think* of myself as depressed would only be to obscure the emotional starvation and confusion under a layer of abstraction, and might give me the idea that there is something particular I can do about it – take drugs, down a bottle of rum, jump in the river – while the real feelings, the internal sensations, the worthlessness and desire to be outside myself are muddled over and blurred, so that real self-reflection would be, as *Narcissus* found to his cost, impossible.

I am in another bind, caught between pure feeling and a poor attempt at reason. Something has to happen to take me out of myself. I look again at my research into the inadvertent death of Leander (accidental, though he brought it upon himself) and the self-sacrifice of Hero (voluntary, though she felt she had no choice). The pursuit of love and desire is a means of escape from loneliness, I suppose, but any perception I might have had that the pursuit was an agreeable Casanovian adventure without victims is wishful thinking; a fiction.

Giacomo Casanova was neglected by his actress mother and brought up by his grandmother while his mother toured the theatres of Europe. As a child he suffered nosebleeds. For a time I resist the comparison. I reject the idea that the librarian I am having an undemanding affair with in Upham might only be an attempt to fill the emotional vacuum left by Lydia, just as Lydia could be seen as an attempt to compensate for Polly, and Polly for the loss of my mother – who else? Instead I should acknowledge the unoccupied space and make a conscious effort to fill it, not with mother-surrogates, as Don Juan, Casanova and the failed romantic in me failed to do, but directly, with the real thing.

> I want to come to India and live with you for a while and feel I am wanted somewhere. Then I shall look for work, any kind of work, to pay Harold back. I am planning to hitch-hike. It will be cheaper than flying or sailing. I will work through the vac here to raise the money.

I take a job as a labourer on a building site. Mother writes back to say she is sorry to hear I am unhappy, that I am welcome to visit and she will help reimburse my expenses. It is a less than heartfelt response, but it is enough.

Then I see a small ad in The Observer: 'Bus Overland to India'. There is a box number. I write and receive a cyclostyled leaflet by return. It looks promising, if I make allowance for the spelling.

ALL NATIONALLITIES

Party Trip to India (Delhi) by Coach (4 weeks stay) and Back Again
Coach leaves Pimlico London on or about 15th July
Comfortable camping. Delhi in aproximately 24 days.

Excellent. I had read of another coach that took two months to get there.

One way £50 Both ways £95
(food inclusive)

£50? Food included? A bargain!

Route: London, Dover, Paris, Basle, Lucerne, Como,
Milan, Venice, Trieste, Belgrade, Salonika, Istanbul,
Baghdad, Quetta, Lahore, Amritsar, Delhi

There follows a long legal piece about breakdowns and compensation, but I take no notice of this. At the end is a note:

> Each one from party will accept alternative route arranged in view of political and diplomatic situation in the world especialy in Middle East

To help raise the fare I sell my duffel coat and books. What remains of my grant pays for the rest. I will not need my duffel coat. I will miss my books. I no longer need Lydia. I will not miss her.

"The winter of our discontent," said Richard, some time before the slaughter at Bosworth, "made glorious summer by this sonne of York." The setting of the sonne is a necessary precursor to his rising again. Leander lives on in the poetry of Ovid, Virgil, Schiller and Marlowe. My new life begins in London, in Pimlico.

♀

Chapter 16

Going Home

I HITCH-HIKE TO LONDON and find my way to a clapped-out tenement building in a run-down street on the poorer borders of SW1. Parked at the back is a brown and cream-coloured charabanc, the bonnet stuck out in front and the body slung low. It looks like a toothless old spaniel wanting to rest its head on its paws and have a good sleep. The owner, K.D. Chopra, had the idea of taking it to India one day while he was running day trips to Bournemouth and Brighton. He is excited and nervous. He waves his hands about. I do not wish to presume on so short an acquaintance, but I wonder if he can be trusted to get us to India.

I meet some of my fellow travellers: four Australian chancers, Dave, Jigger, Bob and Johnny, who having done Europe are making their way home on the cheap; Dougie, an Anglo-Indian chef who has left his wife and children in Milton Keynes; Sammy, a Filipino waiter travelling on his brother's passport and hoping to get to Manila; Pushpak and his family, Hindus from Poona who say very little but giggle a lot; Kathleen, an elderly nun with a cardboard suitcase; Eileen, an ex-Wren who is planning to learn Sanskrit, sit under a Banyan tree and read the *Bhagavad Gita*; and a pale, unshaven man who doesn't want to give his name and has no luggage. He carries all his things in a shopping bag.

Terry, our driver, turns up at the last minute, looking as you might expect someone to look who had been up all night arguing with his wife about whether he should go or not. Terry complains that he is the only driver, he doesn't like the look of the bus and he thinks we should have a rifle in case we have to shoot wild animals or defend ourselves against bandits.

Rattling along and half-way to Dover, we are passed by a police car and signalled to stop. Terry is told he has exceeded the speed limit. "That's an effin' lie," says Terry. "I've been drivin' thirty effin' years, I can read an effin' speedometer." He sits on the verge and refuses to get back on the bus. An air of unease drifts through the party like an unpleasant smell. People who up until now have taken no notice of Terry try cajoling him. Chopra offers him inducements: cigarettes, an extra blanket, a framed colour photograph of our arrival in Delhi. After a long argument, Terry announces he will drive us to Dover and no further.

At Dover he drives the bus up the ramp onto the ferry, hands the keys to Chopra and walks away. Open-mouthed, we watch him go. No framed photograph for him, then. Twenty-three of us are left stranded: four women, fifteen men, three children, an organizer and no driver. Some people are telling Chopra they want their money back. I am unsure what to do. I had been looking forward to an adventure, but more than that, I had been looking forward to going home – to a real home, not a student flat shared with a family of mice, but an air-conditioned mansion with contented servants and high ceilings, a place where I would be welcomed, indulged and given the time to do nothing. I had also been looking forward to happy camping, interesting sightseeing and entertaining companions on the way.

The ferry staff usher us up to the passenger deck while Chopra tries to reassure us. "I will be finding new driver in Boulogne," he says. Not everyone is reassured. From the deck I look down at the sea slipping by, unrelenting and grey. The man with no name tells me we are sailing through a graveyard. "The Channel has the highest number of shipwrecks anywhere in the world," he says. "A punishment from God for the sins of the nation." I wonder if that includes Terry for his treachery or Chopra for his ambition, or me for my insanity in Paris, or Lydia and my mother for – well, everything else.

We dock in Boulogne and Chopra manoeuvres the bus down the ramp and into the parking lot. He asks if anyone in the party speaks French. I say I do, a little. A mistake. He presses me into helping him find a driver of some kind to take us to India. Where should we start? We ask at a snack bar. That seems as good a place as any. They direct us to a car hire firm (*"Aller en Inde? Êtes-vous sérieux?"*), which directs us in turn to a *Fédération Internationale de l'Automobile* office, where the manager is *desolé*, but unable to *aider*. He phones a local haulage firm, who say they will ask their *chauffeurs de camion*, although it is *très improbable* that any of them will be *disponible* and even, if available, *disposé*. Or words to that effect .

Finally Chopra says, "I myself shall drive us to Paris, where we are finding a driver for sure." His hands shake as he takes the wheel and scrapes through the gears. He is negotiating a corner in the car park when there is a loud crack and the back of the bus buckles. A spring has broken. People takes it in turns to look at the back of the bus and shake their heads. Dave is particularly upset. He is on a schedule, he says. He has to get to Baghdad to catch a train to Basra to find a cargo boat that will take him to Melbourne, where he has to see a man about something.

Dave kicks the tyres and takes a cursory look under the bonnet. "I'll drive us to Paris," he says to Chopra. "You can get the springs fixed there." "Do you have PSV licence?" asks Chopra. "No worries," replies Dave. "Where is PSV licence?" asks Chopra. "In the post," says Dave. Dave's friend Johnny confides in me that Dave lost his public service vehicle licence after a court case in Melbourne. "What was he charged with?" I ask. "Manslaughter," says Johnny. He reassures me. "He pleaded not guilty."

Dave opens the driver's door and clambers up. "I'm not driving, okay?" he announces to the bus. "What did he say?" asks the man with no name who is sitting at the back. "He said he's not driving," says Kathleen the nun, puzzled but allowing him the benefit of the doubt, "but I think he is."

Dave drives us to the outskirts of Paris, where we find some waste ground near a dump and set up camp. For three days Chopra scuttles back and forth into town like a squirrel that has lost its nuts, and I tag along behind trying to be helpful. I didn't think I'd be back in Paris quite so soon, and I try not to think that the city might be jinxed.

In fact we fail to find a garage to *fixer les ressorts* (springs), and no-one with the right kind of *permis* (licence) and a secret ambition to drive an old *charabanc* (charabanc) overland to India and back, but we learn about a garage in Geneva that specializes in old crocks like ours and might be able to help.

At this point three members of the party decide to cut their losses and go home, while Kathleen changes her plans and leaves for Spain. We are five fewer than when we left and we've only got as far as Paris.

Dave is dead-set on getting to Melbourne. "Why the hurry, Dave?" I ask. "I owe somebody something, mate," he replies. It doesn't sound like money. Dave tells Chopra he will take over the driving if Chopra refunds his fare, pays for his train from Baghdad and the boat from Basra, buys his beer and pizzas, and promises to say that he, Chopra, is driving if anything happens. They argue into the night. By the early hours Chopra has agreed to fund Dave's train from Baghdad, but not his boat from Basra, and to keep him supplied with pizza, though he will have to buy his own beer.

In the morning Dave mounts to the driver's seat, switches on the ignition, crashes through the gears and we are on our way, chugging, grumbling, lopsided, to Geneva. "Only five thousand miles to Delhi," says Bob. He is trying, I think, to look on the bright side. No one asks what happens when Dave bails out in Baghdad.

The interval between our waking in the morning and leaving is never less than three hours. Breakfast has to be sorted, the washing-up done, plastic buckets, petrol cans, paraffin, mallets, toilet rolls, cooking pots and corn flakes stowed in the boot, and sleeping bags and blankets stuffed in the bus. The big tarp draped over the bus at night as a makeshift tent has to be hauled down, folded and rolled, the luggage passed up to the roof and stacked, the tarp laid over the luggage and roped, the site cleared and a final check made to be sure that no-one is missing. Dougie is usually missing. He is usually to be found in the nearest bar trying to get through to Milton Keynes.

The garage in Geneva can't fix the springs, but they say there is a garage in Venice that can. At this point the man with no name who keeps all his possessions in a shopping bag announces that he will make his own way to India. Chopra reminds him that he still owes for the fare. "I have a Swiss bank account," says the man, which seems unlikely. "You'll get what you're due in the morning." In the morning he has disappeared. Chopra is upset. He goes to the Geneva police. The police are not interested.

Eighteen of us head for the Simplon Pass.

Dave's mate Jigger doesn't want us to waste time sightseeing on the way to Venice. As we approach Milan he draws a little map to show us we need to spend no more than an hour there. "There's not much to see in Milan," he claims. "You park here, check out the *Duomo*, walk through the *Galleria* on the way to *La Scala*, then back across the *Piazza* and you're done." I ask Bob why Jigger is in such a hurry. Bob seems to know, but he won't let on.

We do Milan in forty-five minutes. In Brescia we spend five minutes in a *basilica* (nice frescoes), in Verona we drive past the *Arena* (impressive) and in Vicenza we have a glimpse of a 17th century *palazzo* (no time to stop). We make it to the garage on the outskirts of Venice just as it is closing.

"*Si si, possiamo,*" they tell Chopra. They can do the job, but not until morning. We are invited to park in the yard and spend the night there, which is kind of them. Several members of the party prepare to bed down on the bus, some go to local shops to buy souvenirs and the rest of us lay out our sleeping bags on a pile of used tyres in the yard. Bob and Jigger say they are going into Venice. Sammy the Filipino waiter and I say in that case we will go with them. Jigger doesn't seem too thrilled at the prospect, but says nothing. He takes his big Aussie backpack with him, which I think is odd.

I find the waterways of Venice nowhere near as threatening as the sunless streams of the Yore and the Bease, or the sinister banks of the Seine. The *rivi, canali* and *bacini* of the city are gracious and considerate, and I find the whole experience surprisingly tolerable. It is the time of the *passeggiata* and the locals are strolling contentedly everywhere. If I fall into a canal I might catch something unpleasant, I think, but I will be rescued in seconds.

Bob, Sammy and I sit at a café while Jigger takes his backpack and goes off for a stroll on his own. He hasn't gone far when he is accosted by a prostitute. I have a good idea what Italian prostitutes look like, having seen several of them in films by Fellini. She smiles broadly at Jigger and they walk off together. Bob is unsurprised, Sammy is tickled pink and I am in awe. Is having sex really so easy?

The next morning there is no sign of Jigger. "Things must have worked out," says Bob. He tells us the story: Jigger had met the woman he walked off with when he was on his way to the UK a couple of months ago, she had invited him to stay the night, made breakfast for him in the morning and suggested he stay a while. "First I do Europe," Jigger told her, "then I return." And remarkably he did, as we had seen, and this is the reason he took his backpack into town for the evening. I am slightly shocked. "I thought Jigger was married," I say to Bob. "Well, he was," says Bob

The garage fixes the springs and one or two other things, and several hours later when Chopra has settled the bill after extended negotiations there is still no sign of Jigger. Bob tells the party there really is no need to wait. Dave agrees that we should press on and it doesn't take long to convince Chopra. One fewer to feed. Seven down. Seventeen left.

Five yards inside Jugoslavia the border police discover that Sammy's brother's passport has no visa and they will not let Sammy in. He is sent back through no-man's-land to the Italian side of the border and directed to Trieste to seek the Jugoslav consulate. Dave, predictably, is annoyed at the delay. He drives us into a riverside meadow nearby and we set up camp for the night.

I wake with the sun and make my way to the river to wash. A light mist drifts over the surface as the sun breaks through the trees. It is a shallow, broad and placid river, the water is fresh and forgiving, and for the first time in a long time I feel at peace.

I return to the camp to find Chopra arguing with the Jugoslav police in the same way he argues with shopkeepers, garage mechanics, bank clerks and toilet attendants. Everything is negotiable, from exchange rates to the cost of a cubicle. Today it is camping permits. We have none. Chopra offers the police a contribution to their sports fund, but they threaten to arrest him on a charge of bribery and moral perversion, so, rather unwisely, he increases his offer. But this is one he cannot win. We are ordered out of town and lose the best part of the day driving on a mile or so, driving back and parking in a different spot before leaving, driving on again and returning. It takes Sammy a while to find us, but when he does he is grinning. His brother's passport has a lovely new Jugoslav visa.

We drive on through the night and the next day in an attempt to make up for lost time. The old bus rattles, sways and complains, a few nuts and screws fall off, but for the most part the bodywork and engine manage to hold together.

We drive through Slovenia, stop at a bar in Ljubljana for a break then drive on to Zagreb in Croatia. In Zagreb, Eileen notices that Dougie is missing. Pushpak, giggling nervously, thinks Dougie might be in the Ljubljana bar where he was trying to phone home. We drive back to Ljubljana. Dave is beside himself at the delay. Dougie is not in the bar. We check every other bar in the area. We describe him to the Slovenian police – medium height, anxious demeanour, always looking for change for the phone. Dave suddenly remembers Dougie saying something about going home. That's it, we all agree. Dougie is on his way back to Milton Keynes. For sure.

Eight people missing, sixteen to go. It is beginning to feel like an Agatha Christie plot.

We drive back through Croatia to Bosnia, where we have a puncture, then on to Herzegovina, where we discover a leak, then on to Montenegro where we take a wrong turn looking for Kosovo, and eventually reach Skopje in Macedonia, where we stop for the night. Someone thinks to double-check Sammy's diplomatic status. Although Sammy has a Jugoslav visa, he is found to have no other visas. To be precise, he has no Greek, Turkish, Iraqi, Iranian, Pakistan, Indian, Burmese, Thai, Cambodian or Vietnamese visas of the sort he will need to reach Manila and return his brother's passport.

There is some discussion in the party. Doubts are raised, not for the first time, about Sammy's grasp of the way the world is organized into nation states with border guards, prisoners, torturers, executioners and so on. Chopra proposes we set up camp in Skopje to give Dave a rest and allow Sammy to collect enough visas to get him to India at least.

Dave points out that after only three weeks we are a week behind schedule and nowhere near half-way to Delhi. We are reminded that he wants to get to Baghdad in a hurry, and that the rest of us are depending on him to get us anywhere at all. Johnny quietly suggests that we might be better off without Sammy. Sammy can stay in Skopje to collect his visas, then take the train and meet us in Istanbul. Dave says that at the rate we are going Sammy will almost certainly get to Istanbul before us, which I think about as likely as Chopra getting an award for services to Jugoslav tourism.

Any moral authority Chopra once possessed is draining away from him like fat down a sewer. We take a secret vote on the proposition that we wait in Skopje for Sammy. The result could be closer – thirteen against, one in favour (Sammy, presumably) and one abstention (Chopra, probably). We leave Sammy with a tent, the rest of the corn flakes, some spare Jugoslav dinars and our very best wishes.

Fifteen of us get back on the bus. I shall miss Sammy's grin and unquenchable optimism. I do not expect to see him again.

The bus limps to the Greek border and by the time we arrive in Thessaloniki it is dusk. No-one has Greek money to buy food and the banks are closed, so we park on the sea front and set up camp on the beach. Dave, increasingly infuriated at our lack of progress, goes off to check on trains, while an angry group of us confront Chopra, who looks less like an organizer and more like a limp stick of soggy celery every day. He is visibly wilting.

The complaints come thick and fast. The meals we were promised rarely materialize and we have all had enough pasta to fill a builder's skip. If we are to reach Delhi on anything like the original schedule we should be more than a third of the way after two-thirds of the time. The bus is unsafe: it needs new tyres, new brakes, a new engine, in fact it needs a whole new bus. Everyone is tired after driving night and day in an attempt to make up for lost time and the inside of the bus smells like a corpse. By the way, where is Johnny? Finally and damningly, in case anyone had forgotten, Dave is planning to leave the bus in Baghdad, if we ever reach Baghdad, and not to be alarmist, but he has been seen to nod off at the wheel once or twice while driving at night and that is a bit of a concern.

Chopra responds wearily that if we are to catch up on the schedule we have no time to wait around for inessential repairs, camp overnight or cook three-course meals, and as for Baghdad we should please not to worry, he will be finding another driver in Iraq. Unlikely, I think, in fact more or less *incroyable*. And if Dave falls asleep at the wheel again, he, Chopra, will take over the driving, he says. Though it might, of course, be too late.

Dave returns. "There's a train leaving Thessaloniki for Istanbul at nine-thirty in the morning," he says, "and I shall be on it." It is a pivotal moment. Over half the party – Bob, me, Eileen, Johnny (we find him sleeping in the boot) and the family Pushpak – elect to go with Dave, as we believe that the alternative is going nowhere. We argue for a refund of half the fare. Chopra hedges, bickers, pleads, weeps, crumples and in the end implodes. For the first time I feel sorry for him. "You will get what you are owed as soon as the bank is opening," he says.

The night is hot and humid. I lie under the stars and listen to the sea lapping at my feet. I have arrived in a country I have wanted to visit since first learning about gods and monsters at school and I am already planning to leave. Actually I do not have to travel with the rest of them, I tell myself. I can hang about here for a while and visit the Greek, Roman and Ottoman monuments of Macedonia and Thessaly, see Mount Olympus, sleep under the stars and beg for my food. On second thoughts, that does not sound too appealing. The whole point of me being where I am is to keep going – to go home, to be part of a family, to be comforted and cossetted, to read and relax, to be spiritually renewed and feel mentally well again.

I turn over on the shingle. I miss my mother, in spite of the secrets and lies, and obliging me to walk on the edges of rivers and cliffs. And she will surely be missing me. She will be feeling guilty about her divorce, the confusion over custody, the betrayal in Beasley, not being around to comfort me in my sadness after Paris and so on.

The sounds of the town are keeping me awake. I know this region of Greece as home to the *Strix*, a claw-footed vampire that feeds on the blood of humans then eats their entrails. Is that the sound of slurping I hear? I listen intently, as you do in the night. It is the lapping of the sea. I see the bright reflection of the moon in the water. The infamous witches of Thessaly could draw down the moon from the sky, yet risked being hurled into Perdition if they failed. Why am I so intent on going to a home I do not know? Is the risk worth the uncertainty of the reward? I try to sleep. I understand that the Aegean is micro-tidal, but what if it rises in the night and sweeps me away? That would be one solution. Or if a troop of Thessalian *centaurs* swoops down from the mountains and tramples us to death? That would be another. I know that centaurs are weird, unpredictable creatures. I picture the head of K.D. Chopra on the body of a duplicitous ass as it quaffs a toxic brew while the moon falls sizzling into an acidic sea. Finally the sounds of the town die down and I sleep.

It is nearing nine-thirty when Chopra appears from the bank holding out a handful of drachmas for those of us who have opted for freedom. We scramble for the cash and run for the train.

Twenty-four of us left Pimlico, each with a dream – even, I suppose, Terry, who drove all the way to Dover before changing his mind. Three got as far as Boulogne. Kathleen made it to Paris before settling for Spain. The man with no name will probably be in a Swiss jail by now, awaiting extradition. Jigger will be learning Italian or thinking he has made a big mistake. Dougie might have been mugged in Slovenia or be on the train to Milton Keynes. And Sammy will still be in Skopje with a month's supply of corn flakes. The eight of us who gave up in Thessaloniki left behind a burnt-out, bleary-eyed organizer with a clapped-out coach and six hangers-on. I wonder how far they will get before they abandon the tired beast, and the bus, and hitch-hike home.

The train leaving Thessaloniki is packed and chaotic, and it takes us time to get together and share out the drachmas. Some of us who were beginning to feel sympathetic towards Chopra change our minds when we find he has given us half the sum we agreed. Bob is all for pulling the emergency cord, but can't find one.

We wish harm on our erstwhile organizer now. We heap creative, vituperative curses upon him, of the sort the witches of Thessaly would have been proud. Dave threatens to make a call to a man in Melbourne who owes him a favour and might know a man in Thessaloniki.

After a tedious overnight journey and an extended delay at the Turkish border, the train pulls into Istanbul. The first thing we do is check on overnight trains out, because sleeping on the train means a saving on hostels and doss-houses, and is marginally more homely than bedding down on the station steps. Our aim is to reach Basra in Iraq at the head of the Persian Gulf and there seek a deck passage to Bombay. In Bombay the Aussies will find a freighter to Perth or Melbourne and those of us with destinations in India will take the train. We all have Turkish and Iraqi visas, so we reason that this is an excellent and practical plan. Pushpak assures me I can travel for free in India if I climb to the roof of the train as it is leaving and jump off as it arrives. He giggles. I am learning the difference between Pushpak's serious giggle, which I think this is, and every other kind, including the giggle at things he actually finds funny. As time passes there are not many of those.

The train from Istanbul to Iraq is scheduled to pass through Syria, we learn, but none of us has a Syrian visa. The Syrian consulate tells us that visas can only be obtained from the Turkish capital, Ankara, which is two hundred and fifty miles to the east. We return to the station. "The train for Ankara does not leave from Istanbul," we are told. "From where then?" we ask. "From Üsküdar." "Where is

Üsküdar?" "On the other side of the Bosphorus." "Is there a bridge?" "No bridge yet." "How do we get there?" "You swim, ha ha!" "Ha, ha!"

The office for the ferry to Üsküdar will not take Greek money and none of us has any Turkish money, so Eileen and I collect the party's drachmas and set off to find a bank. We make our way through crowded streets past a pigeon-infested mosque to an area of the city with a profusion of unlit neon signs saying *Bankasi*. An official in the marble halls of the National Bank regrets that they cannot exchange Greek drachmas. He suggests we try the Ottoman Bank. The Ottoman Bank apologizes and advises us to try the Turkish and Eastern. The Turkish and Eastern confirms that our drachmas are worthless outside Greece. In the end I have to give up the last of my sterling and Eileen her traveller's cheques to enable us to buy Turkish lira.

By the time we catch up with the others and share out the lira the last ferry to Üsküdar has left and boats are tying up for the night. None of us has the money for a hotel, so we bed down on the quay on sheets of cardboard we find at the back door of a bar. I lie awake, asking myself if the best way of getting to India is to travel with seven other people with different agendas. It will surely be quicker and easier to travel alone. Once across the Bosphorus I can hitch-hike through Turkey to Iran, through Iran to Afghanistan, from Afghanistan to Pakistan and from Pakistan into India. What could be simpler?

I am having difficulty sleeping, so I get up and go for a walk. Steps take me down from the quay to the edge of the water, where a fishing boat is coming in to moor. I help the skipper tie up. Without thinking I give the rope a turn and a double half-hitch, which puzzles me, as in spite of being brought up by the sea I never learnt to tie nautical knots. My shoelaces were challenging enough.

The skipper speaks some English and we get into conversation. I know no Turkish, but I know my ancient Greek. "*Bos* comes from *bous*," I tell my fisherman friend, Mehmet, over a beer, "meaning 'ox', and *poros* means 'ford'. Thus Bosphorus actually means 'Ox-ford', a university town in England!" I tell Mehmet that my girlfriend Polly went to Ox-ford. He buys me another beer. "I shall tell you something else I know about Bos-phorous," I say. "Okay, but drink!" says Mehmet, which I do, and continue. "It seems that *Zeus*, god of the sky and the weather and all things good and bad, fell in love with the princess *Io*, daughter of the king of the plains." Mehmet looks at me warily. "But *Hera*," I continue, "queen of heaven, consort to Zeus and jealous protectress of marriage, did not approve." Mehmet puts back an ouzo chaser. "This Turkish ouzo!" he declares. "Not Greek! Turkish is *uzum*, meaning grape!" "Very good!" I say, and warm to my story. "Well, Zeus, to conceal Io from Hera, transformed Io into a cow ..." Mehmet pours me another grape. "... which was condemned to long wanderings ..." I pause "... until she crossed the Bosphorus!" "Ah, Bosphorus!" says Mehmet. "Here is to Ox-ford!" I cry, and raise my glass. "Where Polly went!" "Then what happened?" asks Mehmet. "To Polly?" "To the cow." "Are you calling Polly a cow?" "Ach!" he swears. "Oh, the princess," I say, "I cannot remember." "Another uzum!" says Mehmet. "I think she went to Egypt," I say. "Miss Polly?" "No, Io!" "You go to Egypt? Very good!" says Mehmet.

"Now, Jame," he says to me in all seriousness. "I tell you about Bosphorus. This very narrow strait, Europe here where I work and Asia over there where I live. Most narrow strait in the world for navigation – from Black Sea to north," he explains – I interject, "Known to the Romans as *Pontus Euxinus!*" – "to Sea of Marmara" – "*Propontis!*" – "and *Canakkale Bogazi, Dardanellia* to you." "Ah, the Dardanelles, once known as *Hellespontos*, the Sea of Helle!" I cry. "I shall tell you sad story of Helle and Phrixus!"

Mehmet shrugs and gazes over to Asia. He might be wondering how *Hero* felt while waiting for *Leander* to arrive or simply wishing he had gone home ages ago. "Fearful of jealous stepmother," I say, "Helle and Phrixus escape on winged, golden-fleeced ram across Aegean." By now Mehmet is glancing through a newspaper he has found on a nearby table. I carry on regardless. "But Helle falls off ram into sea, which becomes known as *Sea of Helle*, or *Hellespontos*! Interesting, eh? Would you like to know what happened to Phrixus?"

Mehmet shows me something about an accident he has come across in the paper. "These dangerous waters, Jame!" he cries. "Or ram with golden fleece?" I offer. "All Greek lies!" shouts Mehmet and embarks on stories of tankers and freighters, coasters and carriers that collide while navigating the S-bends of the Bosphorus. "In this strait," he explains, "both back and forward sight is blocked during changes of course all ships must make. In addition currents change. They make seven or eight knots." "Well, well," I say, not too concerned. "These dangerous waters!" Mehmet repeats. "Oil spill – ships aground – fires – deaths – wrecks. Drunk and useless captains from Bulgaria, Georgia, Jugoslavia and of course Greece!"

I tell Mehmet of my plan to hitch-hike to India. He laughs out loud. "You crazy, Jame!" he cries. However, he is returning to Üsküdar that night, he says, so as my very good friend he will start me off on my journey, only we must leave at once because the current is favourable. I demur. "I take ferry tomorrow with traveller friends," I says. "No no, you come with me!" he says. "You stay my house! You sleep my daughter!" He laughs a lot. I wonder why. "Is there not a bridge across Bosphorus?" I ask. "Ach, they talk of bridges twenty years, no bridge!" I do not relish the idea of crossing the strait with a drunken ship's skipper who has offered me his … although … no, no … but if I am to leave my colleagues and journey alone there might not be a better opportunity. I hesitate. "Come!" calls Mehmet as he wends his way uncertainly from the bar to the quay.

Half way across the strait the engine cuts out. Mehmet curses. We drift with the current to the apex of a bend. We can see very little ahead or aft. Mehmet tries urgently to re-start the engine. "This is why I come to Istanbul, for more gas!" he says. Suddenly a huge freighter looms out of the night. Mehmet tries to steer out of the way, we yell, we wave, there is a crunch, a collision, we are taking on water. "Be scooping!" screams Mehmet. It is a losing battle. The boat tips, capsizes, I fall overboard, try to haul myself back on the boat, but cannot find it. In desperation, I begin to swim for the shore. How can this be, I think, I cannot swim! Yet the water is holding me. It is blissfully easy.

I am floating now, looking up at the stars, drifting calmly into Bombay harbour, where Mother is waving to me from the shore, wearing a wedding dress and carrying a whip. "Come closer!" she shouts. "I can't!" I cry. I wake on the quayside in Istanbul, wet from rain in the night.

The morning ferry is crowded with commuters. Dave says he was last here a few years ago when a ferry was rammed by a Ukrainian tanker half-way across. "No-one was killed," he says. "A few poor buggers were crushed and some fell in the water." "Not too bad, then," I say, thinking that was quite bad enough. "A few days later," he remarks, "a Turkish sub collided with a Swedish freighter." "What happened?" I ask. "The freighter was okay," he says. I want to know what happened to the submarine. After drowning, I can imagine nothing worse than a power failure underwater and a slow death from suffocation and claustrophobia. "Eighty-odd guys on board, the sub sank, five escaped and the rest went to Davy Jones' locker." He tries to change the subject in a way that does not make it any better. "I don't suppose this ferry has sonar, eh?"

After five or six hours on the train to the Turkish capital, Ankara, my hair is thick with dust and the spots on my face are showing up red in a paste of grey. During an oppressively hot afternoon touring the consulates we learn that Syrian visas will not be granted to travellers holding British or Australian passports. Syria in sympathy with Egypt over Suez has broken off diplomatic relations. Indian passport holders Pushpak and his family are issued with visas and leave straightaway. We giggle together with sadness and regret as we say our farewells.

And so we are five. Bob, a brickie from Sydney; Eileen, an ex-Wren on a cultural mission; Johnny, a sheep-shearer from Queensland; Dave, wanted for questioning in Melbourne; and me, virgin and university dropout. We discuss our options. We could take a train to Syria, hop off at the border, hitch-hike round to Iraq and on to Baghdad and Basra; or we can try our luck in Iran.

To our surprise we are granted Iranian visas. Either the news about Suez hasn't reached them or they don't care much for Syria and Egypt. We find a map of the Middle East in a bookshop and work out that the best way of getting to Iran is via Erzerum in the far east of Turkey. We check the trains. There is one leaving for Erzerum the next day.

That evening Bob and I share a table in the station café with two taxi drivers and Nusret, an off-duty policeman. On discovering our plight – not enough lira, too many drachmas – they ply us with beer and cigarettes in exchange for teaching them to swear in English (the usual profanities, I am almost immured to them) and

Strine (far more creative – siphon the python, water the horse, clatterfart, clutterfuck, etc.). After an hour or so the taxi drivers go off for their evening shift and Nusret, who by now is the sort of friend for life you can make in an hour in a bar, offers to take us for a Turkish bath and a party. At least that's what we think he says.

He drives out of the centre of town and parks on an unsurfaced side road near a high double doorway. "Is this the bath-house?" I ask Bob. "I think it might be the party," says Bob. "Yes yes, girls!" says Nusret and knocks at the door. A policeman he knows lets us in. Inside we find ourselves at one end of a narrow dirt street with single- and two-storey buildings on either side. All the doors and windows are open, women are sitting at the windows and standing in the doorways, and men are walking up and down. I have never been to a party like this before.

We walk up the street and back again, trying not to catch anyone's eye. Bob has a wink with Nusret, but I can see he feels as uncomfortable as I do. I am surprised, having always thought of Bob as a bit of a lad. "Seen better brothels in Bangkok, Jim," he says to me. At the exit we apologize to Nusret for not taking advantage of his hospitality. "Sorry, Nuz," says Bob. "Not in the mood, mate." Nusret shrugs and huffs, and instead of taking us for a Turkish bath he drives us back to the station, where we catch up with the others and spend the night on the station steps. How was I to know it would be my last opportunity for sex for a year and a half?

The following day we take the overnight train to Erzerum, where we plan to take another train to Tabriz in Iran followed by another to the capital, Tehran – six or seven hundred miles in all. At Erzerum station we are told, "No tickets Tehran." "Why not?" we ask. "No train," they say. We are directed instead to an earth-covered compound on the outskirts of town, where a multi-coloured, single-decker Dodgem studded with bright chrome bolts from bonnet to boot is waiting. "Tehran?" we ask the driver. He looks at us. He is promising nothing.

The interior of the bus is full to overflowing with families, pilgrims, bedding rolls and chickens in cages, but as luck would have it the long back seat is empty. As the bus rolls out of town we discover why. Dust blows up from a gap in the bodywork and within minutes we are covered in a fine grey haze. "How long Tehran?" I ask a fellow passenger. "One day, one night, one day more," he says.

The countryside outside Erzerum is desolate and dry. At midday we stop at a café at a crossroads in the middle of a treeless plain. We indicate to the proprietor that we have no Turkish lira, only travellers' cheques and Greek drachmas. He apologizes, he can take neither, but he offers us the pick of his kitchen with nothing to pay. Is he serious? Well yes, we discover, he is. Through school and university I had always taken the Greek side in their quarrels with the Turks, but today in the middle of nowhere I have to admit that the Greeks cannot rival the Turks in their hospitality towards strangers – other than, I suppose, Greeks.

It is dusk as we cross the border into Iran. Snow-topped Mount Ararat is still visible in the distance, fading into a darkening sky. When we reach Tabriz, the driver indicates he is going no further until the morning and no, we cannot sleep on the bus. We split up and search the back streets of the city for somewhere to stay.

I find a French monastic mission and ask *Monsieur l'Abbé* if he might put us up for the night. He reluctantly agrees as long as there are no females in the party. *"Non, non,"* I assure him. *"Pas de femmes."* I find the rest of the party and explain. Eileen is unfazed. She stuffs her hair under Johnny's hat, borrows Dave's jacket, keeps out of the light and we smuggle her in. "You may sleep on the roof," says the Abbé, "but you must leave before six, when the brothers rise. *Attention aux chiens de garde, ils sont très féroces." "Quels chiens de garde?"* I ask. He explains that Christian sects like his have been having a hard time of late in Tabriz and guard dogs are let into the courtyard at night *pour des raisons de sécurité.* We are instructed to remain on the roof at all times.

In the early hours I wake to fierce, unearthly howling and the screams of a fanatical mob – the door to the roof has been left open, we have been mistaken for monks and are under attack! I call out, "But I don't believe in God!" before realizing this may not be the right thing to say to religious zealots, then the hounds are upon us, their fangs dripping with blood and saliva, at which point I wake. It is morning and no-one else has heard a thing. We return to our dust-encrusted bus for the long drive south. Iran feels a long way from home.

In Tehran I seek out the British Embassy for help with my drachmas, but the office is closed for a religious holiday. I catch a glimpse of a man with a trim grey moustache as he passes by in a chauffeur-driven car.

When I meet him in his office the next morning he is wearing a crisply ironed, short-sleeved shirt and a tie. He is clean and neat and smells of Palmolive. I am unshaven and shabby and smell of a long night on the station steps amongst pigeon droppings. I explain my dilemma. "No-one outside Greece will take my drachmas. My companions have travellers' cheques, but I have no other means." "If the banks in Tehran will not take your drachmas," says the man, "then I cannot." I am upset. He is unapologetic. "But there is another way," he says. Ah, he is a decent chap after all, I think, he is going to offer me an unofficial deal. "We can repatriate you," he says. "We can pay your second-class fare back to Britain and invoice your family for the cost." I am appalled. "That does not work for me," I say. "I have travelled through thirteen or fourteen countries (I throw in Yorkshire, the five or six states of Jugoslavia and add Iran) and I have only three more to go. The last thing I want to do is return to Britain. I want to go to India." "You are British," he says. "We cannot repatriate you to India." "It would be cheaper all round if you would simply change my drachmas," I say. "We are neither a bank nor a charity," says the man with the moustache stiffly. "Repatriation is all I can offer." "But my family …" I start to say, but then give up. I have another, quite overwhelming, reason for not taking up his offer of repatriation. I do not wish to be beholden to my stepfather for the cost of my failure.

As I am about to leave the Embassy office I learn of a Scottish doctor from the British Council who is planning to visit Greece on holiday and might be able to help. He is apologetic, he already has his quota of drachmas, but he holds out a note of hope: he has to go away for a day or two, could I possibly hold on and he will see what he can do on his return?

I find my companions and tell them I cannot accompany them to Basra. "I have to stay in Tehran to change my drachmas," I say, "and I have no idea how long it will take. You must go on without me." Before leaving they kindly have a whip-round of their Iranian change and give me nine rials. Dave, Bob, Johnny, Eileen and I have been through a lot together. We say goodbye with some sadness. "I hope you find a good lawyer, Dave," I say. "Jim, mate," says Dave, "good luck. You're gonna need it."

One left. I feel introspective rather than lonely. My main concern is how long I can make nine rials last. I take my rucksack into the station café, order a lemonade (one rial), sit at a corner table and get out my bus, train and kebab-stained edition of Men and Gods. Nearer home I may be, but there is a long way to go.

> I see, but I cannot touch what I desire. And it is not as though there was a great ocean between us, or long roads or mountains or city walls.

I have been drawn to the familiar tale of *Narcissus* and *Echo*.

> We are only separated by a little water. And the face I look at looks back at me with love, smiling when I smile, weeping when I weep. Why then does it always escape me?

My best guess is that my reflection, being ungraspable, will always be unrequited in the love it seeks.

I make it through the day without eating. Weak from heat and hunger, I have no desire to spend the night alone on the steps of the station in this less-than-friendly city. I find a lodging-house that is offering the share of a large room with a threadbare carpet and no beds for five rials. Several pilgrims have already laid out their bedding rolls on the floor and are saying their prayers. It is a hot and heavy airless night.

The next day I return to the station café and buy a packet of biscuits (one rial) to go with my lemonade (another rial). Someone has left a paperback copy of Camus' *Caligula* on the table. To pass the time, I start to translate it.

> First Senator   Always nothing.
> Senior Senator   Nothing in the morning. Nothing at night.
> Second Senator   Nothing for three days.

At midday I make my way back to the Embassy, more out of something to do than with any expectation of help. I loiter for hours in the shade of the gateway listening to children playing behind the high Embassy wall. I can hear the sound of a fountain. So this is how it is to be hungry, thirsty, penniless, homeless and powerless, I think. Not forgetting loveless. This must be what Limbo is like. Dippy appears at the blackboard. "Oblige us with your attention, Seagrave." "Yes, sir. Excuse me, sir." "Limbo is from the Latin *limbus*, meaning what, Seagrave?" "Edge, sir?" "Correct, sir." I am skirting the edge of the underworld in a waiting-place for discarded souls, staring at the Tehran traffic and thinking of nothing. I do not even feel anxious. *Toujours rien. Rien pour trois jours.* If I faint in the dust or die in the night the British Ambassador will have some explaining to do. I will be found with the price of a cheap lemonade in my pocket. I now understand what it means to be stoic. I am immune to misfortune; unaffected by joy, grief, pleasure or pain.

The Scottish doctor returns a day early and invites me into his air-conditioned office, where he offers me iced water and exchanges every one of my Greek drachmas for Iranian rials. He has helped me take a step back from the edge.

On a map in the office of Iran Tour I see a town called Mashhad in eastern Iran near the Afghan border. Afghanistan is on the direct route to Pakistan, so I book a cheap overnight train to Mashhad then seek out the Afghan Embassy in Tehran for a visa.

I have gone about this the wrong way entirely. A plump, perspiring Afghani official sitting under a fan turns me down. "It is the wrong season," she says. "The roads are bad and you do not have enough money." Her office is an oasis from the heat of the streets and I am tempted to extend my time there by questioning her use of the epithets "wrong", "bad" and "enough". I think to ask her, 'What is wrong about the season and, more interestingly, what is right about it?' 'How bad are the roads to which you refer?' 'Does that apply to every road?' 'How much money is enough?' 'What does the average Afghani earn?' and so on. I don't, of course. The woman says if I am intent on going to India I must go via Iran and Pakistan and avoid Afghanistan altogether, and that is an end of it.

The train from Tehran to Mashhad grinds its way through the night and the rest of the next day. Next door to the station in Mashhad is a hotel with a tiny foyer and a notice stating

> *Hotel Ferdowsi* named in honour of Persias national poet author of fifty thousand verses of *Shah Nameh.*

I wonder what the aristocratic author of the Book of Kings would have made of this drab little doss-house that has taken his name. A youth at a counter in the foyer takes my passport. I ask him the best way of getting from Mashhad to Zahedan in the south of Iran near the border with Pakistan. "You must ask the police," he says. "What do the police have to do with it?" I ask. He shrugs, files my passport and finds something more interesting to do.

The next day I have dysentery. I have been living on iced drinks bought on the street from vendors who break up the ice and drop it into unwashed glasses by hand, so I am not surprised. I grow weak, my eyesight begins to fail, my breathing is shallow and I have to concentrate hard in order not to lose consciousness. It feels like the dry land equivalent of drowning.

On the third day of the sickness I am visited by the Chief of Police, who asks me my reasons for being in Mashhad. He speaks in French. *"J'ai une maladie,"* I answer, adding under my breath 'Otherwise I would have left this shithole the minute I arrived.' *"Je dois faire attention,"* he says pleasantly. *"Nous sommes près de la frontière avec l'Union soviétique. Comment puis-je savoir que vous n'êtes pas un espion?"* "How do you I know I am not a spy?" I ask. *"Je suis étudiant des classiques,"* I tell him weakly. *"Je suis malade,* I have no money and I am on my way to India to see my mother." I do not care if he finds this unconvincing. He is affable and polite, but he wants me out of town. He says he will pay my fare on a bus to Zahedan leaving the next day and a constable with my passport will pick me up at five o'clock in the morning. I am as grateful as any agent of a foreign power who intends to abscond as soon as his passport is returned would be.

The constable is late and by the time we get to the bus station the bus has left. The constable is understandably upset. He was under strict instructions to get rid of me, so he commandeers a taxi to catch up with the bus and makes sure I get on it. The bus is full of livestock, suitcases, bedding rolls and babies. I am unwell, but I am on the move again and it is costing me nothing.

The journey to Zahedan takes twenty-six hours. I do not sleep. I am shaken and sick. A fellow passenger by the name of Habib kindly shares his bottled water with me and tells me of a train that leaves Zahedan every Tuesday for Quetta in Baluchistan. "What day is it today?" I ask, having no idea. "It is Friday," he says. "The train is arriving Zahedan Monday, you must buy Inter Class ticket to sleep on this train unless you wish to be travelling Third Class, when you must buy ticket the morning following, though you might not obtain a seat." "Where is Baluchistan?" I ask, thinking I have overlooked a country. "It is in Pakistan," he says. "Many violences, shootings, smugglings and curfew."

When at last we reach Zahedan Habib leads me to the no-star Hotel Melli. "It is cheap," he says, "also clean. Sheets are changed frequently." "How often is that?" I ask, not really caring, just curious. "Every week, I am sure," says Habib. He advises me to keep enough Iranian money for the hotel and the train and to change the rest into Pakistan rupees. "I see you are getting good rate," he says, looking around. *"Aie,* come."

I follow my companion out of town away from the shade. The sand underfoot is yielding and hot. After a long walk he stops at a fruit stall and picks up half a melon. Is this a signal? Can I trust this man? I feel for a breeze that will cool the sweat against my skin, but the air is still and blisteringly hot. A man with grey stubble and wire-framed spectacles comes from the back of the stall where he was sitting cross-legged in the shade. Habib says something, the man looks at me carefully, then beckons. I follow him down an alleyway to a wooden doorway, where he stops and beckons again. "Come," he says.

We are ushered across a courtyard into a dimly lit room. I wonder if I am about to be robbed. I check for my scout knife, but it is out of reach in my rucksack. The man with the spectacles asks me how much Iranian money I want to change. I count out half my rials and he shows me on a calculator how much I will get in Pakistan rupees, assuring me that this is three times as much as I would get from the bank. Habib agrees. I count out most of the rest of my remaining rials. I have to trust these men. I count the rupees I get in exchange. It seems like a lot of rupees. After a glass of sweet tea we leave as quietly as we arrived.

Outside, it is an effort to breathe. I am drowning in dry air. I decide against staying at the Hotel Melli. "I have to save my money," I say to Habib. "That is no problem," he says, and leads me through the streets to a mud-walled compound open to the skies where thirty or forty men are sitting and standing, smoking, fingering their prayer beads, arguing and chatting. "They are waiting for the train," says Habib. Some of them look at me with suspicion, but that could be my paranoia. It likes to pop by for a visit whenever I am tired. I find some shade. All I want is sleep.

Over the next two days I save what I can by eating very little. I distract myself by reading. I am following *Oedipus*'s long journey from Corinth, alone and on foot, to consult the Oracle. The Oracle is uncompromising.

> Unhappy man, keep far away from your father or you will kill him. Then you will marry your mother and have children who will be fated to crime and misfortune.

I can just about believe I am fated to kill my father, but however hard I try I cannot see myself marrying my mother. This must be some kind of simile. Perhaps I am fated to marry a woman who will take the role of my mother – in which case why am I going to such lengths to pursue a transitional object in the shape of my actual mother? Either my ideal of maternal love has substance or it is illusory and unattainable. If it had substance, I would not be questioning it so readily. If it were illusory, I would soon be rid of the vain desire to pursue it. The glittering oasis of motherliness I see in the distance might well be a mirage, I tell myself, but it is all I have. And it might, after all, be real.

On the evening of the third day I trudge through the sand to the station to buy an Inter Class ticket to Quetta that will allow me to spend the night on the stationary train before it leaves in the morning. I have been allocated a top bunk in a six-bunk compartment. One of my companions is a cheerful *chaprassi*, an office worker on his way home on leave from Tehran. With his bushy moustache dyed a dark shade of red he looks like the cowboy in the Looney Tunes cartoons who has an intense hatred of rabbits.

My other companions are pilgrims returning from Mecca. Promptly as the sun sets they go about their prayers; laying out their mats, slipping out of their sandals or sliding out of the flattened heels of their shoes, ceaselessly murmuring while standing, raising their hands, bowing, kneeling and prostrating themselves. There is no room on the floor for the man in the top bunk opposite mine, so he performs a modified version of prayers in the space between his bunk and the ceiling. He is also uncertain of the direction of Mecca and ends up facing the wrong way. I do not think it is up to me to point this out.

The train takes thirty-six hours to reach the Baluchistan capital, Quetta, with frequent stops for water and food. Prayers take up much of the time – after sunset, before midnight, before sunrise, then midday, late afternoon, after sunset again, before midnight again and before sunrise the next morning. The praying is inescapable. I wonder if they all do this at home. It certainly helps pass the time on the train. After a while I feel as if I am praying too. If I were, it would be for a rest from the praying.

Quetta is an oasis. It has orchards. The air in the station is acrid and cool from water sprayed on the ground to keep the dust down. A child is splashing in a shallow puddle left on the platform. I cannot help thinking that an unsupervised infant might drown in such a puddle if they tripped, hit their head and lost consciousness. Morbid thoughts. I can't help them. My default state is 'What is the worst that could happen?' Train crash, terrorist attack, shot, robbed, limbs amputated, I have to be ready for anything.

The train from Quetta to Lahore is due to leave the next day. All Inter Class and Second Class tickets have been sold, Third is unbookable and a ticket for a two-bunk First Class compartment costs ninety-five Pakistan rupees. The clerk informs me that First Class ticket-holders are allowed to spend the night in the First Class waiting room. After what Habib told me about guns on the streets I do not relish the idea of going into town or sleeping on the station steps, so I spend ninety-five of my black-market rupees on a ticket that will allow me to bed down for the night on a padded bench in a locked waiting room. Only one other passenger spends the night there and he does not get up to pray.

The next day I am joined in my First Class compartment by an elderly, heavily-garlanded, corpulent *babu* wearing a spotless white cotton *kurta* and *dhoti*. I am a tramp in comparison. I am even a tramp in comparison with the beggars who besiege the babu as he makes his way down the platform accompanied by a retinue of immaculately laundered young men who shoo the beggars away, stow my rucksack on the upper bunk without asking, arrange their master's belongings to take up the lower bunk, bring him tea and tiffin, and treat him with the kind of respect that is difficult to believe could be genuine. As the train moves off the young men *salaam* their goodbyes, keeping pace with the train to the end of the platform and continuing to salaam until we are no longer in sight – at which point

I imagine them letting out a collective sigh of relief, exchanging high-fives and returning to the office or the ashram for a party.

As the eagle flies it is five hundred miles from Quetta in the west to Lahore in the north, but the railway has to make a two-hundred mile detour south-east to Sukkur on the Indus to avoid the Sulaiman Mountains. It is a dull and comfortable journey. A couple of small cockroaches make a token appearance, but they are nothing compared to the beasts of Blackfoot Lane. I try to make conversation with my companion, but he is barely responsive. He tucks into his tiffin and reads an Urdu newspaper.

I am living on melon and biscuits and reading a second-hand book I bought at the station in Quetta, a slim paperback with the grand title, 'Hugo's Hindustani Simplified, an Easy and Rapid Self-Instructor with Imitated Pronunciation of Every Word'. Here is an example: '*Ram ne apna ghora becha*, Ram sold his master's horse'. That might come in useful, I think. And there is a story that reminds me of the nightmare of fishing with Harold out of Sourness-on-Sea, though it is too endearing to be scary. I enjoy the literal translation that is intended to give the serious student of Hindustani a flavour of its unusual syntax.

> A fisherman one time one very small fish caught.
> This little creature crying said: Me catch from what use?
> Me to grow for time give. Me river in back throwing do please.
> When I more big become, then me catch.

I am hooked. What happens next?

> The fisherman by answer given: Struggling of any use not is.
> Now thou my hand in art, thou my basket in go must.
> Today evening my frying-pan in go must, and I thee supper in shall eat.

Struggling of any use not is. In meantime Sukkur from line to Bhawalpur Indus is following. Bhawalpur lies on the Sutlej, the southernmost of the tributaries of the Indus. From Bhawalpur the track crosses the Chenab to Multan and from Multan to Lahore it follows the Ravi. The fields on either side of the train are battered by monsoon rain. Date palms grow in wet clumps. A damp camel lollops round a Persian wheel. I turn to my classical companion, Rex Warner, who recounts how *Jupiter*, the Roman King of Heaven, brings a Great Flood upon the earth in his anger at man's wickedness.

> Clouds sat upon his forehead; water poured from his feathers and the folds
> of his garments. He squeezed in his fist the hanging masses of cloud, and
> there was a crash.

Water from the skies falls heavily day and night. The train trundles past flooded fields on its long haul north.

> Thick vapours fell from the air, the crops were battered to the ground and
> farmers wept for their fallen hopes.

The farmers I see from my First Class seat on the train may be weeping in the rain as it batters their crops and fills their fields, and if so I feel for them, but I am on my way home. I am as cheery as young *Neptunus*, sea-blue brother of Jupiter and Lord of the Waters, who instructs his charges:

> Open all your doors, let nothing stop you, give free rein to your flowing streams!

We are nearing Lahore when the sun breaks through and the heavens are unveiled to the earth again. For a time Jupiter forgives us our wickedness. He scatters the clouds and instructs the North Wind to dispel the rain. Then Neptune raises his three-pronged spear and calls for the waters to retreat. The rivers have their banks returned to them and the streams run in their proper channels. Let nothing stop me, I pray. Give me free rein. Only one border remains.

♆

Chapter 17
Yamuna River

FROM MY THIRD-CLASS SEAT ON THE ONE TRAIN A DAY from Lahore in Pakistan to Amritsar in India I watch labourers walking barefoot through the fields with sacking held over their heads. Warm rain sweeps through the mosquito wire of the open carriage window. This rain feels redemptive. It is washing away years of muck and muddle. I shall see my mother soon. The fields outside are green with new growth.

While waiting in Amritsar for the connecting train to Yamunanagar I explore the bazaar and find a book with the title Ganga-Yamuna, Myth and Mystery. It tells of how *Lord Krishna* was carried across the Yamuna on the night of his birth. *Yamuna* herself is characterized as daughter of the Sun God and sister to the God of Death, an ominous duality that reminds me of Dippy's depiction of bodies of water as both attractive and dangerous. I read that although bathing in the holy waters of the Yamuna is said to free one from the torments of death, it does not promise to free one from death itself. Freedom from torment, I reflect, would be freedom enough. I might at least dip a toe in the water.

At Yamunanagar I am met by the local agent for Harold's employers, the British Empire Corporation, diplomatically known these days by its post-Independence acronym, BEC. The agent places a garland of marigolds around my neck and puts his hands together in greeting. *"Namaste*. Welcome to India, Mr Jamesahib!" His driver hands him another garland and instructs one of the *coolies* crowding round looking for custom to take my rucksack. I protest. That frayed old thing has accompanied me for almost six thousand miles and we will not be parted. The agent laughs and dismisses the coolie. "Ah, Mr Jamesahib," he says, "you are depriving the man of his wages!" He chortles as if to assure me that this does not matter in the least.

The agent presents me with a light-up plastic replica of the Taj Mahal – "A small gift for your goodself, Mr Jamesahib." I thank him. I wonder if Mother might like it, though she probably has several already. The agent's driver retrieves the stuffed and mounted head of an animal from the boot of his car and hands it to the agent, who presents it to me. "Is spotted deer shot by Mr Sutcliffe Sahib on last visit to Yamunanagar," says the agent.. "*Bohut accha*, very fine antlers you will agree, please to remember me to his goodself."

My rucksack, the dead deer-head and the miniature mausoleum are transferred by another driver to another car, which turns out to be for me. The agent bids me an effusive farewell with many expressions of goodwill. I settle into the back seat of my car. I may look like a tramp, but I have my own chauffeur.

It is dark by the time we reach Chandrapore and the end of my journey. I am exhausted, emaciated, pleased and proud. I don't quite know where I am, but at last I am home. Harold greets me pleasantly, as if he hadn't seen me for a day or two. Never mind, I think. Mother will mark the occasion with more extravagance. "Your mother is in the foothills for the summer," says Harold. "There is a train leaving tomorrow. Everything is arranged." Oh. She is not here. I want her to be here, excited and a'flutter to see me, and deeply concerned for my well-being after the distressing events of the year and my arduous overland odyssey. "Where is Rupert?" I ask. "In Simla, at prep school," says Harold. "Doing very well." I suppose he means academically.

Harold admires the head of the handsome animal he shot in Yamunanagar. He asks for my opinion. I have none. He thinks he might hang it high on the dining room wall for the benefit of guests who will wish to know the circumstances of the kill: the calibre of gun used, the distance to the target, the point of entry, and so on.

Everything is arranged. 'He is saying, in effect, 'You are an inconvenience, but we shall work round it.' The familiar feeling of being left again might not be at the same level of existential threat as it had been in Fourth Street, Rawley or Blackfoot Lane, Beasley, but in my paranoid mind they are inextricably linked. My mother cannot help repeating an unlovely pattern.

She has relocated to a rented bungalow in the summer resort of Mussoorie in the foothills of the Himalayas, high above the heat and humidity of the monsoon-laden plains. It takes a car, two trains, a horse-drawn *tonga* and most of the next day to get there. I am looking forward to being welcomed, however, to being forgiven and comforted, and folded into my mother's arms.

Mother is courteous and solicitous. Have I eaten? No. Am I tired? Yes. Am I disappointed? She doesn't ask that. This is not the homecoming I had hoped for.

I sleep badly that night and in the morning I am wary. I know from monitoring her mood that my mother has something to say and that she is waiting for the right moment to say it. As soon as breakfast is over and the table has been cleared, Mother makes reference to my melancholy last letters from England. I knew they were tactless, but did not believe they were so revealing or that she would read between the lines quite so readily. She is on the verge of tears. "Did you not think, James," she asks, "how much they would hurt me?" Hang on a minute, missus, I think – aren't I supposed to be the hurt one? There is an agonized silence. I have no answer for the hurt I have caused.

In a month in the hills I do little but read (Hemingway, D.H. Lawrence, The Penguin Herodotus), listen to music (Debussy, Rachmaninov), stroll among the pines and make the best I can of being the guest of a woman whose emotional pain is so much more compelling, more present, than mine. I am not yet twenty-one. It is a confirmation of something I have suspected since the age of two: that the world does not turn in my favour. I make an attempt to align myself with my mother's hurt, but I can barely approach it. She fails to get within a mile of mine.

With the passing of the monsoon we relocate to the plains. Our driver Kumar Singh drives Harold's Ford Zephyr through villages of mud huts the colour of the earth, hammering the horn to clear the tarmac strip of pedestrians, cyclists, scooters, cattle and hand-carts, and steering briefly onto the hard-earth verge to overtake bullock carts that ramble along unconcerned in the centre of the road. An elderly cyclist persists along the tarmac ahead of us, his shirt and waistcoat flapping in the breeze. Kumar Singh hits the horn repeatedly, but the old man keeps to his line, so Kumar Singh makes a point of passing him as closely as possible in order to prove that it would have been in the old man's interests to have veered off the tarmac onto the verge well before we arrived. The cyclist is swept off-balance by the rush of air as we pass, but recovers enough to swear at us and gesture fiercely.

As we drive into Chandrapore passers-by salaam. "Are they salaaming you, Kumar Singh?" I ask. He laughs. "No, Sahib," he says. "they are salaaming the car." "Why do they salaam the car?" "Sahib, this is Mr Sutcliffe Sahib car." Mother points out that Harold as manager of the BEC mill is the *Burra Sahib*, the main man, of the area and almost everyone in Chandrapore depends on him in one way or another. *"Salaam, Sahib!"* greets the car everywhere in case the Burra Sahib is in it.

We drive through the bazaar and over the river to a gated compound of bungalows reserved for the senior staff at the mill. Kumar Singh sounds the horn and an elderly Gurkha in the uniform of a private guard ambles over to let us in. "Lazy little man," says Mother to no-one in particular. I am puzzled, ready to be offended on his behalf, but I can't tell if she is being critical or indulgent. I really don't know this woman. The guard salutes and smiles a shy Gurkha smile as we pass.

We stop at The Sheiling, the only two-storey, drive-and-veranda surrounded house in the compound. Three servants – *Bearer*, *Cook* and *Sweeper* – are waiting under a pillared portico to greet us and take our luggage. *"Salaam, Memsahib! Salaam, Chota Sahib!"* The *chota* – little – sahib is me. It is a polite form of address intended to distinguish me from the *Burra Sahib*, but I can't say I like it.

Mother briefs Cook about supper, then takes me on a tour of the grounds. The lawns are as fine-trimmed and flawless as the bowling greens of Thirby. I am invited to admire pink and vermilion *bougainvillea* and purple-blue *jacaranda*. A *mali* is weeding the flower beds. He rises to greet us. *"Salaam, Memsahib. Salaam, Chota Sahib."* Mother asks him about his son, who is pruning roses. Perhaps she does care. I hear the cry of a peacock, the sound of a fountain. I compare all this to the stone-flagged yards of Rawley and the thin brick terraces of Beasley whose doors opened directly onto the street.

Behind the garages at the rear of the house is the servants' compound, a row of low brick dwellings with hard earth floors and flimsy wooden doors. Great-grandma Barraclough might have felt at home in these tiny, tidy dwellings with their simple facilities. She might even have approved of their little altars to *Ganesh, Vishnu, Krishna* and *Shiva*. I notice that one of the religious figurines still has its original label.

> 'The product look like artworks effluxing flavour of cultures and allow the infinite wonderful originalities to burst forth out of confined space of mankind'.

I am touched. These little dwellings have an effluxing flavour bursting with originalities that the big house lacks.

Beyond the servants' compound is a vegetable garden, a pen for poultry and a disused well currently home, I am told, to a nest of cobras. "Do not concern yourself with snakes," says Mother. "They usually get out of the way if they hear you coming." There is something less than reassuring about the conditional way this is worded.

At the far end of the grounds a narrow canal brings water from the Yamuna to supply the mill that Harold manages. A footbridge over sluice-gates leads to his private entrance to the mill.

This is his domain. These are Harold's roses and cobras and his wrap-around veranda. Here are his wife and his chauffeur and a servant for every purpose, including the *ayah* who cares for his son when he is out of boarding school. This is not my family. When Harold cuffs Rupert round the head for being exuberant and Mother slaps him on the thigh for a minor misdemeanour in the same way she once slapped me, I say nothing.

I write to Lydia, though I know there will be no reply. I ache as D.H. Lawrence did for Frieda.

> If she would come to me here
>   Now the sunken swathes
>   Are glittering paths
> To the sun, and the swallows cut clear
> Into the setting sun! if she came to me here!

I tell myself that things would be different if Lydia were here. She would be a long way from her mother, for one thing, almost as far as I am from mine. 'Come to me here,' I write. 'To the sun and sunken swathes, whatever they are.'

I borrow Ashi the Cook's bicycle and ride out of the compound into the countryside with no particular aim. I pass a camel-driven well and a group of mud huts. The camel is blindfold, plodding sightlessly round a circular rut worn into the ground. Outside one of the huts a woman is patting lumps of dung into pancakes for fuel and slapping them onto the wall to dry. In the distance, two vultures are circling. As I come nearer, I see more of them perched on a dead tree watching a cow that is lying on its side, barely alive, its tail flickering intermittently. The vultures are so sure the cow is dying that some wait only feet away. I throw a stone at them and they flap slowly off the ground and come to rest a few yards further on.

I pass a woman in rags carrying a baby on her back and a heavy bundle of firewood on her head. Two naked, pot-bellied children run across the track in front of me. A bullock cart trundles by in the opposite direction, its driver asleep in the back.

'Come to me here,' I write. 'We can make fuel from dung. Our children will run naked and barefoot. The soil is poor and dry and people do not wear shoes.' I need to share my guilt and complicity with someone, even if they will not respond.

That night I fall asleep to music from the bazaar as it drifts across the river that divides those of in the compound from the others in the town. The music can be heard on both sides.

> *Mera joota hai Japani,*
> *Yeh patloon Inglistani …*

The next day I borrow Ashi's bike again and cycle to the bazaar. Some people salaam, some laugh at the sight of a European on an old sit-up-and-beg bicycle. A woman in a bright ochre sari squats on the ground selling sweetmeats from a circular tin tray resting between her knees. *"Sahib, Sahib!"* she calls. I stop. She wafts a fan at the flies crawling over her sticky sweets. *"Kitna?"* I ask. "How much?" I take out a few *annas* change that I have in my pocket. The woman holds out a bony hand to take the money and salaams gratefully. She doesn't give me any sweets. *"Salaam, Sahib, salaam!"* she says. I nod awkwardly and walk on.

I soon find what I have been looking for – a shop selling bangles, oil lamps, brass pitchers, tiffin tins, joss sticks, silver-framed pictures of *Laxmi* and *Ganapathy*, and 45 rpm records. I ask the shopkeeper if he has *'Mera joota hai Japani'*. He joyfully obliges. *"Bohut accha* record, *Sahib!"* he cries. "Very popular song sung by famed movie star Raj Kapoor!" He looks at my trousers: *"Tamara patloon Inglistani?"* he asks and laughs gleefully.

Back in the kitchen at the Shieling I ask Ashi to translate the lyric for me.

Mera joota hai Japani,
My shoes are Japanese
Yeh patloon Inglistani
These trousers are English
Sar pe laal topi Roosi
The red hat on my head is Russian
Phir bhi dil hai Hindustani
But my heart is Indian.

I tell him I want to learn it in Hindi. Ashi spits betel juice into the sink and strokes his bushy moustache. *"Jamesahib,* it is about the new India," he says. At least he is no longer calling me *Chota Sahib.* Ashi cannot believe I might wish to take a step or two into the new India rather than stay rooted and restricted in the old.

Mother storms into the kitchen. "Where is *Bearer?"* Devi Das, the softly spoken bearer, appears as if from nowhere. *"Ji han, Memsahib?"* "Devi Das, ring for the *derzi!* The *dhobi wallah* has ruined my curtains! Come and see!" We follow her dutifully into the lounge. "He has ruined my curtains from Delhi! Look at them! Six inches shorter! He washed them in hot water and I distinctly told him cold water – *kathor pani,* I said!" *"Memsahib,"* says Devi Das gently, *"kathor pani* is unkind water, he thinks you mean hot water, cold water is *kam pani."* "Kathor pani, kam pani! Is he *gadha??"* Mother storms off to phone Harold.

That night I am in my bathroom singing *Meera joota hai Japani* when I see water coming up from the plughole into the bath until it overflows and the floor is flooded with *kathor pani.* I go to Mother and Harold's bedroom for help, but their floor is flooded too. Harold has to get out of bed to drain off the water. I have inconvenienced him. I am hugely embarrassed. I am trying to be a good stepson and an apologist for the new India, yet my dream seems to be saying these are incompatible aims.

The ex-pat wives of the senior staff at the mill are doing their best to keep the old India alive. They are pleased to have a new participant for their bridge, bezique and *mahjong* mornings, tennis afternoons and Scottish country dancing evenings. Scottish country dancing is revived when I arrive. Ever since one of their number retired and returned to the UK the memsahibs have been one short of an eightsome.

Over the last year Sutcliffe, McMurdoe, Gillespie, Butterworth, Plumtree, Priestley and the other British memsahibs have been joined in the senior staff compound by Rajinder Singh and Chatterjee Memsahibs, who are in the process of learning canasta, mahjong and Scottish country dancing too.

Butterworth Memsahib is looking forward to her husband Walter retiring. "Thirty years is too long. But if Walter had his way we'd be buried out here or floated down the Yamuna or whatever they do." "Mind you," says Gillespie Memsahib, "we can always take to the hills when the monsoon arrives." "We never have fires," says McMurdoe Memsahib, "except at Christmas." "Even if it's too warm," pipes up Plumtree Memsahib, who is thought of as a bit of a rebel because she once wore a *sari* to a Chandrapore Club party.

Their favourite topic is servants. "I never hire Indian Christians," says Priestley Memsahib. "I had a cook ten years ago who was brought up in a Salvation Army mission and he was the most dishonest cook I ever had." "Indians are best brought up as Hindus," says McMurdoe Memsahib, who speaks as if she has published authoritative research on the subject. "Madho Ram is honest enough," she says, "but he is so old I worry when I see him carrying anything heavy." "She's been very unlucky with her servants," says Mother after McMurdoe Memsahib has left the room to powder her nose. "She's had six bearers since she came out five years ago." Everyone tuts. "Ajit has been with me for twelve years," says Butterworth Memsahib. "Sometimes I ask him if he does not want a change and he says, 'Memsahib, if I leave you I shall have to go and work for some rich Indian family and they treat their servants like dogs'."

McMurdoe Memsahib returns. She has no need to check if the subject has changed. "We pay them too much," she announces. There is a murmur of assent. "We are exploited," says Butterworth Memsahib as she presses a bell on the wall. A boy of about thirteen appears. "Ranjit, coffee *lao*," she says. *"Jihan,* Memsahib,*"* says the boy quietly and leaves. "Where is your usual bearer, Shirley?" asks Mother. "Ajit? He is sick, or so his wife says. That was his son." "What bad luck," says Mother, meaning, I suppose, bad luck for Shirley rather than Ajit or Ranjit.

Harold and I play squash in the court that the Engineering Department at the mill built for the senior staff. On perhaps the fifth or sixth of our regular end-of-the-day games I arrive at the court early and start to knock up on my own. I tell myself I will not rest until I beat him. I feel co-ordinated. I thrash the ball against the far wall. It comes back in one bounce on the backhand and I thrash it again. This time I skip to my left to take it on the forehand, hit the ball early and it comes back high. I turn and thump it towards the back wall, but it skids off the frame of my racquet and plops to the floor. "Watch the ball," I say to myself. "Winning is a state of mind." I have been assuming that Harold will win and he always does. I whack the ball on the backhand and the tin sheet of failure clangs just as Harold walks in, changed and ready.

"Hello, Harold," I say, "you look tired." I have been reading Stephen Potter's Gamesmanship. "Hard day at the office," says Harold, "I shall be easy on you." This riles me, as he intends.

Harold wins the toss and serves. He is light on his feet for his size and uses his energy well. My will to win fritters away as I find myself losing again. Harold commands the 'T' and controls the game. I run about more than I should. The more points I lose, the more cavalier and careless I become.

After half an hour, Harold stops and says, "Time for a *chota peg*, I think." This always annoys me. He will never say whisky or Scotch. It is always a *chota peg* or a *burra peg*, though he will never suggest a *burra peg* after a game of squash, as that would imply I had made him work harder than he had to for a *chota peg*.

We walk back to The Sheiling through the dusk. Bats flit towards us and veer away. A faint wailing starts up as the music from the bazaar drifts over the river.

> *Mera joota hai Japani …*

I sing along in Hindi.

> *Sar pe laal topi Roosi*
> *Phir bhi dil hai Hindustani …*

Harold is not amused. I may have lost the game, but in siding with the poor on the far side of the river I have my revenge. Not that that is much help to the poor on the far side. I try not to think of them and most of the time I fail. Almost everyone on the streets of Chandrapore is worse off than the poorest of the poor in Rawley and Beasley, and they are impossible to ignore. In my first weeks in India I attempt to discriminate between people who approached me for money – is this child with no legs who propels himself on a home-made board with wheels more virtuous, more deserving, than this toothless old lady, crippled, bent and thin as a twig? It is impossible to say, so I give up trying and give money to anyone who asks. After realizing I can make no difference to their lives I vent my frustration by gesturing dismissively – *"Ar jao!"* – as Mother and Harold do – at every beggar who comes into my personal space. Then I go back to attempting to discriminate, which feels wrong on so many levels.

After a few weeks more of coffee mornings, afternoon teas and drinks before dinner with people who generally are a generation older, socially and culturally conservative and in the main married, I feel not only guilty, complicit and impotent, but bored. I wish desperately to meet someone my age and for something to happen. I make an announcement at supper: "I am going to hitch-hike to Delhi for the weekend." Harold immediately offers me one of the mill cars and a driver, and for a minute or two I contemplate refusing as a matter of principle, but I reckon he still owes me for abducting my mother, disrupting my schooling and leaving me to share a toilet with eleven other people, so I agree. He has won again.

My driver Ramesh takes me to the *Red Fort* and *Humayun's Tomb*, extraordinary buildings worth an hour or two of anyone's time, but then I opt to visit the *Mutiny Memorial,* which I assume to have been built to honour the native martyrs of the First War of Indian Independence. It turns out to be commemorating members of the British Defence Forces who died. Ramesh assumes I am there to honour the British Defence Forces, but I assure him this is not the case. "I wish to honour all the martyrs," I say, "including those who have no memorial." *"Accha, Sahib,"* says Ramesh politely, but I can see he does not understand.

Next we visit the *Kutab Minar*, an 800-year old tower built for a princess, according to legend, or to mark the start of Muslim rule in India with material obtained from demolishing twenty-seven Hindu temples, according to Ramesh. *"Twenty-seven?"* I ask. He is certain of the number. I am curious. "Are you a Hindu nationalist, Ramesh," I ask, "or a Muslim apologist?" *"Sahib,"* he states politely, "in my job I am having neither religious nor political persuasion." "What about at home?" I ask. It is an unfair question. He does not respond and I do not raise the matter again.

The entrance to the tower has a notice forbidding visitors to mount to the top unless they are accompanied by at least two other people. I suppose that too many who came unaccompanied were found dead in the dust at the foot of the tower, but I am past suicide, no-one is counting and I go up alone. The steep spiral staircase narrows considerably towards the top, making it difficult for visitors to squeeze past each other on their way up or down. I wonder if two people ever get stuck together and strike a spark on those steps.

Finally we drive to the ghost city of *Fatehpur Sikri*, where the wells ran dry and the palace was abandoned soon after it was built. "Spirit of a princess is climbing to palace roof every day to pray for rain," says Ramesh. "Every day she is pleading for sun to go down and for rain to fall on the dry city." All to no avail, I understand. The wells remain dry.

In Chandrapore a few days later I am struck by the kind of spark that those squeezing by on the stairs of the Kutab Minar might experience once in a century. After spending weeks praying for rain to fall on the parched city my prayers are answered. I meet someone. She arrives at the Sheiling with her sister to pay a courtesy call on my mother as the *Burra Memsahib* of the compound. Mother introduces them without ceremony as Rupinder and Gudiya, daughters of Rajinder Singh, one of the departmental managers at the mill, then takes them off to the morning room to hear all about their recent trip to visit relatives in the Punjab. I am not invited to join them. I go back to my book. Exciting though it is – the obsessive quest of a ship's skipper for a whale that once bit off his leg – it is not easy to concentrate.

The following evening I go to Film Night at the Club in the hope that the sisters might be there. Gudiya comes alone. She enters the room wearing a flimsy, floaty white sari, her hair tied back in a single, long, lustrous black plait with a white jasmine flower tucked into it. She sits in the row directly in front of me. It is a humid, hot night, the *punkahs* are on full, I have had a beer or two, the lighting in the hall is on the dim side and I haven't been this close to a woman under forty for months, but for the second time in thirty-six hours she seems to me the most beautiful woman I have ever met.

Her father, Rajinder Singh, a tall, stooped, grey-bearded ex-army major, follows her, holding what looks suspiciously like a large Scotch. I am surprised. I thought Sikhs were meant to be teetotal, like Methodists. Perhaps he makes an exception for whisky, as Grandma Lily frequently did for Tia Maria. He goes to sit on his own at the back of the hall and Gudiya turns to check on him. I study her profile – eyelashes, nose, lips that part and come together as she speaks – all standard items, but in the mood I am in they fit together perfectly. The film starts. I hear music. I think angels are singing. I will Rajinder Singh to order another Scotch so that his daughter might turn round again to check if he is still sober.

Mother had been rather offhand about Gudiya after the courtesy call. She spoke of her with a frostiness that reminded me of her response to Polly in Beasley. Does she think this girl is too smart in some way, too young or too beautiful? She praises her older sister Rupinder, who is on the plump side, with a faint downy moustache and a face scarred from smallpox. "Rupinder is a really *nice* girl," says Mother. "What a pity they haven't been able to marry her off. They won't have any trouble with the other one."

When the lights come on at the interval while the reel is changed I lean forward and say something to Gudiya about the film. I can't remember what I say. She smiles and replies. I can't remember what she says. I think she is agreeing.

When the film ends we sit around chatting to other people, then leave without exchanging another word. I am trying to be cool and succeeding far too well.

I can hardly leave it to Mother to invite her to the Sheiling for coffee or canasta, so I send her a *chit* by the Bearer's boy asking if she might like to meet at the Club at the weekend for a walk or a game of badminton. Her *chit* comes back: 'Thank you. Yes. Sunday around two would be nice'. I am thrilled. I say nothing to anyone.

On Sunday after lunch I excuse myself, telling Mother and Harold that I am going for a walk. "I'd like a word, James," says Harold. Mother gets up. "I have to see about supper," she says. Harold hesitates. "I understand you have arranged to see Rajinder Singh's girl," he says. "Gudiya? Yes," I say, surprised. "How did you know?" "This is a small place, James." Oh damn, I think, everyone in the compound will know. The Bearer's boy will have spoken to the Bearer, the Bearer will have said something to Rajinder Singh's Bearer, Rajinder Singh's Bearer will have had a word with Rajinder Singh and Rajinder Singh will have mentioned it, reluctantly, to Harold, his boss, and they would have had an awkward discussion about whether they should do something about it and, if so, what.

Harold goes on. "She is a good-looking girl and I understand you might find her attractive, though some say she is a rather shallow person." "Mother," I mutter. What is it with my mother and a certain kind of girl, i.e. those I like? "I am trying to be helpful, James," says Harold. He is as sensitive to our relationship as I am. "I know there are no other people of your age here, but you must not let a romance develop." I am strangely encouraged. Romance is seen as a possibility. It is all I want. "We have nothing against the girl," he says, "but she is a Sikh." I am surprised. "So what?" I ask, ready to be offended on behalf of all Sikhs, Hindus, Muslims, Jews, Jains, Zoroastrians, Anglicans, Atheists and Aliens. If my stepfather and I are to fight about anything, I think, it might as well be race, religion, ethnicity and socio-cultural principle. "Her family will not tolerate her having anything to do with men other than Sikhs," he says. "And even then only under strict supervision. Rajinder Singh is a very proud man. His religion tells him she must marry a Sikh." "I can grow a beard and convert," I say. This does not go down well. I can see that our differences are not simply about race or religion, but power. Only one of us can win.

Remember this, son, if you and I are ever at odds. For the exercise of power between people to be ethical and honourable it can only be shared. How a father and son can manage that I have no idea.

Harold sighs. His instinct, like mine, is to be in control of the situation, but neither of us has entirely given up on reason. I change my tone. "She is an intelligent girl, Harold. Surely she can decide who she sees for herself." "If she is seen with you it will mark down her prospects of marriage," he points out. "Not with me!" I cry. Harold ignores this. "Her reputation depends on her behaviour," he says. "She must be beyond suspicion. All I am asking of you is to respect local custom." "Jesus, Harold," I say, "all we are going to do is play badminton." If that were the only reason, of course, I could equally have made a date with Rupinder, or with Harold himself. I am peeved. "I'm sure her sister is allowed to go out on her own," I say. "They have given up on marrying Rupinder," he says. "Are you telling me not to go?" I ask. I am trying to provoke him into saying something he might regret, but he is equal to it. "I am asking you to give it your most careful consideration," he says. Have I won, or is this a stand-off? Harold is stuck, reluctant to give me an instruction and determined not to sound racist, but to my mind this is exactly what he and Rajinder Singh are.

I think for a moment. There is a sensitive dimension to the situation that I had not even begun to appreciate. The last thing I want is to offend my stepfather and upset his relationship with one of his senior managers. No, that is the next to last thing I want. The last thing I want is not to see Gudiya. "I'm sorry, Harold," I say, "but I have promised and it would not reflect well on the family for me to renege on that." Aha, I think, there can be no answer for that, never mind that it isn't my family.

It is the first time I have had an explicit difference with my stepfather. I reassure myself that he is not my father – who anyway would not have cared a toss. "You have a decision to make," says Harold. I have already made it. And no-one has won.

Gudiya arrives at the Club twenty minutes after the appointed time. To my disappointment she is accompanied by Rupinder. I wonder if there have been ructions in the Rajinder Singh household and this is the compromise they have arrived at: that the older sister will come along as chaperone and if anyone happens to see the three of us together the encounter can be written off as a coincidence.

We greet each other warmly. I am invited to call the girls by their pet names, Guddie and Roop. I offer them Jim in return, but Guddie says she prefers James. She makes James sound like a really nice name.

The three of us play badminton together. The girls cannot move too well in their saris, but Guddie is willing and giggles a lot, while Roop labours and perspires. Then Guddie and I play Chopsticks on the piano while Roop sits in a corner reading old copies of Punch. Guddie's hand touches mine accidentally. I feel slightly faint. We find an old gramophone and some Victor Sylvester records. I put on a waltz. "Would you care to dance, madame?" I ask and bow. Guddie giggles My arm goes around her waist and my hand touches her bare skin between *choli* and *sari*. We dance. I dare not move my hand an inch either way. I want to say something, but all I can think of is 'Do you come here often?' so I don't. It is the quietest and politest waltz I have ever waltzed. At the end I bow again. Guddie curtsies. We both giggle.

I suggest a game of table tennis. I assume that Roop will follow us to the table tennis room at the far end of the Club, but she stays in the main room reading. I fix the net and look for the bats while Guddie dusts the table. She mentions she is going to Delhi soon to start university. "How soon?" I ask. "Next week," she says. Oh no, I think. "What are you reading?" "English," she says. I say that was one of my subjects at school. It is a pretty thin connection, but I want to find something we have in common other than badminton and Chopsticks. I want to spend more time with this girl. I imagine the possibility – remote, but not completely off the planet – that she and I might become lovers.

The table tennis goes to one game-all and Guddie suggests a decider. This could go either way, I think. If I win she might be impressed, but equally she might be resentful. If I lose I risk dishonour, though she could equally be pleased. I suggest a walk instead. In this gentle flirting, this skirting around each other, these first rehearsals for the possibility of a full performance, a shared walk ought to be less of a risk than a deciding game. "Where to?" Guddie asks, sounding doubtful. "We could walk along the river," I say. To my mind the Yamuna does not carry anything like the threat of the Yore, the Bease and the Seine, even with tales I have heard of freshwater crocodiles. "We cannot do that," she says. "Why not?" I ask. "We might be seen." She hesitates, then says, "We could walk to my father's farm."

We return to the main room. Roop has discarded the last copy of Punch and is looking through Good Housekeeping, which has a picture on the front cover of a slim blonde English housewife in twin set and pearls wearing a neat little pinafore and holding a pie. She looks nothing like Roop.

Guddie speaks to her sister in rapid Hindi or Punjabi, Roop says something back that sounds contradictory, Guddie responds dismissively, Roop says something churlish or shrewish, Guddie comes back with a few words that don't sound very nice, then turns to me, smiles and says, "That's good. Let's go." Roop apologizes to me: "There is something I must do at home." I am pleased that Guddie has asserted herself, though I have no idea if it is because she wants to spend more time with me or to get one over on her sister.

We leave the compound and walk along the river. On the other side boys from the bazaar are flying home-made kites made of balsa wood and brightly coloured tissue paper. A kingfisher swoops down to the river from a telegraph pole. "Let us sit here," I say. "Why?" asks Guddie. She is uneasy. "We can watch the kites and the kingfishers." "No no, we cannot do that." "Why not?" "People will see us." We are on the compound side of the river, well away from the bazaar, but I can appreciate we are treading a fine line. We walk on.

"Guddie, what will you do when you leave university?" I ask. "I will probably teach and then get married." "Will you keep working if you get married?" "Probably not." "Why not?" "My husband would not approve." She says this matter-of-factly. I am surprised. "Would you not like to keep working?" I ask. She thinks for a moment. "Yes," she says. "Well, then?" "James, you do not understand. I am eighteen. My father will not rest until I am married. My education is an interim thing. Instead of marrying me off immediately he has agreed to wait until I am twenty-one."

I realize that the picture I had of the possibility of a romance between us is diminishing rapidly, and it is no longer in colour but black and white. This girl's mind-set is elsewhere. But there is a week before she leaves.

Our path leads away from the river through wheat fields and cane fields to her father's farm. She calls to one of the farmworkers: *"Daddy-ji kahaan hai?"* The man salaams and gestures to where Rajinder Singh is supervising the cane harvest. I have the feeling we ae half-expected. Her father treats me with a mix of respect, condescension and caution. It must be difficult for him. I am the boss's bachelor son and entirely unsuitable as marriage material for his younger daughter. He instructs one of his men to bring fresh cane and Guddie shows me how to strip the bark with my teeth and chew the pith until all that is left is fibre, which she spits out onto the ground. Her teeth are white and sharp. She must have chewed and spat sugar cane many times. before. My teeth cringe on the tart pith. The three of us sit there stripping, chewing and spitting. Not much is said. This is some first date.

As soon as it is polite to leave Guddie and I set off back to the compound. Rajinder Singh assigns one of his farmworkers to accompany us, but out of deference the man lags a long way behind. "Guddie," I say, "let me have your phone number in Delhi." "Why?" she asks. 'Why?' What does she mean, 'Why?' Isn't it obvious? "Well, we could meet," I say. She is silent. It occurs to me there might be a turbaned, bearded young lawyer or doctor in Delhi who is a much better prospect for marriage than this unemployed, clean-shaven *Inglistani*.

At the gate to her garden we stop to say goodbye. This would be a good time for us to kiss, I think, but I am quite unable to make a move. Our hands touch briefly on top of the garden gate as we close it between us. Dusk is falling. I am in a Jane Austen novel. Tonight I will write a wistful entry in my diary about the unrealized moment. Then the bazaar music starts up.

Mera joota hai Japani …

It is the last time I see her, except in a dream. We are kissing on a bridge over the river when the duchess interrupts and I have to leave, though I remember to thank the duchess for the tea. I have a job as a ferryman, taking ex-pats from the compound to cut wheat in the fields and workers from the farm to dance the Gay Gordons at the Club. As day turns to night Guddie sneaks away from the palace to join me. We lie in my boat gazing up at the stars. As the boat drifts downriver the goddess Yamuna orders music to accompany us. A flunkey appears with *chapattis*, a flask of cane juice and a book of verse translated from the Hindustani.

A fisherman one time one very small fish caught …

"No, no!" I cry. "Bring me the Fitzgerald version!"

> Ah, Love! Could thou and I with Fate conspire
> To grasp thy sorry Scheme of Things entire,
> Would we not shatter it to bits – and then
> Re-mould it nearer to the Heart's Desire?

My lover lies in my arms. We are conspiring with Fate to remould the sorry scheme of things when a giant wave sweeps us upriver and overwhelms us. The boat capsizes, Guddie's heavy sari is saturated, she floats face down among lilies and lotus until a young Sikh in a crisp white suit and a magnificent golden turban appears and rescues her.

Distracted by loneliness and unrequited love I seek refuge in reading. Harold has a shelf-full of books on the subject of hunting in his study, including the thrilling and faintly preposterous Man Eaters of Kumaon by Colonel Jim Corbett, a man utterly without fear, I am led to believe. Colonel Corbett sits out at night to kill man-eating tigers by the light of the moon while consoling himself with the promise of a good cup of tea and a well-filled pipe when he gets home. He explains from the start that a man-eater

> is a tiger that has been compelled by the stress of circumstances beyond its control to adopt an alien diet.

The animal and I have much in common, then. I vow never to join one of Harold's hunting expeditions or to take another trip in Walter Butterworth's boat. Harold and Walter like to take a few beers to a birdwatching spot upriver and one weekend I am invited to join them. I am reluctant, but this might be an opportunity to face down my *potamophobia*. Fortunately the river level is low that day, but unfortunately it means that Harold and I have to wade in the shallows in places to push Walter's boat off the sandbanks. As we clamber back on the boat Walter mentions the common krait he saw swimming in our vicinity. This is a snake whose venom contains uncommon neurotoxins that bring on swift paralysis, respiratory failure and death. It occurs to me that it might have been compelled by the stress of circumstances to inject some of that venom in me. I didn't even know that snakes could swim. Next time I am invited to go boating I plead a common cold and stay home.

I find T.E. Lawrence's Seven Pillars of Wisdom in Harold's library. I glory in its exhilarating

> sweep of open places, taste of wide winds, morning freshness of the
> world-to-be, ideas inexpressible, whirling campaigns …

Lawrence and I are outsiders, in a furious struggle with ourselves and the world about us. "All men dream," he writes, "but not equally."

> Those who dream by night in the dusty recesses of their minds wake
> up in the day to find it was vanity, but the dreamers of the day are
> dangerous men, for they may act their dreams with open eyes …

I am the first kind of dreamer, a narcissist, with a vain desire to be the second, who would change the world. I identify with Bengali novelist Manik Bandopadyay, who writes of the struggles of victims of flooding as the monsoon rains fill the rivers until they spill their banks and inundate the low-lying lands of the Ganges Delta. Every year villagers perish, cattle drown, trees are uprooted and homes washed away as the river waters rise. The principal offender, as ever, is the feared and revered *Ganga Mata*, merciless, tender and terrible Mother, who takes life in one mood and sustains it in another. With her sister Yamuna she sustained the British Raj and the Moghul Empire, and long, long ago the legendary Vedic civilization from which the extraordinary mythology and lamentable caste system of Hindu India derive. The sisters brought mixed blessings.

I am surprised to find a gilt-and-leather-bound Introduction to the Vedas in Harold's shelves. How could a man who slaps his infant son around the head without compunction and slaughters duck, deer and peafowl for sport come to own such an illustrious cultural and spiritual tome alongside the bloody oeuvre of Jim Corbett? Does Harold have a hidden metaphysical side, or is the book an unopened gift from one of his BEC agents? That seems more likely.

I dip into its pages. The supreme god of the Vedas, I read, is *Vishnu* – all-pervading essence of things, master of the cosmos and so on, and yet loath to exert himself and, it has to be said, not very bright. He wakes up one morning and thinks to measure the extent of his domain, but rather than get out of bed he stretches out his left leg. He stretches it so far that his big toe pierces a hole in the fabric of the universe. What happens next must come as something of a surprise, because through this hole pour the headwaters of the Himalayas in the form of two mighty goddess-rivers, the Ganga and Yamuna, who join together and course a thousand miles across the plains to create the Causal Ocean.

I want to believe that wading in the waters of the Yamuna to push Walter's boat off the sandbanks has served to wash away some of my fears and frustrations. The logic of the myth of Vishnu's toe is that given the *descent* of the goddesses from the celestial Himalayas to the cradle of the plains they must be the agents of *ascent* too, from earth to heaven. Immersing oneself in either river ought therefore to be a short cut to peace and the extinction of pain.

It hasn't worked out that way for me. I feel drained. I have dallied, dawdled and idled in India. I have pretended, procrastinated, piddled about, played mahjong and tennis, played by the rules, danced, loved, lusted, lost, pandered to the memsahibs, ordered chota pegs of whisky and read every weevil-ridden copy of Women's Weekly and the Illustrated London News. I consider now whether I have gathered the tithes I was owed. I have asserted my right to a family life, of a kind, and Harold has been obliged to provide it, to a point, but I still do not think of myself as having anything other than an associate role in the family Sutcliffe.

I decide it is time to add value to my presence in India. "I'm thinking of going to Delhi or Yamunanagar to look for a job," I announce one evening at dinner. Mother is dismayed. "Oh dear, James. Must you?" Does that mean she will miss me, I wonder. I hadn't allowed for that. "Without you," she says, "we will be one short of an eightsome for Scottish country dancing." Vishnu help me, but I actually feel guilty. "It just doesn't work with seven," she says. Oh no, I have hurt her again.

I can see that Harold would rather my mother had no more reasons for being unhappy than she already has – the state of the plumbing, the laziness of the guards, the cook's air of insolence, the mali's incompetence, the lack of a decent department store in Ludhiana, the list goes on – so he offers to find me a job at the mill. "No no, Harold," I say. "I have to fend for myself." But perhaps he still thinks he owes me and this will finally settle our account, so I temporize. "Only if there is something lowly," I say, "and that I do not take anyone else's job. I am happy to act as a coolie or a clerk."

If T.E. Lawrence can resign his commission and sign on as an apprentice aircraftman as a way of thumbing his nose at the establishment, I think, I can do something similar. Anything that will give my days structure and purpose while involving the exercise of as little authority and responsibility as possible. I know – *ti hypocrisia!* – I want to show solidarity with the masses while continuing to have my shoes cleaned and my bath run. "I'll run my own bath," I insist, but Devi Das makes a point of getting there before me.

Harold's personnel manager, Hallam Purdy, invites me to dinner. Hallam is the only bachelor on the senior staff at the mill, the kind that the married men, with a mixture of envy and condescension, call 'confirmed'. "Meet our confirmed bachelor Hallam Purdy, lucky man, ho ho." Hallam is an amateur artist who came out to India in the thirties to paint, but when war broke out and the Chandrapore mill was working round the clock producing clothing for the Indian army he applied for a temporary job supervising the night shift, enjoyed the perks, was offered a day job and moved onto the permanent payroll. Now he hires and fires people and pays lip service to government policy on Indianization, the gradual replacement of European staff by Indian nationals. It is a policy that seems not to apply to me.

Before dinner Hallam shows me his paintings. There are views of the snow-capped Himalayas as seen from the foothills of Dharamsala and Simla, and studies of half-naked men working the night shift at the mill. Sometimes he paints men entirely naked after they have discarded their *dhotis* in the hot conditions. I think he may have used artistic licence for these paintings, but I am too inhibited to ask. Instead I remark on his technique, which mainly consists of the application of thick swipes of paint with a palette knife. "Bold," I say. "Expressive." Crude, I think. Banal. I think if Lydia were here she would purse her lips and change the subject.

After Hallam's bearer has taken the port away and brought out the brandy Hallam offers me a job as a general trainee at a notional salary of seventy-five rupees a month. I gratefully accept.

And so begins my apprenticeship in the woollen trade. Hallam assigns me a desk in his outer office and takes evident pleasure in taking me under his wing. Perhaps I am the son he will never have. He might even be my idealized father.

"Come, James," he announces. "It is time for your induction." We begin in the Wool Store. It is very quiet in the Wool Store. All I can hear is the intermittent flap-flapping of pigeons that are roosting in the roof. "See those six-hundred pound bales of wool?" says Hallam. "Big bales," I say. Well, they are. "Feel the raw wool." He offers me a sample. "Raw wool contains up to fifty per cent grease and dirt." "As much as that?" I ask, supposing it must be a lot. "Yes, indeed," says my guide. "So first it must be cleaned." "There's a lot to be cleaned," I say. Well, there is. Hallam strides ahead. "Off to the Scouring Shed. Our little adventure continues!

"See the overhead lattice feeding wool to the scouring bowls?" "Big scouring bowls," I say, attempting to look into the first one. "Keep well away, dear boy! Extremely acidic." "Oops!" I say. "Now squeezy rollers deliver the wool to a second bowl, and a harrow takes it to a third and fourth for rinsing." "That's a lot of rinsing," I say. Oh dear, it's time I started varying my responses. "Smells of hot wet sheep in here," I venture. "Indeed it does!" says Hallam. "Any questions so far?" I cannot think of any. It all seems very straightforward. "In that case on to the Drying Ovens!" he exclaims.

"Hot in here, eh?" Hallam is taking a mild delight in my discomfort. A workman greets him: "*Salaam, Sahib!*" "*Salaam!*" says Hallam. He strides ahead. "After drying, the wool is baled again and taken for dyeing or blending. Which route shall we take, I wonder." I have no preference. "The Dyehouses, I think," he says. "Whatever you say, skipper," I respond. He beams.

The Dyehouses are the sheds from hell. "What are those crashes?" I ask. "You'll have to speak up, dear boy! Those are the power winches!" "That high-pitched humming?" "The hydro extractors!" "The rattling?" I can hear loud rattling. Wooden carts full of hot, heavy yarn are being hauled by hand over the concrete floor. The coolies in the Dyehouse are clad only in their *dhotis*. "Hot in here, eh, James? Too hot for the men to wear much, eh?" "Even nastier and noisier than the Scouring Sheds," I say. Oh. That sounded worse than I intended. I wonder idly what it would be like to be tipped into in a vat of dyehouse acid. Would it be better or worse than being sliced by the sword of a Sikh ex-serviceman intent on taking revenge for a daughter disgraced? "Are we done here, James?" shouts Hallam. "I think so!" I cry, having no better idea. "Then on to Blending!" he yells.

"Salaam, Sahib." *"Salaam."* "A bit quieter here, eh?. What do you think so far, James?" "Jolly interesting, Hallam." It might have been more interesting, I think, if the conditions hadn't been so oppressive. "I knew you would take to it," says Hallam. "The dyed wool and waste arrive here in batches, then the blend components are taken via a series of Fearnaught rollers to the pneumatic chutes, where they fall ready-blended to the ground." We go over to watch. "As well-mixed as a cocktail at the Club, eh? Ha ha!" I laugh at his little joke. "Ha ha!" "The *shovel-wallahs* are loading the blends into a machine that oils them with an atomised spray ready for bagging." *"Salaam, Sahib."* *"Salaam."* He puts a hand on my shoulder to steer me. "On to Carding, young man!"

"Carding?" I ask, supposing that a renewed show of interest might be in order. "A mechanical disentangling process that aligns the fibres ready for spinning!" It is noisy in Carding and he has to shout, but I can see he is enjoying himself and doesn't mind in the least. "The yarn is fed to scribbling cylinders surmounted by smaller rollers that strip and feed the parent cylinder, causing the stock to be opened and mixed ready for slubbing!" "Slubbing?" I realize that all I need to do is repeat the last thing he says. "Slubbing extends the slivers of wool and gives them a twist! You're learning fast, James!" I'm not sure I am, but never mind. "Next, Combing!" "Combing?"

"A complex and delicate process that combs the carded fibres for woollen or worsted!" The metallic chatter of the Combing process is as noisy as Carding, so I decide not to ask about the complex and delicate process of Combing. "On to Spinning!

"A relatively simple process, as you can see. Rollers draw off the slubbing, then the feed stops and the carriage continues, reducing the slubbing further." The carriage stops, clank, and the spindles whir, imposing a twist. I can just about follow this. "You will have heard more whirring and clanking here than clattering, eh?" says Hallam. I have heard. He might be mildly disappointed that I seem to be more interested in the sounds things make than the function of the things making the sounds, which is what interests him, but he doesn't show it. "The fallers run on the spinning worm and the process repeats itself, over and over. Get the idea?" "Oh yes," I say, "I think so." I am thinking of all the stuff that repeats in life, over and over, and produces more of the same, but a lot less productively than here.

"Good-oh, you're doing well, James!" "What next?" I ask, hoping we are nearly done. "Good question! Winding and Warping!

"The bobbins are for the weft, the cheeses for the warp. For Warping, the cheeses are placed on pegs of creel – I promise you, I am not making this up, ha ha!" "Ha ha!" "Then the ends drawn through sley, wound into lengths, taken off to a beam and hielded." I decide not to ask about cheeses, creels or hielding. "The yarn is now ready to go to the looms!" he exclaims. "We are about to enter the unceasing, pounding heart of the mill!" He is, I see, thrilled.

It is very, very noisy in the Weaving Shed. "If you think that every process you have seen so far is loud – sorry, can't hear you, you'll have to shout!" There is not so much clanking and clattering here as rattling, clunking, clanging and banging. "So noisy that the weavers have to communicate in weavers' mime! You have heard of weavers' mime?" "Er, yes, I think so!" The men are mostly barefoot, clad only in shorts and vests, perspiring in the heat. They mime to their colleagues. "You'll have noticed that the men here are younger than the men in the Dyehouse!" yells Hallam. I hadn't noticed. "The older men prefer the heat and humidity of the Dyehouse to the sound of the looms!" The noise is unnerving. "The younger men prefer the Weaving Sheds because they are cleaner!" "The sheds or the men?" I ask. "Both!" says Hallam. "Ha ha!" He likes my little joke. I watch the shuttles speeding the weft back and forth across alternating threads of the warp. This is a little more interesting. I can see something that looks like a product. "What are those clicks and clacks?" I ask. "Those are the light looms! The thunks and thonks are the heavy looms! That bang and biff you hear is the carriage as it hammers the weft tight to the cloth between each pass of the shuttle!" I take his dual descriptions of sound and purpose as evidence of some progress in our relationship. I look around. All I can see is line upon line of looms. "How many looms are there here, Hallam?" "Seven hundred, James!" He looks as proud as if they were his. "Seven hundred?" I say. I am impressed. "The box looms are for fancy weaves, the plain looms for twill!" I'm not sure of the significance of this, but acknowledge it nonetheless: "Twill, eh?" A weaver calls to Hallam, *"Salaam, Sah ib!"* as we pass. *"Salaam!"* shouts Hallam. I cannot decide if the men really like him or are simply being respectful. He asks me if I have seen enough. "Thank you, Hallam, I think so." "At least for now, eh? Ha ha!"

Outside it is cooler and quieter. "The supervisors you saw ranging the weaving sheds are on the lookout for faults. Broken warps have to be mended by hand before they show up as faults in the cloth. A weaver's bonus is affected if he lets too many faults through." We enter another building. "And finally," he says, "Finishing." I sigh inwardly. I thought we had finished.

"What is that swishing sound?" I ask. "Those are the scouring dollies cleaning the greasy pieces." "The mumbling?" "Milling machines." He may be getting tired of this game, but he indulges me. "And here they are Tentering, a relatively quiet procedure, I'm afraid!" "Tentering?" I am back on track. "Setting the warp and weft at right angles and stretching the cloth so that it dries evenly. Then away it goes for drying and cropping."

"That high-pitched whirring?" I am off again, making an effort. "What you hear are the cropping blades." I am conducted through brushing, pressing, winding, cutting and burling. I intervene at intervals: "Brushing?" "Burling?" "Burling is a matter of removing knots, lumps or slubs in the cloth. The finished product has to be perfect, you know. We have a reputation for quality here." He shows me examples of knots, lumps and slubs. I examine them carefully and comment on their similarities and differences. It seems the right thing to do, as we are getting to the end.

"Good morning, Sahib." "Good morning, Devi Lal. Devi Lal is responsible for inspection, measuring, order filling, packing and despatch." Devi Lal accompanies us through each of these processes and explains his responsibilities at some length.

"That's about it, James," says Hallam. I am hoping it is. "Back to Admin for a cup of *char,* eh?" "Yes!" I respond. "A cup of *char* would go down a treat!"

"Good morning, Sahib." "Good morning, Moti Lal." It is a relief to be back in Admin, where the only sounds to be heard are the whump-whump of ceiling-mounted *punkahs,* the distant chit-chat of typewriters and the occasional raised voice in the distance as a *sweeper, chowkidar* or *char-wallah* is cursed by an office *chaprassi.* .

"Personally," says Hallam as we take our tea, "I have learnt to look at a bale of cloth in a tailor's in Ludhiana and feel something akin to humility." I respond that I will never again take a suit made by the local *dherzi* for granted. It is absolutely the right thing to say. "Good man," says Hallam. "I think you are ready to join us."

I do not manage to bring much of my classical education into my work as a trainee executive in the woollen trade, other than doing a certain amount of furtive reading – mostly turgid translations of the Vedas that I keep in a pile of technical manuals on my desk for times I am bored, which is often. My heart is elsewhere. What is Guddie up to in Delhi? Will Lydia ever write? How often has Polly had sexual intercourse at Oxford?

Now and again to while away the time I take a walk round the mill in a kind of trance, affecting to inspect the work of scourers, dyers, blenders, carders, combers, weavers and warpers without much idea of what they are doing and with nothing much to say to them other than '*accha*' and 'jolly good!'

"*Salaam, Sahib!*" "*Salaam!*" I receive and reciprocate the greetings of men doing real work and earning a real if meagre living. The mill is so big I can do a tour like this every day of the week and never take the same route twice. In the end I can no longer keep up any pretence to myself that I am gainfully employed, although I seem to have convinced Harold and Hallam, for a few weeks into my apprenticeship Harold invites me on a shooting expedition and Hallam asks me to dinner again.

Over our first glass of port I foolishly raise the subject of labour relations. I have been reading Charlotte Brontë's Shirley. Hallam knows the book. Brontë writes of trouble in a Yorkshire mill town against a backdrop of the owner's battles with his employees over the introduction of labour-saving machinery. Hallam remembers his days under the Raj, when that kind of thing happened with barely a murmur from the workers. Now he has to negotiate agreements with their representatives, who have recently registered a dispute. Hallam casually uses the word Luddite in the context of the dispute at the mill. "Which mill?" I ask. "Brontë's or yours?" "Both," he says. I take exception to this. "Their motives are understandable," I say. "What about the means they choose?" queries Hallam. "Forgivable," I say. Hallam frowns. "Which mill are we talking about?" he asks. "Both," I reply. "Ned Ludd was an idiot and an idler," says Hallam. He gestures to his bearer, Sham Lal, to bring out the brandy. "What is an owner supposed to do if his mill is running deep into debt?" he asks. I defend Brontë's Luddites. "The owner had already laid off a large number of workers and he was awaiting delivery of machines that would allow him to lay off even more," I say. And I take a risk. "Is this not what is happening here? You are exploiting honest workers who can barely afford to feed their families?"

"No, James!" says Hallam. He is a bit tiddly too. "They are using the loss of their jobs as an excuse for upsetting the rest of the community and inciting violence!" "Rubbish, Hallam!" I cry, surprising myself. "This is really about the class war, is it not?" "Not at all!" cries Hallam. He is upset. I should leave it at that, I know, but I can't. "Your privileges are leading you to defend a system that as an impoverished artist you used to despise!" I say. I may have drunk a little too much.

Hallam surprises me by deciding not to respond and going back to the book. "Actually Shirley is more about the role of women in society," he says. "The mill stuff is only background for showing Shirley as an independent young woman at odds with the times." He has shifted the argument sideways and I cannot disagree, so I go off at a tangent too. "You are a talented painter, Hallam," I say. "What happened?" I realize I may sound righteous and bumptious, but I can't help it. Hallam's voice rises an octave and his eyes begin to protrude. Sham Lal takes away the port and brandy and with the merest hint of a disapproving look leaves us to it. Hallam, turning sharply, shouts, *"Yahan ao!,* come back!", makes a wild gesture in Sham Lal's direction and falls off his chair. I realize that if I wish to earn more than seventy-five rupees a month and to be reconciled with my idealized father I should make an attempt to save the situation, so I laugh and say it was all a joke. I help him up, he puts an arm round my shoulder and says, "Actually there is some truth in what you say." He shouts after his bearer, *"Bohut khed hai,* Sham Lal! Very sorry!"

Some time later I learn what everyone in the compound seems to know but no-one ever mentions – some out of antipathy and some, I suppose, delicacy – that there is more to Hallam and Sham Lal's twenty-year relationship than first appears.

I make my way back to The Sheiling. What I must do now, I tell myself, is reach some sort of rapprochement with the *Burra Sahib*, Harold, even if that means taking an interest in woollen manufacture, labour relations and matters of finance. I go unsteadily down to the river and pray to the goddess Yamuna for guidance.

φ

Chapter 18
Guns of Chandrapore

HAVING VOWED OUT OF PRINCIPLE never to go on *shikar*, I am flattered when Harold invites me and surprise myself by agreeing. I know that he chooses his hunting companions carefully. Is he thinking of luring me from academia or the labour exchange into the higher echelons of BEC? Perhaps he sees his stepson and blood-son competing over the role of *Burra Sahib* of the Sutcliffe dynasty when he retires or dies.

Harold demonstrates the operation of the twin triggers of a twelve-bore and encourages me to take pot-shots at tin cans in the garden. I am giving in to the only reality on offer. It is not a question of enjoying it, I tell myself, but of dealing with it manfully. I speculate that being a man is not about emotional indulgence or giving in to gloom or to feelings of inadequacy, but about dealing with things – not brutally or vaingloriously, but as I might now say, modestly and cheerfully.

Harold leads me to the wool store to aim a .22 rifle at pigeons roosting in the roof. The pigeons are a nuisance, he says. Their shit is acidic and bad for the wool. Well, we can't have that. My .22 slugs leave little holes in the corrugated iron roof and sometimes in the birds themselves. I am not a good shot, but the targets perched in the rafters are practically stationary and to my shame – another of the emotional states I am learning to deal with manfully – I kill several birds. I justify this as best I can by the fact that those we retrieve go to Ashi for the pot and any that are excess to requirements are shared among the servants. Yet some wounded birds hide among the bales and if they are not retrieved quickly will die a lonely death. I try not to identify with them. That is not what a man does.

I am unconvincing as a killer. I will eat the meat readily enough, but take no delight in providing it. I cannot decide if it is better to be hypocritical and emotionally distant from death, as I am, or to enjoy the pathological pleasure of dealing directly in it, like Harold.

He wakes me at four in the morning to join his diehard friends, known collectively as 'the guns'. We drive north on unlit roads. The only other traffic at this time is the occasional bullock cart, its driver asleep under a blanket as the animal plods on, dewlap flapping, following the tarmac by the light of the moon.

The headlights of our vehicle sweep the verge. Suddenly the eyes of a rabbit reflect the light back. Harold stops the vehicle and the animal sits mesmerised for a moment, time enough for one of the guns to jump out, ram a couple of cartridges into his 12-bore and blast the animal with both barrels. He retrieves the carcass, sees that it is riddled with inedible lead and tosses it aside. Deal with it, James.

After an hour or so we turn off the tarmac onto a dried earth track, which we follow for a mile or so to our rendezvous with the local *shikari*. Harbans Lal makes a living shooting duck and small game with a home-made muzzle-loading shotgun and hiring himself and his *shikar wallahs* out for the day to people like Harold. We walk through marshland with Harbans Lal leading the way. Sometimes he stops and gestures for silence. There is a faint but intense sound in the distance. It is cold now, a few moments before dawn. The sound grows louder as we wade towards it through pools of marsh water. I am reminded that my limnophobia is an aversion not only to what might be swimming on the surface but also to what might lie in wait underneath.

We reach harder ground and are allocated to a line of dried mud-and-reed hides. First light comes to the sky. We wait in the hides. As the light reaches the ground I can make out a large expanse of wetland in which many hundreds, perhaps thousands, of live shapes are gathered, each one adding to the general chatter that spreads over the water. They are wild duck preparing for a dawn take-off.

The sun appears on the horizon, weakly yellow. I grip my gun and wait for something to happen. The birds are restless. Suddenly there is a loud flapping as the first bird takes off and a dozen or more follow. I am startled at how close above us they fly. They are followed by more and more oblivious birds flying directly overhead to be met by a barrage of shot. I see Harold single out a bird, follow it and shoot it cleanly. Then he picks out another, drops it with his second barrel, quickly reloads and begins aiming and firing again. Harbans Lal congratulates him. *"Shabash, Sahib!"* It is noisy and confusing. I realize I am supposed to join in , so I point my 12-bore at the sky and loose off both barrels simultaneously. Well, that is my intention. In fact nothing happens because I have left the safety catches on. I knock them off, fire at the last bird and miss by some distance.

"The knack," says Harold quietly, "is knowing where to aim. It is a matter of calculating how far in front of the bird you should lead. It is no use following the flight. You must lead the bird on, as it were, with the end of your gun. And don't stop the second you pull the trigger, but feel the movement continuing." This is about the most Harold has ever said to me. He is more enthused by this exercise than by anything else I have seen him enthused by, with the possible exception of Ashi's mutton curry. "How far in front should you lead?" I ask, feigning interest. "That depends on how fast the bird is flying. It depends on how high the bird is. It depends on whether it is flying towards you or away from you or at an angle. Experience will tell you." So I have to miss or maim a few dozen birds before I learn to kill one outright. "Allow a couple of lengths for every ten yards of range to start with and work from there." Hm, I think. I might have neither the interest nor the inclination.

Harbans Lal and his shikar wallahs wade thigh-deep into the water to retrieve fallen birds. They won't get me doing that. One bird that was wounded and fell into the lake is trying to paddle away. Another with a broken wing tries to evade capture by hiding in a clump of weeds. It is found by a shikar wallah, who kills it by hammering its head with the thick stick he carries.

There is a lull. The rest of the birds on the lake are safe at a distance and will not make the mistake of flying over the source of all this commotion. Suddenly Harbans Lal gestures at us to take cover again. He has seen a flock of geese coming in to the lake in a long V-formation. They are flying towards the centre of our line of guns, totally unaware of the violence and havoc that awaits them. As soon as they are within range Harold and the others raise their guns, pick out individual birds, lead-follow and fire. One bird drops straight to the ground; its death is instantaneous. The flight of another falters and the rest of the flock passes. The wounded bird flaps its wings furiously, trying to catch up with the others. For a few seconds it manages to hold height, but then it drops abruptly, wings flapping feebly, and hits the water hard. A shikar wallah leaps into the lake and paddles towards it, but the bird edges away. The man wades after it, but the bird keeps just out of reach, even though one of its wings is trailing in the lake and blood is oozing from its chest and colouring the water. The bird has no strength. Gradually its head sinks and the man, water up to his waist, grabs a trailing wing. Strangely I think of my mother in the North Sea trying either to drown me or teach me to swim. There is a brief struggle and the bird dies in his hands.

When we are back on the track where the cars are parked, the shikar wallahs lie the birds in a line on the verge and the guns take photographs of each other alongside the kill, grinning and grasping their shotguns. This is without merit, I think, and I am a part of it.

Harold gives Harbans Lal ten rupees and one of the geese. *"Accha, Sahib, namaste,"* says Harbans Lal, putting his hands together in thanks. Harold gives a duck to each of the helpers. Each man salaams in silent salute and inclines his head gratefully.

There is a cry. One of the younger shikar wallahs has found a leech on his leg. No-one mentioned leeches as one of the perks of wading in water. There was the remote possibility of coming across a tiger that swam, or a snake or a freshwater crocodile, or catching typhoid or dysentery, but leeches? The slimy black slug attached to the fleshy part of the man's calf is helping itself to his bodily fluids. Frantically he tries to knock it off. *"Aisa mat' karo!"* shouts Harbans Lal, but the man in a panic grasps the engorged animal between his thumb and forefinger and yanks it off, tearing his skin so that the wound bleeds profusely. It is the revenge of the waters. I imagine there are *Naiads* in residence here, pitiless spirits exacting a price for every unwarranted entry into their once-peaceful domain.

A first-aid kit is found and the shikar wallah's wound is treated. Harold suggests we check ourselves. He lights a cigarette and tells me to take off my boots and socks slowly. He examines my feet and ankles, cigarette ready to be held against anything alien. "If you are lucky they will react to the heat," he says, "curl up and drop off, leaving nothing but a hole in your skin so small it will hardly bleed." "And if I am not lucky?" I ask. "It will be a bigger hole," he says without irony.

I am almost disappointed to find that I have escaped the attention of these guardians of the marshes, as I planned on affecting a certain insouciance when showing Mother and Rupert the wound.

This is but the start of our Boys' Own weekend. We drive north for another two hours until we reach a *dak bungalow* at the edge of the forest. We are there to seek bigger game, announces Harold. "Wild boar, chital," he says, "perhaps a tiger or a leopard." Hang on. This is not what I signed up for. I signed up for ducks.

Since reading Man Eaters of Kumaon I have been stalked in the night by an animal that looks like a cross between Lydia and a creature that has been hungry for too long. The only desire of this starving carnivore is to devour me. I attempt to shoot it, but my rifle will only fire slow-motion bullets that fall in an arc to the ground some way short of their target. The dream usually fades at this point, but one night the creature continues towards me and takes on the face of my mother. I fight her off, then wake, perspiring with fear and impotent rage.

At the dak bungalow we learn that the watchman's dog was taken by a leopard the previous night. Not a bark or a whimper disturbed the watchman's sleep. The local shikari shows us the pug marks and a spot of dried blood in the dust. I am astonished that the guns take this news with only the mildest of tut-tuttings and shaking of heads. It is agreed that the shikari will send out a tracker in the morning to follow the trail and that the still-trembling watchman will be compensated for the loss of his faithful companion. Now, what's for supper?

Over *curry, dal* and *chapattis* prepared by the bungalow staff the guns talk of tigers and leopards. "Remember the man-eater in Nepal that was responsible for four hundred people?" Responsible? I don't think so. "And the pair in Gharwal that killed over five hundred between them?" "No no, it was no more than three hundred." Not so bad, then. The guns speculate about the animal that took the watchman's dog. Leopards are normally shy of humans, the guns agree. There is that qualification again: snakes usually stay out of the way; crocodiles keep their distance most of the time. What they are saying is that these felines of the forest, *Panthera pardus*, get over their shyness on occasion and kill people.

Why would one have come so close? It could be old, injured, sick, cubs to feed, broken teeth. One wag says, "At least it took the watchman's dog and not the watchman!" Another: "This time, ha ha!" If leopards are desperate for food, I learn, they will eat anything, from insects to buffalo. It does not take me long to work out that every one of us present comes into this category. A trainee executive my size might stave off a leopard's hunger for a week. "We should go after it or it might end up killing goats and cattle," said Harold. "Or people," I say. I know my Corbett. "It could turn into a man-eater." The guns laugh. Someone says there hasn't been a man-eater in the area for years. Another of those statements that serves no useful purpose. I am more concerned than ever. *Every man-eater has to eat its first man*, and that could be me. What if there were a potential man-eater out there watching this dog-eater and picking up tips? If it comes to defending myself I have no confidence that my aim would be good enough to kill a leaping animal in mid-air with a single shot, as the Colonel claims to have done on more than one occasion. Corbett Sahib describes tigers and leopards as prodigious leapers. I would not trust my aim if the animal were seated five feet away licking its paws. I might admit to the guns to being no great shot, but I cannot admit to fear. Caught between *Charybdis* and *Scylla* again: dead if I miss, cut dead if I confess.

In the morning we check our killing equipment and set off in single file followed by a legion of beaters. I have decided to load one barrel of my 12-bore with number 4 shot for small game and the other barrel with a single ball in case of ... well, in case. No-one else seems to be too concerned about how long it would take to reload if they missed with both barrels and a beast with big teeth and claws were heading for them at speed. They would not have the benefit of a slow-motion replay in which to reload and take aim.

We track quietly through the forest. Try not to be the villager last in line as you make your way home at the end of the day, advises Corbett, because more often than not the last in line will be the first to be taken. And often so silently – seized by the throat, no time to cry out – that they might not be missed until the others get home. I wonder if the villagers take it in turn or draw lots to be the last in line, or is it taken for granted that the last will always be the oldest and slowest and least likely to be missed?

I start our expedition near the front of the file, but then think I should not be too near the front in case we come across something that has to be dealt with, so I drop back gradually and unostentatiously, I hope, to the middle.

The tracker follows the pug marks of the leopard to a narrow track leading deep into the forest, where he finds a trace of blood. He indicates something to the shikari, who whispers to Harold, who tells the rest of us quietly, "He changed his grip." It could still be a she, I think. Equally as vicious, perhaps more so if she has been crossed in love or has a family to feed. I tread on a dry stick. The shikari puts a finger to his lips. I must have missed page one of the How to be a Man manual: 'Do Not Tread on Dry Sticks in the Forest'. A killer could be listening. We tiptoe along the track. I try hard to be invisible, which is fairly pointless.

The trail of blood stops. The shikari and his tracker go some way down the track, but find nothing, so we fan out on both sides of the trail and continue searching. Then the watchman's dog is found. Or rather its remains. It was quite a small dog. "Not much of a meal for a leopard," says Harold. "He'll still be peckish." Thank you for that, Harold. The tracker shuffles around the remains of the dog in ever-increasing arcs looking for signs of a peckish leopard, but finds none. We have the bones of the prey, but no sign of the predator.

It is hot. We break for a smoke in the shade. A small bird perches on a branch nearby. "Rosy minivet," says Harold. Good heavens, he is enjoying himself. He is birdwatching, while I am still looking out for anything with four legs and large incisors. Perhaps the creature has been wounded. It has one eye and a limp, and like the *Cyclops* lives for itself, without laws, its cave strewn with the bones of goats and the remains of babes, limbs torn, bloody, still warm. An animal that crunches human bones and laps the blood of a child will be learning to esteem human flesh above all others. Young flesh. Like mine, say.

We move on and reach a clearing. Harold and the shikari range the guns along the top edge of the clearing and tell us we are beating for chital and sambur. I am posted to the far end of the line, so that the worst I can do is shoot the person next down the line rather than one either side. I acknowledge the logic of this and set myself up behind a tree, insert number 4 shot in both barrels and quietly snap my shotgun shut – an impossible thing to do quietly, I discover.

I am now in a quandary. I have made a sound that could have given me away. I hear the beaters in the distance. I freeze and focus on the forest at the far side of the clearing. I even try not to blink, which is about as silly as you can get. Then the thought occurs to me: what if our one-eyed dog-eater has seen me getting here in the first place? After all, I had to move to get here in order to be able to stand still now. Another thought: it might be about to leap on me from above. I look up. Now I have moved again. I look back across the clearing. I can hear the beaters getting nearer. I strain to detect any sign of movement in the forest at the other side of the clearing, and to either side, and behind me. Yet another thought: which of the two barrels of my double-barrelled shotgun holds the single bloody ball? I check: it is neither. I had put number 4 in both. Okay, then which of the two triggers is for which bloody barrel? I can't remember. I will have to pull both triggers, but then I will have nothing left if, as seems likely, I miss. I check which of the four or five pockets of my hunting jacket holds the cartridge with the ball. It is the bottom left. Should it be the top right? Or would the top left be better? I spend precious seconds shifting cartridges between pockets and trying to remember where the fuck I put them. What is that rustling sound? Have I disturbed a krait or a cobra? I had forgotten about snakes. I can hear individual beaters now – shouting, banging cans, hitting trees. There is a noise not far behind me that sounds like a jeep in second gear. The beaters break through the forest and into the clearing. No game appears, which is a relief. And none of the beaters gets accidentally shot. I move my thumb to put the safety catch on. It is already on. Is this a sign of a subconscious death wish or simple stupidity? What if the animal had been coming for me and I had fired? Click, nothing. Would it be better to die from the bite of a snake or from the jaws of a leopard? An injection of venom leading to paralysis, respiratory failure and cardiac arrest, or hook-like claws tearing at my back, fangs sinking into my throat and my jugular vein irreparably severed? Neurotoxins or throttling? The venom, I think. Harold might have an antidote in his first-aid kit.

The guns are disappointed at the lack of something to shoot at. I am thinking it is time to go home. "I hadn't realized there was a road back there," I say to Harold. "Did you hear that jeep going up the hill?" "There's no road there," he says. "Only more forest. What you heard was a tiger complaining as he moved off." Or she, I think. "We must have disturbed him." Or her, I think. "Oh," I say. And again, "Oh."

I console myself with the thought that if I were to be eaten by a tiger I would go to Hindu heaven, even as an outsider or a sinner. The Vedas tell of a serial wrongdoer *Vahika*, who is killed by a tiger in the forest. His soul arrives before *Yama*, Lord of Death, to be judged, but is found to have no compensating virtues, so his soul is sent off to hell while the body is left to be picked over by vultures. One of the vultures flies away with a foot bone, is pursued by a rival and in the ensuing fight the bone drops into the Ganges. Drama. The river, being holy, confers instant salvation on the owner of the bone, leaving Lord Yama with a huge ethical and reputational dilemma, because as Ruler of the Departed he has already sent the soul of the owner to hell. What should he do? He despatches a celestial chariot to intercept the soul of Vahika and divert it to heaven. The chariot arrives in the nick of time.

This strikes me as a rather chancy a way of achieving redemption and deliverance, but I am learning that anything is possible if a holy river is involved. I vow to stipulate in my will that I should be cremated, preferably at Varanasi or Allahabad, and my ashes scattered in the Ganga or the Yamuna, or in both if it increased my chances.

Back in Chandrapore Mother is arranging to take Rupert out of prep school in the hills of Simla and leave him in the boarding school she has found for him in the backwoods of Yorkshire. She offers to pay my fare on the boat if I will help keep Rupert amused. She is out of practice at that sort of thing, having delegated responsibility for her first two children to a succession of grandmothers, sisters-in-law and ex-husband's second wives, and in the case of the third to nursemaids, servants and preparatory school matrons. Having finally consigned my fantasies of family life in India to a snake-ridden midden at the bottom of the garden, I have no hesitation in accepting her offer.

I speculate that Harold will be relieved to be rid of the three of us. He seems to have given up any idea of grooming me for a corporate career or to become a fully-fledged member of the guns. And he and Mother have not been getting on well of late. There have been rumours of illicit liaisons in the senior staff compound and it is having a generally unsettling effect. Plumtree Memsahib is no longer inviting Priestly Memsahib to her canasta mornings, this year's amateur theatricals have been cancelled and Harold has postponed a longstanding shikar party – just as well, people are saying, given that Plumtree and Priestly Sahibs would have been armed to the teeth.

My main reservation about leaving Chandrapore is the prospect of spending almost three weeks at sea. Dominion over life and death in the oceans is a privilege the gods have long reserved for themselves. Will they allow us through Suez? Britain recently exploded a thermonuclear bomb in the Pacific and the USSR has launched an artificial satellite in orbit round the earth. The gods might task *Nemesis* to track our boat and seek any opportunity – a tidal wave in the Red Sea, a bomb in the souk at Port Said – to wreak retribution for our imperial pretensions. Oh, heck. More paranoia to add to my fears and obsessions.

Mother supervises the packing of cases and trunks, compiles a checklist of everything the servants have to do in her absence and arranges for Rupert to join us from Simla. He is happy to be home again until his *ayah*, Rajani, gently and tearfully reminds him that he has to leave again, and this time it could be forever. I try to reassure Rupert that what he is going through is standard procedure for the colonial classes, he isn't being punished, but he doesn't quite get the point and nor, frankly, do I.

Kumar Singh drives us to Delhi for the train to Bombay, leaving Harold to take pot-shots at pigeons in the wool store and – well, the monsoon is imminent and anything could happen – share a Singapore Sling or two with one of the memsahibs who has elected to stay behind on the plains. No-one is above suspicion at this time of year. The rains will bring the plains-stayers relief from the tension and unbearable heat. It has been extremely humid of late.

Mother is not well. She is carsick and trainsick, and upset by the rumours of goings-on in Chandrapore. Rupert is unhappy. He is leaving behind everything and everyone he knows; not least his ayah who has looked after him since infancy. And as a paranoid, obsessive, hallucinatory thalassaphobic about to embark on his first-ever voyage, I am anxious. I pray to *Poseidon*, Overlord of the Sea, and to *Aeolus*, King of the Winds, to grant us safe passage for our few remaining virtues and please to ignore our multiple sins.

φ

Chapter 19
The Curse of Kunti

WE ARE PROPOSITIONED BY A BEGGAR in Bombay Central Station – not a novel experience, but in a sudden premonition I see this man as the messenger of death. I try to erase the thought from my mind, but it will not go away.

He is an elderly man with one leg, blackened teeth and half an eye. One hand wields a crutch, the other a tin can containing a few annas. *"Baksheesh, Memsahib,"* he mumbles to Mother as he rattles his can. *"Ar jao!"* says Mother reflexively. The man tugs at my sleeve. *"Sahib, baksheesh manta."* I shrug and give him the remainder of my change. *"Achha, Sahib, namaste,"* he says and salutes. He makes the mistake of approaching Mother again. She swears at him: *"Jao sala!"* I understand this oath to be a coarse one. The beggar gestures at her, jabbers something in Hindi and hobbles off. "What did he say?" I ask. "Nothing," says Mother. "It must have been something." "He cursed me." "What did he say?" "Something silly. Count the bags."

I have read about Hindu curses. Like the spells of ancient Greece they are not intended for transient effect, as was my mother's *"jao sala"*. They are for eternity. A good Hindu curse might be deflected, but it can never be negated. There is the classic curse of the son who learns that he has unknowingly killed the half-brother who was born to their mother in secret. When the son learns the identity of the man he has killed he is stricken with grief and curses his mother on the lines of:

Age se koi apane garbhavastha chipa hoga!
Hereafter no woman shall hide her pregnancy!

It is known as *Kunti ke abhisapa,* the curse of Kunti, excuse my Hindi. Kunti is the mythical mother whose bastard son is unwittingly killed in battle by her legitimate son. It is said that for this reason a woman's pregnancy always shows. Has the half-blind seer seen something I have not?

BEC's Bombay agent has booked us into the Taj for the night and takes us for supper in the oyster bar. I have a choice: creamed oysters, oysters with honey, smoked oysters, raw, boiled, beer-battered, roasted, stewed, pickled or steamed. The agent's licence must be up for renewal, as he spares us no expense. I choose Oysters Fresh from the Arabian Sea, which I picture being gathered at dawn by topless young women diving in clear turquoise waters. The agent assures me they have no central nervous system and feel no pain. I check. He means the oysters. Is it true, I wonder. These luscious, lubricious pelecypods are succulent and soft on the palate, and are clearly co-operating in their ascent into heaven, for it is obvious that they – not ambrosia, not nectar, not freshly-cooked doughnuts – are the food of the gods.

That night I am violently sick and have to revise my beliefs. These particular molluscs must have been bred in, and fed on, the abundant effluent in Bombay harbour. As we board our boat, the S.S. Aphrodite, the next morning, I look balefully out at the grey Arabian Sea – no hint of turquoise – and am sick again. The last remaining reminders of supper swill in the gunnels as we pull away from the quay.

I survived a qualified welcome in India, I lived through nightmares and love affairs that never were, I was threatened by predators, attended endless coffee mornings and tennis tournaments, now undiscriminating filter feeders who concentrate in their guts anything they find in the shit-filled waters around them have laid me low. The immortals have issued one more warning.

Idealized pictures of *Aphrodite* abound on board. The Goddess of Love is variously portrayed as rising blandly naked from the foam of the sea; stepping daintily ashore on the island of Cythera; blithely taking to the air accompanied by doves and sparrows; winging her way effortlessly to Cyprus and causing flowers to spring from the soil wherever her tiny feet tread. This is the mother of *Eros*, whose praises I sang at Calverley Grammar. What I intentionally failed to point out in my debate with Polly was that Aphrodite's appearance unclad caused a scandal in Cyprus and she only just escaped being charged with conduct prejudicial to public order; that she went on to marry the deformed god of fire, *Hephaestos*, and was unfaithful to him within weeks with a highly volatile character by the name of *Ares*; that her three or by some accounts four children, including Eros, were almost certainly illegitimate; and that when her husband caught her and Ares *in flagrante delicto* he threw a fishing net over them and displayed them for public ridicule. I would not have blamed Hephaestos if in his anger he had resorted to his personal version of the curse of Kunti:

> Hereafter no wife of mine shall hide her pregnancy!

I recover from gastroenteritis and get seasick, and when I recover from that I get drunk. The bars on board open early and the alcohol is duty-free. Rupert manages to look after himself. His time at boarding school has taught him not to rely on his relatives.

When we arrive in the Red Sea the waters are calm and the days hot and quiet. I have reached the last chapters of Men and Gods, and the bittersweet story of *Ceyx* and his young wife *Halcyon*. You will know Ceyx as the son of *Sirius*, the Dog Star, and Halcyon as the daughter of *Aeolus*, God of the Winds. Not the most promising of pairings. The master of the winds and his minions are unpredictable and dangerous, and the Dog Star is a portent of uncertain change whose rising marks the flooding of the Nile and the hottest, longest days of summer.

As the S.S. Aphrodite makes her way through the Red Sea and the Suez Canal I lie in the sun smoking Senior Service and Craven 'A', consuming India Pale Ale with rum chasers and trying not to think of my father, who in similar circumstances would have been doing much the same. It is blisteringly hot. The lack of even a light breeze begins to feel sinister. I hallucinate in the heat. I am Ceyx, half-crazed by visions and strange ideations, preparing to sail in search of a cure for my disordered mind. My wife Halcyon sobs, "If my father frees the winds and they reach the sea, nothing can stop them! I fear for you!" Unmoved, I sail the length of the *Mare Internum* with a fresh breeze singing in the ropes, but as I enter the *Oceanus Atlanticus* the crests of the waves begin to whiten and the wind to blow more fiercely. I reef in my sail, but the angry sea will not be contained. I am being punished, but for what? For seeking to heal myself, rather than leaving it to the slap-happy gods? I hold on through a wild, black night of howling tempest. I call in vain for my father to come to my aid, but the sea closes over me. I pray for a painless end.

By morning the storm has abated and a tasteless joke is circulating among passengers about returning last night's lobster linguine to the sea. I check on Rupert, who slept through it all, then make my way to Mother's cabin. She is in pain and has a fever. She tells me that she fell from her bunk as the boat pitched and rolled in the night. I ask the ship's doctor to see her and when he arrives and starts asking certain questions I excuse myself and go out on deck.

As I look out to sea I wish for an unconditional love such as Halcyon had for Ceyx. I see something floating in the distance. Each succeeding wave brings it nearer. It looks to be a body. For one shocking moment I think I am viewing my own corpse. Halcyon cries, "Oh, Ceyx, is this how you return to me?" and in her grief she throws herself into the sea to be with him. As she falls an extraordinary thing happens. She is transformed into a kingfisher. She swoops down, folds her husband in her azure wings, sets kisses on his lifeless lips … and he too is transformed.

Shades of the kingfishers on the banks of the Yamuna, where I walked with Gudiya and dreamt of romance. Now I know what they signify, these brilliant birds with their forlorn call and iridescent wings – the sadness of loss followed by the promise of new life.

Ceyx and Halcyon are inseparable. They build a nest upon the sea and every year the gods grant them seven special days of warm, calm weather in which to bring up their young. These are the halcyon days that hark back to a time of idyll and peace.

When were these days for my mother, I wonder, if ever they were? When handsome young Wilfred, her childhood sweetheart, asked her to marry him with the promise of escape from the unrelenting tides of Rawley Bay? Or years later when she sailed to Bombay and for the first time in her life tasted milk and honey? Neither of these, she tells me from her sickbed on the ship. It was the time of carrying her first child. And that was me.

The doctor confides in me that my mother has suffered a miscarriage. He lists the indicators of heightened risk: her age, the anti-depressants she was on, her excessive consumption of caffeine and gin, and on top of it all the physical trauma of her fall in the storm. I feel numb. She has kept this new life and its premature ending to herself. I am mortified to have this knowledge that I cannot share with her.

Had she found herself pregnant by another man in Chandrapore (Plumtree? Chatterjee?) and is returning to England to arrange an abortion or an adoption? Or had she been determined to give birth to the baby in Beasley so that if it were a boy he would qualify to play cricket for Yorkshire? Possible, but unlikely. I am plagued with unanswerable questions. Had the beggar in Bombay seen with his one good eye the child who could not be hidden, but can never be acknowledged? Had my own self-absorption brought on my mother's depression and contributed to her loss? Had I unknowingly killed a half-brother in a storm I created myself?

We dock on a dark day in Liverpool and take the train across wet and clouded moors to Beasley. No garlands of marigolds await us, no azure wings or cries of laughter. Only the beggar's curse, my empty life and what comes after.

φ

Chapter 20

The Lieutenant's Papers

WHILE I WAS AWAY ON SABBATICAL Roy qualified as a builder and emigrated to apartheid South Africa under Auntie Joan's sponsorship. He might be lucky, I think. He might not want to read a book that the censor has banned or to have sex with someone not quite white enough. His brother Ken has joined the regular army, where I imagine he will feel at home when he has to clean the ablutions. Bert has pneumoconiosis and is coughing a lot. Grandma Lily thinks they will follow Roy to South Africa soon – before Bert croaks irreversibly, I suppose.

Mother registers with a medical practice, rents a detached house with central heating in one of the nicer parts of Beasley and leaves Rupert at the boarding school she has found for him. It is far enough away for her not to have to visit too often. I am at a loss. I can think of a few things I want to do – lose my virginity, quit smoking, complete my dissertation – but none of these quite cuts it as a career. I cannot stay with Mother for long. We know too much about each other that we cannot admit to. Among the topics to be avoided are beggars, babies and any hints of divorce, depression or suicide. Fortunately the weather is not on the list.

A letter arrives in a brown envelope requiring me to register for National Service. I have been assigned to the army, not the RAF or the navy. At least it isn't the navy. If it had been the navy I might have had to claim a conscientious objection to the sea. It occurs to me that I do not have to reply to this letter, as it has been addressed to me at Grandma Lily's. I could send it back marked 'N/K at this address until National Service ends'. Here in fact is something I can do without having to decide whether I want to do it or not.

A few weeks later I find myself outside Oswestry station in Shropshire with a group of young men in civilian clothes armed with travel warrants, suitcases and four-shilling postal orders. We are greeted by the last kindly corporal we will ever encounter, directed to a dun-coloured, three-ton lorry and driven to a camp in the countryside surrounded by a high wire fence.

A clerk issues me with a long army number and a service book. I shall be obliged to recite my army number so many times over the next days that I shall never forget it. 23507513. I think that's right, give or take a digit or two. In the quartermaster's stores we are equipped with our kit: irons, eating, other ranks, three; drawers, cellular, green, other ranks, two; blouses, battledress, khaki, other ranks, one. "If it fits, you must be deformed," says the quartermaster sergeant to everyone. As we emerge from the stores we are allocated to a squad and ushered into a Nissen hut with a coke-fired stove. A corporal instructs us to clean the hut spotless ready for inspection, in spite of it having been cleaned spotless by the outgoing squad. He addresses us as 'gunners' rather than privates, and insists we call him 'bombardier' rather than corporal. Henceforth I shall be known as Gunner Seagrave J.H., 14 Squad, 40th Training Battery, 17th Training Regiment, Royal Artillery, Oswestry, Salop. For some bureaucratic reason I have been inducted into a regiment of artillery. Perhaps my record shows I am a poor shot and might be a liability in the infantry. The Artillery has bigger guns and it should not be so easy to miss.

Among my colleagues in 14 Squad are Dusty Rhodes, Ginger Rogers, Sandy Brown and Nutty Cox. There is a tentative attempt by Shagger Evans, a squaddie from Wales, to call me Red Seagrave on account of my mildly radical views, but Nutty comes up with Squire Trelawney (*vide* Jim Hawkins, L.J. Silver *et al*), which is soon abbreviated to Squire, and although I cavil, as most of us do, at our nicknames, I am not displeased. Squire has an air of landed gentry and jodhpurs, far removed from the potato-picking, cockroach-collecting ghosts that haunt me occasionally, even with my Latin and Greek, shikar parties, servants and chauffeurs.

We are a mixed lot, former boy scouts, Borstal boys, boarders, labourers, graduates and illiterates. In 14 Squad we share the same lowly status and eat the same sausage and mash. I have to make an exception for Kit-Kat Connolly, so-called because his mother sends him a weekly supply of chocolate biscuits, which he locks in a suitcase, stows under his bed and keeps to himself.

Basic training is about getting fit and following orders, however arbitrary. Many young men suffer. They are physically uncoordinated or have problems with authority, or have been brought up to believe that it is not very nice to be shouted at. We are shouted at constantly. While square-bashing, hand-cleaning the floors, crawling under barbed wire or simply going from one place to another. We are shouted at while saluting. Sometimes we salute the wrong people. Commissioned officers wear pips and crowns, are called 'sir' and have to be saluted. If they come into your hut you have to stand to attention. If you are ill in bed you have to lie to attention. Non-commissioned officers wear stripes and badges, are called 'bombardier', 'sarnt' or 'sarnt-major' and are neither to be called 'sir' nor saluted. There is an exception to this. The Regimental Sergeant Major is not to be saluted, but has to called 'sir'. I salute him once before I have fully grasped these fine distinctions and he shouts at me. The rest of 14 Squad enjoy that a lot.

Every short-sighted, cack-handed squaddie is issued with a .303 rifle. Even poor Dickie Bird, who was back-squadded after shooting himself in the foot in an attempt to be invalided out. He lost one toe and half another, and after a month on crutches was obliged to stay in and start all over again.

At five o'clock in the morning we are up buffing and bulling our kit for the day and making immaculate beds with hospital corners. Breakfast is at seven, lights out at ten. At night I hear young men whose lives have changed too rudely stifling their sobs. No-one tells them to put a sock in it, although the temptation is there. They are weeping on behalf of us all. Most of my colleagues have made a sacrifice of some kind in order to be there. Marriages have been postponed, further education deferred, jobs and careers put on hold. My own sacrifice is modest enough: it is to donate a pint of blood to the nation, trusting this is the nearest I will get to active service. I avert my eyes as the needle goes in, but can't help glimpsing a nozzle-full of ruby-red fluid being drawn from my arm. My haemophobia is on full alert, but this is not the brilliant scarlet of my bleeding noses or the cardinal red of the carcases in the butcher's freezer. I could swear that the sample taken from me has a tinge of blue, more a mature Burgundy than a young Beaujolais.

My obsessive tendencies help me cope well with square-bashing, even under the beady eye of Drill Sergeant Duffy, 'Plum' to his friends, who fancies himself a bit of a comedian. "If you do not swing that arm parallel to the ground, Seagrave," he shouts when I am not quite managing to do so, "I shall tear if off, stick it up your arse an' 'ave you for a lollipop."

I do my best to iron knife-edge creases in my thick serge trousers, but they invariably end up looking, well, blunt. They can never be as keen as the creases Roy used to create for his Saturday night trousers in Beasley. But I learn to blanco my webbing until it is as smooth as the icing on a khaki-coloured cake and to buff up my brasses, front and back, until the inspecting NCO can see his own distrustful reflection in them.

By far the best at buffing and bulling is Tosser Ball, who used to work in Burton's Menwear. He folds every item of his clothing, including his drawers, cellular, green, as if he were preparing them for display in his High Street store. He is not the most popular member of the squad. Those of us who cannot match the mirror-like finish he gives to the toecaps of his boots are in danger of qualifying for special privileges, like peeling a pile of potatoes outside in the rain – justified on the basis that it simulates battlefield conditions – or cleaning the toilets in the Sergeants' Mess with a toothbrush, a task which has no point I can see other than sheer pointlessness, which may, of course, be the point.

Muddy Waters is a regular candidate for this kind of attention. His kit and personal appearance are so consistently crap that the squad bombardier threatens to lock him in a cupboard for the duration of our next inspection. This alarms Muddy considerably, as he suffers from claustrophobia. I reassure him that the bombardier was speaking figuratively, though I am not entirely sure this is true.

But the best and most beautiful thing about my time in 14 Squad, 40th Training Battery, 17th Training Regiment, etc., beyond all other accomplishments, beyond learning how to cut the lawn outside the officers' mess with kitchen scissors, is learning to swim. And the secret is surprisingly simple. You follow orders. "Swimmers to the deep end, non-swimmers to the shallow end!" is the first. Seven or eight of us cower at the shallow end, believing the air to be a lot colder than it actually is. The next order follows as predictably as abuse follows the least delay in responding: "Get in the water!" Now it is a matter of doing exactly what Sergeant Wilson ('Won'tson' we call him, for some reason) requires of us or risking what might sound to an outsider like a scurrilous attack on our characters. "Get in the water, Seagrave, you lily-livered shit!" I learn to take language like this as near as it is possible to get in the circumstances to loving encouragement.

The water itself is gratifyingly warm. "Face me! Take hold of the edge!" Now we do everything by numbers, literally. "On the command 'One' you will take a deep breath! On the command 'Two' you will immerse your heads in the water! 'Three', heads out! 'Four', under again!" 'Five', out! 'Six', another deep fuckin' breath! Any questions?" "No, sarnt!" "Are you ready, you sad twats?" "Yes, sarnt!" "'Arris, you fat fucker, are you ready?" Poor, plump, impossibly polite Fatty Harris whimpers, "Not quite, sergeant", and gets himself the kind of personal attention he could well do without. "Not *quite*, 'Arris? Not *quite*? Well, you'll 'ave all the fuckin' time in the world when I tie fuckin' weights to your fuckin' ankles and drop you in the fuckin' deep end, you flabby fat fucker! Are you ready, 'Arris?" "Yes, sarnt!"

And on the word of command we breathe in, go under, come up again, under and up again, and when I have done this half a dozen times I am so used to the nasty sharp feeling of chlorinated water filling my olfactory cavities, a feeling that at school I used to associate with aggravated assault, that I begin to think of it as simply unpleasant rather than life-threatening.

On the next set of commands there is a slightly longer pause before 'Five, out!', requiring us to hold our head underwater for a second or two longer. I have to admire this tactic. I realize that I am not wholly at the mercy of the nymphs of the pool. There is an element of control in my relationship with the water that I never suspected was possible.

Next we are instructed to immerse ourselves, push off from the side and *swim underwater*. This sounds ridiculous, but is counter-intuitively easy. We are expressly forbidden from attempting to swim on top of the water. Another turning-point. I find myself moving in a forward direction, apparently alive and not sinking further.

"Everybody out!" Harris is secretly attempting a dog paddle. "Stop that, 'Arris!" "Sorry , sarnt!" "Did I tell you you could fuckin' swim yet, 'Arris?" "No, sarnt!"

In the next lesson we learn the basics of breast stroke (chin into chest, head up, or is it down?) and back stroke (chin up, I think), and make an attempt at a crawl (palms out and back, I'm reasonably certain of that). I learn that swimming is not a matter of coasting elegantly along on top of the water as in my fantasies I had seen others do it, but of sloshing, flundering and larruping along as best you can with practically all of you underwater – a place where most of me would rather not be. But by the end of basic training I can manage a breadth of the pool by doing as I have been told. I am a soapy little sycophant, but I have learnt how to swim.

My fellow servicemen and I divide into three readily-defined camps: the Saddos, the Squaddies and the Nobs. The Saddos resent their two years out of civilian life. It disrupts their lives and puts a strain on their significant relationships. Some simply miss their mums. They do not do well in the army. After vain attempts to feign disabling conditions, they either knuckle under and count the days or find themselves on CO's Orders for simulation, insubordination and absence without leave.

The Squaddies do comparatively well. They resent the first few weeks of abuse and forced labour, but come to enjoy the uniform and the haircuts, and once their personalities have been broken down and remade they cannot wait to be sent to Korea, Kenya, Sudan and Somaliland to keep the peace and shoot at people.

I thrive, it has to be said, in the Nobs. We do as we are told and take none of it seriously, though I learn not to laugh when Sergeant Duffy makes a joke. "Did I *tell* you that was funny, Seagrave? Take that sad fuckin' smirk off your smug ugly mug!" "Yes, sarnt!"

By a leap of imagination or a serious error of judgment the Battery Commander gives me an OR#1 officer rating and I am sent on an Officer Selection Board course. After a weekend of initiative tests, teamwork exercises and obstacle courses ("Make use of the planks and the barrels, avoid anything painted yellow"), there is a one-to-one with an army psychiatrist. "How do you think your parents' divorce affected you, Seagrave?" he asks. "Not at all, sir," I reply without hesitation. "They parted on good terms, they phone each other frequently and we all get together at Christmas." It is by far the biggest lie I have ever told.

At the end of the course we are issued with nondescript slips of paper ready printed with three alternative outcomes: 'Accepted/Deferred/Failed for Officer Training'. My little slip has the second and third alternatives crossed out. I am inordinately pleased.

There is an expectation in the concept of *hubris* that suffering or punishment will follow an excess of self-esteem. I am wholly confident that this will not happen to me. On the second of three days' leave prior to Officer Cadet School I receive a telegram that says, 'Call Upham 810415 now, Lydia'. I am surprised and slightly disturbed. I was sure I had consigned all my unresolved feelings about Lydia to the snake pits and open sewers of Chandrapore. Does she want to return my copy of Virgil's Pastoral Poems? Has her mother been sectioned? I call. She says she just wanted to say hello.

Gradually the truth comes out A year-long liaison with a wispy-bearded architect called Wendell, who I remember from Upham and never much liked, has ended.

"It helped me realize," she says, "how much you mean to me, James." I take a deep breath. I believe her. In a surfeit of self-esteem at being accepted for officer training I suspend all disbelief at this hugely improbable sentiment. I began the call feeling ambivalent and curious, and end it unequivocally thrilled.

We meet the next day in Middlebridge and the year and a half since I last saw her shrinks to a second. There are no apologies on her side and no reservations on mine. Self-deception is a wonderful thing, a trick of the central nervous system designed for the survival of the least fit. I dismiss all those days and nights of despair and frustration without a moment's regret. What happened in Paris happened to a duffel coat-owning near-orphan who had seen too many *films noirs*. The letters I sent from India were written while listening to long-playing records of Rachmaninov at his most romantic and heartsick. There is an irresistible familiarity to our re-acquaintance and a sudden overwhelming deluge of mutual desire, so that at the end of the day we agree we were meant for each other and there is nothing else for it but to be married. It will be on my seven days' leave on commissioning, three months hence in the Spring.

When my mother learns of our plans she is pleased beyond reason. I will no longer be hostage to her conscience. Her guilt and hurt are assuaged overnight.

If only wispy-bearded Wendell had broken up with your mother-to-be a month or two earlier while I was still five or six thousand miles away … if only Lydia had not felt so suddenly and shockingly bereft of attention … if the telegraph service had missed a delivery that day … if I had not been so blind to the chasm that exists between love and desire.

It feels as if there is a poetic inevitability to these events. Our respective narratives have coincided at this particular moment in history because there is something for us to learn that could not have been taught in any other way. Alternatively, this reprise is the result of pure chance, a random event among an infinite number of unrelated events. Either way, the gods have found in our favour. We are young and untrammelled and can do no wrong. On the train back to Beasley I remind myself that these same gods can be frail and cruel; deceitful, lustful, boastful and irresponsible schemers and conspirators. "Ha!" I reply, "but true love conquers all, does it not?"

My first task at Mons Officer Cadet School is to lead a troop of my fellow cadets on an elementary map-reading exercise. I have no difficulty with this. I lead my men to a rendezvous in Aldershot and we arrive well within the allotted time, only to learn that we are meant to be in Bagshot. A small setback, but I have learnt the first art of love and leadership, which is to convince yourself and those around you that even when you are lost you know exactly where you are.

My fellow cadets and I attend lectures on military law and the responsibilities of command alongside exercises in artillery techniques and battle tactics, when we each take it in turn to lead the troop and get it all wrong. And throughout the course our officers call us 'Mister' and our NCOs, incredibly, 'sir'. "Mr Seagrave, sir, 'ave you seen your 'air, sir? Well it's long enough for me to stand on, sir. You are an idle, disorderly officer cadet, sir! Get it cut! *Sir!*"

We are monitored throughout the course. While dining in the Officers' Mess; while advancing on Salisbury Plain to let off blanks with our 25-pounders; while calculating ranges and trajectories; while crossing our fingers and firing live shells; and while giving improvised talks in the classroom or from the back of a lorry, or in the middle of a field, day or night, rain or shine. One cadet who was a lawyer in civilian life gives the troop a talk on the origin of the cherry-red uniforms of a regiment of infantry. It seems that two hundred years ago they ate a lot of cherries on a campaign in Italy, dribbled the juice down their drab jackets and became known disparagingly as the redcoats. The lawyer confides in me that he made most of it up. I had been planning a talk on Death in the Himalayas about cobras, kraits and dog-eating leopards, but after the story about young men picking cherries I realized that my subject was too obviously butch, so I offer instead a treatise on Toilets I Have Known, calling on my experience of relieving myself in a succession of loos, bogs, johns and closets from Rawley Bay to Chandrapore. It might be too obvious to say that it goes down well.

Halfway through the course Lydia takes time off from her studies and we meet in London to discuss plans for the wedding. We wander round the streets of run-down Regency houses near King's Cross station seeking a cheap hotel for the night. We have a tough decision to make: to book two single rooms or a double.

If you have been taking an interest in my sex life, or lack of it, so far, you will recall that your mother and I had not slept together at university. That will sound bizarre now, even deviant, but we had yet to arrive in the swinging sixties, we were still lingering in the bottled-up, button-down fifties, when more couples consummated their relationships within marriage than without it. Really.

As a twenty-one year old virgin the thought of walking into a chemist's shop (pharmacy to you) to ask for a packet of prophylactics ('lubricated or plain, sir?') is as terrifying for me to imagine as walking the plank over a shark-ridden sea at the point of a cutlass. I say virgin. There was an ambiguous encounter with the Upham librarian after Lydia and I split up that blurs the distinction a little, but cannot be counted as actual, um, intercourse.

The Glenorchy Hotel, King's Cross, is the only establishment with a vacancy notice in the window. We peer at the list of tariffs and silently compare the prices for single and double rooms. "What do you think?" asks Lydia. She doesn't wait for a reply. "We might as well book a double room," she says, "seeing that we are almost married." She says this nonchalantly, as if she hadn't been rehearsing it for the last hour or so. "All right," I say casually, as if the thought has only just occurred to me. I almost add, 'It'll save us money', but that would have brought a reminder of Paris when we hadn't managed to save money by sharing a room there, so I don't.

Once we are under the eiderdown at the Glenorchy Hotel Lydia hints at having slept with Wendell once or twice while I was in India. She mentions this not to put me off, I believe – and anyway after all this time nothing but a fire alarm could – but to reassure me that she knows what she is doing and that I can leave the technicalities to her. It is rather like negotiating an obstacle course during officer selection or working out a tricky artillery targeting exercise, but once we get going it is a welcome new experience not to have to worry, not to have to stop, not to agonize, not to be held back by the shackles of centuries. Lydia is pleased with herself at having facilitated this historic event. "How was it?" she asks. "Er ..." I say. I am not entirely sure. I wonder for a moment if it might not be quite as exciting as firing live ammunition on Salisbury Plain.

On my next day off I take the train to Oxford with the uneasy intention of tracking down Polly Unmore. I want to be sure I am over this first great love of my life. After some officer cadet work in the Eng Lit department I am given a phone number that passes me on to another number. "Hullo," I say. "Hullo," says Polly, "who is this?" "It's James," I say. A pause. "Seagrave." "Oh, James. Hello." "I'm in town, I thought we might meet." She hesitates. "Well, yes. Why not?" She sounds about as enthusiastic as a bowlful of soup. Perhaps I have disturbed her in the middle of writing a romantic novel about her schooldays. I could help with her research, I think – what was it really like for me, her first and best love, etc.

We meet in a coffee bar. As she enters, I am unnerved. This is not the butterscotch-sweet eighteen-year old whose memory I have held dear since we said farewell in Beasley bus station. This is her anorexic, sunken-eyed, twenty two-year-old shadow. I have been carrying an idealized portrait around with me, as fanciful as a miniature painting, and I am shocked to see the life-sized reality. Too much sex and drugs, I think, and not enough serious study. Suddenly the suit I have borrowed for the day from a fellow cadet feels too big for me. I have shrunk a little inside it. It is as well I have witnessed this cataplastic change in Polly, I tell myself. There will be no such surprises with Lydia.

Back at Mons my fellow cadets and I are issued with pre-printed invitations to fill in and send to our prospective guests.

> The Commandant of Mons Officer Cadet School, Col. A.H.G. Fortescue, MBE, MC, requests the pleasure of the company of ………. at a passing-out parade to be held on ……...

Having just missed out on the award of Senior Under Officer I am pleased to see our SUO Scottie McAlister stamping his right foot so hard during passing-out parade rehearsals while reporting the troop as ready for inspection, *sir!* that his right trouser leg escapes from his gaiter.

Miss Ripley cannot make it to the ceremony. She has a portfolio to prepare, she is in the middle of wedding arrangements and she has to ensure that her mother takes her tablets on time. I do not invite my father. I have had no contact with him or indication of interest since my sister and I were farmed out to Beasley seven years ago. Mrs Sutcliffe offers her apologies: Rupert was caught drinking shandy and smoking cigarillos behind the bicycle sheds and she has an appointment to see the headmaster. Having encouraged her son to fend for himself in the foothills of the Himalayas and the moors of North Yorkshire she seems to be showing signs of remorse. The Greeks were made of sterner stuff. When they put a child out on the hillside it would either die of exposure or live to be reared by wolves. I am sure that Rupert will come to thank his mother for his lessons in self-reliance. At the very least, like my colds and nosebleeds, he will have found an alternative to tears. In his case, by the sound of it, nicotine and alcohol.

The passing-out parade is taken by Major-General R.L. Bramwell-Davis, CB, DSO, ably assisted by Captain L.H.J. Tollemache of the Coldstream Guards and accompanied by music from the Royal Artillery Mounted Band (*sans* horses on this occasion), conducted by Director of Music Captain W.E. Runcorn, MBE, ARCM, RA. I am pleased to note that among the pieces Captain Runcorn has chosen to play are The Mad Major and a subversive Scottish song The Garb of Old Gaul.

> In the garb of old Gaul with the fire of old Rome
> From the heath-covered mountains of Scotia we come.

So it comes to be that I am commissioned by the Queen as J.H. Seagrave, 2nd Lt RA. It says as much on the certificate on which Her Majesty's signature has been printed. I discard the white tabs on my lapels in favour of brass pips for my epaulettes. In place of a floppy beret I am issued with a stiff-brimmed hat. And I take possession of a polished wooden swagger stick, a symbol of my status that soon proves indispensable. I can swing it parallel to the ground while walking purposefully along, I can thrust it under my left arm prior to saluting with my right, I can leave it with my hat and gloves on desks and tables during important meetings, and strike it rhythmically into my hand while standing around waiting impatiently.

Ubique Quo Fas Et Gloria Ducunt

'Everywhere that right and glory lead' it says on my hat badge. I double-check the Latin for the benefit of fellow subalterns who wish to be confident of the meaning when the motto is called, as it frequently is, into question.

My week's leave on commissioning begins at a register office in Upham, where an unexceptional ceremony ends with the grant of another certificate. I think it fair to describe the reception in Mrs Ripley's front room as low-key. Lydia has told our dozen or so guests that in deference to her mother's condition it will not be a long or elaborate affair and they are kind enough to leave early. The widow Ripley – will I ever call her Gladys? I doubt it – spends the day with a fixed smile that might have been described as a rictus. "What is the secret of a happy marriage?" I ask my friends Frank and Phoebe, who have come to the reception in order to drink. They have been married for three years and seem to me to have a good relationship, not that I would know a good relationship from, say, a canteen of cutlery. "That is easy, James!" cries Phoebe. "Compromise!" Is she serious? Compromise is surely the antithesis of a happy marriage. "Surely the secret of a happy marriage is to do everything together," I say. "You think and feel alike, you share the shower, have similar tastes in wallpaper." "Good luck, James," says Frank. "You are going to need it." Why is he sniggering? I ask myself if I really believe all that tarradiddle about thinking and feeling alike, and I say to myself, yes, it may be cheesy, but I really believe it. Frank and Phoebe can paddle in the lukewarm waters of compromise until the tide runs out, but my marriage will be exceptional; it will be mutual and beautiful.

Our four-day honeymoon in a two-star hotel not far from her mother's begins in embarrassment and ends in disaster. The embarrassing part happens when I am showing some enthusiasm for making love and Lydia makes an odd little joke on the lines of men being predators and women their prey. It feels like a pre-emptive strike. If this is what she really thinks, then my naïve construct of everything being equal and shared, and in particular the mutual and beautiful basis of making love together, collapses. It is also a curious reversal, because in my recurring nightmare the predators (four legs, drooling, angry) have always been female. So who is the victim and who is the perpetrator here, or are we unwittingly acting out roles we have not chosen, but which have somehow been assigned?

The disastrous part arises out of nothing. I really have no idea how it comes about, but I am reminded – how often does this have to happen before it really sinks in – that we might not always be thinking and feeling alike. I have said something unconsidered or left something undone, or insisted on repeating a question that Lydia had already decided did not merit a response. I have committed some unintentional, unintelligible offence, and rather than a minor clash of personality it has resulted in a head-on collision. Lydia withdraws into one of her lock-down, watertight, don't-even-look-at-me states in which she refuses to communicate. I am stranded. My mother has left for Leeds again, my father is missing at sea, believed drowned, and my stepmother has sent me to Coventry and left me there. It is not as though I had forgotten this ability of Lydia to put up the shutters. What I had overlooked was my fatal inability to cope. I denied it all in a heartbeat, in the breathless romance of a few hours in Middlebridge. Trauma caused by denial of this kind can be hidden, just as flowers can cover a grave, but it hurts no less than physical injury, and unlike physical injury may never completely heal.

I interpret what happens to Lydia at times like this as a kind of hystero-cataleptic response to an imagined threat, somewhere between a panic attack and paralysis. Unfortunately, I have no idea how to deal with it. I have tried reason, anger, patience, embraces, entreaties and tears. In my innocence I supposed that marriage would soften the edges of the problem or dissolve it altogether. Marriage was more than the certificate, the fruit cake and the drunken friends. It had an emergent quality, like birdsong, indispensable for pair-bonding and seeing off strangers, but also for so much more than that. For uncritical acceptance, for mutual solace, for sharing the delights and surprises of life. As I thought. In fact when Lydia withdraws all I hear is the clunk of a thick metal door as it closes between us and then silence. We are at another impasse, with nowhere to go except in reverse – back into childhood, infancy, babyhood, beyond. Some tiny neural component has failed and set off a chain of related events, and in a second the whole works has gone into shut-down. My mother's slamming doors, slaps and explosions of anger were blips in comparison.

I want to believe that what happens between us at a time like this is one of the no-fault accidents of life, a random encounter between Lydia's susceptibility and my stupidity, but it dawns on me that there is more to it than that. Her immune system has been compromised by the loss of her father and her mother's mental illness in the same way that my parents' absence and divorce has compromised mine, so that for either of us any new trauma, however minor, is likely to result in deep tissue injury rather more than surface bruising.

How bad do shocks to the system, even tiny after-shocks, have to be before the damage is irreparable? How many no-fault accidents have there to be before the vehicle as a whole is a write-off?

Hours pass before Lydia is ready to communicate again and she gets no help from feeble me. We have created something monstrous between us. In the darkest entries in my diary I speculate that we have given life to a goliath who will devour us one nibble at a time until only the bones of the relationship are left to pick over. Yet in lighter moments I reason that the monster will soon tire of this diet and sink back into the accommodating ocean forever, leaving us to enjoy the guilt-free, undefended, *happily married* parts of ourselves.

We make no attempt to examine what happened. We do not consider how a similar situation might be anticipated or mitigated, or how we might divert or adapt its negative energy. For me that would feel too synthetic, too analytic, too far removed from my ideal of effortless intimacy. For Lydia it would feel unsafe and invasive. So we put on a wary kind of jollity and carry on as before. Lydia returns to her research and I go back to the army.

I have opted for a home posting. The War Office might have sent me to keep the peace in Aden, Eritrea or a dozen other desirable places, but they assign me to my first choice, the Royal Artillery in Woolwich in south-east London. Lydia and I will be no more than a bus or a tube or two and a train ride apart. It still doesn't make for a great start to a marriage, but being sent overseas to be shot might well have been worse.

The Headquarters Regiment of the Royal Artillery occupies an elegant eighteenth century barracks with an imposing arched entrance of mock-Doric columns and a frieze topped by unicorns and griffins. I know these mythical creatures. Unicorns are symbols of purity that can only be captured by virgins (I'm not sure how that relates to the Royal Artillery) and griffins are monsters who are destined to mate for life. Will that be my fate or good fortune, I wonder.

This splendid, elegant and, yes, welcoming building will be my home for the next twenty-one months. I report to the CO and the Adjutant. I am allotted a room in the Officers' Mess and half-share of a batman. There was a time when I might have been concerned at the socio-political implications of owning half a batman, but given my experience of egalitarian ideals in India (there were none), I confess to feeling only mildly uneasy, and that for no more than a day or two. It takes me a little longer to get used to the extraordinary experience of being saluted by gunners, bombardiers, sergeants and sergeant-majors all the way up to the exalted rank of RSM. The first time I am saluted by stately Regimental Sergeant-Major Heskey I think he has made a mistake. He may think the same.

My first official task is to invigilate NCOs sitting for a maths exam. 'A soldier wishes to buy a portable radio costing 18 guineas …' Tricky if you don't know what a guinea is, but the rest of the paper looks straightforward enough. I invite those who finish early to write an essay on what the army will be like in the year 2000. "Use your imaginations," I say. "No need to be serious." "But sir," says one bright bombardier, "we are NCOs, we are not meant to have imaginations." "Today you are meant to, " I say, "because I say so."

I am sent next to a magistrate's court in neighbouring Greenwich to give a character reference for a soldier who is on a charge of common assault and criminal damage. I don't know the man, but I have been instructed to say he is of excellent character and has an exemplary service record. I hope this isn't too far from the truth. He is let off with a warning.

Then I am made Acting Motor Transport Officer when the regular MTO is sent on sick leave after being charged with drink-driving. I imagine I have been given the job because I cannot drive and have next to no interest in lorries. I am, however, qualified to sign things. I sit at a desk adding *J.H. Seagrave, 2nd Lt RA*, to a stream of requisitions, receipts and reports, anything that Battery Sergeant Major Cartwright, who runs the unit, puts in front of me, and spend the rest of the time keeping my diary up-to-date, mugging up on the Officers' Guide to Protocol and Etiquette and strolling round the unit inspecting things and returning salutes. My experience at the mill in Chandrapore comes in handy for this. I stop to watch men in overalls fixing things, murmur "Jolly good" and "Keep at it" ("Thank you, sir" "Yessir"), and move on before they can ask me anything technical. I get a reputation for being pleasant enough and, probably, useless.

Then the Assistant Adjutant of the regiment, Lieutenant Pursglove, resigns his commission in order to return to his first love, the law, and the CO invites me to take his place. Suddenly I am at the centre of things. I have a desk in the Adjutant's office next door to the CO's. If you want to see the CO, Colonel Quayle, you have to go through the Adjutant, Captain Cochrane, and to see him you must first check with me, and to see me it is advisable to first pay your respects to Mr Truscott, the Company Sergeant-Major, who has the office next door.

The Colonel has a brisk and formidable manner, but I get to know his sensitive side and after meeting smiling, steely-eyed Mrs Quayle – the only person other than the CSM who can get away with walking into the office unannounced – I think his marriage might be under a similar strain to mine.

I am positively vetted. I sign the Official Secrets Act. I have the code to a safe containing instructions on what the Royal Artillery has to do in the event of war. I cannot tell you what that is, I'm afraid, as I have signed the Official Secrets Act, but between you and me it might have something to do with moving out of Woolwich and going somewhere else.

One of my duties is to help the Adjutant, Nigel, run CO's Orders, arraigning those who fell asleep on guard duty or were arrested for fighting in Woolwich, or failing all else can be matched to the catch-all charge of conduct prejudicial to good order and military discipline. I draw up the charge sheets, Nigel reminds the CO of his powers of summary punishment – admonition, reprimand, severe reprimand, detention – and accompanies the felon in question as he is quick-marched by Mr Truscott – "left right left right left right!" – into the CO's office.

Another of my duties is to organize the Orderly Officer of the day. Every junior officer in the regiment has to take a turn at mounting the guard in the evening and being on call, preferably sober, through the night, ready to inspect the guard at a time pre-decided in my presence by drawing a wooden token from the velvet bag in my desk drawer. I enter this time in a register and lock the register in the safe. The aim of this elaborate procedure is to maintain the readiness of the guard to spring into action at any time of night or day to keep us all safe from the IRA. To this end the guards are armed with pickaxe handles, as rifles are thought to be too dangerous.

I take advantage of my status as senior subaltern to rig the rotas in order to do fewer Orderly Officers than the other subalterns and to tinker with call-out times in order to stay on good terms with the guard. It is not unknown for my Orderly Sergeants to have a shrewd idea of the time they can expect me to make a surprise visit. That way we can all get a good night's sleep, a condition I deem to be vital, along with the pickaxe handles, for keeping us safe.

There is only one scare during my stints as Orderly Officer when the Orderly Sergeant phones me at midnight to inform me that an unexploded bomb has been found in nearby Plumstead. "Is there a protocol for unexploded bombs?" I ask as I scrabble around on my bedside table for a copy of Standing Orders for Orderly Officers. "No problem, sir," says the sergeant. "I'm dealing with it." "Jolly good, sarnt," I say, and go back to sleep, secure in the knowledge that this is the kind of thing sergeants are for.

While I am settling into my duties in Woolwich Lydia is looking after her mother in Upham, producing a portfolio for the final phase of her MA and taking the train to London at intervals to research her dissertation. There are no married quarters in the Officers' Mess, so I find us a flat in Brixton and have permission from the CO to commute to and from barracks when my wife is in town. The Colonel is sensitive to the challenge of reconciling married life with life in the military and if he ever forgets he has a framed photograph of smiling, steely-eyed Mrs Quayle on his desk to remind him.

The Brixton flat is on the first floor of a disused greengrocer's in a near-derelict street awaiting demolition. There is no formal contract. I have put my name to a handwritten note promising to pay someone I have never met £2 10s a week. "We are really lucky to have found this place," I say when I take Lydia to see the flat. I point to two items of furniture left behind by the previous tenant, a threadbare *chaise longue* and a grand piano that has lost its gloss but still has, I suggest, presence. Lydia purses her lips. I try a romantic line about this being our first ever home together. She is unmoved. "Let me get this right, James," she says. "We have no lease, no bathroom, a smell of old vegetables, a grand piano that neither of us can play and it is only costing us £2 10s a week?" "You're right," I say, acknowledging her reservations, "but it's handy for the bus."

Our first nights at the flat are spent on a second-hand mattress laid over a home-made plinth of disused fruit boxes. The wind whistles through gaps in the sash windows and rattles the bedroom door.

Lydia is busy, stressed and working to a deadline. In the mornings she catches the 159 into the West End to work at the National Gallery and the British Library, while I take the 436 and the 89 in the opposite direction, buttoned up in my uniform, for a day at the office.

I experience a slight wobble when there is a suicide in the barracks. A lance-bombardier hangs himself after his wife leaves him for a civilian tradesman – a general handyman, I understand. The bombardier's death is recorded as 'accidental'. If he had been unsuccessful and survived, I learn, he would have been liable to prosecution under military law, which strikes me as, well, pretty shitty in the circumstances. Trying to kill yourself but failing leaves you open to being charged with a criminal offence against God and the Crown, even if you have nothing much against either. If you do succeed in killing yourself you will be in the ludicrous position of being found guilty without being in the position – alive, that is – to offer any kind of defence.

The Colonel gives two of the soldier's close comrades forty-eight hour passes to get over it. "Forty-eight hours should be enough, eh?" he asks Nigel, who agrees. "You cannot be too generous with compassionate leave, sir," says Nigel, "or everyone will be taking it." I shall have occasion to remember those words.

As a result of the suicide and its ramifications, I express a mild interest in military law and am promptly sent off on a two-day course, followed by attending a District Court Martial as an observer and making two appearances as a defending officer to deliver heartfelt but unsuccessful pleas of mitigation. I am then given responsibility for prosecuting all the Royal Artillery's routine cases. Being thrown in at the deep end is something I have learnt to take for granted in the army. Like those junior officers sent over the top in WWI I am assumed to be competent until proven otherwise – in their case, regrettably, by being shot.

In addition to prosecuting, my job is to recruit three senior officers to make up a panel of judges and to designate a defending officer from any spare subaltern I can persuade or, if not, co-opt. It occurs to me that there must be an eye-popping conflict of interest in the prosecution appointing the judges and the defence, but I am merely going along with the army's way of doing things or, to put it another way, following orders.

Running a court martial turns out to be no more demanding than learning to swim or firing a 25-pounder. It is all done by numbers. And almost every exchange has to be recorded in writing so that cases can be scrutinized minutely if they ever go to appeal, which they rarely do.

The protocols of the court engage my sense of theatre and my budding sense of social justice. A soldier charged with absence without leave, for example, will more often than not plead guilty, as the evidence against him is usually well-documented and undeniable, but if he has gone AWOL because he is desperate to get out of the army I might offer to charge him with desertion instead. Soldiers found guilty of absence without leave are sentenced to a period of detention and find themselves back in the army, disgruntled and itching to go AWOL again, whereas those found guilty of desertion will get a period of detention followed by a dishonourable discharge, which means they will get what they want and be out of the army for good.

It is possible I make rather too much of *prima facie* arguments in presenting these cases. Senior officers acting as judges are inclined to take unsupported 'on the face of it' evidence as sufficient in itself if it is uncontested, because it saves them time and avoids the need for wading through piles of paperwork. I am challenged only once over a prima facie argument. A conscientious major with too much time on his hands interrupts my presentation. "*Prima facie*, Mr Seagrave," he says, "means literally 'at first sight'. I must point out that in the interests of justice today we have time for a second and, if necessary, a third." "No problem, sir," I murmur and present my evidence again, this time more slowly and in a different order.

On our stays at the greengrocer's Lydia and I make our way past the rotting fruit on the ground floor, mount to the first floor, avoiding the missing step, and at night listen to the mice gnawing away at the floorboards. We have no bathroom and there is no hot water. The only sources of heating are a single gas ring and a one-bar electric fire. The window over the kitchen sink has a missing pane. During the night Lydia prefers to pee in a bucket on the landing rather than make her way downstairs to the loo. Going downstairs means negotiating with the mice, who have an apartment of their own on the ground floor and do not take kindly to being disturbed. In addition her dressing gown cord never seems to be threaded and she tends to trip over the missing step.

In the mornings I light the caked black gas ring, put on a kettle of water, arrange my shaving tackle on the draining board and place an enamel bowl in the kitchen sink full of scum-laden water that has failed to drain overnight. Lydia pours hot water from the kettle into the bowl and bravely tries to soap herself while I slosh, scrape and hack at my face. We shiver in the draught from the missing pane. If I were to compare conditions in Waterloo Road, Brixton, to the much maligned slums of Blackfoot Lane, Beasley, I would have to say that this flat over an abandoned shop in SW9 is marginally worse.

We have alternatives, however. Lydia can stay with her mentally ill mother in the shadow of pylons next to a ladies' hairdresser in suburban Upham, while I have the Royal Artillery Mess, with its deep-pile carpets, extravagantly varnished mahogany tables, hand-polished silver service, starched linen napkins and gilt-framed paintings of battle scenes featuring a great deal of smoke. The Mess is considerably plusher and posher than Harold's dusty club in Chandrapore, but my stepfather never makes it to Woolwich, so I never get to entertain him. 'Only members can buy the drinks here, Harold', I would have said. 'You are my guest. No, I insist. It goes on my chit. A *burra peg*?'

As a member of the Mess I attend monthly Mess nights dressed in my stiff-collared blues with a red stripe down the trousers. I hang my blues hat and belt in the commodious washroom, stroll into the lounge to greet my fellow officers and take a generous schooner of sherry ("Dry, sweet or medium, sir?" "Dry, if you please") from a smiling Mess servant holding a shining silver tray. Dinner in the banqueting hall is accompanied by live music from the Royal Artillery Band in their best navy, red and gold uniforms. And after dinner we get to pass the port and Madeira in opposite directions – port left, Madeira right, of course, though after a glass or two of either or both it doesn't seem to matter so much.

After the Colonel has retired for the night a bread roll or two will be thrown at the junior officers' end of the table. As Assistant Adjutant I am expected to keep some sort of order there, but a balance has to be found between a little silliness, which is almost *de rigeur*, and a little too much, which is unquestionably *infra dig*. And however drunk one might get on Mess nights, one is expected to be civil to the Mess servants and turn up for duty the next morning sober, clean-shaven and correctly dressed. Minor infringements of the social order (laughing too long or too loudly, accidentally hitting a senior officer with a bread roll) merit an informal chat with one's Battery Commander, while more serious discourtesies (blasphemy, fisticuffs, throwing up on the carpet) qualify for a frosty word from the CO the next day in his office, which invariably means being subject to the critical attention of the CSM, the RSM and the Adjutant *en route*. A dim view will be taken somewhere along the line if one has left a button undone or shaved without due care and attention.

Lydia, meanwhile, is trudging from one existential crisis to another. Her mother's grasp on reality is increasingly at odds with other people's, her dissertation on Joseph Wright of Derby and the History of Candlelight Painting in Eighteenth Century Britain is overdue, and she is tired of having to pee in a bucket on the landing. "This is the last time," she mutters as she totters out of the room in her flannelette nightie.

I continue to deliver my summaries of the case for the prosecution, mount the guard now and again, pay my bar bills on time and take tea with the Colonel, Mrs Quayle and Nigel whenever a new officer joins the regiment and needs to be screened socially. The Colonel and his lady make a first-class team on these occasions, models of hospitality and affability, although I know better, having heard raised voices from the CO's office followed on one occasion by the muffled but unmistakeable sound of weeping. Whether it came from Mrs Quayle or the Colonel I cannot be sure. What Nigel or I would have done if either party had emerged wishing to unburden themselves I have no idea, as there is nothing to cover that kind of thing in the Officer's Guide to Protocol.

RA Open Day is a key date in the regimental calendar. There are VIPs to entertain. We are showing off, recruiting, making the case for more lorries and guns. Nigel escorts a Minister of the Crown, the Colonel looks after a general or two and I am allocated the Bishop of Woolwich, a prominent pacifist who makes a reluctant guest. I show him an impressive display of field guns down the ages, but he is not impressed. I invite him to join me in a parachute jump off a tall tower, but he politely declines. I mount to the top. "As easy as falling off a tall tower!" I cry, launch myself and land badly. The Bishop kindly accompanies me to the First Aid tent, then we retire to the Mess and end up in the bar debating the merits and demerits of unilateral nuclear disarmament with my Battery Commander, Captain Lionel Porritt.

Something is bothering Lionel. He is ordering round after round of single malts and putting them all on his chit. When I first met Captain Porritt I thought of him as old school, crisp and curt, his uniform pressed in all the right places. Then I noticed signs of what I took to be subversion. The way he knotted his tie, for example – a full double Windsor rather than the usual wrap-around-under-and-through – and his insistence on wearing boots and gaiters to the office in preference to shoes. "*Semper paratum,* James!" he barked when I remarked on his choice of footwear. "Always ready!" He would not say for what, but it must have been for war. Then there was the facial hair – downy tufts left unshaved on his upper cheeks, bushy eyebrows like miniature tussocks of knotweed, and enough growth on his upper lip to stuff a small sofa. As I came to know Lionel better I realized that this raffish display was not his way of subverting Queen's Regulations, but of affirming them. To be sure of official limits Lionel aimed to take a position as close to them as possible.

After a third single malt the Bishop excuses himself. I escort him to his chauffeured car and return to the bar to check on my Battery Commander. Lionel has something on his mind. He orders another round and lowers his voice. "Word in your ear, James." Oh dear, I think, he's planning to grow a beard or the Bishop has converted him to nuclear disarmament, either of which could be a court martial offence. "I've been a captain too long," he says. "Should have had my majority years ago." He looks round. We are the only people in the bar. "All my contemporaries are majors and colonels by now," he confides. I don't know what to say. "Small favour, James," he says. "Wonder if you might exercise your influence with the CO, get him to pen a brief *billet doux* to the War Office, query the delay, put in a good word, that kind of thing. He'll know the drill."

Promotion is fortunately not my concern. When I receive my discharge papers I shall qualify for the automatic rank of Lieutenant in the Emergency Reserve and I have no intention of attempting to go any further. Lionel reminisces about his delight on earning his second pip, followed though it was by an unusually long wait for the third. Wiping an invisible spot from the toe of his boot, he recalls the time a junior officer came to report to him wearing shoes. "I asked the man," says Lionel, twitching a tussock, "where are your boots?" He bristles and barks. "Even as a captain I wore boots for my first interview with the CO!" No wonder he hasn't made it to major, I think. He's a bit doolally. Spent too long on the Northwest Frontier.

Lionel stands, smooths the growth on his upper lip and reaches for his stiff-brimmed hat. "Important to maintain standards, James," he says. Most officers go to some trouble to beat the stiffness out of their hats, as a floppy brim is a sign of service, but to Lionel a floppy brim is a sign of moral decline. I promise to have a diplomatic word with the Colonel about the War Office's deplorable oversight. Lionel is embarrassed. "Good man," he murmurs. "Another snifter?"

My own day of shame comes when I am carpeted by the CO for withholding my batman's gratuity. The batman had complained to the Quartermaster Sergeant, the QMS brought it to the attention of the CSM, who probably thought it none of his business but spoke to the RSM, who felt obliged to mention it to the CO. Small world syndrome again, in the way that gossip used to shoot round the Chandrapore compound faster than the earth round the sun. I explain my reasoning to the Colonel. "His work was below par, sir. I wished to encourage him to improve." "I understand, James," says the Colonel briskly. "You have admirably high standards, but it is simply not done to withhold your batman's gratuity."

Oh, shit. I have broken a tacit moral code. I go back to my Officers' Guide to Protocol and Etiquette, but the entry on batmen and their gratuities is by no means definitive. It must be a class thing. I have some catching up to do. I make restitution with the batman with a casual apology ("Oversight, overdrawn"), but can't help making a point ("Not so heavy on the blanco tomorrow, eh Swinson?").

I make an effort to be generally more nonchalant. I return salutes a little less fastidiously – tipping the brim of my hat with my swagger stick is often enough – and throw a few more bread rolls on Mess nights. Whether this makes any difference to the way I am perceived I cannot be sure, but for two sublime weeks while Nigel takes annual leave the CO appoints me Adjutant.

Lionel is beside himself. He manages to bristle and bark at the same time: "That is a job for a Captain!" he complains. "But you are on the cusp of promotion to Major, Lionel," I assure him. "The job is not up to your pay grade." He harrumphs as he watches me sign Part I Orders as 'J.H. Seagrave, 2nd Lt RA, Adjutant, Royal Regiment of Artillery'. It is the acme of my non-career in the army. And it will all come to an end very soon.

"This really is the last time!" Lydia cries after we have spent another night listening to the mice helping themselves to the floorboards. "This is no place to bring up a baby." I agree. "Luckily, that is not our concern," I say. Lydia looks at me. "This is not the way I imagined telling you I was pregnant." I look at her. It is not the way I imagined being told. "Are you serious?" I ask. She does not respond. She has retired into one of her silences. Well, you know her silences. Legendary, impenetrable. There is no way we can sort this out now. She has a train to catch and I have to get to a court martial.

On our way to the front door, my nose begins to bleed. Dammit, I thought I had grown out of my nosebleeds. Liquid scarlet drips in copious clots to the dusty floorboards of the abandoned shop. Lydia leaves, slamming the door in its rotting frame. A pane of glass falls out.

Is it true? Is she pregnant? On the bus to Woolwich I mop spots of blood from my uniform – there are a few funny looks from my fellow passengers, where is the war? – and go obsessively over what she said: "This is not the way I imagined telling you I was pregnant." She did not say she *was* pregnant.

I swallow my pride and ask the Colonel for compassionate leave as soon as the day's court business is over. "How long would you like, James?" he asks. I do not want to ask for as much as the men whose mate committed suicide were given. "Maybe twenty-four hours, sir. My wife and I have something to sort out." Is this the kind of thing an officer admits to? I hardly care. It is not so long ago that Nigel was suggesting to the Colonel that he should not be over-generous with compassionate leave or everyone would be taking it. I admit to the Colonel what I have difficulty accepting myself, that my wife might be pregnant. "Aha," says he. "Should I be offering my congratulations or commiserations, James?" "Both, sir," I say, smiling weakly. The Colonel glances at the photograph of Mrs Q on his desk. "Take forty-eight hours," he says. "More if you need it." I can't help wondering if he ever grants compassionate leave to himself.

I catch up with Lydia in Upham and we go for a long walk by the river. She is not above pushing me in if I upset her again, I think, but at least I can swim now. She confirms my best and worst fears: yes, she is pregnant. We look at each other warily, then smile. We agreed that it is a surprise. We say we are thrilled. I admit that she is right about the flat, it is in no fit state to bring up a baby.

Over the next months I replace the missing windowpane, clean the gas ring, pay a plumber £6 10s. to fix the water heater, tape and wedge the windows, stuff the chimney flue and the gaps in the window frames with newspaper, buy a two-bar electric fire, fill in the mouse-holes, move our mattress into the living room, paint the bedroom as a nursery, buy an extendable second-hand cot, a collapsible baby bath and an adaptable push-chair, and in a final attempt to be normal attend Queen Alexandra's Military Hospital as a day patient to have a metal wire device heated to a dull red glow inserted into my nose to cauterize the swollen blood vessels that were implicated in my stress-induced bleeding.

In Brixton market I find a gilt-framed picture to hang over the fireplace: three nude, pink-bottomed nymphs gazing at a sunburnt youth with floppy wet wings who lies flat out on the beach, a crimson curtain draped over his genitals. Is this *Icarus*? Had the winged adventurer not drowned after being abandoned by his neglectful father? Where did the crimson curtain come from? The nymphs are trying to revive him. One holds his head from behind, her left breast lightly touching his shoulder. Wake up, man! Is he dead or exhausted? I am about to find out what happens next when Lydia wakes me and tells me that the baby is coming.

We take a taxi to Lambeth Hospital. "A false alarm," they say, "come back in the morning." Lydia insists on staying, so they reluctantly find her a bed and send me away. It is one of those units that operates a policy of the excluded father. "Get some sleep," they tell me, "your wife has hours yet." I phone an hour and a half later and the baby has been born. I hurry back. Lydia is fine.

You are a boy, as I'm sure you know, with big brown eyes and hair as dark as your mother's. It is an extraordinary experience to see you, hold you and watch your every burble and twitch.

If Lydia is upset at having to make it through labour with only a midwife for company, she does not show it. But that is symptomatic of our relationship; we have no vocabulary for feelings. I have always found it difficult to distinguish one feeling from another, in the same way that I can hardly tell one nautical knot from another, even though I clearly should. Challenge me to name some of my feelings and I will probably be able to identify Anxiety and Sadness – and now, to my intense gratification, occasional, if fleeting, Joy, such as I experience as I hold and grin inanely at my son.

We agree on the name Julian. Our models are Lydia's sister, Julia, who is helping look after their increasingly unhinged mother, and my favourite Roman Emperor Flavius Claudius Julianus, social reformer and Stoic philosopher, whose sayings include 'Never yield yourself a slave to your own desires' – I am with him there, if only in theory – and 'Nothing exists that is not by its substance the offspring of ocean'. Dippy said something similar at King's. "We are made of water, gentlemen," he declared one day when our Classics class was discussing the enduring myth of the sea-nymph. "How much water, Faucett?" The class giggled. Four-eyes Faucett was notorious for knowing this kind of thing, but it was not why Dippy singled him out. "How much of us is water, sir? Seventy per cent, sir." "Seventy per cent indeed, Faucett. The same percentage as makes up the earth's surface, interestingly enough. We cannot escape the stuff, gentlemen. We derive from, depend on and ultimately break down into so many atoms of hydrogen and oxygen." "Twice as many of the first as of the second, sir," piped up Four-eyes. "Thank you, Faucett," said Dippy, and moved on.

It is several weeks more before we agree on a middle name. I want something esoteric or heroic – *Eros, Olympus, Jason, Byron* – but none of these finds favour with Lydia. She suggests *Piero, Filippo* or *Domenico* after painters of the Italian Renaissance. I demur. "Words ending in 'o' lack substance and gravitas in English." "Name some," she says. "*Dildo, Fandango, Farrago,*" I say. "There are many more." "Such as?" I have to think a bit. "*Bimbo, Ditto, Sago, Guano.*" "None of these are names." "But they all end in 'o'." I'm not sure where this conversation is going. She challenges me to find a name that embodies both substance and gravitas, and yet is not boring.

It isn't long before I come up with *Pittacus, Protagoras* and *Pythagoras*. Lydia rejects Pythagoras as an appellative on the grounds that you might grow up to love or hate maths, and either would be just as bad. She does not dismiss Protagoras until I point to his doctrine of pleasure as the only true good. That would be to give you too obvious a hostage to fortune, she suggests. Which leaves Pittacus. Pittacus of Mytilene, as you may know, was one of the Seven Sages, a soldier-philosopher credited with the sayings 'Pardon is better than punishment' and 'Forgiveness is better than revenge'. I sense that Lydia might not be wholly committed to either Pittacus or forgiveness, but it is late, the night-time feeding is taking its toll and constantly having to look things up in Doctor Spock, unwilling as we are to trust either her mother or mine for guidance on anything related to children.

Above all else, I think to myself, I want my son to grow up immune to the sorrows and sensibilities of his parents. Julian Pittacus Seagrave, J.P.S., has a sensible, judicial ring. I pray that *nomen est omen*, nominative determinism, will do its thing and inspire him to be sensible and judicial. When I reflect on the extent to which his mother and father floundered in the depths of their unfathomable emotions, I tell myself that sense and reason will, indeed, must give him something of substance to hold on to.

As I register the birth and take possession of the relevant papers I am obliged to acknowledge new responsibilities. 'Father: James H. Seagrave', it says on the birth certificate. 'Occupation: 2nd Lieut. Royal Artillery'. We are living on my salary from the army, but it will come to an end very soon. I consider training in law when my

National Service ends, or returning to Upham to complete my degree, or even, briefly, transferring to the regular army and seeing if I can beat Lionel to Major.

I am in the Mess flicking through the Sunday papers when I come across an article on the London Film School. A montage of memories appears on the page: Saturday morning matinees in Thirby in the breathless company of Flash Gordon and Roy Rogers; sitting in the front row of the Odeon, Beasley, with Grandma Lily, a flask of cocoa and a spam sandwich, totally absorbed in a revival of Gone with the Wind; and unforgettable times at the Art Cinema in Upham and the Academy on Oxford Street, catching up on the work of Buster Keaton, Satyajit Ray, Ingmar Bergman and the French *Nouvelle Vague*.

I apply to the School for a course in Film Principles and Practice and to my delight receive a letter of acceptance. "Have you seen the fees?" asks Lydia, who has found the accompanying invoice. Fees? I had not considered the fees. I had been thinking more of the wealth of material available to be adapted from Eng Lit, the Bible, Greek myth and the Hindu scriptures Lydia wonders, just wonders, if I might find a job instead. "We shall be in need of an income very soon," she says. "The moment you are demobbed there will be practically none." And adds, "I have absolutely no intention of raiding my trust fund to make up the difference." Ah, this fund, that is only ever mentioned in the context of never having to be used. The impression Lydia likes to give is that it is a very modest sum, which may or may not be true, and available to her only in the direst of dire circumstances.

She goes on about J.P. having to be fed, clothed and whatnot. Well, I know that. She mentions a building site she saw in Brixton that was advertising for labourers. "That would not leave you much time for painting," I say. She is not amused. I murmur something about the limited opportunities for advancing my creative aspirations on a building site and the philosophical gap that is opening up between the notion of doing something I really want to do and working at a dead-end job in order to buy extra nappies and cod liver oil. It feels as if a lot more than I know depends on this Strait of Messina-like choice. If I blindly follow my desires we could run into the rocks and be left penniless – with the exception of some secret cache of hers about which I have no information and to which I have no access – but if I do the decent thing and tack to the other side of the Strait I could be sucked into a downward spiral of non-achievement that would be difficult, perhaps impossible, to escape.

A letter arrives from the Ministry of Labour with information on the availability of educational bursaries designed to help smooth the way for young men leaving National Service and returning to civilian life. Without much hope – would a film course qualify, the scheme is surely intended for central heating engineers and chartered accountants – I apply for a grant and barely ten days later receive a cheque for fifty per cent of the fees. Terrific. Thoroughly well deserved. I suggest that though the way ahead might be choppy it is at least negotiable, and if we trim our sails we will get by. As an artist herself I know she will be thrilled at the opportunity that has opened up for me. She is silent. I think she does not have the words to share her great joy.

I do one other thing on leaving the army. I join the Campaign for Nuclear Disarmament, a move that at the time makes sound political sense, but will have a profound unintended consequence.

♀

Chapter 21

A Fine Mist

YOU MAY HAVE NOTICED how little of this chronicle is devoted to the inner lives of others. What do I know of my mother's true feelings as opposed to the emotional ruthlessness I project onto her? What might be at the root of my stepmother's deep antipathy towards me and the world? And most recently and damningly, where are the clues to the inner life of my troubled wife?

I can speculate about young Mildred's abandonment by her mother, Edith's traumatic time in the Blitz, the loss of Lydia's father in the Normandy landings and so on, but that would be like wondering if gods and monsters exist. Of course they do, but what can we do about it?

Sometimes I ask Lydia how she feels about all the travelling she has to do between tutorials, galleries and baby clinics, but even a well-meant remark like "It must be a big deal for you having no time to paint" comes so loaded with presumption – that it *is* a deal, that it is measurable, that she does indeed wish to paint and is unable to find the time – that it is impossible to be sure of getting a meaningful reply. In any case, Lydia has a habit of turning remarks like this, even anodyne questions like 'How are you?', back on themselves. "Is it not plain to see?" she will say. Or the suffocating, infuriating "If you really loved me, you would know". Failing these she has the real show-stopper, silence, to fall back on, when she simply turns away and walks offstage.

As we lie side by side in silence one night after yet another misunderstanding, I tell myself it would be so easy for her to get back on terms if she really cared, if she really … oh heck, that is her line. All I can see is her faint reflection in my solipsistic pool. If only I had the temerity to really reach out to her, to ask her how it really is for her and tell her how it really is for me … but that would be to break the surface of the waters in a way that would almost certainly result in my humiliation or rejection. The gods take revenge on those who interfere in their play. As that creepy old misogynist Dippy used to say, "Water is female, Seagrave. Whether your motives are self-seeking or self-denying, you will be punished."

My two years' service to the nation comes to an end and Lydia has her MA. Now she makes an unexpected gesture of commitment to our life in London by decorating the walls of our room a soft shade of grey and putting up one of her paintings, a moody little study in oils of what looks to me like a ploughed field in the fog, but which she describes as "a conditional representation of latency". "What does that mean?" I ask. She sighs. She does not like to explain her paintings. "It is an abstraction of the interval between stimulus and response," she responds, which is about as chatty as she gets in reference to her work. I translate it as hope.

Well into my course in film theory and practice and with Lydia and the baby on a visit to Upham, I get a letter from the owners of the shop giving us a week's notice to quit. Our section of the street is about to be demolished. I'm sure that the notice we have been given is illegal, but given that we are sub-letting the place from an acquaintance of the original leaseholder it is likely that our tenancy is open to question too. I decide to say nothing to Lydia until I have found another flat. Keeping the stress to myself is the manly thing to do, I tell myself, though whether that makes it self-seeking or self-denying I cannot tell. My models for manliness are a pathetic alcoholic and a man who seeks out animals to kill, stuff and hang on his dining room wall.

After searching in increasing desperation in Camberwell and Clapham I find a ground floor flat in a shared house in a shabbier part of Notting Hill where we will have a room and a kitchen to ourselves. I phone Lydia. She is incredulous. "Why did you not tell me we have to quit Brixton?" she asks. Isn't it obvious, I think – that I have kept the anxiety to myself in order to save her and the ... or it *would* have been obvious, I think, if she really ... oh, leave it. "It will cost us very little," I say, thinking this is in its favour. Lydia is suspicious. "Why is it so cheap?" "The owner is away," I say. "Where?" she asks. I hesitate. I decide to tell her. "They say he is in prison in Thailand." "Who are they?" "Um, the other people in the house." "Is it a squat?" "I would not call it that." "What would you call it?" "A transitional home." "How many rooms does the flat have?" "A bed-sitting room and a kitchen." "You mean we have to share the bathroom and the WC? How many other people have to share the bathroom and the WC?" "Not many," I say. "How many?" "A few." I say we are lucky, it could be worse, but to a girl who has never had to put a lavatory seat down in order to sit on it this is uncharted territory.

Lydia notes the rubble left out on the pavements of Beaumont Road, W.11, the cracked stucco façades and the doorways littered with bells and loose wiring. "The area is in the process of transition," I say. "From bad to worse," she supposes. I mention the lack of through traffic. At that moment a tin-lined works lorry with a shovel loose in the back drives by on its way to a building site two doors down. We look around the flat. "I believe some Chinese students were here before us," I say. Lydia inspects the kitchen. "They seem to have done a lot of frying," she says.

We scrape the kitchen walls free of grease and move in. "We have to see beyond the squalor," I say. "This can be home." I order a pint of milk to be delivered daily, but it keeps disappearing, so I get up early one morning and keep watch on the front porch through a gap in the curtains. A woman from the basement is taking our milk. I confront her. She says, "Oh, I thought it was, like, a communal pint, you know, for the cats." I say, "It's for our baby." "Maybe you ought to, like, order another pint," she says helpfully. She talks as if her mind were not quite connected to her body. "What kind of baby is it?" she asks. "Quite a small one," I say. "Would you like a cup of tea?" she asks. I look at her. Pale, blonde, thin, with tangled hair. She might have been attractive once. "All right," I say, and follow her to the basement. Her room is dark and full of books. There are books on the floor, on shelves, on chairs, in shopping bags and boxes. And there are cats. I'm not sure how many. She pours out my milk for her cats and puts the kettle on. "I'm Jim," I say. "Geraldine," she says. I ask her what she does. "Nothing much. I read a bit." "What are you reading at the moment?" "A book called The Doors of Perception. Far out," she says. "Don't suppose you know where I can get hold of any mescaline?" "Er, no," I say. She finds what looks like a used tea bag. "And I'm getting into The Tibetan Book of the Dead. Really cool. Have you read it?" "I've heard about it." "It's about what follows death, you know, the stages leading up to the Great Liberation, awareness freed from the body to, like, create its own reality." "Wouldn't it be better for it to do that while you're alive?" I ask. "You should read the book," she says.

A man's head appears from under a duvet on a mattress on the floor. "Say hello to whatsiname, Jim, from upstairs, Rick," says Geraldine. "Hi," says Rick. He reaches out for a half-smoked joint. "Hi," I say. It may be the first time I have used the word as a greeting. "Can you spare a couple of quid?" he asks. "Shut up, Rick," says Geraldine. "Take no notice," she says to me. "Er, no," I say to Rick. "Sorry." Why am I apologizing? Rick shrugs and lights his joint. Geraldine brings me my tea in a used mug from the kitchen sink. I move a pile of books and a partially-eaten pizza to make room to sit on the sofa. I offer to help sort her books, thinking I might borrow one or two. "Take what you like, like any time," she says. "I might try the Book of the Dead sometime," I say. "I could do with a bit of liberating." Rick crawls out of bed naked, scratches himself and goes over to stroke one of the cats. "Hello, Josh," he says. "How are you? Yeah. Me too."

I finish my tea. "Well, I shall leave you to it," I say. Geraldine brings me what is left of the milk. "For the baby," she says. "Thank you, no, you keep it," I say. I'm not sure what I am leaving them to other than the sort of thing I have seen in television documentaries. I do not mention any of this to Lydia, but I think we might be living in a drug den.

The previous Easter while I was still in the military and had a day off I came across a crowd of people marching along Whitehall to Trafalgar Square. I stayed to hear speeches about nuclear disarmament and I was moved. Now it is Easter again. Geraldine and Rick invite Lydia, me and the baby to join them on a two-day march to London from the atomic weapons establishment in Aldermaston. They plan to spend the night of Day One in Rick's tent on Chiswick Common.

The idea of spending the night in a tent with Geraldine and Rick does not have quite the same sense of adventure for Lydia as it has, in passing, for me. I argue the case for going on the march. "It is for J.P.'s future," I say. "The Bishop of Woolwich will be there. I know him a little." Lydia is unmoved. "J.P.'s future does not depend on finding our way to Aldermaston and walking back to London, with or without the Bishop of Woolwich, but on finding a decent place to live." I acknowledge the point and offer a compromise: forget the tent, we'll just go on the second leg, from Chiswick to Trafalgar Square. Lydia refuses, so I go alone. I am upset that she does not share my commitment to unilateral nuclear disarmament. Well, she hasn't been in the army, she wouldn't have to press the button. Nor would I, but if I were entrusted with the code for the safe in which the button was kept I would have some serious thinking to do.

Over the next months we find ourselves sharing Beaumont Road with a succession of vegetarians, vagrants, students and street entertainers. There is a fire-eating actress who is teaching herself to juggle while riding a unicycle, a woman in a kaftan who sells crystals in Portobello market, a man with a dog who sits on the pavement outside Holland Park tube all day, and an extreme vegan who only eats grass, which he cultivates in pots that he keeps on his windowsill. Some of these people are there longer than others. The man who eats grass is the first to go. He dies, unfortunately.

It isn't long before Lydia has had enough of London. When I finish my course at the Film School, she declares, she will use some of her trust fund to rent us a cottage in the country. This must at long last be the direst of dire circumstances for her. She will get back to painting, she says, and I can write or research or go for long walks. "Excellent," I say, "I was thinking of writing a script about Alexander the Great and his failure to conquer India. I could adapt it for a book." "Fine," says Lydia. "Or I could write it as a book and adapt it for a script." "Whatever," she says. There is a tiny bohemian part of Lydia to which the idea of artist, writer and baby in a thatched cottage in Dorset appeals. We check out the small ads in The Observer. Thatched cottages in Dorset are rather expensive, so we end up renting a redbrick shack near a pig farm in Hertfordshire. It rains a lot and niffs a bit whenever the wind changes, but it is quiet.

I sit in the kitchen in front of a portable typewriter while Lydia sets up her paints and canvases. We are getting on well enough, but there always seems to be something between us – a thin layer of mist that intensifies or subsides to a greater or lesser degree, but is ever-present, like a recurring disease. Occasionally I glimpse a pale light of ease and trust through the mist, but it never grows brighter and the haze never clears. I am committed to someone I will never really know. I look at my typewriter. Rather than write about Alexander the Great in India perhaps I should write about our marriage. It would mean changing all the names. I switch on the radio.

> "This is the BBC Light Programme, the time is twelve thirty and here is a summary of the News. Mr Macmillan told the Commons that he was still

looking forward to meeting Mr Kennedy, but that it was too early to make plans."

Alternatively, I could write about my mother and the memsahibs, and how they witnessed and did their best to resist the end of Empire.

> "That is the end of the News. And now for Have a Go, with Wilfred Pickles. This week's Have a Go comes from the pleasant town of Duckford. The only thirst you can quench here is a thirst for knowledge at the technical college. There are seventeen places of worship and no pubs! So with Mabel at the table and Harry Hudson on the piano, let us meet some of the good folk of Duckford!"

I can hardly write about the intermittent appearances in my life of my mother without bringing in my absent father and abusive stepmother. Oh dear, this is all getting too personal.

> "Are you Miss or Missis?"
> "Missis."
> "Have you any family, Missis?"
> "Yes. Two boys and two girls." (Applause)
> "And how long have you lived in Duckford?"
> "I've lived here for thirty-five years." (Applause)
> "Well now, that's grand. Now who wears the trousers in your house?"
> "We all do." (Laughter)
> "Give 'er the money, Mabel!" (Applause)

If I were to write anything like the truth about my family, Lydia and people like Polly and Aunt Ada, it would have to be a fiction.

> "Well, good evening, sir. I've got a gentleman by me. Will you tell me your name?"
> "Ron Pickering."

In which case even if I knew nothing about the real psychopathology of these people, I could make it up. That might not be so difficult.

> "Ron, what do you like about living in Duckford?"
> "Oh, well it's convenient, isn't it?"
> "Do you consider the rents here reasonable?"
> "Oh, reasonable, yes, for what you can get, aren't they?"
> "Now I keep saying this town's beautiful, what do you think?"
> "Oh, yes."
> "If you could get on a soap box at Hyde Park Corner, what subject would you, well, get hot under the collar about?"
> "Well, that's kind of awkward to answer, you see I'm a civil servant, I've got to be careful what I say." (Laughter)
> "Ha, ha! Ron, I'm going to ask you the running question. If I am not what I shall be what am I? Do you know the answer?"

"No."

"Mabel, give 'im the money!" (Laughter and applause)

There is another problem. It would be difficult to write about the people in my life without bringing myself into it too, and I don't want to do that. I don't know myself. I wouldn't know what to say. Then I realize I could make that up too. As with Geraldine and The Book of the Dead my awareness would be free to create its own reality.

Lydia returns from the shops. "So what is it about?" she asks. I need to have something to show for the two weeks I have spent listening to the radio, making pots of tea and staring out of the window at the pigs in the adjacent field, so I improvise wildly. "What I have so far is a scene where this chap is asleep in bed with this woman and this other woman comes in." Lydia is in no mood to listen. "I did not get on well with the attendants at the launderette. All I did was ask them for more soap." I ask her why that is a problem. "Because they did not give me enough in the first place. I think they didn't give me enough soap on purpose, it has got to that state." I try to show interest. "Did you get on with the launderette lady in Notting Hill?" I ask. "No. All her other customers came in wearing suede jackets and fur coats. How far have you got?" "I told you," I say. "This chap is asleep in bed with this woman and this other ... no, man, it should be a man who comes in. He lives in the flat – well, I don't know if he lives in the flat with them or not. And the man who has been sleeping with this woman found this other man who committed suicide because he had been abused as a child." "Oh no," says Lydia. "Something like that," I say. "And the man who comes into the room has not been sleeping with anyone." "Why not?" I suppose she is trying to be helpful. "Well, it is not necessary to the plot." "Why not?" This is getting annoying. "Perhaps he has a wife or something. Anyway, this woman comes round and says, 'Go and get Fred'. She does not like to go herself, you see, because Fred is in bed with someone." "Oh, I see," says Lydia. I don't think she does. "Right, so he comes downstairs – " "Or goes upstairs." "Or goes upstairs and says, 'Get up, Ron has committed suicide', or Ned, 'Ned has committed suicide', and the man in bed with the woman is not shocked, you know, he is quite excited, as it is quite thrilling in a sick way to hear of someone committing suicide."

"Is that the story?" asks Lydia.

"So far."

"When do you think you will have it finished?"

What is the hurry, I wonder.

"Are you saying it does not sound right?" I ask. "The fact that she has been sleeping with him? I mean, would it not make her more distressed if she had not been sleeping with him?"

"I don't know."

"Well, the reason is the night before, you see, she said I am not going to sleep with you anymore."

"Why not?"

"Because fidelity is the thing and I am going to stick by Fred, or Ned."

"He committed suicide for that?"

"It is a bit implausible, isn't it? I think I shall have to think of another reason."

"Get on with it, then. Would you like some cocoa?"

It is a lot harder than she thinks, this writing business. I notice that I seem to be thinking about sex and suicide a lot. "Shit!" exclaims Lydia. "He has swallowed too much castor oil. Look it up in Doctor Spock, will you? It might be under emoluments or ointments." I find our baby Bible. "There is something here about vitamin D," I say. "Is he getting enough vitamin D?" "Oh god, he is being sick!" she says. She finds a nappy to wipe it up. "He has brought up three lots, one after the other. And he only had stewed apple and fried bread and milk."

After four weeks of feeding you, washing your nappies and listening to the rain rattling on the roof, Lydia is getting restless. She has not been inspired to paint much. And I have not been very productive. I have written six pages about Ron and Fred, but Alexander the Great and his mother keep coming into it. I read somewhere that Alexander's mother slept with snakes and I thought there might be some mileage in that.

It is clear that neither of us has enough to show for our month in the country, so we return to Beaumont Road and look round the flat. No-one seems to have squatted in it while we were away. I acknowledge that it could do with fixing here and there. "Have you noticed, James," says Lydia, "that we have no bathroom or toilet to ourselves?" I infer that this is no place to bring up a baby. "I will look for a job," I say. "Good," she says. "I shall take Julian to my mother's for a few days."

When they have gone I sit at my typewriter and switch on the radio. It has become a habit when I have nothing better to do. I am hoping that something will emerge.

> "The Royal Philharmonic Orchestra under Sir Thomas Beecham were playing Elgar's Serenade for Strings. We have been reading the book Wake Up Stupid – Fred Majdalany?"

I wonder if I might fit Ron Pickering, Alexander the Great's mother and Fred Majdalany into a sex and suicide scenario.

> "Well, do we like Lee Youngdarl? It seemed to me there was a good deal of adolescent bounce and juvenile humour about this book that I found alarming. Basic situation: man slips on banana. Well, I hate wags and I hate waggishness and it seemed to me a waggish book."

It might all culminate in Alexander the Great's humiliating retreat from the plains of Ganga-Yamuna. Then I remember I am meant to be looking for work.

> "Splendid. Well now, to the film. Metcalf?"

> "Yes, it's a good job of its kind, but it's not a very good kind. Why, one asks, did Sellers decide to do this film? Is this the proverbial desire of the clown to play Hamlet?"

I feel guilty. I leave the flat and go for a walk. Why am I so lacking in direction? Who can I blame? Alexander's mother comes to mind. Anybody's mother. Easy targets for my failings and the ills of the world..

I am walking past the Commonwealth Institute in Holland Park when I see a poster advertising for porters. I go in and to my surprise get a job. A proper job. I will be paid. I phone Lydia. "How much are they paying you?" "Not very much." "For how long?" "I don't know," I say. "When do you expect to be back?" "I'll call you," she says. "We don't have a phone," I remind her. "I'll write," she says.

My responsibilities at the Commonwealth Institute consist of putting chairs out in rooms, putting them away again and moving portable screens between one room and another. It is not too demanding and doesn't take long. My porter colleagues and I spend the rest of the time in the basement listening to the radio and playing cards. I think that this experience of having a pointless job will come in useful some day in my life as a writer.

> "And it's Evans coming in to bowl to Savile, bowls to him, long hop, played straight out to silly mid-on to Wooller, who fumbles it. Neither the bowling nor the batting – nor the fielding, really – has been of a very high standard today."

The Institute is preparing an exhibition of contemporary sculpture and between moving chairs and screens between rooms my porter colleagues and I contribute an exhibit of our own. We put a random pile of chairs together and type up a notice.

> EMPTINESS Voldemars Vrublevskis 1939 – Latvia:
> 'I see through vacant eyes. All is interim. All is indigent'.

Not many visitors get to view this radical new work before it is discovered by the management and the artists who created it – me, Biff, George and Dingo – are summarily dismissed. I phone Lydia from a phone booth with the news. "Did you get my letter?" she asks. "No. What does it say?" "It says I am not coming back to London. It says I will live with you only on condition that you get a job up here and buy a house." I ask her if she is joking. She confirms that she is not. I can hear her mother in the background. It all feels very unpleasant.

I have to talk to someone, so I go down to the basement and ring Geraldine's bell. She is tense, but lets me in. Several other people I do not know are there. She is busy doing something on the gas stove with a spoon and silver foil. This might not be a good time, I think, so I go back upstairs and look out at the street through the dirt on the window. The sun is lighting every speck of dust in the air. I go outside and sit on the front step. A toothless old man I met when we first moved in comes by wearing a long army greatcoat with no buttons. He complains that someone in the Post Office has been telling his neighbours that he lives with married women. He is upset. I suggest he might be mistaken. He insists it is so. "Oh, well then …" I say, and he walks on, stopping now and again to pick up cigarette butts. I watch him, thinking that some day that could be me.

Geraldine appears, looking more relaxed. I tell her that Lydia has left me and taken the baby and I have to go after them. Geraldine is not too concerned. "Let's, you know, go for a walk," she says. We wander the streets and squares of Notting Hill and end up in a bookshop on Holland Park Avenue. I look at all the books I would like to own, but cannot afford. When we leave I notice that Geraldine's shopping bag is full of books. "I didn't see you buy those," I say. She gives me a 'My God, Jim, but you are naïve' kind of look.

Who is this woman, I ask myself. I know nothing about her. If I were a real writer, I think, I wouldn't care so much, I would make her up. "I really don't know you, Geraldine," I say. "Are you saying you want to sleep with me, Jim?" she asks. "No, no!" I protest, though I probably do. What is stopping me being honest and saying, 'Well, now that you mention it, yes'? "I don't know Lydia either," I say, "and I don't know myself." "Your problem, Jim," she says, "is that you think there is something to know." She is right, I do think that. Hardly anything is transparent between Lydia and me and that just isn't good enough. "Relax, Jim," says Geraldine. "You have to go with the flow." Suddenly I have had enough of her stupid hippy-talk. "What fucking flow?" I cry. "There's no fucking flow!" She laughs. I calm down. "I have to pack," I say. "All I know is I have to go, but I could be back."

φ

Chapter 22

Crime and Punishment

I TAKE THE TRAIN TO UPHAM about as enthusiastically as a lamb that has had a whiff of the abattoir. There is no room for me or my single suitcase at Mrs Ripley's, I am told, though there obviously is, so a friend from university days puts me up on his sofa. What Lydia and her mother are saying by their conditions – get a job, buy a house – is that this is my last chance to join them in the aspiring lower-middle classes. Having been raised in the outside-toilet, cockroach-shovelling class, spent time in the port-and-Madeira class and dropped overnight into the living-in-a-squat (did I mention the rats?) class, I am not too bothered either way. My priority is to see my son.

The only way I can get to see you is by making an appointment forty-eight hours in advance and waiting at the Ripleys' back door for you to be brought out in your pram, ready dressed and fed and, more often than not, asleep. I am not invited in.

Lydia informs me that if I am not back by four o'clock her mother has threatened to call the police, social services and the environmental cleansing department. Mrs R is as pitiless as a Greek goddess with a grievance and her daughter, unexpectedly, is proving almost equally severe. I have no choice but to conform to their petty conditions. I behave nicely. I am as nice as pie.

I look in the local phone book under three headings – Film, Publishing and Museums – and write to three organizations: to Corinthian Pictures – the allusion to the most noble of classical orders and the highest standards of sportsmanship appeals to me; to Philemon Press – perhaps I shall pursue a career editing books on arcane subjects of educational interest; and to the Council Department of Leisure and Libraries, where I see myself translating ancient *papyri* and *pergaminae* in the basement of an Institute of Learning for the benefit of generations of students and researchers to come.

To my surprise I am offered three interviews. The first is with the Council, where a junior administrative post is available in Urban Traffic Management. "Nothing in museums?" I ask. "We have the occasional vacancy for an attendant," they say. Well, one has to start somewhere. "Though not at present."

Almost before I sit down at Philemon Press I am offered a job selling Encyclopaedia Britannica. Bless me, but for a moment I am tempted. The Sales

Director ("call me Steve, Jim") assures me that my education and experience are perfect for the job. For several minutes I imagine they might be. I ask Steve for twenty-four hours to think it over.

The next day I have an interview with Corinthian Pictures, a small film company specializing in documentaries and television commercials. They seem impressed by my course at the London Film School, discover that I know one end of a Bolex from the other and after little more than half an hour offer me a job as a general trainee at £12 10s a week.

For a split second I compare a career in film-making to the possibilities of urban traffic management and encyclopaedia sales. I cannot say that Lydia is pleased that I have landed a job with prospects so quickly. She is more grimly satisfied that her first condition has been met. She wastes no time fulfilling the second condition herself. Within a fortnight she has found us a three-bedroomed end-terrace twenty minutes' walk from her mother's and I have signed up for a mortgage that will take £3 3s a week from my wages.

My colleagues at Corinthian (Dan, Stan, Ed and Ted) teach me to operate 16mm Arriflex and Bolex and 35mm Caméflex cameras, hump lights, record sound, edit film with a cement splicer, cut negative, write scripts, add music, thread projectors, make tea, sweep the studio and drive the van. Dan is producer-director-writer-editor and occasional cameraman, Stan director-cameraman and occasional sound recordist, Ed sound mixer, technician and stand-in stills photographer, and Ted heavy lifter, general factotum and sparks. Together we make documentaries about shipbuilding, the manufacture of crisps and the demolition of a large chimney, and commercials with taglines such as Domestos Kills All Known Germs, Upham Best Bitter Is The Best By Far, and Ackroyd's Plumbing Services Will Not Send You Round The Bend. Dan, Stan, Ed and Ted are patient, knowledgeable and generous with their time, and I learn quickly

The company is commissioned to record the maiden voyage of a gargantuan tanker round the coast to Falmouth in Cornwall for fitting-out. Director-cameraman Stan is unavailable. He has been booked to film a critical scene in the studio involving two large dinner plates, one of which will show the effect of germs left on the surface after it has been washed in an ordinary liquid, the other the remarkable difference after it has been washed in water to which a small measure of Domestos has been added. Stan is an acknowledged expert at this kind of thing and cannot be spared to film on the tanker, so I have my first break. I am sent on board with a hand-held Bolex to film whatever takes my fancy, while producer-director-cameraman Dan records the launch from the shore with the big blimped Caméflex, then drives down to Falmouth to record the tanker arriving and docking.

I lurch around the ship aiming my camera at nothing very exciting while the half-empty shell makes its way through the waves. I feel as queasy as I had in the Bay of Biscay on the voyage that saw the loss of my mother's unborn child. As we approach the Straits of Dover there is a shudder in the deck and the ship's engines stop. I hear voices from the bridge. I imagine an episode from the wartime life my father led as a German destroyer approaches at speed off the starboard bow. Guns are firing, shells explode, there are screams of pain, lifeboats are launched. I hear the note of drama in the music as I come to edit the sequence.

This sense of detachment stays with me as Dan opts to drive us home from Falmouth through the night to save on hotel bills and I wake on my back by the side of the road with a severe headache. It is dark, there are unintelligible sounds, I see firemen and ambulance men moving around the scene of what looks like a terrible accident. As I am lifted from the grass verge I have a glimpse of Dan slumped behind the wheel of his car. What is he doing there?

Shards of glass are picked from my hair and cuts to my head and lip are stitched. They say my colleague is unconscious in intensive care with a ruptured spleen and that we have been involved in a head-on collision with a car that was coming towards us on the wrong side of the road. The other driver died at the scene. Either I was asleep at the time of the accident or the trauma of the impact has wiped the event from my memory.

I phone Lydia, minimizing the unpleasantness as best I can, discharge myself from the hospital and make my way home. "I was worried when I didn't hear from you," she says. She somehow omits to ask me how I am. "Why didn't you phone earlier?" "A bit tricky," I say, "as I was unconscious at the time." This was uncalled for, I realize. "There is no need for sarcasm, James," she says, and goes on about my failure to keep her informed.

Dan never recovers consciousness and dies in intensive care. I do not go to the funeral. I have survived, Dan has not, and I feel guilty and ashamed.

Director-cameraman Stan has no interest in taking on the roles of producer, writer and editor too, and in any case is planning to emigrate to New Zealand. The owner of Corinthian calls me into his office and asks me if I am up to the job. I have been with the company for not much more than a year and feel inexplicably confident. He says he wants continuity. I ask for a raise. He offers me £15 a week, I ask for £17, we split the difference and he hints that this might go up incrementally, but to no more than £19 19s, as that was Dan's salary.

Lydia seems slightly impressed. It means that we can move out of the suburban shadow of her mother into a Victorian terrace in a trendier part of town. Our mortgage repayments double, but my income goes up too. A television producer friend auditions me for a weekly programme presenting excerpts from viewers' letters. I am certain it has nothing to do with the fact that I am giving his actress wife a lot of voice-over work at the time. The fee is twelve guineas a programme, a posh way of not paying very much, but it makes a significant difference to the Seagrave household.

Lydia is reluctant to acknowledge my television work publicly. Television is not very cool among her artistic and academic friends. They might admit to watching

What's My Line? or an occasional episode of The Forsyte Saga, but only as a respite from their painting, sculpting, composing and writing obscure poetry.

We hold a housewarming party. The date coincides with one of my pre-recorded Saturday evening television slots, so I switch on the programme to run in the background while people are partying. I want to be noticed, though only in a self-mocking, ironical kind of way, of course. No-one notices. They are too busy networking, flirting, smoking *Gauloises* and watching a live event that Lydia has organized. She has asked an artist friend, Fitz, to create a mural on our dining room wall and he is splashing and slapping away to *O Fortuna* from Carmina Burana while consuming pint after pint of my Upham Ale. The result is what Lydia describes as "a seminal *chef d'oeuvre*", or dog's dinner, as I think of it, but it is typical of the kind of thing we find ourselves doing in the sixties. When the fuss has died down I plan to paint it over with magnolia.

Another thing we find ourselves doing in the sixties is having sex rather freely, as most young women are now on the pill. I say 'we' are having sex rather freely. I have to exclude myself and your mother. We are having sex exclusively with each other. It is hardly a chore, but I am beginning to feel I am missing out on something in the *zeitgeist* that is almost obligatory. Am I expecting too much? When *Hera* reproaches *Zeus* for his infidelities, he argues that when he does share her couch she derives far greater pleasure from what they get up to than he does. "Nonsense," says Hera. "How would you know?" asks Zeus. So they call in a mediator, *Tiresias*, to adjudicate. Tiresias recently had a sex change and seems to be speaking from personal experience.

> If the parts of love-pleasure be counted as ten,
> Thrice three go to women, one only to men

says he. That is pretty much my impression too. What am I missing? To reward Tiresias for his insight, Zeus gives him long life and the gift of prophecy, but Hera is upset that her secret is out and strikes the poor soothsayer with blindness. There you go, the truth will not always set you free. Whether Tiresias is right or not in his assessment I find myself wondering if sex might be more varied or fun or fulfilling, if only to compensate for the nagging sense of *ennui* I tend to feel when it is over.

And so it comes about one evening that I embark on what I intend to be an amicable exchange with Lydia on the subject of what everyone else is up to – everyone, that is, but us. I go on about sexual expression being a creative force akin to the need to paint, sculpt, compose and write obscure poetry, and that there is a cost to be paid in constraining it. "How lucky we are," I say, "to live in an era in which it is possible to explore oneself freely in relation to others while still remaining committed to one special person," and so on.

Well, you know your mother, if not in these terms, so do you think she buys into any of this?

Lydia argues that sex is a primitive, preliterate activity that marriage was expressly designed to contain. She describes the times we are in as loose rather than liberating, an unwelcome return to the pox-ridden practices of the eighteenth century. I object to the appearance of the word 'pox' in our discussion. "What would you prefer?" asks Lydia. "Sexually transmitted diseases that can kill you, infect others and cause serious social disruption?" The mood deteriorates. She starts using words like supererogatory, retrogressive, prurient, deviant, phallocentric and atavistic, but they only serve to provoke me, because I'm not sure what some them mean. I call on Jean-Paul Sartre and Simone de Beauvoir as witnesses in my appeal against a life sentence of sexual fidelity imposed by the Court of Stagnation. I argue that society as a whole benefits from our personal freedom, and add that I am determined not to be embarrassed by this simple truth. The problem, I am reminded, is that there is no such thing. The truth is never the same for any of us.

Lydia speaks emphatically to hers. "Real freedom brings moral responsibility, James," she says. "You are talking about wilful interference with the precious principles and intimacies of marriage." "If by wilful you mean voluntary rather than contrary – " I start to say, but she interrupts: "Call it what you like, James, it's adultery!" The temperature in the courtroom is rising. "There is no such thing as adultery in the Age of Aquarius!" I cry portentously, and add, "I am talking about love in all its colours!" Lydia isn't. "Pff!" says she. I fear that that might be it. I know from bitter experience there is no answer to "Pff!"

I try a different approach. 'We are fortunate to be living in a time of cultural and political transition with an unprecedented opportunity to explore and express revolutionary new values of love, brotherhood, unity and community' is what I wish I'd said. In fact I burble on about freeing ourselves from the stuffy inhibitions of the fifties. "It is time to fling open the windows to experience!" I cry. "No no!" cries she. "There is an irritating wind outside and it is causing too much turmoil!" She purses her lips, never a good sign. I huff and haw. And what began as an adult discussion deteriorates into childish whining on my part and an habitual tight-lipped retreat into silence on hers.

Then two things happen that will have a chilling effect on our lives – and yours too, I'm afraid – forever. The first takes place at the housewarming party while *Carmina Burana* is playing *ad nauseam* and Lydia's pompous friend Fitz is hurling paint at the blank canvas of our dining room wall. I find myself sitting on the stairs with Fitz's girlfriend, Nina, who is making the kind of roll-your-own that was Rick's speciality in Notting Hill. She takes an extra-long cigarette paper into which she drops and distributes shreds of a brownish-green substance that looks very much like tobacco. It is marijuana, I realize. It has arrived in the regions. Nina twists one end of the paper into a pointed shape and talks about feeling neglected. I confess to something similar and at the same time to feelings of frustration. Nina looks at me. "You mean sexually or professionally?" she asks. I look at her. I'm sure her pupils dilate. Either she is showing interest in me or anticipating her first drag of the day. "Both," I say. She lights her spliff, draws deeply and offers me a turn. I pretend to know what I am doing. We talk, inhale, cough, exchange, talk some more, no idea about what, I begin to feel hazy, doesn't matter, we kiss, fumble, stumble upstairs and fall into bed. The room is circling round my head. I feel euphoric, then ambivalent, then incapable, then ridiculous, then we stop and stumble downstairs as though nothing has happened, which is almost, if not quite, the case. It is my first sexual encounter outside marriage since Lydia and I booked a double room and eiderdown at the Glenorchy Hotel, Kings Cross.

The second thing happens a few months later. I am upset at the government's continued refusal to contemplate nuclear disarmament and determined to go on the CND march that year. Lydia will not come. Even though our relationship is far from smooth I still want to believe there is a basic affective affinity between us, but her refusal to accompany me to an event of such personal, national and global importance leaves me feeling isolated and deflated. At least that is my excuse for what happens next.

I take the train to London, turn up at the squat and doss down with Rick and Geraldine. They are kind enough to clear the needles and takeaways off the sofa to make room for me. The next day the three of us go on the first leg of the march together, but in the evening Rick disappears. He has taken his tent, so Geraldine and I return to the basement and I join her under the duvet.

Sexual intercourse with Geraldine is nothing like the liberating psychedelic experience I had been anticipating. She is only the second woman I have slept with (I exclude Nina and the librarian in Upham on technical grounds) and I learn to my dismay that the business can actually be – well, the word that occurs to me is mundane. My partner is nothing like as excited as she might have been and the cats on the duvet do not help. But I have finally broken the adultery duck – another cricketing analogy, bear with me, in terms of soccer you might call it a no-score draw after extra time – and I am able to convince myself that I feel no differently about Lydia.

I say nothing to Lydia for months. You might reasonably suggest it would have been better to say nothing at all. The fact is I wanted to prove to her that it hadn't made the slightest difference to our relationship, had it, just as I said it wouldn't, hadn't I?

Lydia once vowed that she would never vote Labour, but when I join the local party she comes along to meetings and when I am elected Branch Secretary she agrees to stand as Treasurer. She knows less about accounting than she does about socialism, but the members who vote her in don't seem to mind at all. I speculate that she might be wanting to compensate for our disagreements over sex, CND and Pythagoras (as a secondary name for Julian, not in a geometric sense), so I reciprocate by accompanying her to her friends' exhibitions and concerts, and being as forgiving as I possibly can be with her mother.

The fact that we have more of a life together outside the house can only be a good thing, I think. There will be more trust between us, I think. So one evening when we are onto our third *margarita* and with music by a new group called the Pink Floyd playing in the background the talk turns to the innovative times we are in and from there to some of the unconventional things that our friends and neighbours are up to. Lydia tut-tuts, but from her involuntary smile and a brief appearance of the dimples I can see that she finds the subject mildly arousing, so I speculate that this might be a good time to come clean. "Okay," I say. "I can prove to you that the occasional extracurricular fling can be a good thing. At our housewarming a year ago Nina and I fell into bed together, but nothing much happened, it was a bit of drunken fun, and six months ago Geraldine put me up for the night after the CND march." The air suddenly turns cold. "You mean you had sex?" asks Lydia. "Well, define your terms," I say, in a misguided attempt to be amusing. "I guess you could call it that." I go on. "I didn't enjoy it much, as it happens. Actually it was quite …" No no, I think, this is too much information, but I blabber on. "… unpleasant." "So it would have been all right if you had enjoyed it?" "Er …" I think hard. What is the point I was trying to make? "The important thing is that it did not affect my feelings for you. In fact I have enjoyed our Sunday mornings in bed with the papers even more." "Even more than what?" she asks. 'Than Monday mornings', I almost say. "Than before," I say, lamely, then pause. Is this the right thing to say? Is it even true?

Pink Floyd comes to an end. Piper at the Gates of Dawn, I recall, though it could easily have been the Gates of Hell. There is an ominous silence, a silence so thick and clotted that it clings to everything in the room. Okay, I say to myself, I have been clumsy. I have not expressed myself as elegantly as I might have done, but she will question me, I will clarify things, we will mix another margarita and continue our mature discussion. I am not confessing to anything criminal, after all. The serial adulterers you hear about are no better than fraudsters, conmen and timeshare salesmen. I am an amateur in comparison. "All I have done is exercise a little liberty," I say. "Non-threatening. Unifying, in fact. In the spirit of community." There is no response to this desperate argument. Have I said enough, I wonder. Almost certainly. But I can't help myself. I try another line.

"It's a male thing," I say. "They call it the biological imperative." "Who does?" snaps Lydia. "The girls at the checkout in Sainsbury's," I reply. This was a poor choice. "Social scientists," I say. "Is that so?" she counters. She is getting dangerously monosyllabic. Silence is almost certain to follow. "We are programmed for the widest possible continuance of the species," I continue, adding hastily, "Not that I intend to continue it with anyone but you." Something more is needed. "I do feel guilty," I say, "if that helps."

Lydia gets up from the sofa and goes upstairs. I curse myself. Where did this need for honesty come from? I blame the shame that my forebears attached to their lack of education, their poverty and lack of opportunity. I blame them for their shame-driven evasions and deceptions, as I have many times before when I needed something to deflect me from myself. With all my fancy arguments against the tyranny of the nuclear couple and for the open joys of polyamory, Great-grandma Barraclough would have taken me for a simple adulterer, no more acceptable in the 1960s than I would have been in the 1890s. And yet there is an anomaly here. Yorkshire folk were meant to be straightforward, sometimes cringeworthily so, even to the point of causing not entirely unintentional offence. We called it bluntness, a word pronounced with a plain, no-nonsense 'uh'. Bl*u*nt. It was supposed to be a virtue rather than, as I see it now, a shield against weakness. In Rawley Bay you would sooner expose yourself to the ravages of the sea than to raw feelings.

Unusual sounds are coming from upstairs. I go up. It is dark outside. Rain is beating on the windows. Lydia is working conscientiously, taking the contents of my wardrobe from the bedroom and throwing them into the spare room. I watch as she empties the contents of my sock drawer onto the spare bed without a word being said. After my pillow has made the involuntary journey, I can contain myself no longer. "Have you nothing to say?" I ask. She continues to walk back and forth, silently dumping. Dumping turns to flinging. Eventually she speaks, coldly and precisely. "Do not ever think about sleeping with me ever again." I think about this for a moment. I am tempted to point out that her second 'ever' duplicates the function of the first unless her intention is to provide convincing back-up in case I missed it the first time and fail to grasp the seriousness of the situation. And I do. I grasp the seriousness of the situation and say nothing.

It is the start of a three-day silence between us, nowhere near the record, but a serious attempt at it nonetheless. And then we talk. And a limited if coherent agreement emerges. I will sleep in the spare room for three months – I negotiate this down from six – after which we will see. It is a separation that preserves the appearance of the marriage for the sake of – what? who? J.P.? Her mother? The postman?

I remember my adolescent ideals about Polly Unmore that were crushed when she left and extinguished altogether when we met again. And I wonder, does all love comes to this – a raging sickness that begins in desperation and ends in despair? Who or what is at fault here? Me and my incoherent sentimentalism or Lydia and her unrelenting idealism? Both, I say now, but I could not see it so at the time.

Polly tried to show me that Don Juan was not such a terrible fellow. He was in the tradition of roguish young men of low birth who made their way in a corrupt society via their cunning and courage. There are elements of that analysis that both attract and repel me. After all, Byron had not fixed in his mind whether Don Juan would end in hell or in an unhappy marriage – 'not knowing', wrote the author, 'which would be the severest'. Either way he knew that his protagonist was predestined to fail.

Any cunning I had once is no longer working for me, that much is obvious. I do have some courage remaining, however, some patience. A couple of weeks after moving into the spare room I see a television interview in which a psychologist recommends that former Minister of War John Profumo should "clear the air" with his wife, actress Valerie Hobson, over his affair with Christine Keeler. The psychologist maintains that good relationships are not built on self-ideation, but on telling your partner how it really is for you. I am trying to do just that, I tell myself, so perhaps I am in the vanguard of progressive thinking in these matters. There is a sympathetic review of the programme in The Observer that I plan to discuss with Lydia, but she throws the paper out the same day.

Three weeks pass. A month. We make an effort to be civilized and polite with each other, and most of the time we succeed. Then Lydia seems to be having second thoughts. "This is not working," she says. "It is totally untenable." I am relieved. My patience and progressive thinking are about to be rewarded. "It *is* a crazy arrangement," I say. "I shall move my pillow back where it belongs." "Are you insane, James?" she exclaims. "Or just very, very stupid?" I admit to the possibility of being stupid. "What have I missed?" I ask. "You must move out altogether. It is the only way." And she adds a sentence that echoes in my head still: "If you do not move out you will come home from work one day and find I have left and taken Julian with me." For a moment I cannot compute what she has said. I am wondering if that shift from the simple future ("you will come home one day") to the future perfect ("I will have left") might be indicating a marginal shift in her position, but she reverts to the simple future so that I should be in no doubt. "I will take him while you are out and you will never find us. You will not know where we are." I know she is entirely capable of carrying out such a threat. "You have hurt me beyond healing," she says. She is not expressing her hurt in the past, but in the present perfect. Rather like my mother, she continues to hurt.

Now normally when someone speaks in such extreme terms we understand it is the voice of the deep disappointment they feel about themselves and the world that is making itself heard, and that sooner or later they will come round to a more philosophical or forgiving position. But there is this thing about Lydia, and you will know her well enough by now to know what I mean: she will carry out her threat *in order to prove to herself that she means it*. It is not a wish, but a promise. This may be a sign of terrible emotional insecurity, but I take it as nothing less than a brutal declaration of war. Finally I understand that love, for Lydia, is a practical, not a sentimental, matter. It is the first thing, not the last, to be frightened off by difficulty – by unemployment, say, or illness, or extramarital sex.

I have a choice. I can call her bluff and ignore her or I can take her to court. Both carry the certainty of a total breakdown in communication between us and that does not seem to be in anyone's interests, least of all our child's. Yet I have to face it: the relationship, or certainly this phase of it, is over. We are no longer the wide-eyed young gods who believed ourselves made for each other. We are monsters. I am a goat-footed *satyr* with a single useless eye, my blind romanticism turning out to be an excess of conceit. Lydia is a pitiless *Medusa* whose desire for revenge will poison a man and suck the life out of him. In the wider scheme of things we deserve each other.

Damocles only had to make it through a single evening with the sword of the tyrant hanging over his head. I have to live night and day with Lydia's threat. If I do not move out she will take our child and disappear. The likelihood of this happening hangs over me by a single thread. The threat is repeated unequivocally. And finally I give in. "All right" I say. "I shall find a flat nearby for a while. I shall come every evening to tell J.P. a story and put him to bed, and I shall continue to pay the bills on the house." My plan is to maintain as much contact and continuity as possible while this silliness sorts itself out. In return Lydia agrees that we will not divorce unless the decision is mutual. I convince myself that as the arrangement becomes predictable and tolerable, perhaps even amicable, we can be friends again and get back together.

And some of this happens. I find a one-room flat ten minutes' walk away, I continue paying the bills on the house, I come every evening to play with you, read to you and put you to bed, and we do stuff together on Sundays. The only variables I have left out of the equation are your feelings – I want to believe you are too young to notice or be troubled by what is happening – and my feelings – I feel lost and cursed – and Lydia's – though why should I be so surprised? She meets someone else.

I had not expected this. I believed that our agreement allowed us to lead our lives independently but adjacently, with the potential for renewal once we knew ourselves better and were more able to negotiate the relationship. Within a month of moving out I receive a solicitor's letter informing me that my wife has instituted proceedings for divorce. I confront her. We had an agreement. She refuses to discuss the matter. Her solicitors have told her there can be no hint of collusion or the legal process – still adversarial, mediation is not an option – will be compromised.

Had I known that her solicitors needed more evidence to make the case against me I might have been more circumspect about supplying it. I meet a journalist, Renata, at a party. She asks if she might interview me for an article on the swinging sixties that she is preparing for a Czech magazine. I am flattered, agree, and we meet at her hotel the next day for lunch. She mentions she is only here for a few days, but the hotel is expensive and she needs to find somewhere cheaper, do I happen to know of a place? Without thinking, I offer to put her up. "Oh no, James," she says, "I couldn't possibly." I insist, and that evening she moves in with a large suitcase. Well yes, we sleep together. It is the friendly thing to do, as there is only one bed.

Oh dear me, I hear you say. I deserve whatever tricks the gods might play on me for this ingenuous gesture in the middle of legal proceedings. It does not occur to me that if Lydia hears of this she will have ample grounds for the divorce I have been at such pains to avoid. I learn, too late, that you can be done for adultery even if it is not malicious or wilful, even if your wife has threatened to abduct your child, even if you have been blackmailed into leaving the family home and are living in one room, feeling lonely, paying two sets of bills and doing a good deed for a stranger. Lydia's analysis of the situation is almost certainly simpler than this: she plans to remarry and wants me out of the way.

Two days after Renata moves in there is a knock at the door. A small, tubby man stands there, perspiring from climbing the stairs. He wears a mac and a trilby. How did he get in the locked street door, I wonder. He shows me his card.

G. Truelove, Esq.
Quartermain Investigations
100% Confidential

"I'm sorry to disturb you, sir," he says. "Mr James Seagrave? Could I come in for a moment?" I realize how he has managed to gain entry to the building. Quartermain & Pumfrey are the managing agents for the flat. I remember something else. Quartermain, and Swindler is the name of Lydia's solicitors. Something like that. Though it could all be a coincidence.

I let Mr Truelove in. Politely, with a hint of apology, he explains how grateful he would be if I could offer him evidence of some kind along with a statement voluntarily admitting to – "How shall we put this, sir, fornication?" I am taken aback. It sounds a lot worse than the friendly coupling Renata and I have been enjoying. "My apologies," he says when he sees my reaction. "Fornication is a technical term we use for extramarital sex. Should you prefer, sir, we can call it adultery." I feel some relief. It is almost as if he has let me off the more serious charge and is offering to proceed with a lesser offence. "Some evidence that will give your wife straightforward grounds for an uncontested divorce," says Mr Truelove, "and make the whole thing that much easier, speedier and indeed, sir, and it is not to be sneezed at these days, is it, sir, cheaper." I offer him a cup of tea. "How very kind. Milk and two sugars." "What kind of evidence would be helpful?" I ask. He looks round the room. I am the hapless victim of a pitiless sting. Lydia is *Scylla*, her six vicious jaws reaching out to take me whichever way I turn. If I attempt to escape I shall only be sucked into the Charybdian vortex of the law.

Renata appears from the bathroom clad only in my dressing-gown. "Bit of a situation here, Renata," I say. "I wonder if you might help." Mr Truelove explains the responsibilities of a co-respondent, a legal nicety that requires her signature to a statement, nothing more. Renata is due to fly back to Prague in a day or two and does not mind in the least. Her only condition is that she should be free to write an article about the experience, though she promises to change all the names. That seems entirely reasonable. So the man in the mac and I set up a scenario in which he finds a neatly folded nightdress under the pillow and writes out statements for both of us to sign. He finishes his tea, doffs his trilby and bids us farewell. It is all very polite, if on the sleazy side, so I'm sure Renata will have enough material for a humorous article or two.

As part of the settlement drafted by one or other of the Quartermains and Lillicraps I sign over my share of the house in the expectation that this will give mother and child the security and continuity they need. The divorce goes through as a formality, though it soon becomes clear that Lydia has read every word of the Truelove Report, because shortly after receiving her solicitor's bill I get a letter from the managing agents for the flat giving me a month's notice to quit. Lydia goes on to sell the house I half-wittedly signed over to her, pockets the profits and moves in with her boyfriend. And exposed and bemused as I am, I let it happen.

It occurs to me that Lydia might have met this boyfriend of hers months ago and has been using my pathetic confession of a night in Notting Hill as an excuse for doing something she wanted to do anyway. Delusions of persecution, James. On reflection, I think it more likely that her actions were motivated by sexual revenge.

Either way, I have been punished. Hung, drawn and quartermained. When *Clytemnestra* took her epic vengeance on *Agamemnon* it was not because he had sacrificed one of their children to the gods, it was for nothing so prosaic, but because after looting Troy he brought home a female slave to be his mistress. The subsequent imbalance of sexual power tipped Clytemnestra's moral and mental scales. She murdered, not the slave, but the enslaver, a man of poor judgment who had been traumatized by war.

Lydia's retaliation seems to me more squalid than epic, but no revenge is ever sweet. Before setting out on such an undertaking the revenger is advised to dig two graves – only one of them for the intended victim. Clytemnestra herself was the next to go: murdered by her own son, no less.

It was entirely predictable that you would grow up to be rid of your mother too, Julian, by moving to Mexico. This greatly upset her. But was that any different to the anguish I caused my mother, the hurt my mother caused her mother and the heartache her mother caused hers? May the rot stop with you. Don't have children. If you do, don't cheat on their mother. And if you do feel the need to express yourself elsewhere, don't feel such remorse that you allow yourself to be butchered, chopped into small pieces and fed to the fishes. It could be said that your mother and I came together at this particular moment in history in order to learn something about ourselves and the human condition that could not be learnt in any other way, and in one way or another to pass that learning on. Well, for what it's worth, there you are.

After losing my flat I rent a cheap room in a damp basement nearby and tell myself it is no more than I deserve. Lydia marries her boyfriend, Bernard, and moves into a detached house with central heating and parquet flooring. I understand that she considers whether to offer her mother the granny flat in the garden, but finds her a place in a care home instead. It is around this time, by the way, that your mother gives up painting – an uncertain loss to the world of Abstract Art – and starts collecting antiques, which is less messy and potentially more profitable.

I affect indifference to all these events, but feel badly betrayed. I have been ripped off over the house, forced out of my flat, separated from my son and denied the remote but not inconceivable possibility of a reconciliation with my wife. Please do not tell me I brought this upon myself. I know.

It is not a good time and has a negative effect on my professional judgment. I turn up at the studio one day to direct a commercial for a DIY store – having foolishly agreed to a thirty-six hour deadline to shoot, edit, dub, cut the neg and deliver a print to the TV station – only to find that the cameraman has called in sick, the recordist overslept and the sparks has been taken into custody for an offence involving grievous bodily harm. Rather than postpone the shoot – clearly the sane thing to do in the circumstances – I have a divine revelation about the nature of reality. Inspired by my subject, I believe I can do it all myself.

The first shot, 'CU pensive housewife', requires the actress I have cast for the part to look at an unconvincing tear in the wallpaper on the studio living room set with a quizzical expression. The voice-over line in the script ('Thinking of wallpaper?') is simple, not to say simple-minded, enough, but getting the right oh-dear-what-shall-I-do-about-the-wallpaper look from the actress is proving unexpectedly difficult. The problem is the positioning of her forefinger, which she is holding delicately poised on her lower lip to indicate uncertainty. It does not look natural. "Try it a little to the left, dear," I say. "A little more, too far, back a bit. Great." I skip round the studio switching on the lights, nip into the sound booth to start the reel-to-reel, nip out again to turn on the big blimped Caméflex and pop in front of it to operate the clapperboard. I am in a half-crazed state, but don't know it. "Standby!" I call. "Action!" The actress puts on her pensive look, raises her forefinger to her lower lip and frowns slightly. "Cut!" I call. "Great!" I cry. Terrible, I think. The finger should be nearer the corner of her mouth – or should it be further away? – and the frowning eyebrows are not quite right. "One more take!" I skip around the studio switching everything off, nip back to direct the positioning of the finger and the eyebrows, then nip away to switch everything on again. The actress watches. "What am I thinking of?" she asks. "You're thinking of wallpaper," I remind her. "Ah yes. And exactly where do you want the finger?"

Seventeen takes. Skip, switch, shoot, knock off, nip back, fix finger, direct eyebrows ("up a bit, down a bit, can you move them independently?"). Finally I convince myself that the right take has to be in there somewhere, it will be all right on the night, so I move on to the next shot, 'CU wallpaper'. And this is how I come to make what is probably the worst commercial in the history of independent television. I manage to get the print to the TV station on time, only to discover while watching the transmission that I have forgotten to allow for the obligatory second-and-a-half of silence before the sound kicks in. The whole thing is out of sync, which means I have to re-edit, pay for another transmission and apologize to the agency and the sponsor, who are understandably inclined not to employ me again.

I cannot decide which is – to be a crap director or a homeless divorcé with a poor credit rating. In the absence of a sensible friend or a friendly barmaid to offer support, I revert to my allegorical worldview in which the entire pantheon of Greek gods is available for consultation. I begin by asking *Prometheus*, god of Reason and Wisdom, for his advice. He admits to being exhausted by recent events and suggests I slow down, make us both a cup of tea and pay my respects to *Hestia*, goddess of Hearth and Home. Hestia looks around my basement flat. "You need to clean and tidy the place from top to bottom," she says briskly, "and remember to dust the chair legs and hoover under the sofa." I protest, I am meant to be resting, but I do as she says. Now what? Should I descale the kettle? "How long is it since you re-ordered your books?" she asks. I am doubtful about the books. Should that be by size or by category, subcategory and so on, I ask myself, or by colour-coding – black spines, orange, white, etc?

It isn't easy for a true obsessive to decide on this kind of thing. Prometheus intervenes. "Your preoccupation with detail is leading you nowhere," he warns me. "You need to let things be for a while." Hestia is upset, but she is the lesser god, so Reason prevails over Cleaning and the pressure on me to do everything perfectly eases. The dust settles again. The books sort themselves randomly. And gradually my muddled ideals about life, work and relationships resolve into something more sensible and credible. I go out more and expect less, I make a half-decent film or two, I am nice to Lydia and Bernard without thinking they have to reciprocate, and I get to see my son. It is all very promising, but the gods are not done with me. Something is missing.

φ

Chapter 23

In the Shallows

THERE IS AN IDYLLIC STRETCH OF THE RIVER that runs through Upham and skirts its mediaeval cathedral, and one summer Sunday I am picnicking on the banks of the river with friends when I find myself in conversation with a Frenchwoman, a teacher on sabbatical. She is introduced to me by a mutual friend as Céline. "You and Céline have something in common," says the friend. "You have both been unlucky in love." "Until today!" I exclaim and chortle, and get away with it because the day is warm and forgiving.

Céline and I lie on the grass sipping chilled Mateus Rosé and talking compulsively. She has seen all the films of the *Nouvelle Vague* I have seen and more. The day wears on and becomes hot, so we strip to our underwear and go for a dip-low-ma in the river. I explain my father's joke with a packet of Woodbines and Céline is generous with her laughter.

What is it about the Upp this day that makes it so much more agreeable than the Yore, the Yamuna, the Bease and the Seine? Its waters are shallow and placid. There are no hidden depths. No Pollys, no Guddies, no Lydias, no mothers. Céline breast-strokes into the flow and I am tempted to follow, but I remember the rapids downriver and I do not want to get carried away – and yet I do, it is impossible not to. I swim over, we circle round each other, splashing and laughing, then turn and breast-stroke back to the bank. I lie on my back to dry off in the sun. Céline lies on top of me and kisses me gently and lightly, then kisses me again, fully and softly.

This lack of restraint is what I have been missing. Making love that night is like letting go in warm, supportive waters, going out of my depth at times, but only far enough to get back safely, exhausted and refreshed.

Céline has to return to Normandy and I feel bereft. I write long letters. She reciprocates. I discover the French for 'I miss you' is *Tu me manques*, 'You are missing in me', which is both poetic and real.

As soon as I can take time off I travel to Newhaven, catch the ferry to Dieppe and hitch-hike in the rain to the village in Normandy where Céline has an apartment over the school at which she works. She gives me a shower, puts on relaxing music by Saint-Saëns, then something less relaxing, then takes me to bed and makes love to me in ways I have only read about in books.

It is the school holidays and we have the place to ourselves. Over the next few days I meet one other person, a former *petit ami* of Céline, a *fromager* by the name of Michel who brings fresh Camembert and invites me to visit his farm. But I have no time, I am spending my time in bed with his former *petite amie*, though occasionally we take time off to talk and to cook.

It is all one, *la cuisine, le discours et l'amour.* We make a frothy *Omelette de la mère Poulard* (*oeufs fermiers,* splash of *calvados,* touch of *crème fraîche*) and a tasty *Tripes à la mode de Caen* (*pied de veau, tripes, cidre,* splash of *cognac*), a welcome change from Grandma Lily's *Tripes à la mode de Beasley,* which was eaten cold with salt and vinegar. No-one liked it, but it was preferable to sheep's brains and pig's trotters.

I find Sartre's *L'Être et le Néant,* Being and Not-Being, in Céline's shelves. For all my preoccupation with my life being preordained or at the disposal of others, Céline and Jean-Paul persuade me that *oui, bien sûr,* I have free will. And if I really am the architect of my own design, if the world really is as I make it and not as I find it or fear it to be, there is no sense in my being unhappy. I am not my past, Céline is not hers; *le moment présent* is our reality. It helps me to acknowledge it consciously – *mais oui, Jean-Paul, d'accord,* the present moment is the only one in which one can possibly be present.

On a sunny morning after several days of *manger, discuter et baiser* we decide to exercise our freedom of choice by doing something different. Céline suggests a drive through the forests and fields of Normandy in the general direction of Paris. If we get that far, she suggests, we can visit her mother and pick up her six-year old daughter Sabine from Sabine's father. Ah. Céline's past is about to catch up with us. The idea of collecting her daughter strikes me as one of those afterthoughts that actually came first, so that any earlier (in fact subsequent) decision – in this case to drive in the general direction of Paris – would not have been made freely, as an unconscious bias in its favour already existed.

I am uncertain about Paris. The city, the Seine and I have history. But I tell myself it is an opportunity to rewire the negative circuits triggered by the word 'Paris' and replace them with something more *positif,* more *bienfaisant.* So it is not a free choice for me either, but one activated and informed by the past. Is it possible that the attractions of acting as if only the present exists are a distraction from the requirement to discover who we really are?

You might think that your move to Mexico was entirely voluntary, but you can be sure there were unconscious factors involved. Getting rid of your mother – forgive me, putting distance between you – might have been one of them.

I offer to drive. Céline's car is an old *deux chevaux,* a thin, tin, rackety donkey-cart of a car with a clunky black knob of a gear-shift sticking out from the dashboard. I feel like Robert Louis Stevenson on his travels in the Cévennes with an amiable but obstinate animal he could never quite get the hang of. But this soft-top, big tin can and I manage to come to an accommodation of sorts and we rattle happily along together. Sunlight flickers through the trees. Delibes and Debussy accompany us through countryside that inspired Millet and Monet, Sisley and Pissarro, Seurat and Bonnard.

Dusk is falling as we reach the city and drive to the *dix-huitième*. We rumble down cobbled streets past cafés and bars where people sit sipping their *pastis* and *Pernod*. I hear an accordion playing.

> *Il me dit des mots d'amour,*
> *Je vois la vie en rose …*

At Céline's mother's building we take the little gilt *ascenseur* to the *sixième étage*. Her mother has left a note: '*Aidez-vous au bon fromage dans le frigo, mes chéris, je serai en retard*'. And after a glass of wine and another omelette – this with shavings of mature *Gruyère* and a sprinkling of *estragon* – we go to bed *et fait l'amour à nouveau*.

In the morning *Maman* brings us *cafés au lait* and fresh *pains au chocolat,* and sits on the edge of the bed, completely unfazed, for a chat. Is this really happening, I ask myself. Is this what all mothers will be like in fifty years' time? Where am I but in existential heaven?

There is no sign of the Seine from the airy *atelier*, no rain on the pavements. The anti-hero of a *film noir* set in the mean streets and seedy hotels of the *Rive Gauche* is transformed into *Jim le Flâneur*, urban explorer, *promeneur nonchalant*, browsing the bookshops, galleries and cafés of Montmartre. Céline and I stroll by day and make love at any time of day or night.

On the morning of the third day we drive to Montparnasse to pick up her daughter Sabine from her ex-husband, Raoul. Raoul *est très amical*. He introduces his *charmante petite amie*, Annick. She and Céline chat. Raoul makes *thé anglais* in my honour. I am inwardly congratulating everyone on their *sang-froid* and enlightened attitudes to sex, exs and live-in lovers when existential hell catches up with us. Céline and Raoul start arguing. The *sang* quickly turns *chaud*. They are furious and foul-mouthed with each other. I cannot follow everything they say, but it seems to centre on issues related to Sabine and her father's girlfriends. Annick bursts into tears and shuts herself in the bathroom. Raoul gestures at me at one point. What have I got to do with it? I feel impotent and awkward. Sabine plays with her dolls behind the sofa.

On the drive home Sabine is carsick. Céline speaks impatiently and harshly to her daughter in a different tone of voice to the honeyed notes she has been using with me. That night she scolds and slaps Sabine in a spat over bedtime. I am shocked by this sudden explosion of violence. *"Mais il n'est pas là!"* she yells as she slams the door of her child's room. My physical memory feels the full force of that door. This *crise de colère* feels like another case of the mother punishing the child for the sins of the father. I know something else at that moment, and this beyond question, that I could never be father to someone else's child.

I miss my son. It is the first time I have been away from him for more than a day or two and I am surprised at the strength of the physical feeling of separation. *Tu me manques.* You are missing in me.

Céline and I do not make love that night. A gap has opened between us and I do not have the reserves of patience, benevolence or simple decency to attempt to bridge it. The sensual bubble we inhabited has burst. My nymph of the river is an angry mother with a traumatised daughter whose father lives in the city with a succession of girlfriends. And I – what am I? An intruder, a fantasist, a shallow opportunist.

I cut my holiday short and hitch-hike home. I feel regret, but no remorse. For a week or more I have lived of my own free will in a dream. Was I free or acting under an unconscious compulsion? I cannot tell.

Back home I resolve to establish a pragmatic and if possible amicable relationship with Lydia and Bernard so that I can get to see my son without upsetting the *status quo* and having to fill out an application in triplicate. I visit you all in your new house by the river, trying to forget that it was partly bought with my money.

Bernard is a lecturer in the historiography of the Dark Ages, a pleasant if diffident fellow. I genuinely hope he is coping with his wife's silences and denials better than her first husband, who was by all accounts a difficult fellow. When Bernard and I are alone I express the wish that we might be friends. I call him Bernie. "Would it not be nice, Bernie," I venture, "if you, Julian and I could get together now and again here on the banks of the Upp just as Mole, Toad and Ratty did on the Thames?" Bernie looks startled. I go further. "My son would have two dads," I say. "A nice normal one and me." It is an odd little joke and doesn't go down well. "We only have to put our minds to it to make it happen," I say, more in hope than expectation.

I have floated what I believe to be a perfectly feasible idea, but I can see that getting everyone on board is not going to be easy. Bernard is too afraid of Lydia and wary of me, Lydia is too uncomfortable with me and uncertain of Bernard, and I am too liberal and peculiar for either of them. I recall that not everything in Mole's pastoral idyll was perfect. Mole himself got lost in the woods, Toad stole a horse and was placed under house arrest, and Ratty thought seriously about running away to sea.

Lydia gets pregnant. And she comes up with a surprising – and for me shocking – proposal. For two-year-old Julian to be fully integrated into his new family, she says, Bernard should adopt him. When I am eventually able to contemplate the idea without tearing at my hair I have to concede that she might be right – and she might also be terribly wrong, because it would run completely counter to my ideal of a laid-back alternative in which we would all come and go as we pleased and everything would be informal and genial. Yet the more I compared my fantasy of an extended family to the existing reality – implacable Lydia, fearful Bernard and unpredictable me – the more implausible it appears and the more improbable it becomes.

I meet a lawyer at a dinner party and put a hypothetical case to her. She concedes that the hypothetical stepfather in the case might be detached enough and the hypothetical mother pragmatic enough to tolerate occasional visits by the hypothetical former husband, but that before long they would come to resent the intrusion and find reasons for changing any arrangements we made.

And this is what happens. Lydia asks me to postpone my next visit on the grounds that our son was too upset after the last. She offers no evidence to substantiate her assertion and I am too pudding-headed to ask for specifics. It seems to me that Lydia is the one who was upset. All the same, the suggestion that you might not be coping well with the idea of two fathers, one who lives away from home and another who is sleeping with your mother, leaves me feeling as you must be, confused.

The lawyer and I become friends, then lovers. Roz is serene and sensible, and I heed what she has to say. My picture of the ideal extended family is exposed as the impossible dream of a deprived infant suffering from chronic attachment disorder. Given the characters involved it is as unworkable as my former fantasy of marriage as the melding of twin, inseparable souls.

In terms of intimate relationships, Roz convinces me that the non-exclusive alliance she and I share is the perfect arrangement. "It is practical, progressive, unpressured, and above all it makes sense," she says. I agree, although at the same time I want to believe that our particular intimate relationship is special and exceptional in a way that our other intimate relationships are not. This puts me in a familiar bind, caught between sense and sentimentality and unable to make peace between them.

I am upset at Lydia's suggestion that Julian should be adopted by Bernard, but Roz argues that in the circumstances it is justifiable. "But it is not just!" I cry. Roz quotes Plato:

> What I say is that 'just' or 'right' means nothing but what is in the interest
> of the stronger party.

"You are not the stronger party," she reminds me. She points out that the divorce settlement to which I agreed gave me only the most imprecise of rights to consultation over Julian's future. And Lydia could legitimately argue that she is consulting me over the adoption, even if her version of consultation is to paint me into a corner and ask my opinion as to the colour of the paint.

I withhold my signature to the adoption papers in the hope that I can keep this ship at sea until its supplies run out, but it is becoming clear that Lydia and Bernard are unwilling to endorse anything like the progressive model I have in mind and that I will either have to accept their more orthodox version or take them to court. Roz argues that going to law on such a fuzzy premise will get me nowhere. It will put my son's relationship with his stepfather in jeopardy and destroy any vestige of goodwill that might remain between his mother and me. "Reason has to override your repugnance, James," she says. "A simple adoption will entitle Julian to all the legal and moral privileges his siblings will have, including the right to inherit, without excluding your right to remain an essential part of his life." She argues convincingly that it is the least undesirable solution.

Over the next months my repugnance shades into reluctance. I just wish that Bernard's surname had been something other than Willey.

> Bernard and Lydia Willey are delighted to announce the birth of their
> daughter Gillian, sister to Julian

says the printed postcard. So you have a sister. And if yours is to be a full-on happy family, goes the argument, you all ought to share the same surname. I acknowledge the limited thinking behind the proposition, though I don't much care for it. My reluctance softens into sufferance. I am disposed to accept the change. And gradually, reluctantly, agonizingly slowly, sufferance slides into acquiescence, like slurry into a hole in the ground. Complete acceptance, however, remains buried in a secret, inaccessible place, where it lies to this day.

I can appreciate that J.P. Willey has a certain ring to it. You might grow up to be a celebrated crime writer like P.D. James or a professor of medieval literature like C.S. Lewis. The fact that you left home at the age of eighteen to become an apprentice bullfighter is all right too. I am sure it will be temporary. And the name Julian turns out to be secure enough, though I understand they call you *El Inglés* in Guadalajara. However, Lydia lied to me about retaining your secondary appellative, Pittacus, a name that would have distinguished you from every other J.P. Willey on earth. As soon as the adoption goes through she wipes Pittacus (patrician, judicious) from the files and replaces it with Peter (lumpen, plebeian). Her thinking seems to be that at the tender age of two you will not know the difference and in my attenuated state I can say what the hell I like, it will make no difference.

At least my portfolio of recognizable emotions is growing. To Anxiety, Sadness and fleeting Joy I can now add Anger and Frustration, with Uncertainty, Restlessness and Resistance up there too, though I am unsure if these are feelings in themselves or variations on Anger and Frustration. It is no consolation, but I wonder if Lydia might find herself suffering from Guilt and Contrition later in life, having alienated her children, sent Bernard to an early grave and pissed me off greatly.

With no more than a week's warning the Willeys move to Henley-on-Thames near London. Lydia tells me that Bernard was offered a research fellowship at Reading and they had to make an instant decision. I think the move has actually been brewing for months and they see it as an opportunity to establish themselves as a smug, sorry, snug little self-contained unit well away from my malign (to them), benign (to me) influence.

Then Roz is offered a position at a law chambers in London, a wonderful opportunity for her, but if she takes it up I will be deprived of an undemanding relationship on which, ironically, I am beginning to depend. I consider my work at Corinthian. Running a small company in the provinces has its rewards, but it could be time for a change. For one mad moment I contemplate volunteering for that job on a deep-sea trawler from Hull that I once secretly planned then had to abandon. It is that or move back to London.

φ

Chapter 24

Typhon in Sicily

THE REBELLIOUS MONSTER *Typhon* dares to attack the gods in heaven. In revenge they drop him into the Mediterranean and pile the three-cornered island of Sicily on his back. He struggles to free himself, but is pinned down by the weight of Mount Etna. In his anger and frustration he spews out ashes and flames, and in an effort to push the mountain off his back causes severe earthquakes. At such unsettled times the gods fear lest the earth might split and allow light to enter the underworld, where it would disturb the trembling ghosts of the dead that lie there.

My ghosts are uneasy. There are times when the weight of expectation I put upon myself threatens to fracture the ground on which I stand and out pop spectres of the past in odd and unwelcome ways.

Roz moves to London and urges me to follow. The Willeys have already moved within commuting distance of London. I am approaching the limit of what Corinthian will pay me (£19 19s a week), so when I see an ad in the trade press for a film job in London, I apply.

I am called for an interview at the Department for Information, Media and Communication (DIMCO) and hugely pleased to be offered a job writing and directing programmes for home and overseas television. There is a theory that children deprived of information find their way into journalism or broadcasting, while those denied attention become actors or megalomaniacs (there is often a difference), and abused children become psychiatrists or patients (and frequently both). If the theory is correct I qualify several times over.

I promise myself that London will be different this time. I am less encumbered, I know the difference between a Moviola and a flat-bed Steenbeck, and I will be earning substantially more than I earned as a second lieutenant or a Commonwealth Institute porter.

Roz moves into an apartment in Bloomsbury that her parents use as a *pied-à-terre* for their trips to the theatre from Surrey. She finds me temporary accommodation in a basement flat in South Kensington, sharing with a friend of hers, Roger, who works in the City and has one leg. This is awkward for both of us – not, initially at least, because of the missing leg, but because I know that she is sleeping with Roger and Roger knows that she is sleeping with me, so although as a woman of principle she makes a point of not sleeping with either of us while we are sharing the same apartment, we find ourselves treading carefully around each other, whether on one foot or two. When voices are finally raised it is over a trivial issue, the question of what one does with the tea bags after they have fulfilled their purpose: drop them in the sink or on the worktop (Roger's cavalier habit) or take them to the bin ensuring that they do not drip on the floor (my obviously more responsible choice) – but it leads to a tetchy debate on the topic of taste and social responsibility, which further leads, I really do not know how, to taking up different positions on the subject of two-legged versus one-legged sex. For me it is not the spectre of jealousy that rises Typhon-like through a crack in the basement floor, but one of guilt – the man is clearly disabled and I should be welcoming, even facilitating, or at the very least not discouraging, his sexual fulfilment. But with my girlfriend? My relationship with Roger quickly deteriorates and after a few weeks I move out, even if that means they can copulate freely.

I find a studio flat in West Hampstead. I am busy, Roz is busy, sometimes she stays over at my place and sometimes I stay over at hers. Sometimes, I suppose, she stays over at Roger's. I cannot help wondering how they get on with – or indeed without – his wooden leg, though I am determined not to get obsessed with the idea. Too late, you might think.

At intervals I take the train to Henley-on-Thames. After one of these visits I write to my mother.

> Lydia, Bernard and I are on friendlier terms, which makes things easier. Julian is happy and bright. He is up to page 14 of his first reading book. Jigsaw expert too. They might be coming up to London for a visit at Christmas.

Most of this is lies. Lydia and I are not so friendly. And I have decided it is unlikely that Bernard and I will ever be on Jim and Bernie terms. I am paying maintenance and solicitors' costs, I have had to borrow money for moving, the deposit on the flat, the estate agent's fees and an electric kettle. And as far as I know the Willeys have no intention of coming to London for Christmas or for any other celebration, and certainly not to see me.

Mount Etna is in grumbling, pre-eruptive mode. I suggest to Lydia that as she is living in some comfort on Bernard's salary, the proceeds from her antiques business and the profits on the sale of the house that I kindly if stupidly signed over to her, she might be able to manage without my £3 10s a week child maintenance payments.

I write again to Mother, hinting that I might not be as content as I had claimed. She writes back, hinting that she prefers not to hear that I might be depressed again as it feeds her remorse. My reply is a touch on the sour side.

> My dear Mrs Dinwiddy,
> You worry too much. I never meant to be hurtful. You are a splendid mother
> and that is why you are hurt by everything about me. I am a bad son and
> instead of keeping you in ignorance of my febrile ways, I hint at them. I shall
> reform and in future say nothing.

I am struggling to have some kind of adult relationship with this woman who was
such a marginal part of my childhood and yet so often claims the right to be hurt
by me. A letter or two later, in an exasperated mood, I let rip.

> I love you. I have no desire to hurt you, I have never tried to and never will.
> What hurts you about me are the things that happen to me. You should be
> sad for me, not hurt. FORGET IT. If we cannot understand each other, we
> might at least be accepting and care a little more. I cannot understand Lydia,
> Harold or Alec Douglas-Home, never mind you. ENOUGH.
> Love, James.

That will hurt her for sure. I can't help it. The free will I felt I was exercising in
Normandy and Paris was no such thing. I can only be as my mother and father
with their lies and surprises made me. And it must be better to let my anger and
frustration out now, I tell myself, and live a year or two longer, than repress it all
and die of congestion. It is a moot point.

When I hear from Lydia again it is an exceptionally distressing letter that she
couches as a contribution to the continuing debate over our son, but which I can
only read as a deadly escalation of her campaign to weed me out of her life – and,
by extension, yours.

> I think it would be a good idea if you held off visiting for a while longer until
> we get into a different routine.

I ponder on the ambiguity of that 'we'. She means the four of you – you and your
sister, your mother and stepfather – but she also wants me to think of that 'we' as
me too. I should get into a routine of not visiting while you get into a routine of
not noticing and managing perfectly well without me. The awful thing, again, is
that she might be half-right. I am overwhelmed by crippling self-doubt. The whole
of Sicily is on my back. If I insist on regular visits, am I compromising your
integration into a family of which you have an absolute right to be an equal
member? I don't want you feeling as I did in Thornton Moor and Chandrapore –
peripheral, no house key, forever knocking at the back door and hoping to be let
in.

From the Strait of Messina at Sicily's north-east corner the spectre of *Scylla* raises
her six vicious heads again. If I engage my ex-wife in direct combat I risk being
dismembered in seconds, but if I turn the other cheek I shall be up against hideous
Charybdis, who threatens to drown me in my own guilt. To escape the open jaws
of one is to be caught in the outrageous demands of the other. As I flail around in

conflicting currents for something to hold on to I stub my toe on a half-submerged wreck. I had forgotten my father.

What happened between him and my mother and my stepmother all those years ago and is there anything there that might inform my present state? I phone Jenny and ask if she might be interested in going to see him. My sister and I have kept in contact over the years, but only just – birthday cards, Christmas cards ('love Jenny', 'love James'), infrequent phone call ('how are you?', 'good, how are you?', 'bye for now'). The shame of the past has kept us apart, the presence of the other a reminder of times we have been trying to forget. Jenny is fiercely unwilling to see her father. She has taken his disengagement from his children more acutely than I have, or perhaps I have reconfigured my dismay with him into disappointment with myself. I write.

> How are you, Dad? You might be interested in what I have been up to the last seventeen years or so. And I would love to learn something about what happened between you and Mother and what was going on with Edith.

He writes back.

> It would be good to see you again, Jim boy.

He has a condition.

> But I don't want to talk about the past.

This is uninspiring but unsurprising.

> By the way, Edith died five years ago.

I am enormously cheered by this news and do not feel in the least guilty.

> I got married again last year. To Norma who is a patissier, she makes cakes and fancies. She is a lovely lass, she looks after me.

He encloses a photograph of himself in the arms of a plump Victoria sponge of a woman with chubby white arms and rosy red cheeks. He is looking a bit chubby himself, presumably from all the cakes and fancies, while she looks inordinately pleased, as if she has been given a cute little white-haired koala to cuddle. Perhaps when I am next in the area I will take him to the pub on his own and get him to talk. I write back.

> Sorry about Edith, look forward to meeting Norma. I will give you a call.

This is the Christmas I give everyone a copy of Erich Fromm's The Art of Loving. I'm not entirely sure if Mother and Harold, Jenny, Lydia and Bernard or Dad and Norma appreciate the gift unreservedly. I have been reading a lot of self-help books of late, having figured that I am not getting what I want in any of my relationships – other than with Roz, that is, from whom I have the precious gift of acceptance. Roz's one small but significant condition – never articulated, but well understood – is that I will neither comment on nor question her freedom. Her philosophy is John Stuart Mill's, that the only freedom deserving of the name is that of pursuing your own good in your own way, as long as you do not deprive others of theirs or impede their efforts to obtain it. I have to admit that, with the exception of Lydia, my parents and the government of the day, I do not feel deprived or impeded by anyone but myself.

Lydia returns her present unopened. She is exercising her freedom to make a point, I suppose. Roz is the only person who thanks me. Everyone else must think I am dropping them a hint about how they got it all wrong, but can still make amends. They're right. My message is Fromm's: never mind the guilt and confusion, love is the only sane and satisfactory answer to the problems of existence. But what kind of love do I mean? Love of repressive great-grandmothers, reluctant mothers, lukewarm fathers, abusive stepmothers, vengeful wives? Or love of one's tactless, thoughtless, preposterous self? Or love that in my pursuit of its distant cousins fascination, attraction, attachment and arousal has become compulsive – worse, addictive – because I can never get enough of it.

I wonder if the problem might be one of categorization. Fromm and I have only one word for love, whereas the Greeks, as you may know, had three: *eros*, or love of that which we lack; *philia*, or love of oneself and those close to one; and *agape*, love of all others, including those we do not know – useless love, one might say; love without reason, love for its own sake. Where will I find myself and how far can I go on this endless spectrum?

Roz and I go to a party in Kilburn and as sometimes happens on these occasions we pair off with other people. I am getting on well with a yoga teacher called Elsa, who comes from Sweden, or it might be Norway, and Roz is dancing a lot with a slick-haired, greasy-looking guy in a 'King of the Twist' T-shirt. They leave the party together without saying goodbye, so I ask Elsa if she would like to come back to my place for the night.

Now if I were to describe the situation in ancient Greek terms it might go something like this: my love for Roz at that moment is a friendly *philia*, continuing but distant, renewable when it suits us; my love for the stranger she left with might just be squeezed into the all-embracing category of *agape*, though I try not to think about him; while my love for Elsa this evening is unequivocally *eros*, the desire for something I lack.

Elsa and I are in bed together in the early hours when the doorbell rings. I go to the door and peer through the letter flap. Roz is peering back at me. "Hello, James," she says. "Oh no," I groan. I explain the situation. Roz says she is tired and doesn't want to go all the way back to Bloomsbury. "Hold on a minute," I say. I go to explain things to Elsa. I apologize. She shrugs. I go back to the front door, let Roz in and introduce them. There is only the one bed, so I invite Roz to join us, thinking a threesome might alleviate the tension, but Roz says she would prefer to sleep in the bath. It is too late to debate the absurdities, sensitivities and erotic possibilities of the situation, so I take her at her word, make up a bed for her in the bath and loan her my pillow. Elsa and I fail to get back to where we left off. It is not a good night.

In the morning we have breakfast together. The girls are polite. I try to jolly them along. My intention is to buy a spare pillow and get the three of us back together sometime. Elsa returns to Malmö or Tromsö soon after, however. It is the last I see of her.

I tell you all this – having no idea how you arrange this kind of thing in Mexico – as a warning. It is an example of the kind of idealistic mix of *eros* and *philia* that Roz and I would like to believe is a part of our aggregate state of *agape*, but which rarely works out as lovingly as we would wish. Indeed, you could argue that in an excess of self-love, or *autophilia*, we are confusing individual *eros* with indiscriminate *altruismos* and thoroughly deserve the unsatisfactory compromise, or what the Greeks might have called emotional *xaos*, that results.

Meanwhile my work at DIMCO is going well. I am one of three writer-directors working on the documentary series This Week in Britain, featuring anything remotely interesting that our researchers can discover about life in these isles – an anniversary of one of the Brontës, a new kind of Cheddar, seaweed farming in the Hebrides, that kind of thing. I have a week in which to research and write the scripts, a second week for filming and a third for editing and dubbing. Our overseas television audience is gratifyingly huge, 100 million or so.

One of my director colleagues is a posh titanium blonde by the name of Margot, who lives in Chelsea, and the other is an ex-East Ender called Arthur or, as Margot and I like to call him, Arfer. Arfer smokes cigars, dresses in three-piece suits, wears a modest gold bracelet and makes soft-porn films on the side. He asks me if I might be interested in writing the occasional script for his company, Art Films.

I ask Margot for her advice. If I accept Arfer's offer can I retain my artistic integrity? This is not a meaningful question for Margot, whose interest in film-making lies less not so much in creative expression or professional advancement as in the opportunities it affords her for blagging invitations to parties and sleeping with celebrities. The *Nouvelle Vague* is something Margot would expect to find in a boutique on the King's Road. Her advice with regard to Arfer's offer is to go ahead as long as it is fun. She offers to help me with storylines from her personal experience.

I am in a quandary, wanting to meet several potentially incompatible aims: to do reputable work, to explore the darker side of the human psyche and to achieve, in addition to creative expression and professional advancement, unilateral nuclear disarmament. The ground is not yet shifting beneath me, but it is threatening to open up soon.

Roz finds herself spending more time at my place than she does at her own, but the proximity of her parents in Surrey means that my idea of moving in together –

something I have floated in order to save on the rent and the rates – is really not on. "Mummy and Daddy might be moderately impressed by your status in the Army Emergency Reserve," she proclaims, "but not by the pony-tailed, floral-shirted, bell-bottomed phase you are going through, and certainly not by your shady acquaintances in the film business." "For my part," I counter, "I am unmoved by your father's chauffeur-driven commute into the City and your mother's preference for Harrod's and Fortnum's over John Lewis and British Home Stores."

Mount Etna is rumbling again. I am disappointed that a woman of Roz's intelligence and independence should feel under such an obligation to her parents, but there is a lot I do not know about families.

Roz has an announcement to make. She is apologetic. There is no way of breaking this gently. She is pregnant. "Oh, *merde*," I say, "this is not in the plan." "There's a plan?" asks Roz rhetorically. "There is no plan. If there had been a plan, then not getting pregnant would have been the first item on it." She has been taking a rest from the pill, the responsibility for contraception passed on to me and I have been diligent, but you can never be sure. "Is it mine?" I ask, assuming it must be. "I don't know," she says. "You don't *know?*" I am incredulous. "No. It might not be yours, it might be Roger's." "*Roger's?*" This turns out to be the self-same hopalong Roger with whom I shared an apartment in South Kensington. "I thought you had stopped seeing Roger after the business with the tea bags," I say. "I might have slept with Roger once or twice around the same time," she says. "You *might* have?" "I think I did." "Jesus, Roz, was there anyone else?" "No no, there was no-one else." "Are you sure?" She thinks for a moment. Why does she have to think? "No, I am sure." I ask her what happened with Roger. She hesitates, then admits they forgot to use contraception. "You *forgot!!?* You got so carried away you *forgot!!?*"

The underworld opens up a crack or two. I see flames. "How could you be so feckless, so irresponsible?" I ask. "There is no problem," she says, "I have the number of a man on Harley Street."

Now I feel bad. Abortion is illegal, but widely available, and Roz is resilient, but is there no other way? "I have thought about this a lot," she says. "I don't want to go through with the pregnancy. The timing is all wrong." I experience a feeling of relief, followed immediately by guilt, followed after a second or so by dismay. "How much will it cost?" I ask. "Eighty pounds." "Eighty pounds? That is a lot of money." I know she does not have that kind of money. I do not have that kind of money. There is no way she will ask her parents for the money.

I consult Margot, who turns out to have seen a man on Harley Street herself. Margot confirms that give or take a fiver eighty pounds is the going rate. She sympathizes. "I'd lend you the money, James, but you know how it is." I do know how it is. It's a lot of money. We agree to put our soft-porn collaboration on hold for a while, as this does not seem to be quite the right timing.

I suggest to Roz that she asks Roger for a contribution to the fee in line with his contribution to the problem. "I can't do that," she says. "Well, I can," I say. I'm furious with both of them. "Does fifty-fifty sound about right?" I ask, distantly. I am trying to be rational. She thinks for a moment. "Yes," she says. I would have preferred something more like ninety-ten in my favour, but fifty-fifty reduces my share of the fee to forty pounds, which I can just about afford if I cut down on smoking and cancel my subscriptions to Private Eye and the Wine Society.

I trust that you are able to make allowances for the situation, Julian, but I have no doubt it will sound a bit sordid to some, a bit sleazy. Well, we were young and foolish, and arrogant too. We thought we were doing everything for the first time, and in some respects we were. The Sixties was a special moment in history, I'm told. People power, the counterculture, sexual liberation and all that. I just wish I had known it was so special at the time, I might have enjoyed it more.

I take the Underground to South Ken, working myself up to what I know will be an embarrassing confrontation. As I turn into the street of mansion flats where Roger lives, the ground beneath me trembles and hisses. Steam rises from the cracks in the steps as I descend to the basement and ring the doorbell. I am sure this time it tolls.

Roger hobbles to the door. I inform him of the situation. Startled, he denies any part in it. I make reference to the evidence Roz has supplied: a credible date, the name of the restaurant in the Old Brompton Road, how very relaxed they had been when they went back to his place, etcetera. Roger cavils. He quibbles. He is sure he was somewhere else that night. I pile on the pressure. I know the colour of the boxer shorts he was wearing that night. He is startled. But the clincher, the one piece of evidence I am almost, but not quite, too embarrassed to present, is that Roz is sure of the date because it was the first time Roger had worn his new aluminium limb, the Legolite Premium, and he had had some difficulty unclipping it. His mouth drops open. I appeal, none too politely, to his sense of responsibility. He whinges, he niggles, but in the end he does not contend. He will find forty pounds. "Without admission of liability," he adds anxiously, a line he must have learnt from his friends in the City. I give him a stony look and leave.

A few days later I am driving along the Cromwell Road with a film crew on our way back to Soho to drop off the day's rushes. I promise the crew an extra pint at the Nellie Dean if they will hang around outside this gaff in Cranley Gardens looking moody while I press this geezer, this chiseller, this butcher's hook I know, for a gambling debt. That much is true. Roger gambled and lost.

His face drops when he sees my associates hanging round at the top of the steps. They are a heavy looking lot, mainly because of their beer bellies. I ask him for the cash he promised. He apologizes, he is entertaining friends, can we sort this out tomorrow? "No!" I cry, kick his walking stick away and push past him into the apartment. Roger hobbles hastily after me. Six or seven of his guests are starting dinner. In an infuriated voice I tell everyone exactly why I am there and point out that my friends outside are as outraged as I am. His guests are shocked and silent.

Roger ushers me anxiously to the door and promises to come up with the money tomorrow. If he does not produce it within 24 hours, I declare, I shall be back with my friends and this time I really will be angry.

Pot-bellied, beetle-browed Wally, the sparks, appears at the top of the steps. "Everythin' all right, guv'nor?" he asks. "For the moment, Wally," I say and make a dignified exit, spoilt only slightly by stooping to retrieve Roger's walking stick and returning it to him. To make up for this lapse I slam the door behind me, in the hope that the sound makes Roger wince as much as it does me. The next day he gives Roz forty pounds in used notes. Sleazy, as I said. It is not our finest hour.

Roz is pale when she appears from the clinic. I take her home, help her to bed and make her a cup of tea. The phone rings. Mummy is coming to town and wants to meet up with her daughter to go shopping. Roz replies that she is not feeling too well and Mummy says in that case she will come round and look after her. Roz demurs and arranges to meet her at Fortnum and Mason's for tea.

For a year or more Roz and I have been commuting between my place and hers, paying two lots of rent and running two refrigerators. For a second time I bring up the idea of moving in together. "It would be purely for the convenience and economy," I say. "It will make no difference, no difference whatsoever, to the way we run our lives and relationships." Roz apologizes. She is perfectly willing in principle, but Mummy and Daddy have always wanted their daughter to marry into banking or the law, have a white wedding in Westminster Abbey, if it were available, and a reception at the Savoy or the Dorchester. The idea of their only child moving in with a divorced film-maker who is almost an orphan is not a realistic alternative.

I find Roz's attitude baffling. How can a sentimental duty to her parents take precedence over simple common sense? She is earning a pittance as an intern and feeling increasingly uncomfortable at Daddy meeting most of her bills, while I am preparing to leave my safe haven at DIMCO to set out on the uncertain seas of the freelance film business. The argument for sharing expenses is becoming compelling. I have work on offer from Arfer, but the deal he is proposing – no fee, a pseudonymous credit and five per cent of the unlikely profits – is far from convincing.

We agree that the last thing we want to do is get married. Roz's reservations about marriage have always been consistent and coherent: it is a nasty patriarchal trick aimed at the suppression of women. I concur, more or less, but for me it is more a matter of loyalty. Marrying again would feel like a betrayal of my allegiance to my son. I accompany Roz on a Women's Lib march carrying a placard that reads, 'End Human Sacrifice: Don't Get Married'. We applaud an anarchic academic at the rally in Trafalgar Square who calls the institution of marriage "a chimera, a monstrous construct, an ill-conceived child of the bourgeois imagination."

I know the original *Chimera* as the son of bad-tempered Typhon of Mount Etna fame and deep-dwelling, foul-smelling *Echidna*, mother of all monsters. Between them they created a mutant with a predator's head, a satyr's body and a liar's tail, a freak who would cheat on you, fry you alive or hold your head underwater without the least hesitation. Marriage is just such a monstrosity, we agree. Roz asks me not to mention any of this to her parents.

We are faced with three equally undesirable alternatives: continue to live separately (inconvenient, expensive); move in together (alienates her family, risks the inheritance); or marry (against the laws of nature and my *a priori* loyalty to my son). Roz comes up with another line of reasoning. "There is no obligation on a lawyer to believe in the innocence of the defendant," she reminds me, "in order to argue the case for the defence." I agree, but how is that relevant? "Even demons have their redeeming features," she says. I try to think of one for Typhon, Echidna or Chimera, who between them embody so many disagreeable qualities, but come up with none. Learned counsel points to the need to be freed from the notion of marriage as an entity, like tax, insurance or government. "It is an *activity*," she argues. "A verb masquerading as a noun. 'Marrying', 'taxing', 'insuring' and so on describe things people *do,* which means they are endlessly variable." She goes on. "It is possible to book a bishop and a 21-gun salute, and go the full Monty, or turn up at the town hall for a ten-minute ceremony, sign a form that no-one will ever see again, then go home, read out a few humanist quotes and get a friend to play the recorder." The legitimacy of one's choices, she argues, depends on the judgment of one's peers, and that comes down to their opinion, and the inescapable thing about opinions is that they differ. They are verdicts not founded on fact and can be neither right nor wrong.

I realize to my surprise that Roz is arguing the case for a marriage of sorts, but she is doing it in such a way that she can claim it is not a belief she is advancing, but a brief she has taken on. I could concoct an equally tortuous counter-argument, but I no longer have the heart. The temptation of saving on overheads overrides every one of our political and ethical reservations. We book a registry office in Surrey, exclude gods of all kinds from the ceremony – including, to my regret, the Greek and Roman pantheon – and elect not to exchange rings. We are players in a masque devised for the entertainment of her parents, but only we can read the unwritten small print on the back page of the script, the tacit terms and conditions absolving us of all responsibility for the assumptions of others about what we are doing. If Anthony Wedgwood Benn MP can swear public allegiance to the Crown while adding, *sotto voce*, a caveat affirming that his prime loyalty is to Parliament and the people, we reckon we can do something similar for a simple civil ceremony.

And so although reason is denied we can argue it has triumphed. It is the contradictory logic at the heart of every judicial plea and counterplea, that what is true for one party may not be so for the other, yet like the wave-particle conundrum both can exist at the same time. The mental stretch required to construct this proposition – that a makeshift commitment can equally be viewed as a permanent union – leaves us feeling uneasy, but that is what it is like to be grown-up and conflicted, we tell ourselves, and it is time to move on.

We rent a second floor flat in Marylebone and hold a housewarming party. Arfer gives us a dinner service made up of seconds he acquired at a discount while filming in Stoke-on-Trent and Margot gives us a £10 voucher for the Peter Jones store in Sloane Square. We do not tell our friends we are married. It is a perverse act of denial, like adopting a small child or a pet that you keep hidden from visitors.

One of our guests is Todd Ramsay, an independent producer who supplies most of the crews for my Department of Information filming. I am pleased to see that he and Roz get on well. Todd tells me he is setting up a short film for the cinema and asks if I might be interested in writing and directing it. I am thrilled. Short films are a stepping-stone to features and are still being shown in cinemas before slides for second-hand cars and Indian restaurants. On the strength of the fee and the promise of further work for Todd's company, Longshot Films, I decide this is an opportune moment to give in my notice at DIMCO.

"I love the treatment you wrote, Jim," declares Todd. "I love it." I know Todd well enough by now to treat anything he repeats with caution, but I am pleased. The film will be sponsored by the International Federation of Cotton Manufacturers, IFCOM, and I have gone all moody and romantic on the subject – exotic locations, curtains of *voile* wafting gently in the breeze, lovers in slow motion, that kind of thing. I look forward to developing the script and directing the film. I remind Todd of the fee we agreed for the treatment. "Of course, Jim," he says. "The cheque is filled in and ready to be signed. Ready to be signed, Jim, the minute the funds are in place." He has sounded the first sour note. "When will that be, Todd?" I ask. "When will that be, Jim? That will be soon. Very soon." I feel a physical pain. 'Soon' is the diversionary shot my father used to fire whenever I asked him when he would be coming again and he had no intention of saying when. 'Soon' is a word that wounds and it has infected every promise made to me since. "How long is soon?" I ask Todd feebly. "Trust me, Jim," he says in a hurt voice, repeating, predictably, "trust me." "Of course, Todd," I say. "Of course I trust you." Now I am repeating myself.

I could have withdrawn my notice to DIMCO during the IFCOM saga, but out of pride or conceit I let it stand. Roz cannot understand why I should be so concerned at the prospect of having no income for a while, accustomed as she is to the idea that something always turns up, usually in the form of a cheque from her father. I have to explain that I cannot depend in the same way, or in any way, really, on mine.

I plan to sell my car in order to meet my share of the outgoings on the flat, but a freelance musician friend recommends that I do as he does and use it to earn money from mini-cab driving. What an excellent idea, I think, and sign up with a firm operating from a temporary hut at the back of Kings Cross station.

Kings Cross Cabs and I have a flexible arrangement. I work if they have the work and stay at home by the phone if they don't. The manager came across this scam long before it was called a zero-hours contract.

I am determined not to be the kind of mini-cab driver who has ripped me off in the past, so I am up-front with my customers about the fee per mile and make a point of indicating the mileage at the start and end of the journey. My driver colleagues tell me this is quite unnecessary – or, not to put too fine a point on it, foolish. What they do is think of a price, double it, and if the customer complains they knock off a few quid, which they invariably get back as a tip.

A month into mini-cab driving, Todd – full of apologies for the IFCOM film, which might still – might still – he says, be going ahead, and he is so charming, so chummy, that I almost believe him – offers me a job directing a cinema short on the Post Office Tower, a new telecommunications hub nearing completion off Fitzroy Square, W.1. To my surprise it turns out to be a genuine job. As the first building of its kind in the world it is generating a lot of publicity and Todd has the finance and a distributor already lined up.

I do some good work on this film. Heart-warming scenes of engineers and their families, tracking shots through banks of computers and striking new views of the London skyline. The final scene is set in the revolving restaurant at the top of the tower – actors, extras, tricky lighting, time constraints – but I finish principal photography on time and on budget. I go over on stock, but make significant savings on overtime.

After a wrap party in the tower for the cast and crew, Todd invites me to join him and his new girlfriend for dinner in Mayfair. He is intent on impressing her with his status, taste, wit, maturity, generosity and charm – something of a challenge for him in most of those areas. He leads the way in his MGB through the streets of Fitzrovia and Marylebone, and I follow in my Ford Cortina. As we approach the junction of Montague Street and Dorset Street the lights change to amber, Todd continues, and in a heartbeat I make a decision not to hit the brakes and risk losing him in the traffic ahead, but to follow. I do not see the car that jumps the lights to my left until it hits me at speed. BANG! For a few seconds I am disorientated. My car flips over. Another bang as the roof hits the ground. I hear the crack of the spring of a bus in Boulogne, the thwack and bam of a 25-pounder, shouts echoing in the school baths, the sting of the slap of my mother's hand, my head held under water, my lungs being pumped, glass picked out of my hair, the sound of water and metal, gurgling and slamming. I have defied the gods once too often and this is it. The car comes to a stop and in the sudden silence I hear a drip-drip which I take to be petrol. I reach out to switch off the ignition, but can't find it. I crawl out, limp away, there is a solicitous passer-by, a fire appliance, an ambulance.

I am checked over at St. Mary's, Paddington, and found to have a few bruises. The police tell me the car is a write-off, but they are dealing with it, so I hail a black cab and continue to the restaurant. I don't want to let Todd and his new girlfriend down. They are half-way through their meal when I arrive. "What happened to you?" Todd asks. "Sorry," I say. "Bit of a problem with the car." I am being ridiculously *blasé* about an accident that could have done for me, but I want to come across as the sort of director a producer can depend on in a crisis. "Gosh, I'm hungry," I say "What do you recommend?" As I study the menu my hands are shaking. Todd's new girlfriend is concerned. As her attention shifts from her peeved producer friend to his traumatized director I can see I have upset Todd's plans for the evening.

I supervise the rough cut of the film between stints with Kings Cross Cabs, but Todd finds a way of excluding me from the fine cut and the sound mix by the simple expedient of not telling me when and where they are taking place. "The distributors had a deadline, Jim," he tells me when I phone to find out what is happening. "I couldn't get hold of you." He is lying. "The film is looking great, by the way," he says, adding, "trust me."

I do not trust him the very short distance between one film sprocket hole and the next, but there is not much I can do other than express my great displeasure, which has absolutely no effect. In any case I have other concerns. The insurers are suing me for the cost of writing-off the car on the grounds that I am not covered for driving for hire; I am heavily involved in a domestic drama featuring an actress from the revolving restaurant scene; I am researching a film about rally driving in Wales, which does not interest me in the least; and Roz is breaking up with Roger and his prosthesis, which is fine by me, but there are rumours – incredible, sickening – that she has been having an affair with Todd. Even in the context of the open relationship I have with Roz, this is more than teetering on the edge of acceptability, it is falling off it spectacularly. I ask her if it is true. She will neither confirm nor deny the affair, murmurs something about my actress and waitress friends, reminds me of the convention that we do not inquire into the private life of the other, and assures me that nothing has changed between us. I go off to Wales feeling betrayed and hypocritical, because I wouldn't have hesitated to sleep with Roz's sister, best friend or grandmother if I had fancied her and she were available.

On my return I discover that my New Tower of London film is being shown at the Rialto in the West End as a supporting short to The Dirty Dozen before going out on general release. I am excited to see a film of mine on the big screen for the first time. The opening shot is one I am particularly proud of – a view on the zoom with the street lamps of Primrose Hill in the foreground echoing the top of the tower beyond – but the opening titles have been superimposed on the shot in a bright yellow drop-shadow font that obscures what should have been a brilliant effect. Not a good start. The rest is adequately done, but when the end titles come up I am astonished to see 'assistant director James Seagrave' followed by 'directed by Todd Ramsay'. The bastard has stolen my directing credit! It is my first West

End showing and he has stolen my credit! I phone the underhand, overweight, smarmy, lying, oleaginous bastard. "That's the way it is, Jim," he tells me. "No, it bloody well isn't!" I cry. "You took my credit!" "I took the director's credit," he says, "because the sponsor wanted the producer's credit."

I make a formal complaint to the film's distributors and the technicians' union. I say I want the prints withdrawn and the credits re-made. There is a long negotiation at the end of which the union rep reports that Todd has agreed to an apology and a correction. Excellent. I thank the rep. It takes a month for a barely legible notice to appear among the small ads in the union journal.

> The credits for the film *New Tower of London* should read 'A Longshot production, director James Seagrave, producer Todd Ramsay'.

It is a cheap two-line correction that could just about be defended as an apology, but it is really no more than a notice of fact that no-one will notice. The film stays the same. The distributors say it will cost too much to remake the titles and manufacture new prints, and when all is said and done I have no contract.

Which is how Todd comes to live in a big house with a garden in Barnes while I rent a second floor flat with a view of the traffic in Marylebone. I am outraged, but I can hardly go round to his place with a film crew and threaten to beat him up, because he employs all the film crews I know.

My next job is with a relatively reputable company, Perforated Films, directing a series of cinema shorts on fishing, sailing and riding in Britain. It is a well-paid job and I am prepared to put my aquaphobia and nausea to the test for the summer and hope for the best.

The fishing film turns out to be a succession of death scenes: trout in the River Piddle in Wessex being fooled into thinking that the fly they are being offered for lunch is an actual fly; salmon in the River Tay being played with a high rod tip to prevent them from what the ghillie calls, 'throwing the hook' – that is, escaping; and sharks being bludgeoned to death with a heavy rubber mallet off the coast of Cornwall. And what happens during these scenes is that I put aside my aquaphobia, my nausea levels increase ten-fold and I develop an unexpected fellow feeling with fish.

As a child in Rawley and Scarmouth I was accustomed to trawlers bringing in dying and newly dead fish every day. The trawlermen did it for a living and I took it for granted. Then in my teens in Sourness-on-Sea as I witnessed the thoughtless slaughter by tourists that served no useful purpose other than 'sport' I was sickened. What is sporting about the indiscriminate exercise of superior force that causes actual bodily harm and leads to the death of the weaker party? In India to my shame I went along with the shooting of pigeons and peafowl, sambur and chital – pretty much anything with wings or legs that couldn't shoot back – because of the status to be enjoyed as a member of Harold's elite gang of killers, euphemistically known as 'the guns'. And I insulated myself from the reality of what they were doing by calling it, as they did, *shikar*. Shikar is an old Urdu word for harvesting wild game in order to feed the local community. It was never intended to describe or objectify trophy hunting or target practice by overfed expats and their aristocratic Indian chums.

In Britain this summer as I watch the deaths of goggle-eyed perch, pike, salmon and trout I am appalled. I am appalled at myself for directing these scenes of living beings forcibly prevented from breathing, drowning from lack of water. It is piscatorial pornography. Even Arfer would have carped – sorry, objected. But what concerns me even more than the ethical choices I am making is my own survival. Where are the lifejackets? How far are we from the bottom of the river or the lake or the bay in the boats we are chartering? I am a long way out of my comfort zone. How can I justify the forcible removal of these hapless aquatic animals from theirs?

Like the rebellious Typhon I struggle to free myself from the weight of guilt that the gods have placed on me in revenge for my challenge to their supremacy over life and death. There is no place for *agape* – love of all things, ideal love, faultless love – here. The perfect love of human beings for anything at all is unimaginable.

Meanwhile Roz and I are doing our best not to let living together dilute our values around sex, friendship and freedom, but it is becoming increasingly obvious that we have not thought the relationship through in practical terms. Having multiple partners takes more than trust and sensitivity, to which I am not naturally disposed anyway, it takes time, attention and energy. Everything has to be subject to negotiation in a way that it hardly ever was when we were living apart. If one of us wants to bring a friend home, for example, should we expect the other to go out or to sleep in the spare room, or is that unfair? Should we only bring someone home if the other has already arranged to go out? I am asking these questions, because Roz is staying at home more and going out less. She doesn't complain out loud about my social arrangements, but she is raising her eyebrows more than usual.

It is left to one of my casual girlfriends to accuse me outright of being a philanderer, an emotional parasite, a Byronite. I argue in vain that the god *Philandros* simply loved people, all people, equally. He was not lacking in moral restraint. And soppy old Byron and Don Juan were not heartless womanizers, but amiable, amenable men doing their best to meet the emotional demands of demanding women.

The amenable amiability defence does not go down well with everyone. On one occasion I am assaulted by the husband of a woman with whom I am having what I take to be an innocent affair. I feel aggrieved – not at him, but at her, because she swore they had separated. The attack takes place in the reception area of Galaxy Pictures, the company I am working with at the time. No blood is shed, but there is a certain amount of furious shoving and shouting until the receptionist tells us to stop being silly. It is the kind of thing that happens in Soho and seems to do no harm to my reputation, so I am not as ashamed as I am sure I should be.

In any case everyone is at it. The Galaxy Pictures receptionist is having an extra-marital affair with the production manager. The secretary who invites me into the stationery cupboard at the Christmas party is already intimately involved with her boss, the managing director. Their affair develops into something of a scandal when the boss's wife hears of it and threatens to leave him unless his secretary gets the sack. The secretary takes the company to an employment tribunal, wins her case for unlawful dismissal, the managing director suffers a heart attack and his wife leaves him anyway. Professionally, though, the company is doing quite well.

Roz's silent eyebrow-raising is beginning to have an effect. "It's time we had a talk, James," she announces one day. My heart sinks. "First let me acknowledge," she says, "that we are both free to stick by the same polyamorist principles we embraced at the start of our relationship." She pauses. What is coming next?. "I wonder if it might be time to agree how we put those principles into practice." She looks at me for a response. I feel defensive. "You mean revise the terms of an unwritten, unspoken, non-existent agreement by defining parameters and agreeing constraints that are almost certain to prove impossible to maintain. For either of us." She stays calm. "I agree that it might require a little discipline, but I believe that will have a generative effect in other areas of our lives." It is an interesting point made with admirable restraint, but I am not in the mood to hear it. My affairs are expedient illusions, I can acknowledge that much. They have a lot in common with the films I make: simulations of reality that only come to life in the flickering world of the imagination. Both socially and professionally I am insulating myself from the real world. "I am not jealous, James," says Roz, "but I wonder if we might make more time together when it comes to organizing our diaries." I understand what she is saying, that she is ready to settle down. She might even be implying that she is ready to have a baby.

I am trapped in the Strait of Messina again. If I stay on the same course I shall be under increasing threat from the green-eyed monster on the Sicilian side, but if I allow myself to drift into the placid waters of monogamy on the Calabrian side I could be dragged down by fierce undercurrents of expectation and drown.

I tread water and consider my choices. For the last year or two Roz and I have been living amicably side by side, like neighbouring nations with a permeable border, but now one side is putting up warning signs and posting unarmed guards. I accuse Roz of not sticking to the spirit of our unwritten, unspoken, non-existent agreement. "You are right, I am not," she admits, "but it has passed its time." At first I protest, then I have to agree. "I guess we have failed," I say. "No, James," says Roz, "we have simply not lived up to our fantasies." We agree that the principle of non-exclusivity we shared had been nobly intended but poorly monitored and inadequately managed. I feel rather sad. I believed that because our friendship was permissive it would go on for ever.

Roz moves back to her parents' apartment in Bloomsbury and I take over the Marylebone flat. My work is continuous and for the first time in my life I can afford to meet all the outgoings with something to spare. Yet in the hassle and hustle of filming and travelling I am finding it difficult to sustain a lasting relationship. What I mean is that I am finding it difficult to sustain a relationship with anyone else while continuing to struggle with my relationship with myself. I ought to be trying harder, I know. It isn't long before I find myself involved in yet another silly, sad, overlapping affair.

I am spending the night in Kirkcaldy with a female friend I met on an earlier visit when an ex-lover of hers comes knocking at the door. "Let me in, Fran" he pleads. My friend Fran freezes. It is one o'clock in the morning. "Oh no, it's Hamish!" she whispers. "He left me a month ago in order to go back to his wife." "I know you're there!" calls Hamish. "You have to forgive me!" Fran frantically dashes in her nightie to the door and bolts it from the inside. The last thing she wants is for Hamish to discover her in bed with another man, even if that would have served him (well, both of them) right. Hamish hammers at the door. I offer to hide in the bathroom. "No no!" my friend whispers. "How about the wardrobe?" I ask. It is the kind of farce that is only hilarious if you are not involved. For Fran it is a genuinely mortifying experience. I guess that Hamish is feeling guilty, suspicious, and mortified too, but I don't care. I don't need any more stories to tell my grandchildren.

It really is time for me to make a few changes. I vow to take up some kind of physical, non-sexual, exercise and go on a diet. Asparagus and broccoli are the coming things, I hear. I might also try to be more meek and less unteachable, which will not be easy. This will not be a sudden or a simple metamorphosis, but I have to start somewhere.

Since cross-country running at school and being left by my travel companions in Tehran I am out of practice at being alone. Now whenever I am in Soho I make a point of visiting the Marshall Street Baths with the aim of working up to six consecutive lengths of the pool. I reason that ploughing back and forth in that implacable Victorian hall with no other purpose than mindless routine will be good for my moral and physical renewal.

And what happens is that the demons I expect to intervene in my new regime retreat and the nymphs of the pool take over. They ensure that the waters are warm. They tease and caress me. We flirt together and take our time.

A man swimming close behind me complains that I am blocking his lane. "Then swim in the next fucking lane!" I call and am admonished by the pool supervisor. No-one takes any notice. I am swimming amongst bleary-eyed, shagged-out commuters who are more concerned with office politics and missed deadlines than what is going on around them. I breast-stroke, crawl, paddle and rest, doing my lengths, swallowing and spewing, floating, coasting, idling and dreaming … that somewhere out there on a distant shore lapped by the *Mare Aegaeum* is the perfect beach for me, a golden strand blessed by *Apollo Helios* himself as he rides the chariot of the sun across the sky, a beach where I shall be content to be alone and feel the sun-kissed sand caress my feet, and smell the faint, fishy tang of a safe, soft, silvery sea ...

The phone rings. It is Roz. She wants to tell me she has decided to have a baby. Oh God, I think, why is she telling me? "But I do not want to be beholden to the father," she says, "or for the father to have any claim on the child. In fact I do not even want to know who the father is." Yet she is sure she does not want the impersonality and absence of passion involved in artificial insemination. "So how are you going to conceive?" I find myself asking and immediately wish I hadn't. She says she plans to sleep with three of the brightest and best of her men friends during her next fertile period. This is years before paternity tests were routinely available. I assume she has earmarked me to be one of the three lucky fellows. She begins to explain the twisted thinking behind her appalling plan, but I am too trapped in my own tangled web to want to hear more. I ask to be excluded from her short list. She tells me I never made it and puts the phone down.

My mother writes, wanting me to be settled again and showing signs of anxiety. I reply

> I am more settled, but not in your terms, Missus. I want to have more control
> of my life, but I do not think I shall ever feel how I imagine you grown-ups
> feel – sure of your place in the world and with the incredible ability to channel
> your needs of a partner through one other person.

I attempt to quiz my mother about what was going on between her and my father when I was too young to understand, but she claims to be unable to remember. It is an evasion so blatant that it has to be filed under Deliberate Deceit. I suppose she is avoiding my questioning because she is still being stalked by that odious, wide-eyed, suffocating companion-for-life shame. I write again.

> I want to know why I am the way I am – how much is down to chance and
> how much to my, let's say, varied upbringing. I want to understand the past
> in what might be the vain hope of feeling more secure in the present.

I am getting used to spending more time on my own, though it means I have more time to be lonely. I phone Roz. She invites me to dinner. She cooks. We drink red wine. And kiss. Suddenly I wonder if I am being seduced. I ask her if she is pregnant yet or if I am back on the short list. She laughs and says no to both questions. Even so, I tell myself, this intimacy between ex-lovers is not the right way to behave – it is too prodigal, too casual, too ... what is the word I want? Wanton. I get up to leave. "This does not feel right," I say, and apologize. "This is not like you, James," she complains. I erupt. "If *I* do not know who the hell I am, how the fuck can *you*?"

Earthquakes are unpredictable, an expression of pressures building up over time, sometimes millennia, from deep underground. "You know what, Roz?" I say. "All the time we were together I behaved like a ponce and you were a whore. The only difference between us and the ponces and whores in Soho is that we tried to rationalize our behaviour in an attempt to make it intellectually respectable, but it was no less sleazy and shabby." In my struggle to be free of the weight on my back the earth's crust has finally split. A void opens beneath me. I am looking into a bottomless pit.

φ

Chapter 25

Angel Grace

THE ROAD FROM SELF-LOATHING TO DIACRITICAL SELF-LOVE – the ability to distinguish between negative *narcissismos* and affirmative *philia* – is a long one, full of twists and turns and unavoidable potholes. I promise myself it will lead in the end to the glittering sea, where I shall finally hope to feel at one with the world.

Meanwhile rather than look into the void and consider what I might find there, I ignore it. I am like the cartoon character who runs over the edge of a cliff and carries on running as if the ground were still there. We know that the moment he looks down he will hang suspended in mid-air for a second (will he by some miracle be saved?) before plummeting helplessly and for some reason hilariously to the ground. I do not look down. I carry on running. I organize parties, I go to museums, concerts, seminars, previews and political rallies. It is implicit that every occasion holds the potential for meeting the perfect partner.

They say this of Don Juan, that his quest was never about sex or seduction, but as a distraction from existential despair. I want to believe that my own quest relates more to universal *agape* than individual *eros*. I want to believe that the special relationship that exists for me out there somewhere will be effortless – no seismic differences, no airy idealism, no second-hand dialectic about what a relationship should or should not be. I am dimly aware that my search might therefore be endless. I am stuck in a compulsive pattern. I might actually be ill. To my unquiet mind compulsion leads without let to addiction, and addiction is a sub-category of insanity.

I know that getting well again is not simply a question of willpower. Addiction is either a disease of the brain or a character flaw. If it is a disease, it is something I have caught inadvertently. If it is a character flaw, it is one I inherited and for which I cannot be held responsible. I cannot help being a sex and relationship addict in the same way that my mother cannot help her addiction to self-pity and my father to drink. The illness is not unlike my experience of flu and suicidal depression. There is no readily available cure and I must follow the course it takes. And so I find myself involved in a succession of affairs, sweet and bittersweet, serious and frivolous. A nervous disorder lies behind the energy and flair I bring to these pursuits. I have a certain *élan*, dash, panache, an air of assurance and zeal.

I behave agreeably and also appallingly. I am erratic, deceitful, I profess love when I mean *amour propre*. Married friends invite me to dinner to meet their unattached female friends who are looking for love, or sex, or a father for their children. It is a beguiling time and I am surprised when the goddess of righteous indignation punishes me for it, though it is more of a reprimand, a gentle rebuke: a course of antibiotics as prescribed in the Special Clinic at St Mary's Hospital.

The consultant who advises me to avoid sex for a month is an attractive woman and I wonder if she might be available for a date when my month is up, but I decide on balance – and it is a finely-weighted judgement – not to ask.

This might be the start of my rehabilitation. I have a word with myself about making the most of this time of denial. There is no expectation on me to renounce desire, after all. It as an opportunity to experience the spiritual satisfactions of disavowing desire. Monks and ascetics have been banging on about celibacy for centuries. If I succeed in controlling my addictive behaviours, I tell myself, I will be better placed to redirect them into my work, or collecting tea caddies, or into something I have always wanted to do but found too intimidating, like translating the twelve thousand hexameters of The Odyssey from the original Greek.

Acknowledging sexual desire rather than pursuing it is like settling for the simple pleasures of pootling round the Norfolk Broads at five miles an hour, say, observing the speed limit and the rules of right of way, to para-gliding in the Mediterranean in a state of high arousal. The para-gliding might be instantly rewarding, but brings with it risks, while pootling around allows me time to appreciate the incidentals, the details, to be a part of what is going on around me without the compulsive need to perfect or direct it.

A week into my celibate month I am invited to dinner with friends in Camden Town and meet Aurelia. I realize quite soon that if I am to have any kind of relationship with Aurelia it cannot be an affair. I am drawn to the unusual combination of her unworldly look and a direct manner. "I like your frizzy hair," I say, and she smiles and says, "Actually I did not have time to iron it." She reminds me of one of those pre-Raphaelite paintings that are both sentimental and realist. If you have ever contemplated the impenetrable gaze of *Penelephon*, the Beggar Maid, in the painting by Edward Burne-Jones you will know what I mean.. The subject sits erect in a black diaphanous slip that hints at her navel and nipples, but the effect is not erotic. She is all but asexual, looking through the viewer to a world of her own that lies somewhere beyond. The young soldier-king *Cophetua* can only sit at her feet and gaze.

> So sweet a face, such angel grace, that beggar maid shall be my queen

wrote Tennyson on Cophetua's behalf. The young man is unable to see beyond the maid's other-worldliness, but does she see him and, if so, what does she see? Aurelia is a nurse, so it is possible that she identifies me as an addict in recovery with a need for understanding and support.

The model for the unearthly Penelephon was a tempestuous artist by the name of *Maria Zambaco*. Burne-Jones and Zambaco had a passionate affair, but he would not leave his wife and when he attempted to end the affair Zambaco tried to drown herself in the Regent's Canal, not far from Camden Town as it happens. A dull place for a drowning, you might think, on a par with a wet night by the Seine, but if your lover had rejected you and you were by nature self-destructive you would have no choice but to go with the moment. Such a perfervid act of love and loss might have spoken to me once, but not here, not now. Aurelia's orbit is a million miles from the planet Zambaco.

The following week I call at the flat in Shepherd's Bush that Aurelia shares with three other nurses. I am earlier than arranged and she is about to iron her hair. She is unperturbed. I have never heard of, let alone witnessed, a woman ironing her hair before. She adjusts the controls on the iron, kneels down, lays her head on the ironing board and runs the iron along the length of her hair to smooth out the kinks and the curls. It is one of the strangest hair-related sights I have seen, stranger even than Donald Nudds with a chip pan over his head or Bert applying his quick-drying cement gel. And yet this, like those, is perfectly ordinary. There is nothing soulful about the scene, no beggar-maid myth, only a gentleman caller in a roomful of girls with their make-up, coffee and curlers, as chatty and happy as a family of sparrows. For twenty minutes we are all one. *Thales of Miletus* had a name for the unity of things: he called it water. In the cycle of the seasons, in birth, sex, flirting, nursing, death and decay, we are all made of the same stuff.

In a Greek restaurant nearby I return to the subject of hair. "I preferred it the way you wore it when you had no time to iron it," I say. Aurelia smiles and says nothing. On our next date her hair is frizzy again. I remark on it. She smiles one of her wry little smiles and says, "I did not have time to iron it." We laugh. And now we are bound together in a myth I have created, that we are creatures of the same nature. "You shall be my Penelephon," I say. She looks at me. I have no idea what she is thinking.

On our third date I go further. I can be really pretentious when I try. "When the winged horse *Pegasus* touches his hooves to the ground on *Mount Helicon*," I say, "he causes three sacred springs to burst forth. And from these three springs three muses emerge. You, dear Aurelia, embody all three." I honestly believe that the attraction I feel for this enigmatic woman is more spiritual than physical. "*Melete*, spring water, brings continuous refreshment," I say. "*Mneme*, memory, gives me access to knowledge only you possess. And *Aoide*, or song, tells me of what is joyous and new." Aurelia looks at me. How have I skewed my desire for simplicity and the joy of the ordinary into this unnecessary paean of praise? I should be soberly assessing what I experience in the relationship rather than getting all poetical about what I would like it to be. "Oops," I say. "Got a bit carried away there." Aurelia smiles. I need no other encouragement.

A month or more passes before we sleep together and another month before she moves in with me. I can see it is easier for her to go along with my initiative in these matters rather than having any clear preferences of her own. I am gratified to find that her grace and elegance survive the move and that in spite of my readiness to romanticize, to want to see more than is there, we remain friends. I write to my mother.

> Aurelia likes Bezique, though she does not win much. She takes losing equably, not like me. Her mother visited recently and stayed overnight in the spare room – oh, did I mention? Aurelia moved in with me a few weeks ago. Her mother doesn't think Aurelia should settle down yet, so she treats the arrangement as a sensible compromise. She is originally from Malta and makes pots. Aurelia's father is a Commodore in the Royal Navy.

I am promoting her father (literally, I think he might be a Captain or a Commander) as a model of respectability, and I am using Aurelia's mother as a model for what I trust my mother's acceptance of the situation will be.

> I would marry Aurelia if that were what she wanted, but for the time being we are content together in a way I have not experienced before.

I am uncertain who I am trying to convince.

> If we decided to have a family we might review the situation, but I think it will be a few years before Aurelia is ready to have children. I have some regrets about this, but I can live with them.

> P.S. Sorry if some of this reads rather pompously. I am only trying to convey that there is nothing unconsidered about what is going on.

I have an agenda. Mother and Harold are on leave from India, renting a cottage in Yorkshire, and I plan to take Aurelia to stay with them and Rupert for Christmas. I am playing down any suggestion of a great romance in case the relationship doesn't work out, but at the same time I do not want any nonsense about separate bedrooms.

> Aurelia as you will see is a responsible person, not careless or facile.

Enough already.

> P.P.S. I would like to call you Mildred. Would that be all right with you?

What got into me to make this cockamamy suggestion – of course it would not be all right with her. The fact is that I have long given up on the idea of a conventional relationship with my mother, because I do not know what that is or how to achieve it, so it seems to me that we should try something different. I want us to be friends.

Mildred replies by return of post – a long, sorrowful letter (signed 'Your Mother') about how hard she has tried, how often she has held back from commenting on my life in a way that I might have construed as disapproving. She is equating being a good mother with feeling critical, but not expressing it. I understand the mad, sad logic of this. I imagine her weeping while composing this letter, trying not to be negative while finding it impossible to be kind. I understand more the sort of semi-detached relationship she wants with her children and vow to do what I can to assist. And the first thing I do is give up trying to be her friend.

The point at which my relationship with Aurelia begins its inevitable decline is around the time I give up on the idea of making friends with Mildred and settle for a more formal association with the woman who wishes to be known as Mother. I am open to the idea of having children again and imagine making good not only my mother's and father's mistakes, not only my own and Lydia's, but those of generations past who were too troubled by ignorance or poverty, or lack of opportunity, or inadequate exercise, or a poor diet, to know any better. Unfortunately, Aurelia is not ready to have children, or anyway not mine.

By 'mistakes', by the way, J.P., I mean decisions attributable to ignorance or to assumptions that at the time seemed well-founded, but which later turn out to be false. Think of them as careless interventions by the fickle unpredictable gods who know perfectly well what is good for any of us, but take a perverse pleasure in twisting it to their own ends. They will tell you stories, but you can test those stories, reflect that you do not have all the information necessary to judge their veracity and adjust your responses accordingly. Here endeth today's lesson.

Aurelia and I plan a holiday together. It is the kind of mistake that could be attributed to ignorance, for if we had taken the trouble to find out what each of us wanted of a holiday we might have arranged things differently. I am keen to fulfil a dream I have had since first reading Homer – to take a ferry from Piraeus and seek the warm sands and hospitable bays of the *Isle of Ogygia*, one of the sanctuaries where Odysseus is said to have rested during his travels, the island where he was seduced under the shade of the vine by the goddess *Calypso*.

> Over the isle there was a fragrance of cleft cedar and juniper, and round
> about soft meadows of violets and parsley.

Is Ogygia actual or mythical? Some say it might be Gozo, off the island of Malta, which might be of interest to Aurelia's mother. I reckon there is a better chance that Odysseus stopped off at one of the northern Ionian islands on his way back to Ithaca. Ogygia might be Corfu, Kefalonia, Lefkas or Paxos.

Aurelia is unenthusiastic about Greece. She read of a ferry that sank while doing an about-turn in the harbour because the captain forgot to close the bow doors. He had skipped Page One of the How Not to Sink a Ferry manual. I have fears about ferries too, but I would have known where the lifejackets were stored.

We book a week on Ibiza instead. After checking in at the hotel we take a stroll along the beach until Aurelia finds a place to lie on the sand. This turns out to be all she wants of a holiday. It hadn't occurred to me that she might not want to reconnoitre the island and find a remote cove where we would seek treasure together and have sex on the shore. Exotic exploration and erotic improvisation are not her thing. What is? In London we tried working our way through the senses

– olfactory, auditory, visual, kinaesthetic – to see which if any held more potential for arousal than the others. We lit frankincense candles, leafed through a book of Modigliani nudes, attempted Seven Sensual Yoga Poses, listened to Jane Birkin and Serge Gainsbourg murmuring *'Je t'aime'* to a background of moaning, that kind of thing. It became more of a cultural than a sensual journey. Here on Ibiza we try the local white wine – light and fresh, with a faint taste of thyme. As an aphrodisiac it is about as effective as the candles, yoga, moaning, etc., that is, not at all.

I readily acknowledge there is a lot more for me to learn in these matters. I am too restless, I think, too ready to explore the wilder shores of arousal, to lose myself in waves of desire without ever quite going under. What Aurelia needs, I realize, is time. Lots of it. So I attempt to be patient while continuing to be attentive, but there is a fine line between attentiveness and intensity, and if I cross that line for a moment it sets off alarms. So I stop, take a breath and gaze into the face of this elusive daughter of a Commodore in the hope that she knows something I do not know about the human condition. Sometimes I interrogate her – what is she thinking, how is she feeling, what works, what doesn't? At other times, unforgivably, I fall asleep.

In the final analysis it is Aurelia herself who makes the decision to move on. She responds to my gaze with the same angel grace she had from the start, but it has become clear to us both that she would be better off with someone who is less concerned to know what is going on in her mind. After all, it might be nothing. We part without recrimination. There is a measure of regret on my side and I am not quite sure what on hers. Relief, I think.

A few weeks after we separate Aurelia moves in with a junior doctor from the hospital where she works. He is an anaesthetist, which seems kind of appropriate. At my suggestion the three of us meet for a drink. David is courteous and kind, and I hope that the three of us might be mates and hang out together. Another of my ill-conceived ideas about the universality of *philia* and *agape*. I tell myself it might have to be the last. I don't call him Dave. "David is very possessive," Aurelia tells me. "But he has you," I say, "and I do not. It is my job to be jealous, which I am not."

I am familiar enough with feelings of professional rivalry and personal envy, but I have hardly, if ever, known sexual jealousy, not even with Roz. I used to reframe Roz's promiscuity as a generosity of spirit, a healthy curiosity and a commitment to psycho-sociological principle. Was that odd, I wonder, even deviant? Jealousy is a normal feeling, isn't it? Why should I still be so determined to be different?

> Thank you, Mother, for your thoughts about my relationships. Your generalizations sound sensible, but when you apply them to me you get it all wrong. I wonder why if we are so closely connected should there be such a distance between us? Is it because we want too much of each other?

> When I came out to India after what had been an emotional crisis I wanted uncritical acceptance. I wanted to be part of a family of the sort I was deprived

as a child and which in the normal way of things I might have grown out of by now. Meanwhile I had invested all my unconscious emotional needs in Lydia, who could not possibly fulfil them and who took the world from under my feet. So I turned to you, but you could only say how much I hurt you by my unhappiness, even though, God knows, I had tried not to express the extent of my despair because I knew that would *really* hurt you.

I miscalculated. I learnt that one cannot depend on anyone else's resources, only one's own. It was a painful lesson. Today I can feel bad that I tried to involve you in my problems, but I was retarded, a twenty-year old with the emotional development of a ten-year old, and I never gave a second thought to *your* problems, your guilt or your hurt.

I know you did not want to interfere with my life and tried not to question it, because you feared to break the tenuous connection between us. And so you resented what seemed to you to be my selfishness because you did not understand my sadness, and in turn I resented your apparent lack of interest in my life. I guess neither of us wanted to risk tipping the balance of an already precarious relationship. Well, dearest mother o'mine, I do not want to go on like this forever, because expecting nothing of someone seems to me as bad as expecting everything of them. We do not want to go the rest of our lives viewing each other through darkened glass.

Though this is pretty much what happens. I give up on my desire for a close relationship – that is, I make an effort to give up, though putting all those ideals of forgiveness, acceptance and living in the moment into practice is hard work, which is surely not the point. What I have to do, I decide, and it is all I have to do, is let things be. Not to be so driven. And this leads to realizing a long-held ambition.

φ

Chapter 26
Entering the Labyrinth

I FLY TO ATHENS. I have wanted to visit the city since Dippy first showed us his holiday slides of the Acropolis, but I didn't manage it before the military coup of '67 and after that I stayed away, unwilling to give political legitimacy to a bunch of thugs who had violently usurped the democratic process. Now I am in a dilemma. Chelsea have reached the final of the European Cup Winners Cup and are scheduled to play Real Madrid in Piraeus. I hesitate. I vacillate. I know that as an Arsenal and Henley Rovers fan you will affect shocked surprise, but I have been a Chelsea supporter for fifteen years and this is the season I attended every home game and collected the programme vouchers that gave me priority in applying for tickets for the Cup. There is a package on offer that includes the flight, a seat for the game, a hotel for the night and – this is the clincher – the morning free in Athens. I pray that the gods of forgiveness will excuse me this one small betrayal of principle. It is only for the one night. I vow to tell no-one.

It doesn't work out quite so simply – predictably enough, you might say, knowing me more, I'm sure, after reading so far. In Athens I meet an enchantress. I shall tell you how we meet and its meaning for me in a moment, but first I have to get to the end of this mawkish, defensive letter to my mother.

> No more generalizations – please! When you say Melissa is too young for me, think again. You don't know her, you hardly know me and you know nothing of the complex interaction of our needs and aspirations. Look at all the relationships you knew that seemed ideally suited but did not work out, and those where the differences were far greater than ours and worked perfectly. I hope you are having good weather.
> Love, James

Melissa is a sea-nymph, enticing, persuasive, high-spirited, quick to take offence and quick to forget. She has the fickleness and irresistibility of water. Meeting a woman like Melissa is the kind of thing that can happen in a labyrinthine world of cause and affect where the path newly taken looks familiar, but is really quite different. Ah, I am ahead of myself. Lost and found again. I have to retrace my steps to the evening of the Cup Final, as the outcome of the game has a direct bearing on what happens afterwards.

A mazy run by dribbling genius Charlie Cooke ends in a typically delicate dinked pass to Chelsea's lofty, lordly centre forward Peter Osgood, who scores with an unstoppable volley. One-nil. 20,000 Chelsea supporters, including me, go wild. "Osgood *is* good!" we chant. Then in the very last minute of the game Spanish midfielder Zoco appears out of nowhere to level the score for Madrid. One-all. Curses. No extra time or golden goals in those days. And I shall miss the replay, which is in two days' time.

But I have something very special indeed to look forward to in the morning. I know the Acropolis so well from my studies that I feel as if I have been reared among these stones. I arrive before the crowds and for a blissful half-hour have the citadel to myself. I know every detail of the Doric temple of *Athene Parthenos*, including the many metopes and fragments of the pediment that were stolen by the temple wrecker Elgin and are now displayed — completely out of context and the wrong way round — outside-in, if you can imagine it — in the skyless halls of the British Museum. It really is time we took plaster casts of these sculptures, returned the originals and put right a long-standing imperialist wrong. My philhellene hero Lord Byron witnessed the conspicuous spaces left by the predator Elgin and wrote

> First on the head of him who did this deed
>   My curse shall light, – on him and all his seed:
> Without one spark of intellectual fire,
>   Be all the sons as senseless as the sire.

The curse seems to have lighted on Elgin's senseless son, the eighth earl, who as High Commissioner to China bombed Canton, looted the Summer Palace and wrote in belated disgust to his wife, "I never felt so ashamed in my life."

Yet this morning it is not the Parthenon but the elegant *Erectheion* that takes my breath away. Six Ionic columns support a porch with a view to the *Agora* below, while a smaller porch of six captive caryatids faces inwards to the citadel and is the knock-out attraction. I have only seen illustrations of this elegant *belvedere* before, never the living — still living, I am certain — reality. Some say that six maids of Sparta were made to hold up the roof of the porch as punishment for their role in betraying Athens during the Greco-Persian Wars, yet these gracefully-draped ladies look to me to be loyal and firm of purpose. I think they were chosen because they were the most handsome in all Greece. Only five of the original six remain, the sixth having been removed by sticky-fingered Elgin to decorate his Scottish mansion. In the light of day these gracious ladies do not appear to be suffering, but I believe that at night they can be heard wailing for their abducted sister and praying for her safe return.

From the Erectheion I look down at the network of alleys and streets in the *Plaka* below. Is there a clue here as to why the celebrated inventor *Dædalus* came to throw his talented pupil *Talus* off the Acropolis to his death?

It is hot. I sit in the shade. My attention wanders. Two men come by and stop to look at the intricate pattern of alleyways below. "Something of a maze," murmurs the older of the two. The younger man takes a notebook from his satchel and starts to sketch. "My labyrinth will be so ingenious," he says, "that no-one will be able to solve it but myself." What a plonker, I think. The older man is upset. He confides in me that the younger man took all the credit for a temple design they undertook recently. "He went too far," says the older man, "and it was not for the first time." His companion climbs onto a low wall, absorbed in his drawing. The older man approaches from behind. I want to intervene, but my limbs will not move. I call out, but no sound comes. I can only watch in horror as the older man snatches the drawing and shoves the young man off the wall to his death on the rocks far below. The young man screams as he falls. I wake in a sweat, having fallen asleep in the heat.

A long way below in the Plaka I see a small taverna with a vine-covered patio that looks like a perfect place for lunch, so I take the path down and search through the warren of streets I saw from above. When I find the taverna, I feel that mix of relief and delight that comes from perceiving a problem, working towards a solution and surprising oneself by succeeding. This was not Talus's experience. The talented designer believed he had a sketch for the perfect maze, but died at his master's hands before he could put his invention to the test.

I sit out on the patio of the taverna in the dappled light with a view back to where I was. It is early and I am the only customer. I order Greek salad and a glass of white wine. Bouzouki music is playing quietly on a tape in the background. I wonder idly how Lydia and Bernard are getting on (there are rumours of a split); and I think of Roz and her misbegotten child (no no, I should be more forgiving); and Aurelia and her anaesthetist lover (someone told me they had started drinking); and my father and Norma (fattening up on her pastries and spending their winters on the Costa Brava); and the producer at Galaxy Pictures who is waiting for my script for a documentary film on the cattle tick; and the actress I had an affair with that upset her husband, who was already being unfaithful himself. It is a long, long time since I felt so content to be on my own.

Are those rocks I can see at the foot of the Acropolis the site of Talus's terrible death? Rather than stay in Athens and face trial for murder, Dædalus takes his son and flees to Crete, where he is granted asylum by *King Minos*. Minos has a condition: that the master designer construct a labyrinth to contain the savage *Minotaur*, part-man, part-beast, without any possibility of escape. Now I understand the mystery at the heart of the story. Dædalus uses his assistant's sketch for an insoluble maze as the basis for his design and Talus, now deceased, will never be credited. Such presumption by the murderous Dædalus has its reward. The labyrinth he builds is so perfect that he becomes trapped in it himself, unable to escape his own vanity.

My mind is just such a tangle of pride and ingenuity that I might never get to unravel. Solving one puzzle leaves me trapped in a far larger one.

My wine arrives in a metal pitcher. I pour a little into a glass. It is oddly yellow in colour and tastes like a blend of disinfectant and petrol. I take another sip. It is my first encounter with retsina. I am not at all sure, but I think I like it. At some time in the future, I promise myself, I will bring my son to Athens to see the great ladies of the Erectheion, eat feta cheese drizzled with Greek olive oil and taste this pine-flavoured wine in the dappled light of a vine-covered patio with laundered check tablecloths and one of the world's iconic views. Mexico might be wonderful, but it surely cannot compare. I look forward to seeing you before long. This bullfighting thing is surely only a phase.

I order another pitcher of retsina and think about the choices I have – not life choices, I know nothing of those, but the day's. There is no immediate need for me to return to London. The producer at Galaxy can wait a day or two. In any case I am in no hurry to continue contributing to a culture in which it is accepted without question that a serious documentary about the problems facing subsistence level cattle farmers round the world should be sponsored by a global pharmaceutical firm. As a born-again, retsina-sipping scholar I wonder if it might be time to take a rest from commercial and ethical consideration and have another look at my unfinished thesis. As for the Greek colonels, they are a temporary blemish on the body of democracy and if I can cope with my residual guilt I can ignore them a little while longer. My hero of the day shall be *Diogenes of Sinope*, whose philosophy of simplicity and virtue leads him to take up residence in a bathtub in the centre of Athens. His big idea is to subvert the corrupt practices of the day by *doing nothing*, naked, in a bath. The symbolism appeals to me. I am free, it is hot, I shall go to the beach.

Half an hour on the bus takes me to the long, soft sands of Vouliagmeni, where the waters are clear and bathwater warm and the sea no more than waist-deep for a hundred metres out. I swim, float, paddle, breathe easily. For the first time in a long time I feel serene. The skies above me are clear, life is simple and I am virtuous.

I go for a stroll and come across the ruins of a temple dedicated to *Apollo Zoster*. I know Apollo as a conscientious god who has taken on a large portfolio of responsibilities, including medicine, music, archery and prophecy, and who has many high-flown titles – *Helios, Lyceus, Acesius* – sun, light, healing, and so on – but the epithet *Zoster* meant 'girdle', so what is the story here? Are we talking about a waistband or the kind of elasticated undergarment Auntie Joan and Grandma Lily used to wear? I shall tell you what I discover, because it brings us right back to the beach and my meeting with Melissa.

You will know that gods can only reflect the flaws and foibles of men, but it is also the case that men can only reflect the defects and imperfections of gods, which leaves both parties in a perfect bind, the nature of one being inescapably determined by the other. So when one of *Zeus's* mistresses, *Letos*, falls pregnant, his legitimate spouse *Hera* – goddess of motherhood, protectress of marriage and so on – cannot help herself: in a jealous rage she sends Letos flying – literally, in the air – and puts a curse on her, that she *might never give birth on terra firma*.

Letos circles over Attica, unable to land. In some discomfort she loosens her waistband (it is that kind of girdle) and it falls to the ground, but because of the curse she is unable to descend and retrieve it. She flies out to sea, to the islands of Kea, Kithnos, Siros and Mykonos, but their citizens refuse her permission to land on the grounds that their islands are attached to the mainland via the sea-bed, so are still *terra firma*. Desperate to give birth, Leto arrives over the tiny island of Delos, whose inhabitants have always maintained that their island is *floating*, unconnected to the mainland above or below the sea and thus neither terra nor firma. Letos lands, Hera's curse is evaded, and Apollo and his twin sister are born. As soon as he is old enough to fly Apollo makes his way to the mainland to retrieve the girdle for his mother and finds it near the beach at Vouliagmeni. Which is how a temple to Apollo Zoster comes to be built by the people in these parts. There is a cynical view – mine, I confess – that the locals made up the story several centuries later in order to attract visitors to Vouliagmeni in preference to the rival resorts of Voula and Glyfada, which are nearer to Athens and handier for tourists.

How does Melissa come into all this? As I sit on the beach near the ruins of the temple I become aware of what the god of the sun, *Apollo Helios*, has been saving for me: the sparkle of sunlight on gently moving water, a transcendent effect much greater than the sum of its parts. Why have I never noticed these brilliant coruscations before? As I give myself up to their radiance I feel the first faint stirrings of renewal. The god of healing, *Apollo Acesius*, takes heed and makes room for me in his diary, and I do not have to make an appointment three weeks ahead. What a fine physician he is, I reflect, wholly devoted to the restorative arts and to keeping them free at the point of need.

I see a disturbance at a distance in the sea, a head, then the shoulders and arms of a young woman swimming towards me. As she reaches the shallows, she rises – slim, olive-skinned, in a brief black bikini, her outline back-lit by the sun. It could be a scene from a film. Cut! Print! No need for another take. She wades to the shore, hips swaying, then stops and shakes her hair. I can almost count the bright beads of water as they fly in glittering arcs from her head. She looks up and down the crowded beach, notices me, smiles and exclaims, "I cannot remember where I put my things!" "You are English!" I say. "You do not look English." "You do!" she says, looking around. "Here they are." A towel, a T-shirt, a multi-coloured sarong and blue flip-flops are in a pile nearby. "Where are you from?" I ask. "I'm not sure," she says as she dries herself. I ask, "How so?" She looks at me. "Who are you?" "My name is James," I say. "I am a Chelsea supporter." She laughs, sits a few feet away and rubs at her hair. "My name is Melissa." "Melissa," I say, "as in *meli,* honey?" "Yes!" she exclaims. "It is a beautiful name," I say, hoping I am not sounding too smarmy. "Thank you," she says, and smiles. I say, "I know who you are." "Who am I?" "You are a nymph, a daughter of *Poseidon*, you come from the sea." She laughs and says, "My mother is Greek, my father was English." "Was? Is he dead?" "I don't know. He was a long-distance lorry driver. When I was born we went to London to live, then he drove away one day and never came back, so my mother brought me to Athens." "So you are Greek," I say. "I was Greek, then I was English, now I think I am trying to be Greek again." "You are free to be who you want to be, Melissa," I say. Me too, I remind myself. Free to bring the self I wish to be into being. But how? Melissa looks at me. "Tell me about sea-nymphs and Chelsea supporters."

"Sea-nymphs are not goddesses, but spirits," I say. "Chelsea supporters are neither, but we seek divine inspiration for the replay on Friday." "Who are you playing?" "Real Madrid, the champions of Spain." "In that case I shall support Chelsea." "I am honoured," I say, "but I must also be careful." She asks why. I explain. "Nymphs are unmarried maidens who love to sing and dance. They hide in mountains and groves, rivers, springs, the sea and so on." And I add, "They emerge from their hiding places to seduce young men." She laughs. Why am I babbling on like this? I was perfectly content sitting there, absorbing the sparkle on the surface of the sea and thinking of nothing. I have absolutely no intention of getting involved with this girl. I go on. "They are not chaste, these spirits, and nor are they wanton. They mate with men and women as they choose." "Is that so?" says Melissa. There is something in the light and heat and the sparkle on the water that is bypassing my higher brain functions. Self-sufficiency is a recreated value, I tell myself; it isn't natural. I can't help myself relating to this person. "Along with their beauty, youth and passion," I continue, "they are capricious, these nymphs. The monsters Scylla and Charybdis were sea-nymphs once. Do you recognize yourself in any of this?" "No, no!" says Melissa, "I have no desire to mate with women!" She laughs. So do I.

We take the bus back to Athens together, walk in the Plaka, buy fruit, look at T-shirts, jewellery and models of the Parthenon. Melissa gestures to a hairdressing salon we are passing. "That is my mother's." "I would like to meet the mother of a sea-nymph," I say. "Are you sure?" "Why not?" "Well, okay." I follow her into the little gilt-and-green salon, where she speaks to a preoccupied woman in rapid Greek and introduces me in English. "James, this is my mother, Sophia." "You are English?" says her mother, looking at me sideways while busying herself with a customer. "Yes," I say. There follows a polite conversation about the Elephant and Castle area of London, where she and Melissa used to live, and about Brixton and West Hampstead, where I used to live. I speak of Chelsea and the replay in two days' time and ask them if there is a cheap hotel in the Plaka they would recommend. Melissa speaks to her mother rapidly, like an express train rattling over the points. Her mother shrugs and says, *'Ne,* okay". Melissa looks at me, smiling. *'Ne',* I know, means 'yes'. "You can stay in our apartment," says Melissa. I am about to be polite and say, 'That is very kind of you, but I shall find a hotel', but Melissa gives me a look and says, "It really is all right." I check my phrasebook.

"Eiste poly evgenikos," I say to Sophia, who smiles at my pronunciation. "You are very kind," I say. *"Eferisto."*

Outside in the street Melissa says, "It is her night off to see my grandmother in Nafplion, she will be away for the night." "Oh," I say and Melissa says, "Do not worry, I am not going to seduce you!" I laugh. So does she.

That evening we take a bath together. Well, what happens is that I am having a bath and Melissa comes in, exclaims, "I emerge from my hiding place!" strips and gets in with me. We giggle and soap each other. And then go to bed.

In the morning Melissa prepares a breakfast of thick Greek yoghurt, toast and rich Greek honey. She asks me what I would like to do that day. The sun is up and it is already hot. I think for a moment. "I want to visit *Delphi*," I say, "and *Mycenae, Mount Olympus, Epidaurus,* go scuba diving in the submerged city of *Pavlopetri* and take the ferry from Piraeus to the *Isle of Ogygia.*" "What about the replay tomorrow?" she asks. "What replay?" I ask. I have an afterthought. "I would also like to swim the *Hellespont.*" "When is your flight?" Melissa asks. "And where is Ogygia?"

We look at a map and discuss our options. The replay is tomorrow, Friday, and I have to be at the office in London on Monday, but these things are aeons away. "Ogygia," I say, "is the island where *Odysseus* was borne alone on the wreckage of his raft after it had been destroyed by a thunderbolt." "I do not think there is such an island," says Melissa. "The name may have changed," I say. "It is where the goddess *Calypso* detained Odysseus for seven years. I think he was a willing prisoner." "We shall consult the Oracle at Delphi," Melissa says, "and hear what she has to say." Not only about Ogygia, I think, but about James and Melissa, and while we are at it I will ask for a prophecy about the replay in case I don't make it back to Athens in time. I am contemplating the possibility of what might be a close-run thing: attending the European Cup Winners Cup Final or spending more time with this girl.

We hire a car from Zorba's repair shop round the corner and drive to Delphi, stopping short of the town and making directly for the palace itself. For me it is another homecoming, second only to the Acropolis on my list of places to see before – that is, to see soon.

I know the Oracle of *Apollo Delphinius* as the sacred centre of the earth, the place where Apollo came in the shape of a dolphin to slay the dragon *Pytho,* who had ravished his mother. The myth does not explain how a dolphin managed to make it half-way up a mountain, but there you go, when revenge is on the agenda anything is possible, as I know too well. Here at this scene of gloomy grandeur hewed from the stone of Mount Parnassus *Oedipus* learns that he has killed his father and married his mother, and it is here that he blinds himself with the pin of his mother-wife *Jocasta*'s own brooch, a chilling detail. Why is Oedipus so eager to pursue the knowledge that will lead to his downfall? Because he believes, as many before him and since, that only the truth can set us free.

Is that really the case? Did Lydia feel suddenly liberated when she learnt that I had spent the night with a heroin addict? I suppose it helped her feel free of me. And how did my mother feel when she learnt that her son had attempted to take his own life? She would have felt hurt, for sure. Then anger. At me. Then self-pity, because after blaming me she would not have been able to escape from herself. Free? I don't think so.

I could have lied to them both, of course. It would have saved them some pain. Yet however expedient a lie or the intentional avoidance of the truth can be, I reckon it is a perversion of an ecumenical ideal: that we are all entitled to real information, even when the possible cost is impossible to calculate. In Oedipus's case the truth leads to his wife-mother Jocasta hanging herself and to her husband-son gouging out his own eyes before going into self-imposed exile. Freedom of a sort, I suppose.

Am I free, with my inherited values and involuntary responses – am I really able to act at will and not under some predetermined set of unconscious compulsions? Sitting on the beach at Vouliagmeni absorbed in the brilliance of the light I had thought so. Walking up to the entrance of ancient Delphi holding hands with a girl I met only yesterday I am not so sure. The Skeptics and Sophists called into question *all* knowledge, belief and opinion. *Question, quibble, assert nothing, inquire into everything.* I should even doubt what was until now the undoubted warmth of my feelings for Melissa.

Carved into the entrance to the temple at Delphi were said to be three popular sayings of the day: *Gnothi seauton,* 'know thyself' (ah, if only, and then what?); *Meden agan,* 'nothing to excess' (that is, there is nothing to excess that is truly desirable); and *Engya para d'Aate,* 'beware certainty' (or as Socrates might have put it, 'be advised of your own ignorance'). 'Please do not tell me I will enjoy this or that play you saw recently', the sage might have said, 'or that I will enjoy this or that wine you drank last night, because I might *not* enjoy them, and I will think less of you for presuming to know me'.

Aate is a peculiar goddess, a model for devilry, perversity, delusion and ruin, having been condemned by her tyrannical father *Zeus* to wander the earth in perpetuity as punishment for some imagined offence. So upset is Aate at her father's readiness to punish her without just cause that she refuses to tread the earth as instructed and treads on the heads of men instead, wreaking mental and emotional havoc that persists to this day. So *Engya para d'Aate* refers to the mischief that befalls those whose unqualified certainty leads to their downfall or – and I hesitate to mention this again quite so soon, but it does seem to be popping up everywhere – death.

As we arrive at the sanctuary, a group of tourists surround a cleft in the rock reputed to be the source of the sacred vapours inhaled by the priestess *Pythia*, the original Oracle, to assist in her polysemantic pronouncements. Several of the group are photographed pretending to inhale the vapours, accompanied by much laughter. Melissa and I climb the slope above the temple and with a long view over the valley prepare our own little *adyton*, a sacred space for the true acolytes of Apollo.

"You shall be the Blameless One," I announce to Melissa, "and I shall be your supplicant." "You must first perform the sacred ritual," utters the Priestess, "or I cannot speak." "What is the sacred ritual, O Prescient One?" "That is not for me to say," the Seer replies, "but for the truly virtuous to know." I gather herbs and grasses and waft them over her. "It is good," she intones. I waft some more. "I have before me two roads," I say. "Which shall I take?" I am wondering if I can get away without returning to London quite so soon.

The Oracle falls into a sacred trance. "*Apollo Delphinius* possesses me," she says in a sacred monotone. "And now he speaks." There is a momentary silence as she listens to the inner voice of prophecy. And then she says, "The two roads are distant from one another. The one road leads to the house of friendship, the other to the house of slavery." "Where is the house of friendship?" I ask. "On the sacred isle of Ogygia," is the surprising response. I already know where the house of slavery is: in Soho, temporarily occupied by Galaxy Pictures working for Globechem. I start to ask about Ogygia, but the Oracle interrupts. "You must find your own Ogygia," she says. "Your heart will take you there."

We spend that night in a hotel in Delphi, have supper under the stars, make love, sleep late, make love again and eat breakfast outside in the sun. We take our time driving in the mid-day heat back to Athens, where we drop off the car at Zorba's and call at Sophia's salon. Her customers are getting their bouffants, beehives and tints for the weekend. Melissa's mother comes to the door with me to say goodbye. "Sophia," I say, "I love your daughter."

It just came out. I thought I would be showing them my Cup Final ticket and saying 'Wish me luck'. I must have been affected by the sacred vapours. Sophia looks at me and looks at Melissa. Melissa is smiling at me. There follows one of those moments when no-one knows what to say, so nothing is said. "I shall phone you from London," I say to Melissa. I embrace them both and go off to the game.

Inspired centre-forward Peter Osgood scores after thirty minutes, followed five minutes later by equally inspired centre-half John Dempsey. Two-nil to Chelsea. At half-time I ask myself, '*What* did I say? What in heaven possessed me?'

Real Madrid come back in the second half, but Chelsea hold on until the final whistle and several hundred of us who stayed on for the replay are delirious. On the flight home I curse myself for being a Chelsea supporter and making such a fool of myself in Sophia's salon. *Assert nothing, question everything*. If I had not been so committed to Chelsea, if I had followed Fulham or Queens Park Rangers, I might never have set foot in Athens and I would not be in the fix I am in now.

Back in London I acknowledge that the questioners and quibblers have taken a tumble. I was seduced by the glittering sea and the pine-flavoured wine, and all too soon, like Odysseus, I shall wake in a cave and long for home.

I have no home. I have a second-floor flat on a limited lease, a job that is no longer fulfilling, two failed marriages (all right, one and a half), one live stepmother, one dead one (what did she die of – bitterness? witchery?), an estranged son, a hurt mother and an alcoholic father with his head in the sand.

> My dear Mother:
> I know, I know, you say what you say only because you want the best for me. I respect your motives. What you must understand is that when I wrote expressing my doubts and uncertainties, I was writing at my lowest ebb. But the tide has turned. I am confident that at least three of your four principal conditions for a good marriage are fulfilled.

Ah, I am ahead of myself again. I need to retrace a step or two, as you have to do in a maze. I forgot to mention that a few days after returning to London I phoned Melissa. "I miss you," I say. "I miss you too," says she. "Come to London," I say. "I cannot afford to." I offer to pay. She refuses. "No no, I will borrow it from my mother." "I will go halves with your mother." A silence. Then, "We will see."

I have some research to do in County Durham, so I phone my father, mention that I will be passing through Thornton Moor *en route* and ask if he would like me to visit. My session with the Oracle has helped me realize there might not be much time left to resolve my relationship with this enigmatic old man who has refused to talk about the past. He sounds, I think, pleased at the prospect of seeing me and insists I stay overnight. I am reluctant, I would much rather stay in a hotel, but I agree.

As I park in the spot where Harold once parked to pick up his stepchildren twenty-five years ago, a deadening feeling descends like a shroud. This is a place of anger and shame. Too much happened here. Gravy was thrown.

My father's plump new wife Norma gives me a hug. She is different in every way from her skinny, grim predecessor, but I sense that at heart she does not trust me. I come from the posh-accented, drug-fuelled, wife-swapping metropolis. Will she be any easier for me to get along with than the witch that was Edith? Edith played the role of wicked stepmother in my life; she deserved an award for the conviction she brought to the part; but I wonder how we would get on now if she were alive. In her cold-hearted, critical way she must have loved my father. I look at this walnut-faced, ruby-nosed little man with soft white hair who wears casual patterned sweaters and almost always has a squiffy smile. Who is he? Everyone seems to like him. Half-seas-over or almost sober, he does not have a bad word to say about anyone, not even my mother.

Norma takes it upon herself to mediate the space between my father and me. She does not leave us alone for a moment, a tactic aimed, I guess, at protecting him from the third degree. I invite him to The Jolly Tar for a tot or two of fermented molasses, thinking this might ease his way into talking on an informal mates-in-the-pub rather than awkward father-and-son basis, but Norma comes along too, orders him a lemon and lime, and talks like a running tap with a faulty washer.

I want to understand my father on his own terms and for him to know me on mine, and I fail on both counts. Why can I not take the imaginative leap that will allow me to leave him be? Instead I wish to question him on the premise that he is guilty as charged, but can still get off lightly. Norma ensures that we get no further than talking about my stepbrother Emil, who qualified as a plumber, married a hair stylist and moved to Merthyr Tydfil.

That night I sleep in the attic where I spent so many winter nights – in three or four years it never seemed to be summer there – when my overriding aim was to get ready for school and get out of the house before Edith appeared. This time I have a two-bar electric fire, but the floor is covered in the same old linoleum. Nothing is resolved.

I drive back to Marylebone disappointed in myself, frustrated at my father and deeply, unfairly, resentful of Norma. There is a letter from Melissa: 'My mother says there is nothing for me in Athens. I should come to London'.

She comes. I am pleased to see her. She is pleased to see me. Our relationship does not have quite the same sense of innocent excitement it had in Athens and Delphi, but we have the memory of two memorable days and nights on which to build.

We visit my mother and Harold in Yorkshire. Harold has taken early retirement. Melissa quizzes him about his bachelor life under the Raj in pre-Independence days – "Really? Amazing!" – and seems genuinely interested. "Intelligent girl," he says to me later. Mother and Melissa talk recipes for curd tarts and parkin. "A nice girl," says Mother. "Too young for you, of course." My mother seems not to feel as threatened by Melissa as she did by Polly (too smart), Lydia (too elusive), Gudiya (too beautiful), Roz (too capable) or Aurelia (too cool). She might be thinking that this spirited half-Greek girl – who is almost all but not quite any of these things – and I are clearly unsuited and that the relationship will never last.

On the drive back to London we divert to Thornton Moor and I phone my father. "I thought we might drop by and say hello," I say. "Norma isn't here," he says. "She's at the shops." Good, I think, I shall get him to myself and put the screws on. We are there in ten minutes. As he fills the kettle, I can see that he is nervous. "Norma won't be long," he says. Does he really think I want to talk to bloody Norma? He is confused and uncertain without his chatty fat partner to protect him, so I choose not to ask him about his blighted childhood, the ill-fated marriage to my mother, his wartime traumas, the endless smoking and drinking, what on earth he had seen in Edith, why he had thought that Emil could pass as his son and how come he had given up Jenny and me without a fight. Instead I listen to the latest about Emil and his wife Shirl and little Selwyn, who turns out after one or two misunderstandings ("He has to beg for his supper" "He pees on the carpet") to be a dog. Uneasy as he is the whole time we are there, Melissa finds him charming and afterwards says, "But he is really sweet!"

Two days later Norma phones to say that my father had a stroke and was taken to hospital, where he had another stroke and died.

I killed him. That is my first reaction. I feel responsible. Then I am angry, because now I will never get to know everything he knew that I didn't. Norma blames herself. They had their first row on the evening of my visit and she believes that this was the cause of the stress that killed him. I believe it was the stress of my visit and the fear of the inquisition that killed him, that the Oracle's warning to *Oedipus* after his long journey from Corinth has been fulfilled.

Unhappy man, keep far away from your father or you will kill him.

Nota bene, Julian: this does not apply to all sons and fathers, unhappy or not. Do visit soon.

So my father has left again and this time for ever. I recognize that my loss is less that of a father, which he had hardly been anyway, and more of what he knew about matters that affected me profoundly, still do, and which he would not discuss because of the painful condition he shared with so many of his class and generation: deeply-ingrained, foolish, gratuitous, contagious, mind-rotting shame. His death has deprived me of something more important, in this case, than love. Information.

Mother offers to accompany me to the funeral, but on the morning in question she comes down with a mysterious condition – scurvy, flatulence, a wart of some kind – which means she can stay at home. Harold comes instead. He dons a brown suit and his second-best overcoat. He may be making a point of his own about my father, that this is a death of no importance. I resent the implication that there is nothing of importance in it for me.

A few weeks after the funeral I write again to my mother in response to her recipe for a good marriage. I want to be positive about Melissa, but I cannot help including the odd caveat.

> To your four ingredients. Compatibility? Yes. We get on well, mostly. Respect for each other? It goes without saying. Loving awareness? I am not sure what that is, but I'm sure we have it. I'm only unsure about your fourth condition – a readiness to compromise.

Not the most effusive endorsement of the relationship, I can see now, though it is at least realistic. It hasn't been bathed in a romantic glow. What I do not say is that Melissa is as jealous and covetous as *Hera* on a bad day. She will sulk or fly into a rage if I talk for more than a minute to another woman at a party or at dinner with friends. Her problem seems to be more about control than a lack of trust or a fear of displacement. Fortunately her sulks and rages manifest rarely, because we do not go to many parties or have many mutual friends.

I ask only that you wish us well. Melissa is aware of your reservations about the difference in our ages, but I hope that will not prejudice your readiness to be open-minded and accept her as you find her. I am sure you will come to appreciate her as I do – generous, cheerful, lively, frank, bright, kind, loving and forever in the moment. I could go on, but I don't want to put you off.

What I feel unable to describe is the quality of the divine in Melissa that holds me in its spell. She has the will to possess without the need to be possessed. I tell myself I can cope with the stormy side of this daughter of *Poseidon*, because all my life I have wanted to be an object of desire. It is a feeling well beyond wanting to be loved. Melissa is my *Maria Zambaco*, with all the ardour and awkwardness, but without the delusions and paranoia.

So what is new is that we are engaged. I have given the lady a ring.

Well, sort of. We were in Selfridge's, as I recall, and found ourselves in the jewellery department admiring a silver ring with a flying dolphin motif. I knew that Melissa was missing Greece and the sea, that she had had enough of waitressing and hairdressing, and that her mood swings were beginning to irritate her as much as they did me. I bought her the ring as a gift from the goddess of consolation.

We will let the idea of commitment sink in before going any further. I think Melissa's mother is fairly fatalistic about what her daughter gets up to.

The flying dolphin goes from being a token of solace to representing the ambivalence Melissa feels, living in some comfort in Marylebone while aching to be free to go to the beach at Vouliagmeni. Gradually her need to return to Greece overtakes every other consideration and becomes compelling enough for me to re-examine my life in London. Professionally and politically the culture is changing. Film is giving way to video, budgets are getting tighter and no-one is making cinema shorts or second features anymore. I feel creatively constrained for the first time since leaving Corinthian and I am only too ready to blame it on a general decline in standards and a government I hadn't voted for.

For some time I have been entertaining a fantasy about finding an unspoilt Aegean island on which Melissa and I will do our own thing for a while. Then military rule in Greece collapses overnight and the idea suddenly becomes feasible. But what should we do on our unspoilt island? There is plenty to do. I will learn modern Greek, Melissa can grow her own zucchini, we will become regulars at the local *Kafeneio* and drink *ouzo* with the village priest and a retired ship's captain or two. More importantly I will work on my dissertation on the incidence of drowning in mythological and modern-day Greece and do my research on the spot. We can take the ferry to Piraeus now and again so that I can visit the Athens Academy and the Museum of Anthropology while Melissa catches up with her family and friends.

On a Spring walk around Regent's Park I convince myself that this is a perfectly reasonable and viable plan. The god of the west wind, *Zephyrus*, whispers in my ear that at some time in the future my girlfriend and I might wish to be married, for anything is possible on our unspoilt island. I hesitate. I put it to him: 'In order to be married in an Orthodox church wouldn't I have to abide by the doctrine of a single God who is not only One, but also Three (how does that work?), not to mention the Resurrection of the Dead (oh, come on) and other such articles of faith?' 'No, no,' Zephyrus assures me. 'Religion is relatively relaxed on the islands, people stroll in and out of the services and believe pretty much what they want to believe. If you are prepared to accept an entire pantheon of Greek gods, including myself, as the figurative equivalents of good and bad and the aspirations, arbitrariness and oddness of people, as apparently you are, it should not take much of a mental shift for you to open up the proposition to One who is also Three. It might also help you to remember,' he murmurs, 'that Orthodox priests, like vicars, rabbis and medicine men everywhere, have as great a propensity for pride, sloth, wrath and original sin as the rest of us.'

I ask myself if this credo of evasion and equivocation he is advocating is really the best way to reconcile my beliefs with my behaviours. And I answer, well, it will do. Everything is relative, as Tony Benn showed when he came up with his highly qualified oath of allegiance to the Queen that allowed him to serve his constituents in Parliament.

I ask my mentor Protagoras and his Sophists for their opinion. Feel free to do anything you like, James, is their consensus – kiss icons, cross yourself, pray if you must – *but believe none of it*. You have no responsibility for the script or for directing the show, only for acting it out for the benefit of the audience, whose only desire on such occasions is to be distracted from reality and entertained for a while.

I suggest to Melissa that we dip a toe in the water and go for a fortnight's island-hopping holiday, but she rejects this damp offer. She wants total immersion. We attempt to negotiate, but my idea of negotiation is to stick with what I first came up with, and Melissa's is to sulk. It ought to be all or nothing, she says. I balk at this. She sulks. Finally we agree to go for a month, with the option of staying a week or two longer (my version) or forever (Melissa's).

If you have formed the impression that we are not communicating particularly well and are not unequivocally committed to each other, you would be right. We might be ready to keep goats and harvest our own olives in a year or two, but for the time being it makes more sense to act as if only the present exists. It is pointless to wonder if what we are doing here and now relates to a coherent idea of the future. Whether we split up in a month or stay together forever is impossible to tell and therefore irrelevant. Melissa is a creature of the seas, elemental and fickle, and I am still working out who I am and what I want. I might return to film-making, or adapt my thesis for a book, or join the navy, or take up dry-stone walling. My life is the result of a thousand such capricious decisions, some tinged with necessity, some by desire, but none by any idea of an ultimate goal.

Diogenes of Sinope reappears. *Keep it simple and virtuous,* he says from his bathtub. I allow it is easier to make decisions based on how one is in the moment rather than on what one might hope to become. Whether that is an excellent or morally defensible position is another question.

My adventure with Melissa is inexplicable in my mother's terms, she makes clear, but it is energizing and in the end undeniable in mine. I resist any comparisons with my mother's wartime adventures or with my father's escapes into alcohol, forgetfulness and the high seas, though there is one regrettable parallel with both: I will be moving further away from my son.

> Forgive me, J.P. I realize you are in Mexico of your own choice, but you might want to bring Maria or Conchita or Carmen back to England at some juncture to see your family, such as it is, and to show everyone videos of the bulls you have killed, and I might not be here. I write to remind you that Greece is only a couple of hours further and that you are more than welcome to join us and to stay as long as you like, if we're still there, of course. You will love Melissa, if we're still together, that is.

I might be clutching at straws, but I have convinced myself that any disadvantages to this trip with Melissa are outweighed by its potential rewards. I work through my existing commitments, Melissa gives in her notice at the Oxfam shop, I sub-let the apartment to a friend of friends, then we take our back-packs and flip-flops and catch the night flight to Athens.

φ

Chapter 27

The Captain's House

WE AGREE TO TAKE THE FIRST FERRY FROM PIRAEUS and go wherever it takes us. Then I remember something the Priestess said in Delphi: "You must find your own Ogygia." Could well-favoured, hospitable Ogygia, with its fragrance of cedar and juniper, be the Ionian island of Kefalonia? Homer records that *Odysseus* had only to build a small raft for the last leg of his journey back to Ithaca. It is clear from the map that Kefalonia and Ithaca are close, separated only by the narrowest of narrow straits. Yet Odysseus only just made it. I may bring him into my thesis as one of the near-drownees who survived. "In which case forget the ferry from Piraeus," says Melissa. "We can get a bus to Patras and a boat from there to Kefalonia."

Kefalonia does not feel all that well-favoured to us. It is mountainous. It has few Homeric soft meadows of violets and parsley. We speculate that Ogygia might be one of the smaller Ionian islands like Lefkas or Paxos, but we are now so near the end of Odysseus' journey that we decide to travel directly to Ithaca.

A *kaïki* ferries us across the Ithacan Strait to a small quay on the rocky west coast of the island. From there we hike inland to the hilltop town of Stavros. I am gratified to find a bust of bearded Odysseus in a shady parkette in the centre of Stavros, and a restaurant nearby named after his long-suffering wife Penelope. So the legend is alive and well on the island as it should be.

We trek downhill from Stavros to the east coast, fill up on wine and cheese pie at Frikes, and take a winding coastal road around half a dozen deserted bays until we arrive at the fishing village of Kioni. Kioni has just the kind of tranquil fishing village feel I always imagined finding in Greece. We make enquiries at the village shop and are directed to a house available to rent at the far end of the quay.

The Captain's House is sixty steps up from the quayside, a spacious demi-mansion at the end of one arm of the bay. It has uncertain plumbing, an old-fashioned kitchen and a stunning view from the terrace over the turquoise waters of the bay to three ruined windmills and a headland that stretches its long rocky fingers out to the Ionian Sea. The shop owner phones the house owner, a retired ship's skipper who lives with his daughter in Patras, and we agree on a deal.

Kioni has next to no beach. It has no discothèque, no high-rise hotel, no pools, no para-gliding and no banana boats. There are a few couples holidaying independently, three or four yachties who sit on their sailboats tied up to the quay and the odd island-hopping backpacker en route to Corfu or Zakinthos. The days are hot, but a breeze drawn down from the mountains brings relief to the evenings. From the Captain's House high above the bay all we can hear is the intermittent chug-a-chug of a fishing boat leaving the harbour or the subdued mutter of a cabin cruiser motoring in quietly to anchor overnight.

Melissa's ready smile and fluent English and Greek get her a job at a waterfront taverna, while I set up under a sunshade on the Captain's terrace to research and write. I am thrilled to find English editions of the classic Greek texts in the Captain's library, including *Apollodorus of Athens'* anthology of classical myth and a copy of the Rouse translation of the Odyssey, the one that begins 'This is the best story ever written'. I wouldn't wish to quibble, but I wonder if Rouse had ever read Treasure Island, the Gospel According to St Matthew or Man-Eaters of Kumaon.

It is less than a ten-minute walk to Melissa's taverna, so most days we meet for lunch and share the small events of the day. On one such occasion I am pleased to report having met Odysseus himself, a stubble-chinned middle-aged man who runs a hardware store in the village and was kind enough to help me with the Captain's plumbing.

After lunch Melissa and I take an afternoon walk or a nap, or make love, or swim, and some days we do all of these things. I happily swim out of my depth in these warm and sheltered waters. On one exceptional day I make it all the way across the bay.

I have brought with me a draft of my thesis on the incidence of drowning in ancient and modern Greece. I find a note in the file stating that three-quarters of all deaths in ancient Greece occurred at sea. Three-quarters of *all* deaths? That is extraordinary. How does it compare with present-day pathology? I plan to cast my net wider than *Hero* and *Leander,* bring in more drownings and near-drownings, actual and fictional, accidental and intentional, and relate it all to my personal experience of the North Sea, King's School pool and not quite jumping into the Seine. It will be an historical, mythological and autobiographical mix. With not many laughs, I have to say, but after being warmed by the Ithacan sun and restored by the view from the Captain's terrace, the comforts of working in my own time and the affectionate attentions of Melissa, I make a critical decision.

I will not limit my theme to death and loss, but open it to rescue and redemption too. This raises a question mark over Odysseus, who survived a violent storm on his crossing from Kefalonia, but might or might not have redeemed himself on reaching home. I hope to discover more about his controversial return by finding the actual locations – the beach, the Palace, the Cave of the Nymphs – that Homer identifies. It might cast a light on my own struggles and discoveries, indeed those of any of us who identify with the metaphor of life as an incredible journey.

I have a provisional theory: that it is the morally ambiguous like Odysseus who are best equipped to survive the tempests and trials of life, while generally speaking it is the nice guys and the real rotters who succumb. The nice guys are crippled by self-doubt and the rotters by the weight of conceit they carry. I am inclined to count myself among the morally ambiguous, but it is conceivable I fit into the real rotter category, in which case I might not have long to live. I am not sure how the theory applies to your own journey, Julian, from grammar school in Henley-on-Thames to the bullrings of central America, though you might turn out to be the exception that proves the rule, that is the nice guy who survives.

Well, it is only a working hypothesis. By the way, do they still kill the bulls where you are or do you dance round them as I understand they do in Costa Rica? I am not being critical, just curious. Costa Rica does sound safer.

> Thank you for your letter. You kill them. Okay. Yes, *please* visit soon. Of course your friend Juan Carlos will be welcome too. Would you require one bedroom or two?

I come across another statistic. 38% of Greeks who get into trouble at sea live to tell the tale. That is a surprise – who are they, do they have anything in common? – though it leaves an alarming 62% who perish, often bizarrely. I am particularly struck by what happens to *Aegeus* and to *Ino*.

Aegeus reminds me of my father. They were fools who drank too much. But did they drink too much because they were foolish or were they foolish because they drank too much? Was the state of my father's brain the result of a disease or a character flaw? If it was a disease, how would that have affected his character? If it was a character flaw, how might that have affected the disease?

Aegeus is a sometime King of Athens who is in despair of ever having a male heir, so he goes to the Oracle at Delphi for advice. "Do not loosen the bulging mouth of the wineskin," utters the Oracle, "lest you die of grief." That might seem to you or I to be a clear warning to lay off the retsina, and in Aegeus' case to go to bed early, for the Oracle, having taken a large dose of the vapours, has come up with an unusual and ambiguous metaphor.

That evening Aegeus is entertained by a friend who introduces him to his nubile daughter and plies him with food and drink. Nine months later Aegeus' friend's daughter gives birth to a son. Aegeus, overjoyed, presumes himself to be the father and names the boy *Theseus*. Theseus grows up to be something of a local hero. He kills a rampaging bull that is devastating the city of Marathon and on the strength of that feat is entreated to sail to Crete to dispatch the *Minotaur*. He promises his father that on his return he will hoist white sails on his black-sailed ship as a sign of success. Theseus succeeds in killing the Minotaur, but in his glory and pride forgets to change his sails when he reaches home waters. His father sees black sails on the horizon, believes his son to be dead and in his grief throws himself into the sea. And as is usual in these stories in which portents are ignored, promises not kept, and the gods of indignation and retribution are involved, he drowns.

My own theory is that Aegeus had been at the bulging mouth of the wineskin a few times too often while his son was away and he was either pissed or mad from the pox. And yet I am struck by his unqualified devotion to his bastard son. I cannot see my father doing anything like that for me, even if he were totally trashed and in the throes of tertiary syphilis, but I hope I would not have been so full of myself as to forget to change my sails.

So the congenial Aegean that holds the shores of the greater part of Greece in its embrace is named after a dissolute tosspot. Not many people know that. My father Wilf is unlikely to give his name to anything much – a half-tot of rum, perhaps, or a damp cigarette butt – but at least I managed to visit him before he died.

My own son makes a move. I write in reply.

> Thank you for your letter! I'm excited that you and Juan Carlos plan to check out the bullfighting scene in the South of France before travelling on to Greece, although here you will know we only fight inflation. I'm afraid we don't have a spare double bed, but we can put two singles together. And yes, you will have a sea view.

The case of Ino of Thebes is another instance of needless sacrifice to the sea. Ino reminds me of my stepmother, the pitiless witch who missed by a whisker being known to the world as the Yorkshire Ripper. The equivalence between Ino and Edith does not come to me while working contentedly on the sunlit terrace of the Captain's House, but an hour or two later as I watch a slimy cephalopod being slapped onto a chopping board in Melissa's taverna, sliced without ceremony and its parts dipped in batter and fried. I chew on this leathery *kalamari* with some distaste and leave what remains of my stepmother on the plate so that she can be fed to the fishes.

Ino is the second wife of *King Athamas* and stepmother to his twins, *Helle* and *Phrixus*. Ino detests her stepchildren with the kind of milk-curdling loathing that only a woman bent on establishing patrimonial preference for her own children over her husband's by his odious first wife can feel. She is determined to be rid of the twins, if possible permanently. How does she proceed? She pays a serf to set fire to the store that holds the crop seeds of the region. She knows that without seeds for the people to plant, there will be no crops; that without crops, the people will starve; and that in a bid to ward off famine they will send their representatives to the Oracle for advice. This happens as planned. And when the people's representatives return, Ino bribes them to say that the recommendation of the Oracle is that famine can only be averted if the King's first-born, Phrixus, is sacrificed, and to make doubly sure his twin sister Helle should be dispatched as well.

You have to admit that Ino deserves a twisted kind of respect for this evil, devious, preposterous, protracted scheme, even more devious than my stepmother's plan for ridding herself of my sister and me.

When the twins' birth mother hears of the imminent threat to her children she sends a flying golden-haired ram to save them – an improbable stratagem, but it works, to a point. You know what happens. The children are about to be slaughtered when the animal appears, Athamas is distracted (a golden sheep? with *wings?*) just long enough for the twins to jump onto the back of the ram and fly off. They fly for many miles until Helle loses her grip and falls to the sea in a narrow channel of water that comes to be known as *Hellespontos,* the very same strait in which the lovesick Leander will perish in his wooing of reluctant Hero and across which Byron, in pursuit of his own ideals of beauty and mystery, will swim.

The stories of Aegeus and Ino fit my hypothesis that it is the morally ambiguous (Ino, Athamas, Odysseus, Byron) who survive, and the thoroughly deserving (guiltless Helle, tireless Leander) and undeserving (the crackpot despot Aegeus, among others) who succumb.

Ino is recorded in the literature as being no worse than a misguided mother who makes errors of judgment, while Athamas, not unlike my father, is prepared to sacrifice his children by his first wife after yielding to the outrageous demands of his second wife. Athamas, nevertheless, entertains doubts – doubts so severe that he descends into madness. Voices in his head tell him that his infant sons by Ino are lambs who must be slaughtered. In an insane act of atonement he kills one son and goes after the other, but Ino seizes the second child and in a bid to evade her crazed husband throws herself and the infant into the sea. Handily for such desperate people, the sea is always close.

So Ino gets her comeuppance after all, although if you really have it in for stepmothers you might prefer the version in which she first boils her baby in a pot and then jumps into the sea. Either way, I cannot bring myself to condemn her unreservedly and, despite the similarities, I would not have wished her fate on my stepmother for plotting to be rid of Jenny and me. As far as Edith is concerned, a public flogging and permanent exile to somewhere like Tristan da Cunha would have been enough.

After lunch I sit on the quayside and watch the local children fishing with their hand-held nets for the tiny translucent fish to be found in abundance in the bay. There were not many diners in the taverna today. A gay couple from Denmark and four portly Germans who rowed across the bay from their yacht, The Enchantress.

When Melissa's shift is over we stroll round the harbour to the tiny town beach, where we lie in the shade of a solitary olive tree. I have brought Apollodorus' anthology of mythical tales to read. It is hot and still. Melissa searches for bouzouki music on her radio. I look up to see the Germans rowing back to their yacht with six-packs of Amstel and Mythos. Ripples from their rowing lap towards us and sink softly into the sand. Melissa lies close. We share a caress. I wonder if those men on the yacht know the legend of the original enchantress?

φ

Chapter 28
The Enchantress

THERE IS A NEWS FLASH ON MELISSA'S RADIO.

> The winged ram that rescued *Helle* and her twin brother *Phrixus* has been
> traced to the barbarian region of Colchis at the eastern end of the Euxine. The
> animal was killed and its golden fleece seized by the usurper *Aietes* for its
> magical and medicinal properties. The goddess *Athene* is said to be angry. She
> is reported as saying that the fleece belongs rightfully to Athens.

I am young and need a noble deed to my credit. It will be for the same reason you
took up blood sports rather than follow your mother into the antiques business.
"I shall recover the fleece," I say. Melissa laughs and kisses me gently. "Go back
to sleep, James," she says. Slow *Tsamiko* music is playing on the radio. I get up to
dance in the sand, twirling my handkerchief in the air in the Greek way. The
Germans in their yacht at anchor in the bay think I am waving to them, so they
wave back and beckon me to join them. I swim over and clamber aboard.

Over several bottles of Mythos I explain my plan and to my delight the Germans
agree. We row to the shore for supplies and meet the Danish couple in the mini-
mart. They agree to join us on condition that we take a generous supply of sun
lotion. Back on the Enchantress we weigh anchor and make our way to the head
of the bay into a balmy Ionian breeze. The sun is high and the sea a cerulean blue.

We sail through the Gulf of Patras and the Corinth Canal, journey north and
make first landfall on the island of Andros, where we take on more lager and pick
up three island-hopping Dutch hippies. We call in briefly at Chios and Lemnos,
successfully navigate the clashing rocks of the *Symplegades* by the simple expedient
of releasing a handkerchief to flutter between them – it hadn't worked with Lydia
at Uni, but does here – then sail through the Euxine and finally reach Colchis.

King Aietes receives me warily. "I am *Navarchos* James Hawkins," I say, using the
Greek word for Admiral I find in my dictionary. "I come as ambassador of mighty
Athens to reclaim the Golden Fleece." Aietes look at me in disbelief. "I have fifty
valiant men under my command," I announce. I have instructed the crew to
mooch around on deck looking mean while I negotiate. Aietes is less than
impressed, but he does not want to risk upsetting my sponsor in Athens by refusing
outright, so he offers a compromise. "Complete three tasks I shall give you," he
says, "and you will earn the fleece as a prize." He outlines three tasks that he

probably thinks are impossible, but in my disconnected state in which anything is possible they merely sound tricky. The first is to yoke six of his bulls and plough a four-acre field; the second requires me to kill a three-headed dragon that is guarding the fleece; and the third is to sow the teeth of the dragon in the field I have ploughed. All before teatime. Showing more bravado than sense, as a young man must, I agree.

On my way to the cattle pens I am approached by a young woman. "Take care," says she. "My father's bulls breathe hot flame, they will burn you alive, and the jaws of the dragon will tear you to shreds." I have seen the local dragons, they are no more than large lizards that eat insects and mice. "I shall cope," I say. Aietes' daughter looks at me. "You are naïve, Jason," she says. I correct her. "My name is James." She takes no notice. "Even if you succeed in dispatching the dragon, my father will turn its teeth into an army of warriors who will cut you down." I laugh out loud. Fire-breathing bulls and three-headed dragons are one thing, but teeth turning into soldiers is really not credible. She sighs. "What do you call your teeth but little soldiers?" "No, no," I say. "Little soldiers are the slivers of toast you dip into your soft-boiled eggs." She snorts. "Not here in Colchis. We boil them hard." She drops her voice. "Listen, Jason …" "James," I say. "I am the only one who can help you. I know my father's tricks and have a few of my own." "What do you want out of this?" I ask. "If you succeed," she says, "you will take me and my brother with you to Athens. My father is insane and Colchis is a dunghill." I look at her. Long, lank hair, unblinking eyes, a bit on the intense side. She reminds me of Melissa on a bad day. And someone else, but who?

She leads me to what she proudly calls her poison-garden, where she mixes a concoction that succeeds in sedating the bulls and making the task of yoking them and ploughing the field appreciably easier. She then feeds the same stuff to the three heads of the dragon, effectively trebling the dose, anaesthetizing the beast and enabling me to get my hands on the fleece it was using as a comforter. All I have to do now is extract the teeth from its six jaws – an unpleasant task, far harder than it sounds – and sow them in the field I have ploughed. "The meaning of 'sowing the dragon's teeth'," Aietes' daughter remarks with a certain smile as I am wielding the pliers, "is to bring conflict to the land." Within minutes every furrow I have sowed begins to bubble and heave as armed men rise from the earth and turn on each other. In the ensuing chaos Aietes' daughter, her brother and I escape with the moth-eaten fleece and run for the boat.

When we are well under way I look at the weird young woman I have taken on. I do not even know her name. "I do not know your name," I say. "*Medelena*," she says. I start to say – here I go again – "That's a nice …" but she interrupts, "You can call me *Medea*." Medea? "And this is my brother, *Absyrtus*." Where have I heard the name Medea before? Isn't she a character in a play? "Look lively, Jason!" she calls. "Set course for Piraeus!" I hear myself calling back, "My name is James!", yet how completely I identify with the naïve idealist, Jason. Is it too late to warn him that he is embarking on an impossible journey with a difficult woman and it will all end in tears?

I check over the fleece. It looks like one of those filthy sheep's fleeces they stretch over sluice boxes in gold mining operations on Thassos and Sifnos. The fleeces filter the water and collect flecks of the metal. This one must have had all the gold combed out before Aietes gave it to his pet dragon to use as a duvet.

Back in Athens I am accused of stealing the genuine fleece. I have to bribe a lot of people in order to prove my innocence. There follows a difficult year. Medea becomes pregnant. My boat-building business falters. Medea suffers post-natal depression and I have to take her to the temple of *Asclepius* for an expensive course of opium therapy. On our return to Athens she gets into depraved and disagreeable ways, which I shall not go into here. There is a shortage of alder and poplar for boat building. We have another child. There is a carpenters' strike. And ill-advisedly I have an affair.

Medea throws a fit. She blisters with rage. The next day the lady I have been seeing is found dead – poisoned, unsurprisingly. I confront Medea. "What happened to your brother, Absurdus," I ask, "when we stopped at that island for supplies?" She looks at me coldly. "Absyrtus. I killed him, dismembered his body and scattered the parts." "What?" I cry. "I knew that my father would delay his pursuit in order to retrieve every last piece." I am appalled. "It was to save you and your crew!" she exclaims. "Are you mad, Medea?" I cry. "Or irredeemably evil?" "Eat shit, Jason!" she yells. In a fit of anger she picks up a vase and smashes it to the floor. It was a valuable urn from the late Geometric period that I used as a wine cooler. I am very upset.

I go out to the Plaka, down a few ouzos, get into an argument with a drunken philosopher about good and evil – do they exist? – of course they do! – and wander around in a daze. What next, I ask myself. If she really is insane, what else is she capable of? Oh no, the kids! I race back to find them dead in their beds in a shocking act of unspeakable revenge. I phone the police, then hear myself calling out, "But the telephone has not been invented!" I look around. Where is Melissa? My research has merged with my fears in anticipation of some nameless misfortune to come.

Melissa is swimming topless in the turquoise waters of the bay while a widow in black gestures angrily at her from the quayside. Melissa waves cheerily to the woman and swims back to the beach. She dries herself. "Do you love me?" she asks unexpectedly. I suspect a trap. Professing love has got me into a lot of trouble in the past. "Love is an addiction to which none of us is immune," I say cautiously. She laughs and says, "I'll take that as a yes." I ask her to ask the staff at the taverna if they know anyone with a spare double bed. "Julian has written to say that he and his friend are not too keen on single beds," I say, "even with a sea view."

The sound of bouzouki music comes from Melissa's radio. I look for the Enchantress and her crew in the bay. Were they ever there? What is the meaning behind that mouldering fleece and the murdered infants?

I go back to my sources to seek out stories of deliverance and redemption as a counter to the sadness and sorrow I have uncovered so far. And all I find is more disorder: the tragic tale of *Taras*, a young boy lost at sea while playing with dolphins; the unsolved mystery of *Hylas*, a youth lost in a lake while being teased by nymphs; and the sickening story of a psychopath, *Sciron*, who sits on a ledge high above the sea on the coastal road from Athens to Megara and begs passers-by to wash his feet. If they stop to oblige he kicks them off the cliff and laughs at their screams. Their motives – curiosity, compassion, foot-fetishism, whatever – were mixed, but what happens to them is unjust. They are, after all, only travellers.

Is this how all our journeys end, in disappointment and death? It would seem to be so, for who dies totally fulfilled? My quest for the fleece is another lost cause, like wanting to make a friend of my mother or finding the ideal woman. There are no ideal relationships, J.P. Remember that if you and Juan Carlos ever plan to marry.

What my thesis and I need now are happy endings. Tales of shipwreck and rescue, suffering and healing, exile and return, perhaps even a bullfight ending with the award of an ear or a tail. It's never a happy ending for the bull, though, is it? If the bull wins the fight it will be slaughtered anyway. I pray that you return from your exile fulfilled and victorious, Juliano, *El Inglés,* before you are gored.

Sadly, my research fails to come up with a single unequivocally redemptory story. Even the labours of *Heracles* end in terminal violence or deviousness and deceit of some kind. My onetime hero *Jason,* having made some really bad choices, dies destitute and alone. *Odysseus?* I need to know more, but I do not expect him to win any prizes. *Byron* dies of a violent fever, having denied his *alter ego* Don Juan salvation by God for his sins. *Amyas Leigh* is blinded by a bolt of lightning at the end of Westward Ho! and his true love, *Rose,* is burned at the stake. Surely *Treasure Island* ends happily? In fact only five of the ship's company that set out with Jim Hawkins return with him, and they bring with them a stark warning: drink and the devil have done for their comrades, they say, along with skewering, keel-hauling and – I hesitate to bring this up again, but there is more to say about it – drowning.

φ

Chapter 29
How Odysseus Came to Ithaca

How SHOULD I DESCRIBE THE REALITY OF DROWNING to those who have never given it more than a passing thought or who live far from a lake or a river or the sea? It can happen without warning. Children have perished in baths and buckets. Drunks and drug addicts have drowned face down in puddles at the side of the road. If you are unable to keep your nose and mouth out of water as a result of a loss of consciousness, exhaustion or a medical condition you will suffocate in seconds. Even if you can swim you can become overwhelmed or hypothermic. In 1970 almost five hundred thousand Bengalis, swimmers and non-swimmers alike – HALF A MILLION, there is no escaping that number – died as a result of a cyclone-driven tidal wave that inundated the low-lying lands of the Ganges delta.

My researches on Ithaca have come up with what to me is the most frightening notion of all – that drownees might not seem to be drowning. Their attempts to attract attention can be mistaken for waving. They are not waving, but drowning. They are unable to cry out for help or to alert swimmers even feet away because *they cannot obtain enough air to call out.* The instinctive desire to inhale leads to taking in water until the protective reflexes the body employs – coughing, the gag reflex, tracheal spasm – are overwhelmed. To put it another way: your involuntary attempts to stay alive can kill you.

I survived as a child, paradoxically, by panicking – something you are strongly advised not to do. Arms flailing, inhaling, sinking, seeing nothing but water above me, convinced for several terrifying seconds – an age, an aeon – that I was dying, until I managed to grab hold of something or someone and haul myself clear. Only seconds had elapsed, but the memory is forever.

Now I am eager to defy the odds while exploring the island by swimming with Melissa from every beach we can reach. *Odysseus* capsized somewhere off the coast of Ithaca at the end of his eventful voyage from Troy and I am determined to discover how and where he came ashore and what happened next. Did his long-overdue return end in his redemption or rejection?

There are any number of bays and beaches on the coastal route from Kioni to the site marked on the map as Odysseus' Palace, and each beach and bay on the way has a character of its own – fragrant, foul, barren, bleak, stony, sandy, sapphire-blue and what Homer, having no word for deep blue, calls wine-dark. My own view is that the ancient Greeks were more sensitized to light than to colour. You have only to spend a little time on the islands to understand why this might be so.

Most of the bays Melissa and I explore are deserted and their beaches are empty. One or two have a single shuttered villa overlooking the sea; one has a solitary rowboat tethered to a dock; another a small shrine with an unlit oil lamp and a faded photograph of the painting of a saint. I am searching for any indicator of the return of the King of Ithaca. Homer's story of closely fought wars, near-death experiences and episodes of excess of one kind or another so nearly, at some level, mirror my own. And yours too, I warrant.

It would have been an arduous voyage from Troy. Odysseus and his men would have had to make their way from Anatolia via the Hellespont into the Aegean, set course via Lemnos for the Sporades, tack along the coast of Evia to Cape Sounion, head round the cape to the Saronic Gulf, follow the coast past Piraeus and Salamis, make landfall on the Isthmus of Corinth, haul their boats along the portage road to the Gulf of Corinth, re-embark, sail to the Gulf of Patras and thence into the Ionian Sea. That would have been the quickest route home. In fact they seem to have voluntarily extended their journey by calling in on the Dodecanese, the Cyclades, Karpathos, Crete, Kythira, Cyprus and Sicily too, encountering a succession of one-eyed *Cyclopes,* savage *Gigantes*, flesh-eating *Laestrygones,* seductive *Sirens* and intoxicated *Lotus Eaters* while having to cope with the sexual demands of a variety of spinsters and widows whose menfolk had been killed at Troy or were missing at sea, or were away seeking work in Athens or Thessaloniki. Odysseus and his men having been traumatized by war were not above exploiting the peace. They were in no hurry to get back to Ithaca.

On our next day out swimming across every bay we can reach as we work our way round the coast, Melissa wonders out loud if my obsessive quest for evidence of Odysseus' return might be, let's see, how can she put this nicely, pointless. "Does it matter in the least," she asks, "if it was all a myth anyway?" I am indignant. "Myth, legend, allegory, history ... the borders between them have always been porous. In any case," I say, "the story *has to stand for itself.*" "But it isn't true!" exclaims Melissa. "You mean like all of history is true?" I bang on about events beng reshaped with every retelling and you only have to add a few more twists to the original narrative for history to become myth. I make an offer: "Let's say true enough." "Not enough for me!" cries Melissa, then, "Sorry. Can we just have a nice time?" "In a minute," I say. I want to make my point. I want to say that Odysseus may or may not have existed in readily verifiable space-time, but there is a fundamental measure in which he thrives – conceptual space, the space we go to in our minds, the space in which a dozen or more dimensions of imagination, emotion, belief, intuition and conviction combine so powerfully and transcendently that the result may be no less real than in the conventional four.

That is what I want to say. "Odysseus exists," is what actually comes out. "He is not illusory." Melissa rolls her eyes. "There is compelling evidence," I say, "that an individual of that name reigned over the kingdom of Ithaca, fought in the Trojan Wars, returned after an extended time ..." I pause."... and is in Ithaca still." "Still?" says Melissa scornfully. "Where?" "In his statue in Stavros! In the tamarisk trees and the olive groves of the island!" I am away. "In the faces of shepherds in the hills and widows in black. In the memory of poets and philosophers down the ages. In the imaginative eye of every traveller in history!" "Oh come, James," she cries, "Odysseus is fictitious! Homer invented him!" *"Odysseus is as real as his palace on Ithaca!"* I cry. It is a curious proposition, but I know what I mean. "Really, James," says Melissa, unmoved. "It is a story for tourists. There is no Odysseus here other than a fanciful bust in the park and the man who owns the hardware store in Kioni." "I shall prove you wrong," I say. "And I shall begin by identifying the beach on which he came ashore."

Melissa is sceptical. She suggests that all this immersion in seawater is softening my brain. "There are a hundred-and-one beaches on Ithaca," she says. "How will you know which is the right one?" "When I find it I will know," I say. "There will be a cave where he sheltered, a path taken only by goats, a certain sweep of the shore ..." She snorts. I am offended. This girl has no soul. Can she not see that Odysseus' encounters with nymphs and monsters, his persistence and perseverance, and, yes, his outlandish behaviour and moral ambivalence, are not only of the utmost relevance to my life but hers too?

The next day while Melissa is at work I set off alone and trek to the Gulf of Afales, a partly-enclosed arm of the sea near the site of what is said to be Odysseus' Palace. I find a long, steep path winding down to a broad, bleak, treeless bay. The beach is rocky and desolate, not the sort of place you would want to be washed ashore in a storm. Dark mountains loom over the bay and drop in sheer cliffs to the sea.

I cannot conceive of a woman so foolish or devoted as to spend ten or twenty years – accounts vary – weaving, waiting and gazing out over such a desolate place. If Penelope had any spirit at all she would have been spending her time in Stavros, testing the sweet wines and syrupy desserts of the island, and enjoying the attentions of a succession of lovers.

The cliffs of Afales have no cave, I discover. I suppose that centuries of erosion or the infamous earthquake of '53 have done for it. But there is a cleft under overhanging rocks and I rest there in the shade as Odysseus may have done from the storm. I imagine how he must have felt: worn out physically, delicate mentally, fearful of what he would find on his unannounced, ludicrously long-overdue return.

Some way above the beach I come across a small church, its exterior ringed with scaffolding. Inside, high on a platform, an artist is restoring a mural. *"Yassou,"* I say. *"Yassou,"* he replies, absorbed in his work. "Er, *Archaeologiko* site?" I ask. *"Ne,"* he says, and gives me directions in Greek. I do not understand all he says, but I follow his gestures. I thank him: *"Eferisto." "Parakalo,"* he says matter-of-factly, and continues painting.

I climb a hill through scrub, wild thyme and briar in the general direction the mural painter indicated. After half an hour I come to a vehicle track, which I follow to a dead end. Why does it end here? A few metres on, half-hidden by brush, I find a weathered stone terrace set into the side of the hill. Worn steps lead to another terrace. This must be the place! A buzzing sound comes from a field nearby. A young man is clearing weeds with a petrol-driven strimmer. He stops when he sees me. *"Kalimera, ti kanete?"* I say. "Hello, I am good, how are you?" he replies in English. I ask him if this is Odysseus' Palace. He shrugs. "The sign on the track from Stavros reads *'To Scholeio tou Omirou',"* he says. "The School of Homer." "That might or might not be a clue," I say. I ask him if anyone is working on the site. "Sometimes they come from Athens or Patra," he says. "I think they do not have enough money." I ask him if it is all right to look around. "Why not?" he says, as if to say, 'This is Greece, don't ask.'

There are no archaeologists on the site; no fences, no volunteers, no sightseers, no signs, but there are wooden walkways over hollows and rocks, trenches with makeshift corrugated iron covers, an alleyway, a doorway, crumbling walls, the floor of a hall. And every part of the site has a view through the trees to the Gulf of Afales with its gloomy grey cliffs and sullen green sea. I sit on a rock and rest. I know those cliffs, these stones, that long view to the sea. After all this time I am home.

An elderly shepherd comes by with a flock of sheep. *"Kalimera,"* he says. *"Kalimera,"* say I. He stops to allow his animals to graze. I ask him how things are on the island. There has been trouble at the palace, he reports. Drunken ruffians from Exogi, the village higher up the mountain, have been plundering the cellars, importuning Penelope and making a nuisance of themselves with the maids. I wonder how long it was before Penelope presumed me dead. Three years? Four? The buzzing of the strimmer is louder now. I feel angry and fractious. At what point did she stop discouraging the attentions of the men from Exogi? Too soon, I surmise. I interrogate the old man. "Names!" I insist. "I want names!"

My blood lust is high and undeniable. I stalk from the palace possessed and seek out the offenders the shepherd had identified ... a sword into the liver of one, an arrow through the throat of another, throwing one man off a cliff (I learnt that from *Dædalus* and the psychopath *Sciron*), lopping off feet, hands, heads ...

then crazily I arrange for the maids from the palace who entertained the men from Exogi to be hanged and strangled, slowly, with a ship's cable.

I know how bad this sounds, how really bad, how undue and excessive, but I have come to think of it as the collateral damage of war; what the palace physician diagnoses as delayed battle fatigue syndrome. "What is that?" I ask. "I have no idea," he says. "I read about it in Hellenic Shipping News." I look at him. You are next, I think.

I blame the goddess of devilry and delusion for these terrible events. *Aate* has been at it again. The unwarranted assumptions I have made about Penelope, her maids and the men from Exogi were the work of a vindictive spirit condemned to wander the earth while treading on men's heads and causing no end of trouble. Aate has twisted the Delphic maxim *'Beware certainty'* into the cynical *'Assume the worst'* in my mind, and the inoffensive *'Nothing to excess'* into an obscene *'Revenge is sweet'*. I am a victim of mischief that is none of my making.

I return to my senses and make my way back to the track. A goat grazing on the grass verge looks up at me. What does it see? A man with no certainty in his own sanity, too ready to let gods and monsters take the rap for frailties in his own nature. That other Delphic imperative comes back to me: *'Know thyself'*. Is that possible, even remotely? Like every other being on earth I am a ludicrously complex creature with an uncertain grasp on reality, constantly obliged to adjust to events over which I have next to no control. I am not Odysseus. Of course not. But he must be as much a part of me as Jason, Medea, Long John Silver *et al* or my violent fantasy would not have been so credible and compelling.

As I make my way from the site of the palace to Stavros, I am plagued by a suspicion that I really have killed someone in the past. Was it in an accident with a 12-bore in the forests of Uttar Pradesh? Or the result of miscalculating the range while firing 25-pounders on Salisbury Plain? Or deliberately with a pillow in my Marylebone flat while the balance of my mind was disturbed? The memory trace of murder pre-dates the Odyssean fantasy and is accompanied by a distinct sense of guilt and the imminent fear of discovery. It begs a critical question: how can I – how can anyone – distinguish for sure between a dream, a waking reverie, a delusional mental representation and a genuine memory? The brain generates them all. Our neural networks are in constant flux, bombarded with input, generating output that either combines to make a coherent whole or fragments into thoughts and experiences that seem real enough but are really not to be trusted. If my memory of killing someone is false, as surely it is, then it opens up the likelihood that I am prone to delusion, and if that is so – and if I have *not* killed anyone, it is axiomatic – how can I consider any of my memories real? My life, this story, your existence, J.P., could all be a total fiction.

The track from the excavations joins a narrow surfaced road that takes me past the *Scholeio tou Omirou* sign and further on to a small building with a sign over the door that says *Archaeologiko Museio*. It is closed. I guess that not enough artefacts have been found to generate enough money to fund the search for more artefacts. I speculate that it might not always be good to dig up the past. My father may have been right, that some things are best left interred under layers of denial.

The shallow pits, makeshift covers and lack of information in the palace excavations serve to support this gloomy conclusion. Given all that I will never know, can I settle for not knowing? And my response is the same it has always been: no. I have been haunted from the start by a lack of information – *too many questions, lad, tha'll understand when tha's older* – and it has left me in a half-empty, disheartened state from which I may never fully recover.

I am in need of a treat. On reaching Stavros I seek out Penelope's under the lemon trees and enjoy a moist and redemptive roast lemon chicken flavoured with garlic and rosemary. Penelope turns out to be a motherly, plump woman whose name is actually Thelma – not the sort, I imagine, to take a succession of lovers when her husband is away, though I should make no such assumption. Her crisp-skinned chicken is roasted to perfection. I promise to return ere long.

After lunch I continue my research. From the square in the centre of Stavros I take the track that leads downhill to Polis Bay, where Melissa and I disembarked on our arrival on the island. It seems a likelier site for Odysseus' return than the other beaches I have seen as it lies directly across the strait from the coast of Kefalonia.

There are no signs of an ancient *polis*, or city, in Polis Bay. There is a small quay, a disused hut, a stretch of coarse sand and the swollen carcass of a goat. If this ill-favoured place had once been the port for Stavros it might explain why the former capital of the island had lost its status. Or it might be because the nearby palace had to be abandoned after the King of Ithaca's brutal, outrageous return.

The rocky shore of Kefalonia looks close, only a mile or two from where I stand. The channel between the islands is no wider, I reckon, than the Hellespont or the Bosphorus. Is it possible that Odysseus *swam* across from Kefalonia? It would have been easier and quicker than building a boat.

Next day Melissa and I take the bus south along the mountainous spine of the island, across the high narrow isthmus of *Aetos*, the eagle, and down a winding, vertiginous road to today's capital, Vathy. From Vathy we trek into the hills behind the town. I am seeking the Cave of the Nymphs, where Odysseus is said to have stored the treasures he brought back from his travels. I say nothing of this to Melissa, as I want no more scorn for my imaginative adventures. I am a boy who sailed to Skeleton Island with Squire Trelawny, after all, stalked man-eating tigers with Colonel Jim Corbett, fought in the Ottoman Wars with Lawrence of Arabia, married a multiple murderess and poisoner – that didn't work out well – and most recently occupied the mind of a man who slaughtered dozens of his own people in a fit of stress-disordered lunacy. My dream world knows no bounds.

Homer hints that the Cave of the Nymphs is to be found

by the Rock of Corax and the Spring Arethusa

I am thrilled to find a freshwater spring surrounded by wild olive and myrtle that could well be the Fountain of Arethusa. And there is a rock by the spring – the Rock of Corax, surely – with a narrow opening fringed by hairy fronds of bearded grass that almost obscure it. What could this be but the half-hidden entrance to the Cave of the Nymphs? How readily we assign meaning to fit what we find! On a sultry day it is a shaded place for Melissa and I to eat our lunch of feta cheese and tomatoes, and make love. And then we doze.

In the late afternoon heat we hike back to Vathy and make our way through dusty streets past pastel-painted houses to the bay. There is a little isle in Vathy Bay that guards the harbour. Byron is said to have swum out to it. I surprise myself by suggesting we do the same.

Melissa swims steadily ahead of me. It is the longest swim I have ever undertaken and her presence is reassuring. I read somewhere that unintentional drowning is the third leading cause of accidental death worldwide, which is kind of astonishing.

What would it be like if the motorboat I hear in the distance were to run over me and the propeller slice my head open? Swirls of blood and scraps of brain in the sea. Would that come into the category of unintentional drowning or dangerous driving? I swim on.

Alternatively, what would it be like to drown voluntarily – how would you go about that? It was partly the uncertainty around deliberate drowning that put me off immersing myself in the Seine and made me settle for a bottleful of aspirin instead. Premeditated submergence could not be anything like as straightforward as it sounds. The instinct would surely be to fight to take in air, to tread water or drift with the tide. Would you only go under when you were too tired to stay afloat or could you simply choose to lie back and let water into your lungs – it can take less than a cupful, apparently. It would not be a pleasant end. What would? I think there is no life that ends happily.

I have no intention of putting my uncertainty on these matters to the test in Vathy Bay, but all the same I am curious. Did *Icarus* have a death wish that led him to fly wilfully high so that the impact on the water when he fell would kill him *before* he drowned? Drowning would obviously be less traumatic if you were unconscious first. I swim on in the warm waters of the bay, wondering at my own challenge to the gods. Am I being foolish or courageous? Is there a difference?

It must be a question you ask yourself every time you enter the bullring.

I reflect on the fate of *Ajax*, obstinate in his bravery to the point of stupidity. My father would have called him three sheets short of a breeze. After the death of *Achilles*, undisputed hero of Troy, Ajax and Odysseus are in contention for the honour of receiving Achilles' arms. When these are awarded to Odysseus, Ajax goes berserk, accuses a flock of sheep of being his enemies and slaughters the lot. Why is it always the sheep that suffer?

In his shame at this delusional episode Ajax falls on his sword, but misses his vital organs and survives, only to be shipwrecked on his voyage home. And here is the really silly part: he swims to land boasting that he has escaped his brushes with death *in spite of the gods* rather than as a result of their exceptional benevolence.

When *Poseidon* hears of this boast he strikes the blasphemer on the spot and Ajax sinks without trace. I see this as a passive drowning. He would have been struck by the Lord of the Sea with a heavy trident and with any luck would have been unconscious before going under.

Melissa is leading me from the little island back to Vathy. The water continues to hold me. I am euphoric. I have swum much further than I imagined I could.

Back in Kioni I continue to divide my time between the Captain's library (lots of books, nice old desk), the Captain's terrace (wonderful view, huge sunshade) and Melissa's taverna (free house wine and all the chips I can eat).

I look again at the note in my files stating that three-quarters of all deaths in ancient Greece occurred at sea. An extraordinary three-quarters of *all* deaths. I should look into the epidemiology of drowning today. An article in Marine Quarterly points to the death rate from drowning in modern-day Greece as double the rate anywhere else in the world. *Double* the rate. Why would that be? Are the waters of Greece so inviting that swimmers and non-swimmers alike find themselves less inclined to be cautious? Do the countless islands and inlets and jetties and bays and beaches of Greece mean that the sea is that much more difficult to avoid?

I sit on the terrace reading and making notes while Melissa flits happily round the kitchen making moussaka. She sings along to Mikis Theodorakis.

> *I have the sun in my heart*
> *Skies are as bright as your eyes …*
> *Love is the ceiling*
> *Feelings free as the air …*

Suddenly she comes up behind me and wraps me in a fierce embrace. "I love you!" she cries. "I love you too!" I declare. It seems the right thing to say at that moment, in the cloudless light, being held by this ardent, demonstrative woman. In moments like this it is an effort to recall her jealous rages, the tempests that blow up out of nowhere and rip the tiles off the roof. They are easy to forget when she is as sunny as the day. Even so I have made a commitment to be here, to be with her, to immerse myself in the maternal waters of Greece, to feed off the energy that she and the seas that surround her possess.

I consider the theme of my thesis: the continuing relevance of the emotional muddles and spiritual difficulties of the characters in the drowning-related myths of Greece, and the universal experience of loss and rejection that drove them to their deaths. I am particularly drawn to the stories of those who leapt into the sea voluntarily: *Hero* in despair over the loss of her lover, *Ino* fleeing an abusive partner, *Aegeus* grieving his son while riddled with the pox, allegedly. There are many similar stories. The Aegean and Ionian Seas are filling up fast.

I should also consider those who kill themselves by other means. Hanging is popular – *Phaedra*, *Jocasta*, *Ariadne* and others. *Lucretia* knifes herself. *Anchurus* rides his horse into an abyss. Perhaps my theme should be more about suicide in general than drowning *per se*.

No-one lacks a good reason for suicide, I shall say, although the death of *Socrates* is a puzzle. He is recorded as saying that a man should not kill himself unless God has sent some compulsion upon him, which to my mind excuses any act of self-harm. *Plato* is more equivocal. "What ought a person to suffer if they kill that which is truly their own?" he asks, which sounds to me as if he believed we have the right to do anything we like with our lives, although I concede that the question, being both ambiguous and rhetorical, is open to interpretation: *What ought a person to suffer if they kill that which is truly their own?* Plato might be saying that although the perpetrator could not suffer in death any more than they had in life, there is a price to be paid by the family and society in terms of the legacy of the act. His unanswered question remains.

Is *Jocasta* right or wrong to hang herself when she finds to her horror that the man she married, *Oedipus*, is her long-lost son? Can *Arachne* be forgiven if in her injured pride at the rejection of her tapestry by *Athene* she is led to put a noose round her neck and hang herself? Is it for good or ill that Athene in revenge turns Arachne into a spider from whose thread she will hang forever? What ought a person to suffer?

Hannibal makes plans to take poison in order to escape the unbearable shame of surrender to Rome. Despairing *Dido* curses the Trojan general who deserted her and casts herself on a funeral pyre she has already prepared for the purpose. How far does the act have to be from the impulse for it to be questionable?

When Socrates finally knocks back the hemlock, does he suppose he is doing it voluntarily or has his God has sent some compulsion upon him? If we feel a compulsion are we compelled to act on it? No! Compulsions are ten a penny. They are strong, often very strong, impulses to do or say something that might be better left undone or unsaid, and we give in to them or deny them every day. *Scylla*'s compelling hunger led her to devour innocent sailors, but there were days when she would have waited for a shoal of red mullet to come along instead. My stepmother might have felt compelled to beat me with a rolling pin or a coal shovel, but if so she resisted and went for the arguably more lasting alternative, sustained psychological abuse, instead. I know, I know, she must have had her nicer side. Let me think. Well, she loved her own son, cooked meals for us all and had a soft spot for robins. There might have been something else I wasn't aware of.

My own compulsion to kill myself came only after what I believe to be due diligence. The impulse arose from an overwhelming feeling of inordinate emptiness, but in the hour or so that passed between the impulse and the act I can claim to have given full attention to my state of mind and to have given it a degree of reflection and care. You could argue that a suicidal state of mind is hardly the best state of mind in which to consider a suicidal state of mind, but it was the only one available to me at the time and, given the fact that I was in it, no other state was realistically possible.

I am inclined to accept that the choices I make are not wholly mine to make. They are the result of a caprice of the gods or – much the same thing, really – to fluctuations in my complex neurology over which I have little control. And if that really is the case, it is arguable that I have no real responsibility for *anything*.

Do those who are driven to suicide in response to the suicide of a loved one bear any kind of responsibility, and if so of what kind and to whom? *Amenias* kills himself after his advances are rejected by *Narcissus*, who in sorrow or shame kills himself in turn. *Eurydice* runs herself through with a sword after her son *Haemon* has done the same – and he does that in response to his fiancée *Antigone* hanging herself. A rare triple suicide.

Disquieting stuff, these reciprocal acts, both romantic and tragic. Whether they are more forgivable or less than the originals that inspired them is an impossible moral conundrum, although I resolve that my thesis should reflect the wider distress caused by these retroflexive acts. Then Byron returns to haunt me.

> We live and die,
> But which is best, you know no more than I.

In other words, does it matter? I am inclined to believe that it does *not* and yet I wonder. I look again for examples of rescue, redemption, recovery, reprieve or relief and finally come across a few. *Arion* is saved from drowning by a dolphin and carried back to land. *Aura* jumps into a lake and is transformed into a fountain. *Halcyon* metamorphoses into a kingfisher, *Cygnus* into a swan, *Daedalion* into a hawk, *Menippe* into a heavenly comet. They are a mixed bunch: a poet, a huntress, a princess, a thief, a killer, a weaver. There are some virtuous souls among them and some out-and-out villains. Is real redemption possible for even the most monstrous and badly behaved of us? *Ino* and my stepmother, say.

It does seem possible. At the moment of Ino's drowning an extraordinary thing happens: she metamorphoses into a goddess devoted to protecting sailors from the ravages of the sea. She even comes to the aid of Odysseus when his boat capsizes by wrapping him in her buoyant, voluminous shawl.

I consider what would have been an appropriate line of work for my stepmother if she had been reprieved. Running a refuge for abused children, perhaps, or a charity for misunderstood stepmothers. Yet even if in the unlikeliest of unlikely circumstances Edith were to have been reborn as a good mother, say, or a mermaid, the transformation would have to have been so complete that any representation of a past life would have been wiped from her memory, leaving her with no motive for making amends with the world. I suppose that a human being cannot pass on the contents of their mind to a comet or a fish. The tales of renascence I come across feel like more of a sop for those of us whose death is yet to come.

I am saved from my fevered imagination when Melissa returns from the taverna, skips up the steps, swoops onto the terrace and wraps me in her arms. She is my kingfisher, my saviour, my iridescent herald of change. Perhaps the possibility of redemption or recovery is a better theme for the conclusion of my thesis than the finality of death.

In that squalid hotel by the Seine I honoured a part of me that did not care, that did not even consider the possibility of rebirth or renewal. Here on Ithaca I can celebrate a part of me that for the time being at least feels that my life – every life – matters. I consider updating the working title of my thesis from The Modern Tragedy of Hero and Leander to something like Rage, Shame and Deliverance. It will mean rewriting the opening and while I am at it a substantial part of the middle and the conclusion too.

There is no need for me to return to London to work on these revisions, I decide. Ithaca and its citizens are amenable, the Captain's House is affordable and our time is our own here. The mini-mart, the mountains, the beaches and the bakery are all within easy reach, the bright lights of Kefalonia and Corfu are a leisurely ferry away, and the resources of Athens not quite half a day.

Melissa is pleased at the prospect of staying on. She plans to open a shop selling painted driftwood and shells, and T-shirts with slogans like 'Greek Goddess' and *'Nosce te Ipsum'* (my idea this, Latin for 'Know thyself', a bit pretentious, but there you are). She also plans to teach English to Ithacans and Kefalonians, and Greek to people like, well, me.

I phone the friend of a friend who is sub-letting my Marylebone flat and offer her a reduction in the rent if she will stay on a month or two longer. I plead an attack of *cyanopsychosis*, summer madness brought on by an excess of blue. Then I, or my unconscious, or the random neural firings that at any given moment have to pass as my mind, make an unexpected decision. I will respond to Byron's 'which is best, you know no more than I' life-or-death question and my 'does it matter?' response by doing something entirely meaningless. Having spent the greater part of my life attempting to do something with meaning – pass exams, prosecute deserters, satisfy sponsors, accumulate awards – I shall prove to the world that none of it matters, that the need for meaning is no more than the long shadow cast by our anxieties, inadequacies and fears for the future. I propose to Melissa that we make, as did Byron, a grand, nonsensical gesture.

φ

Chapter 30

Swimming the Hellespont

THE SEA OF HELLE IS A LEGENDARY, NOT A MYTHICAL, WATERWAY, one of two straits – the other is the Bosphorus – that divide the continent of Europe from the mainland of Asia. It is the body of water whose Asiatic shore was the focus for the Trojan War, but more especially for my purpose here it is the strait that Leander has to cross in order to reach his great love Hero – and it is in that romantic attempt to bridge the gap between what we do not wish to settle for and what we might, just possibly, attain, that lies its symbolic attraction for me. Perhaps the grand idea of swimming the strait is not so nonsensical, neither for me nor for George Gordon Noel.

> For me, degenerate modern wretch,
>   Though in the genial month of May,
> My dripping limbs I faintly stretch,
>   And think I've done a feat today.

Byron is too modest. In May the waters are still cold from the melting of the mountain snows and the rapidity of the currents is such that it is impossible to swim across directly. You must set a course and constantly adjust it, as in life. As for Leander:

> But since he crossed the rapid tide,
>   According to the doubtful story,
> To woo, – and – Lord knows what beside,
>   And swam for Love, as I for Glory;

The waters in the Hellespont flow in contrary directions: southwards in a cool, freshwater surface current and northwards in a warmer, more saline undercurrent. Hero's state of mind is similarly conflicted. Her shifting moods are driving her lover crazy. Leander is not only having to deal with the swells and currents of the strait. Byron compares Leander's frustrations to his own.

> Twere hard to say who fared the best:
>   Sad mortals! thus the Gods will plague you!
> He lost his labour, I my jest:
>   For he was drowned, and I've the ague.

The strait is not a safe one, if such exists. Ships under sail have to wait at anchor for the right conditions before navigating their way across. The word itself is a metaphor for difficulty.

> Once more upon the waves! Yet once more!
>   And the waves bound beneath me as a steed
> That knows his rider.

A powerful *terzetto* that reminds me of being locked in an embrace with Polly Unmore, tormented beyond understanding. Byron finds freedom, even with his withered leg, in the Hellespont. I am keen to attempt the crossing, partly because the poet was there before me; partly in recognition of five hundred thousand Bengalis who died in a terrifying tsunami; partly to honour every intentional and unintentional drowning in myth and history; and partly also, perhaps even mainly, because the strait – the difficulty – is there. Crossing it will inform the conclusion of a thesis that began with Leander and will end with myself in a way that no imaginary crossing ever could. As for meaning, well, like climbing K2 or crossing the Atlantic in a kayak, there is none, but in the mood I am in that makes it more compelling than ever.

I consult Melissa. There is a problem. The Hellespont is a long way from Ithaca. To get there we would have to take a taxi to Vathy, a ferry to the mainland, a bus or a train or two to Athens, a plane or a ferry to Samothraki, Lemnos or Lesbos, another ferry or a *caïque*, if there were one, and another bus or a taxi or a lift, if we could find one. Allowing for ferry schedules, the weather, delays and overnight stays it could take two or three days, with another two or three to arrange and effect the ritual and another two or three to get back. We would have blown a week's rental on the house, I would have lost writing time and Melissa would have fallen behind with her plans for painting driftwood and pebbles. We have a decision to make. If swimming the Hellespont is a meaningless act, as I accept that it is, then not swimming the Hellespont is equally meaningless. After an hour or more tying ourselves in metaphysical knots over the question we agree to consider it again when we have more time, even though, as we know, we have as much time as we choose. To celebrate this mature decision we agree to treat ourselves to a long lunch under the lemon trees at Penelope's.

Friendly, plump Thelma greets us with a broad smile – *"Yassas, pos ise?"* – and invites us into her kitchen to check the dish of the day, *xifias*: fat, fresh steaks of swordfish, landed only that morning in Frikes. We make our selection and go into the garden to pick the yellowest of Thelma's lemons to squeeze over our succulent steaks.

After deep-fried *Saganaki* flamed in *ouzo*, a bottle of the local white *Perachoritiko* with the *xifias*, a glass of 5-star *Metaxa* and a dessert of home-made *Rovani* dripping with Ithacan *méli* – it would only be a minor overstatement to say we had tasted ambrosia – we wander contentedly to the little park in the centre of the village, where we pay homage to the bearded bust of Odysseus and from the terrace nearby look out over Polis Bay and the Ithacan Strait to the shore of Kefalonia. The air is warm and welcoming. The sea is calm and still.

They say that mortals who have tasted ambrosia believe themselves to be immortal. "That is not so far," says Melissa. "For what?" I ask. "To swim," she says. "Instead of the Hellespont." I shade my eyes from the sun. It looks pretty far to me, even after a bottle of Perachoriwhatnot. "We could take a fishing boat back," says Melissa. I consider this. "After Shelley died in Italy," I say, "Byron chartered a boat to take him to Greece to fight in the War of Independence." "So?" "He landed on Kefalonia." "And?" "He may have swum the Ithacan Strait instead of the Hellespont and come here to Penelope's to eat under the lemon trees." Melissa looks at me. "Say more," she says. "If my son can dance with bulls," I offer, "I can go for a paddle in the bay."

In the end it feels like an entirely voluntary decision. No Socratic compulsion came upon me. Undoubtedly there were influences – my dissertation, Melissa, Byron, the 5-star *Metaxa*, my foolhardy son, the cloudless sky – yet I hear no inner voice telling me this is something I *must* do. There is a faint reminder that the weather might change. "I suppose we do not have to go all the way across," I say, to prove to myself that we do not have to go all the way across. "Don't be scared!" cries Melissa, and sets off downhill. "Ha!" I cry, striding after her. "Once more upon the waves!" What else can I do? The psycho-social system of which my unconscious is a silent but undeniable partner has decided for me.

The sea shines and shimmers like liquid silver. The beach is deserted. The carcass of the goat has gone. We leave our outer clothes in the old beach hut and pick out a landmark on the coast of Kefalonia – that distinctive rock or the stunted tree? – at which to aim.

There is something in the air and the light and the lunch and the lemons that day. Some kind of ideal of excellence. Beauty and truth are involved too, and as I stride into the sea, a certain god-free, *Ajax*-like defiance.

φ

Chapter 31

The Glittering Sea

SUNLIGHT REFLECTS ON THE SEA. I breathe easily and cleanly. Today I am at one with the islands and oceans, and best of all I have no known purpose – or several self-cancelling purposes – for entering the water. What I am doing has a quality unlike anything else I have done in Rawley, Chandrapore, Upham or Soho. It is a meaningless act, which makes it an almost effortless pleasure.

I stretch out my arms into the sparkle that dances in the waves ahead of me. I am reaching for a gift that is ungiveable. It is a part of me, but beyond me. I cannot possess it.

Melissa is swimming ahead and I am trying to keep no more than a few metres between us. She cannot see that I am synchronizing my stroke to hers, but the rhythm we generate is reassuring. I would prefer to be swimming alongside her, but I cannot quite catch up.

With very little warning, the skies cloud over and the sea turns grey. It is colder now. Windier. The waves slap at my face. I plough through them, concerned about the best way to breathe. I am taking in mouthfuls of water and spewing them out again.

Every few strokes, I look up to check if we are still on course. Were we aiming for that odd–shaped rock or the twisted tree? The rock, I think. But is that the same rock we agreed? Melissa turns round to tread water and look for me. I wave her on. She is swimming more slowly now. Is she tired of waiting for me or just tired? Her head appears and disappears in the waves.

I am shivering. How far should we go? What the fuck were we thinking of? We weren't even thinking. I try to get some kind of rhythm back into my stroke. I have no idea how far we are progressing, because there is nothing against which to measure our progress. We might only be countering the current and going nowhere.

For the first time I notice how steep are the cliffs on either side of the strait and how high are the mountains behind them. I picture how deep the water must be beneath me. There might be a surface current that will carry us to Kefalonia. Or a deeper current that will sweep us the length of the strait and into the Ionian Sea. Something we did not consider before starting out on this madness.

All my concentration now has to be on staying afloat and moving ahead. I look up again for Melissa. Are the waves hiding her or she is so far in front I have lost sight of her? Perhaps she has succumbed. I should make an effort to catch up, but I can't see her. To turn back now would be to break our agreement, which was to stay together. But is there any point in continuing if she has already drowned?

My legs are tired. I clench and unclench my hands to keep the blood flowing, but that makes it difficult to swim. How long is it since we started?

Every time I look up I feel more alone. Kefalonia is too far ahead to go on and Ithaca too far behind to go back.

My whole body is cold now. Too cold. Hands and feet have no feeling. An awful numbness and weariness. Is this hypothermia? Neither going on nor going back will save me. No point in waving. If anyone saw me, they would not know if I were waving or drowning. In any case there is no-one to see me. It's kind of how my life has been.

It starts to rain. I pray to *Leukothea*, goddess of the sea, saviour of *Odysseus*, save me! *Poseidon*, dark sea-lord, terrible father, how I feared and longed for thee, save me!

Shedding salt tears. Reaching for the unreachable. Slosh and splash on. The guilt of witches was determined by their ability to float. Would *Ino* or Edith have floated? Only the innocent drowned. Ironic? No, tragic. If I float am I guilty? Of what? Of wanting to give my life meaning, where none exists?

Am I dreaming? I will only know if I wake. I am making no headway. Cannot roll over to float. Arms and legs will no longer do as I tell them. Cannot raise my head. Mouth opens for air, but takes in water. Let go or fight? Easier to let go. Helpless acceptance.

They say drowning is quick and silent. It is not quick. It is silent. It is silent cause I cannot scream. I cannot scream because my lungs are filling with water. I feel helpless. Is this the drowning sensation terminally ill patients suffer when artificial ventilation is withdrawn? A seagull cries. Faint slam of a door. A snatch of music – Stormy Weather? The Wreck of the Hesperus? I miss Grandma Lily, Melissa, Polly, Aurelia, Roz. My mother? I remember who else Medea reminds me of. Lydia. The look of revenge and death in her eyes.

Smell lemon trees. Faint sound of a motor boat. If I were hallucinating, this would not be real. It is real. It is *not* real. I feel pressure on my chest as if something or someone is holding me down. I am helpless and drowning. I am four years old.

If I am to be transformed by death, let me return not as a monster or a god, but as a boy on a dolphin. An ordinary boy, with a sister and parents who love each other and are together for certain.

Sorry, Julian.

ΨΨ

Author's Note

This book began as a letter of explanation and apology to my son, who hardly knew me until he was twenty years old, when we became friends. His mother and I hadn't been able to make a good marriage, and for my son's benefit and my own I wanted to explore the reasons for that and the background to it. But the story soon took on a life of its own. Omission, conflation and compression were unavoidable. Characters began to speak for themselves. And not only names changed, but also personalities, motivations and events, so that what I offer here is not a memoir, but a fiction expressed in the way memory and imagination work, in a mix of metaphor, fantasy, truth and myth.

Recommended Reading

Byron, Don Juan
Jim Corbett, Man-Eaters of Kumaon
Daniel Defoe, Robinson Crusoe of York
C.S. Forester, the Hornblower series
Erich Fromm, The Art of Loving
Homer, The Odyssey; The Iliad
Charles Kingsley, Westward Ho!
Diogenes Laertius, Lives and Opinions of Eminent Philosophers
A.J. Merson, A Book of Classical Stories
Ovid, Metamorphoses
The Oxford Companion to Classical Literature
H.J. Rose, A Handbook of Greek Literature
Robert Louis Stevenson, Treasure Island
Virgil, The Pastoral Poems
Rex Warner, Men and Gods

Front Cover

Hylas was a handsome youth who accompanied Heracles and the Argonauts on one of their expeditions. When the ship stopped at Chios to mend a broken oar, Hylas was sent to a local spring for water. The water-nymphs enticed him into the spring and he was never seen again.

About the Author

Philip Harland was born in Yorkshire, studied architecture at King's College, Durham, and wrote and directed for theatre, film & television. He is a psychotherapist, author of five books and numerous articles on Clean Language, Metaphor and the Psychology of Change.

Non-fiction
Trust Me, I'm The Patient
The Power of Six
Resolving Problem Patterns
Possession and Desire
How the Brain Feels

www.wayfinderpress.com

Theatre includes
Fertility Dance (with Carol Thompson)
A Comedy of Sex, Surrogacy and Emergency Plumbing

Film & Television awards include
Grierson Award for Best Short Film of the Year
Gold Award, British Film & Television Festival
Silver Award, New York International
Film & Television Festival
Official British entry, United Nations
Conference on Human Settlements
Best Director, Best Editing and Best Soundtrack
nominations, British Film & Television Festival